SPARRING PARTNERS

When Allan saw the fellow who had been occupying Maidie's attention at the tea table for such an unconscionably long time walk off, he approached.

"Would you care for a cup of tea, sir?"

"Yes, please, with milk. I'm not partial to sugar, you will perhaps remember."

Maidie smiled. "I do remember, and it's just as well, if you and I are to be on speaking terms, is it not?"

Allan looked down at her speculatively, and to his own astonishment replied, "Sugar soon cloys, and the system rebels, but an artful sweetness . . . I can't believe it could ever tire the appetite."

Her eyes widened, her lips parted, and a faint blush touched her cheek as she stared up at him. As he looked down into the grey, dark-lashed eyes, he felt his own cheeks reddening. What had led him to deliver such a foppish gallantry?

Maidie applied herself to pouring his tea, while desperately searching for some reply. The despicable man had left her bereft of words again! She had been in the world for years, and was perfectly conversant with the conventions of flirtation, so why was she so unbalanced? It was mortifying past endurance. She heartily hoped that Mr. Gilmichael would go away.

Allan was no less anxious to escape than Maidie to have him go. Sparring with the chit was one thing; gallantries such as he had just uttered were another. He quickly downed his tea and was on his way . . .

ZEBRA REGENCIES
ARE
THE TALK OF THE TON!

A REFORMED RAKE (4499, $3.99)
by Jeanne Savery

After governess Harriet Cole helped her young charge flee to France—and the designs of a despicable suitor, more trouble soon arrived in the person of a London rake. Sir Frederick Carrington insisted on providing safe escort back to England. Harriet deemed Carrington more dangerous than any band of brigands, but secretly relished matching wits with him. But after being taken in his arms for a tender kiss, she found herself wondering— *could* a lady find love with an irresistible rogue?

A SCANDALOUS PROPOSAL (4504, $4.99)
by Teresa DesJardien

After only two weeks into the London season, Lady Pamela Premington has already received her first offer of marriage. If only it hadn't come from the *ton's* most notorious rake, Lord Marchmont. Pamela had already set her sights on the distinguished Lieutenant Penford, who had the heroism and honor that made him the ideal match. Now she had to keep from falling under the spell of the seductive Lord so she could pursue the man more worthy of her love. Or was he?

A LADY'S CHAMPION (4535, $3.99)
by Janice Bennett

Miss Daphne, art mistress of the Selwood Academy for Young Ladies, greeted the notion of ghosts haunting the academy with skepticism. However, to avoid rumors frightening off students, she found herself turning to Mr. Adrian Carstairs, sent by her uncle to be her "protector" against the "ghosts." Although, Daphne would accept no interference in her life, she *would* accept aid in exposing any spectral spirits. What she never expected was for Adrian to expose the secret wishes of her hidden heart . . .

CHARITY'S GAMBIT (4537, $3.99)
by Marcy Stewart

Charity Abercrombie reluctantly embarks on a London season in hopes of making a suitable match. However she cannot forget the mysterious Dominic Castille—and the kiss they shared—when he fell from a tree as she strolled through the woods. Charity does not know that the dark and dashing captain harbors a dangerous secret that will ensnare them both in its web—leaving Charity to risk certain ruin and losing the man she so passionately loves . . .

Available wherever paperbacks are sold, or order direct from the Publisher. Send cover price plus 50¢ per copy for mailing and handling to Penguin USA, P.O. Box 999, c/o Dept. 17109, Bergenfield, NJ 07621. Residents of New York and Tennessee must include sales tax. DO NOT SEND CASH.

A Lakeside Season
Cleo Chadwick

ZEBRA BOOKS
KENSINGTON PUBLISHING CORP.

ZEBRA BOOKS are published by

Kensington Publishing Corp.
850 Third Avenue
New York, NY 10022

First Printing: January, 1995

Printed in the United States of America

To
John, Jessica, Zack, and Abby
and to
Tina and Paul

Author's Note

I have inserted a range of high, steep mountains, a lower range, and a lake into the map of England's Lake District, no doubt contrary to all geologic sense. The features of my invention lie between the body of water called Windermere and the Kent Valley.

The Lake District in Regency times was visited for its sixteen lakes and the sublime scenery. Although the lakes were the first interest of the tourists and the "lake-loving gentry," a few people were beginning to find enjoyment in the mountains among which the lakes lie. The most famous of these forerunners of modern campers and hikers were the poets Samuel Taylor Coleridge and William Wordsworth, and the latter's sister, Dorothy Wordsworth.

The highest peak in the Lake District is Scafel at 3,206 feet, which to those of us in North America may seem insufficient height to merit the name of mountain. This is half the highest Appalachian summit (6,680 feet); but it is greater than the highest peak (2,800 feet) in the Ozarks, which latter are often described as hills rather than mountains.

Yet these Lake District hill-mountains experience great variations in temperature; and land form varies from green and pastoral valleys to alpine summits, while the deep weathering, long unwooded slopes, and sudden precipices more than make up for the lack of height. They are unique, and it seems right that they should have their own name, from the old Norse: *fells*.

There are many terms from the period of Viking settlement that are still in use in the Lake Country. A few I have used in this novel: mere (lake), ghyll or gill (ravine), beck (stream), and tarn (pond).

One

The silence in the library of the house on Bedford Square was broken only by the distant sound of a passing carriage and by the rustling of pages as Samuel Worthing, Esq. scanned his newspapers. Numerous candles cast a glow over the rich furnishings of the comfortable room, and the fire, now reduced to shimmering coals, touched Mrs. Worthing's high cheekbones with pink as she turned another page of her novel.

An ormolu clock, elegantly decorated with chubby cupids aiming arrows at unsuspecting maidens, ticked away another fifteen minutes before Mr. Worthing put down his newspaper and removed a watch from his pocket. The confirmation that it was now two hours past midnight did not please him.

"Just what does that lisping nincompoop think he's up to, keeping our little Maidie out so late?" he demanded irritably.

Mrs. Worthing looked up from her novel. "You know perfectly well, Sam, that Lord Calvette is not a nincompoop. And in any event, Fanny will be keeping a close eye on the two of them."

"Trust that sister of mine? Nobody's trusted Fan since she learned to talk!" Mr. Worthing paused, considered. "No, even in her cradle she was unreliable."

Mrs. Worthing rose from her chair, and with an arch look at her husband stretched her arms over her head. Her figure was still lithe and fetching, as she well knew.

Mr. Worthing, succumbing willingly to her ploy, removed the glasses from his nose, and patted his knee invitingly. "You're a minx still, aren't you Tish? Come sit on my lap a minute."

Another silence ensued, broken only by a few murmured endearments, which abruptly ended at a soft knock on the library door. "Goodness!" Mrs. Worthing exclaimed, leaping from her husband's lap and hastily smoothing her hair. "I didn't hear them come in, did you?"

The door opened a crack and a low, sweet voice called, "Anyone home?"

Mr. Worthing cleared his throat. "Well, come in, Maidie, come in! Fan with you?"

Fanny Worthing Clarke stepped into the room directly behind her young niece. "And where else would I be?"

Mrs. Worthing crossed the room to bestow kisses, first on her sister-in-law, and then on her daughter. Her heart gave a beat of motherly pride as she kissed Maidie's glowing cheek. She believed firmly that a cultivated mind was of greater value than a beautiful face, but she couldn't help being pleased that her only chick was pretty.

It had to be admitted that Maidie had never been called beautiful, except by an occasional gentleman in temporary throes of adoration. Nonetheless, her features were oddly winsome. High cheekbones like her mother, and eyebrows that slanted up at the corners brought ideas of pixies to the fanciful mind. Gossiping dowagers, always willing to criticize an heiress, thought her lashes darker than was quite stylish, but admitted that her face was "interesting."

Except, of course, that her nose was rather too long.

Maidie, had she been interested in what the dowagers said, would have agreed that her nose was too long. At fourteen she might have sold her soul for a different nose—something pert and snubbish. At twenty-three she was wiser, having imbibed of the philosophers, and thereby learned to pursue and accept

Truth. Lord Calvette, her current admirer (who had no notion at all of philosophers), might have admitted that Maidie's nose was too sharp, but he would have countered that the lips below were delectable.

Maidie was not tall, but the dowagers were forced to admit that her carriage was elegant. For this night's ball, her new maid had caught her hair up in a psyche knot, leaving a few carefully errant and wispy curls to frame her face in a most enchanting suggestion of disarray. Her ball gown, a simple affair that the dowagers estimated had cost her father two pots of gold, was a sumptuous pink, which by the rules of fashion should not have so exactly suited her. But, they agreed, her mother always could wear clothes well, and Maidie was certainly her mother's daughter.

"And just what kept you so late?" Mr. Worthing asked sternly of Fanny. His heart, unlike his wife's, had not swollen with pride, but with ire as he surveyed his troublesome daughter and his possibly more troublesome sister. "I'd be grateful to learn—if a mere father is permitted to ask."

Fanny gave Mr. Worthing's cheek a robust kiss, which he did not appreciate, and then tossed her silvered evening reticule on the nearest chair. She pulled off her gloves. "Really, Sam, two o'clock is a remarkably early hour to leave a ball unless one has an engagement elsewhere! Aren't you a little . . . er . . . *medieval* in your rules?"

Mrs. Worthing smiled at Maidie. "Did you have a lovely time, dear?"

"Oh, yes, Mama! Lord Calvette is *so* amusing! We're going to Richmond tomorrow for an evening sail on the river. Aunt Fan has already promised to go." Maidie turned to Fanny and threw her arms around her. "You're so much more fun than Aunt Seraphina! I know I shouldn't say it, but it's true."

Mr. Worthing cast his sister a suspicious glance. "That doesn't sound just right to me, Fan. What have you been letting this baggage do that Seraphina doesn't?"

Fanny sank down on the sofa. "We've spent a fearsomely proper evening, I assure you. Even Phina would approve. I must say, Lord Calvette is all gentleman!"

"Even if he did try to kiss me when Aunt Fanny wasn't looking," Maidie said, an impish gleam in her eye. She took a waltzing twirl around the room. "It was a wonderful ball! I could have danced, and danced, and danced—"

"What's that?" Mr. Worthing asked from under lowered brows. "Tried to kiss you, did he? And just where had you got to that he could make such an attempt? By thunder . . ." Mr. Worthing, whose head had been gyrating uncomfortably in an attempt to keep track of his daughter, lost patience. "Damn it, Maidie, *sit down!*"

Maidie laughed and dropped a kiss on her father's cheek as she waltzed away to the door. "Oh, but I didn't let him. I won't let him kiss me until after the sail. We'll be picnicking by moonlight . . ." At the door she crossed her hands delicately over her breast, and with eyes rolled heavenward departed the room on a gusty sigh.

"Maidie, you come back here!" her father shouted, but the door had closed and Maidie was gone. "That girl!"

"Sam, she's just teasing you," Mrs. Worthing said pacifically. "I doubt Lord Calvette did any such thing. Did he, Fan?"

"Well, it's possible. He's quite taken with Maidie, you know."

Mr. Worthing slapped the chair arm. "A damned *aristocrat!*" Then, finding the chair too confining for his state of annoyance, he got to his feet and began to pace the room. "It's not enough that the young fool's a nincompoop, but he has to be an earl besides!"

Fanny, unaffected by her brother's show of temper, kicked off her slippers and wiggled her toes. "Ah," she sighed. "What inadequate affairs dancing slippers are for the strenuous demands of a ball! Another time I believe I'll wear my walking shoes." She stretched comfortably. "You might give me a nice spot of brandy, Sam. I may be perfectly capable of walking forty miles in a day, but an evening of dancing has rather done me up."

Mr. Worthing turned on her. "And about all this walking around the countryside without any chaperon, Fan . . ."

Fanny, imitating Maidie, rolled her eyes upward and sighed.

With a frown, he desisted, and bent to stir the coals into a little life . . . it was a chill night for so late in the season. He had never been able to approve certain aspects of Fanny's conduct, and unaccompanied country walking was one of those aspects. Of course, he preferred her company to that of his older sister, high-principled Seraphina, but on the other hand he approved Phina's conduct above Fan's. Just went to show, he thought, as he poked the fire into a blaze, that the world will love a charming rake while scorning his virtuous brother.

Mrs. Fanny Worthing Clarke, the younger of Mr. Samuel Worthing's two sisters, was a handsome rather than beautiful woman, with strong features and classic profile. She was tall like her brother, standing five feet, ten and a half inches in her stocking feet. Which was certainly too tall, the gossiping dowagers declared. And if it wasn't just like her to be dancing—when her place as a chaperon to her niece was to sit beside them and contribute to their observations on their fellow creatures. Her sister Seraphina would have known what was proper. But Fanny Worthing had always been too forward, which undoubtedly came from her low family connections. (The dowagers always conveniently forgot that Seraphina Worthing, in whom they could only with difficulty discover fault, came from the same low connections.)

Fanny, unlike her niece, was well aware what the dowagers said of her, but she cared not a rush. A recognized journal writer and as famous an essayist as her husband Emery, she was now, in her mid-thirties, at the height of her creative powers, commanding the respect of such large minds as Mr. Godwin, Mr. Coleridge, and even of Mr. Hazlitt, who had once been heard to remark that if she weren't so much of a woman one would think her a man, her brain was so acute. At the moment, however, following a pleasurable evening of dancing and a bit of matronly flirting, her acute brain was comfortably at rest.

Mrs. Worthing poured a glass of brandy for Fanny, and then, after a moment's consideration, poured one for herself and another for Mr. Worthing. As she handed her sister-in-law her brandy, she said, "You've been a dear to chaperon Maidie while Seraphina's been gone. I know it's not what you intended when you came down to London."

Fanny made a deprecatory gesture. "Maidie's a delightful young woman. And it does me good to occasionally taste the high life. Makes me aware of what I'm not missing."

"Do sit down again, Sam," Mrs. Worthing said, as she settled once more in her own chair, "You know, dear, it's your fault that Maidie has admirers like young Calvette. It was you who insisted that she attend that school where she was certain to make friends with daughters of the aristocracy. And girls will have brothers who will sometimes court their sisters' friends. Unfortunate, but there you are!"

"Well, perhaps I did choose the wrong school for her. But she needed at least a year or two of normal education."

"I, for one," Fanny said, always ready to take up an argument, "think Maidie's education under Tish's tutelage just what it ought to have been. She has an independence of mind, an originality, and a curiosity about the world that simply is not fostered in those insipid female academies."

Mrs. Worthing smiled at her sister-in-law, pleased with the compliment. "Nonetheless, Fanny, I do believe we should concede that Sam had a point. I am of course convinced that the progressive principles of Rousseau, if correctly applied, are vastly superior to Miss Hannah More's notions of a proper female education. But one must live in the world as it is. I'm sure it's just as well that Maidie's learned to converse for an hour at a time about absolutely nothing and to paint perfectly ugly flowers on velvet. And above all, to write a declarative sentence with no fewer than six clauses."

"Absolutely. Nothing more worthwhile for getting on in the world than a sentence with six clauses." With this statement, Fanny awarded the last word on female education to her sister-in-law. "Anyway, Sam, history repeats itself. I wouldn't have liked it at all if you'd married that worthy young woman—what was her name? You know, the one you were so remarkably, and if I may say so, foolishly yearning after before you met Tish. *Her* father hadn't a speck of nobility in his blood." Fanny sipped her brandy appreciatively. "In fact, I was never certain he had any blood at all."

"Yes, Sam. You married into the aristocracy. True, my father was only a lowly viscount, but the rank is sufficient to admit his granddaughter into lordly circles."

"I wonder why no one ever says 'ladly circles'?" Fanny asked.

Mr. Worthing ignored his sister. "That's true, Tish, I did marry up in the world. But with or without your father's permission I'd have married you, and no difference to me whether you were a viscount's daughter or a coal heaver's."

"I wonder where Maidie gets that touch of the headstrong?" Fanny mused.

Mrs. Worthing favored her husband with a loving glance. "Oh, Sam, you know very well that Papa grew quite fond of you!"

"Well, I've always said to the credit of your family that they're enough ashamed of me that they've never tried to drag us into Society." Mr. Worthing, with an answering loving look for his wife, turned a sterner face to his sister. "But damn it, Fan, it's different with Maidie than it was with me. We've only this one girl chick to pass it all on to. No aristocrat is going to take over my bank when I'm gone, let alone change his name to Worthing! And I haven't worked as hard as I have just to see Worthing's Bank go out of the family. Why, we're as sound as the Bank of England! Sounder, by thunder. We didn't have any run on our reserves during the invasion scare back in '97. Or before we got the news of our victory at Waterloo, either. I wasn't taken in by Rothschild's maneuvering . . . in fact, did him one better, if I do say so. You remember, Tish, Fan, how—"

"I *have* it!" Fanny, who had been slouched comfortably in her chair, suddenly sat up and snapped her fingers. "Let me take Maidie back to Westmoreland with me!"

She leaped up to stride stocking-footed around the room, excited by her own brilliance. "There are all kinds of new people at Krigsmere, now that the Lake District's becoming so unbearably fashionable. And the very *latest* addition to our society is a rich Manchester textile manufacturer and his family. The Califaxtons. Oh, just fantastically, fabulously—*famously*—rich! Emery says they're *very* progressive. That is, in the way they use capital. Although what I've seen in some of the manufactories . . . well, no need to think about that right now. The Califaxtons have investments in any number of profitable ventures all over the world, and monopolies in all sorts of things. I think they have the exclusive right to supply buttons to the Royal household, or some such thing—"

"Hold on, Fan. Hold your horses! Aside from interrupting me, d'you think I wouldn't know the Califaxton enterprises? Old Josiah Califaxton—two generations back it was . . ."

"Really, Sam! Who cares about two generations back? My point is that they're rich *now.*"

"Unitarians, I believe," said Mrs. Worthing thoughtfully.

"Yes, yes. So they are, to be sure. But they've also four unmarried sons. They've built a place—frightfully drafty, but simply magnificent prospects from the terrace and drawing rooms! So they aren't just seasonal renters, you see."

Mr. and Mrs. Worthing, grappling with the sudden shift in the conversational topic, and still not comprehending such an outlandish suggestion as letting their one girl chick leave the nest, stared at her.

Fanny sat down again, beaming at them. "Do you understand me?" She leaned forward and held up four fingers to emphasize her point. *"Four—unmarried—sons!"*

"Four," Mrs. Worthing dutifully repeated.

"That's right. Four. Excessively gentlemanly, all of them, and so very agreeable, and they show no sign of any interest at all in any specific female, at least that I've noticed so far. And there's a daughter too, a little younger. They're all close in age; it must have been depressingly tiring for poor Mrs. Califaxton, having so many babies in such a short time! But with sons to spare it seems unlikely that they would object to one of them becoming your successor in name, Sam. And all brought up in business! I wouldn't doubt but that the youngest is just Maidie's age. And the girl is terribly well-brought up and would make a good friend for Maidie. We won't tell Maidie that we're dabbling in matchmaking. And Emery and I would dearly love to have her. Do say she may come!"

"No aristocrats up there?" her brother asked warily. He was suspicious of Fanny from long habit. However, the Califaxton fortune and enterprises were certainly worth thinking about.

"Not one aristocrat!" Fanny assured him. Then, in the interests of truth, she added that there were of course the great aristocratic landholding families—the Lowthers and Howards—but their seats were not actually in the Lake District, and in any event, there were no eligibles among them.

"Well," Mrs. Worthing said hesitantly, "I suppose we could think about letting Maidie visit. Perhaps for a month or two.

After all, Sam, once Maidie marries we'll have to get along without her."

Mr. Worthing's suspicious eye was still fixed on his sister. "What she's not saying, Tish, is that that house of hers is always full of crazy poets and radicals. Damned odious democrats, half of them. Maidie has enough notions. All that radical reading when she should have been learning how to embroider slippers for me! And"—Mr. Worthing's agile mind had been seeking the telling argument—"if she goes to Fanny this summer, who'll accompany you to the seashore?"

"Oh, well . . ." Mrs. Worthing hesitated. "Perhaps cousin Winifred would be willing."

"Tish is hardly a young girl needing a chaperon, Sam. And she has dozens of friends at Margate. In any event, if I remember correctly, it was a close thing two summers ago, with that American. Now you *would* have been put to it if Maidie'd given *him* any encouragement! She'd have gone off to America!"

With this shot across her brother's bows, Fanny set her empty brandy glass on the nearby table. She pulled up her skirts and began to roll her stockings down. "How I hate garters! They can't be healthful—so tight under one's knees." Intent on her task, she observed, "Maidie has to marry someone. For goodness sake, Sam, I couldn't count how many bankers and lawyers—and I'll wager you can't either—you've thrown in her way. And without any success at all. So why not let me try my hand at it?" She pulled her stockings off and breathed a contented sigh.

"Well, go ahead, Fan. Just take everything off and be done with it. Shall I call a maid to loosen your stays?"

"Stays!" Fanny snorted. "Catch me in stays!"

Mrs. Worthing, accustomed to this sibling bickering, interposed. "Maidie's been asking to visit Fanny and Emery for a long time, you know, Sam. And for all her high spirits, she has a good head on her shoulders. I don't think we need fear that it will be turned by some romancing poet. Remember how she handled that young moon-calf last year? Most unsuitable, but he was nonetheless a pleasing young man, and he could be quite witty when he forgot that poets are supposed to suffer from an excess of melancholy." Mrs. Worthing frowned. "I'm sure I don't know why. Lord Byron never seemed exactly *melancholy.* Of course, I've never met Mr. Wordsworth . . ."

"No," Fanny said. "I wouldn't call William melancholy. Clumsy as a tipsy hen, and without a teaspoon of humor, but not melancholy. And of course Southey is the most gentle and tolerant of beings, except so horribly conservative. Poor De Quincey of course, with his terrible opium addiction . . ."

Mr. Worthing hummmphed. "Now I've nothing against poets. But all this la-de-dah about birds and butterflies that that fellow Wordsworth puts out . . . Give me a solid verse by Pope any time. But I don't suppose either of you would argue that some spooney poet would be prepared to take over Worthing's Bank? No, Fan, I'm not about to let Maidie loose in your sideshow."

Fanny shrugged. "Really, Sam, we seldom see any radicals anymore. Nearly all our acquaintances are become disgracefully conservative. I don't know why, especially now that the war against Bonaparte is concluded, and all the thrones of Europe sat on by legitimate kings—or so they claim to be. But in truth, one must ask if *kings* are legitimate."

"Now, Fan, you know what I think of such radical talk! If you don't look out . . ."

"I can't understand why nearly everybody in England is so terribly afraid of treason, or revolution, or goodness knows what! Why even you, Sam, have stated that by rights Manchester and Birmingham should have representatives in Parliament. Now if that isn't Parliamentary reform, I don't know what is! And when you were younger . . . I distinctly remember how Papa shouted at you when—but never mind that. I see by your stern face that it's better forever forgotten! And Cobbett's fled to America rather than go to prison again for seditious libel. So dreary and disgraceful!" She had pulled off her earrings while she was speaking, and now jingled them in her hand. "Oh, I can see you puffing up, Sam, ready to have at me about Cobbett, which I give you leave to do tomorrow. But what I want you to think about now is that I'm offering four prodigiously rich and handsome young men as marriage prospects, all raised in trade, and as sober as bankers already. I'd keep my mind on *them* if I were you, and not some imaginary steam-powered radical." Fanny stood and gathered up her shoes and stockings and other personal items. "Goodnight, my dears, and you think about it a little longer, Sam, before you deliver a categorical no."

Maidie, on leaving her parents and aunt, had waltzed up the stairs humming one of the tunes to which she had danced that evening, to find her maid dozing on a straight chair beside the door to her dressing room.

"Clarice!" she exclaimed. "You are not to be waiting for me here in the cold. And not even in a comfortable chair! Really, what am I to do with you?"

Clarice, too proper to rub her eyes, reached up to straighten her cap instead. "My duty is to assist my mistress in preparing for the night," she stated flatly.

Maidie sighed. Her friendly and easy-going Jane, who had attended her since she was thirteen—and who had been hardly more than a child herself when she first came to them—had the month before married, and now assisted her new husband in his small tailoring shop at Charing Cross. Jane's replacement, the proper Clarice, had been chosen by proper Aunt Seraphina, a duty Seraphina felt called upon to undertake in order that Maidie not fall into the clutches of another slapdash girl like Jane.

Miss Seraphina Worthing, the family maiden aunt, was a lady of high principles, whose chosen service in life was to guarantee the same order and discipline in her brother's household as in her own, and to see to it that her only niece have a social life befitting her station as a viscount's granddaughter. Over the years Mrs. Worthing, whose health had always been delicate, had gratefully turned over many of those duties, as well as the duty of chaperoning Maidie, to orderly and businesslike Seraphina. She had been pleased to be able to conserve her energies for attending to Maidie's education, which she firmly and steadfastly refused to put in Seraphina's hands.

Maidie had cheerfully accepted both her mother's progressive educational theories and her father's conservative ones, and similarly she accepted her Aunt Seraphina's regulation of her social life and the choice of her maid. Nonetheless, tonight's gay mood was dampened at finding Clarice so tired and so uncomfortable, and she did wish sometimes . . .

But Maidie was nothing if not forever hopeful, and so she made a wistful attempt, as Clarice helped her prepare for bed, to find an opening from among the girl's carefully proper responses to advance a friendship between them, until at last she admitted herself defeated and subsided into silence. Jane, she reflected, would have been waiting for her comfortably asleep before the fire, but would have awakened to exclaim over the evening's events and flirtations as she helped her prepare for the night. And then, both sitting cross-legged in the middle of the big bed, Jane would have told her about her own latest flirts and they'd have talked of life and love.

Maidie was not a young woman given to discontent, but occasionally she did feel that she wanted something she didn't have, although she didn't know what that something might be. However, having been taught that she was an exceedingly fortunate young woman, she always felt vaguely guilty for wanting it, whatever it was.

Nor was she of a romantic inclination, and her mother's progressive principles had not favored an educational program that would uncover any buried romantic strata. Maidie was taught her letters and then was let free—with unobtrusive but judicious guidance—to read what she would. She was expected to exercise regularly, as Dr. Erasmus Darwin recommended, and was sent outdoors in all weathers. She was taught never to presume that because her father was wealthy and she an heiress that service and deference were her due. And above all else, she was taught to judge people not by their station in life, but by what they proved themselves to be.

Since she had been taught to judge character and actions by practical observation, she knew only too well that her principal admirer, Lord Calvette, was a shallow young man dominated by an irascible father and three maiden aunts. He was amiable, and everything that was proper; she was really very fond of him. She considered it a duty to make him kiss her either before, during, or after the moonlight picnic. She'd have to be clever indeed to provide him the opportunity. Aunt Fanny was less strict than Aunt Seraphina, but twice as knowing. But really, Maidie thought, as she climbed into her bed, once that goal was accomplished she must find a way to cool his ardor and to escape from his attentions without inflicting a wound.

She knew that scheming to get herself kissed was above all a symptom of boredom—for which, if she chose, she could feel guilty. She was tired of London, and of parties and balls; she was tired of amiable and proper young men, whether lords or bankers. Although trained to independence of mind in religious as in other matters, her mother's theological battles with Church of England clerics didn't interest her. Although expected to exercise regularly, she had never enjoyed riding. She liked seabathing, but was forced to admit that she was tired of summer holidays at Margate. If they could just once try a *different* seaside resort. And she took no pleasure at all in making pen wipers, or painting on velvet, or any other approved female pastime, which she had also been taught to do, according to her father's more conservative educational principles. She sometimes wondered if she was capable of anything useful at all.

She did enjoy walking, but she was as tired of chaperons as she was of amiable young men. It sometimes seemed that she was never without someone watching—parents and maids and chaperons and grooms and Aunt Seraphina. She wished her father would purchase a country property; other bankers did so. But her father was London-bred, and he often said that he didn't need landed property just so he could sit in Parliament. Power, when all was said and done, rested with the financial interest. How many lords were up to their neckcloths in debt? he asked. How many mortgages on fine estates did he hold? And even kings needed permission to enter the City . . .

But she would love living in the country. She liked to be out of doors, but London was so full of soot and smoke . . .

Maidie drifted off to sleep. She was a cheerful young woman, with none of the morbidity in her nature that so easily led to brooding. Maidie always had the idea that a new day might bring something exciting, but if the new day passed much like any other, as most did, she was seldom disappointed. The end of one day was always the eve of another.

The following day, as Fanny and Mrs. Worthing settled themselves to some homely tasks in Mrs. Worthing's dressing room, they were surprised by the announcement that Miss Seraphina Worthing was below.

"But Seraphina's at Bath!" Mrs. Worthing exclaimed.

"No, dear, she's downstairs. But before she arrives upstairs, do we dare to place my proposal for Maidie before her? Or shall we present it *fait accompli?*"

"Oh, I do think, even though she may object, that it would be better she know beforehand. That is, of course, should we decide that Maidie may visit you."

"Then I shall make the proposal," Fanny said, returning calmly to her task.

Seraphina, of Mr. Worthing's two sisters, had the more stately figure. Her erect carriage and controlled movements gave the impression of a great ponderous ship, all canvas spread, moving majestically before a light breeze. She entered the room with quiet dignity, disposed businesslike kisses on the cheeks of her sister-in-law and sister, and sat down. Not a hair was out of place, not a spot of dust marred her hem, nor a single blemish her fair chin.

"You're looking well, Tish," she remarked with approval. "But you, Fanny, seem just a bit hagged. Perhaps the Lakes have not been as beneficial as you had hoped?"

"You forget, Phina, that I've been in London these four weeks and more. It's London air, not Lake air, that I fear has robbed my cheek of its bloom."

"Always ready with sarcasm, I see, so I may presume that your spirit, at least, does not falter."

"I'm delighted to see you, Seraphina," Mrs. Worthing said, "but what brings you so soon from Bath? I had thought that you intended a longer visit."

"I returned because I began to feel I was the only person alive in the whole of the city. That is, of course, an exaggeration, for a great many people still frequent Bath for pleasure. Be that as it may, I've put my house up for sale, and will look for another in Brighton. I'm assured by Sissy Donlopper—you remember her, Fanny, she was often at our house when we were girls—she assures me that Brighton is much livelier. And it has the further advantage of sea-bathing."

Mrs. Worthing loathed drinking the waters at Bath and other such spas, and therefore chose the seaside for renewal of vigor and zest. A discussion followed on the subject of resorts, during which Seraphina revealed that she did not expect her estate agent to find a house or property immediately in Brighton, and since as they knew she despised rentals—so many rented properties were allowed to become damp—she would be accompanying Maidie and Tish to Margate for her summer holiday. She was quite of a mind to take up sea-bathing.

Fanny could not have asked for a better introduction to her scheme, and the moment Seraphina's pronouncements showed signs of dwindling she launched her proposal. To the surprise of both Mrs. Worthing and Fanny, Seraphina was not opposed to the plan.

Not to say that she approved it—only that she did not oppose it. In fact, she saw a certain advantage in it. One really should be in town in May, and especially in June if one was of the fashionable world, but on the other hand, that silly Calvette was showing dangerous symptoms of attachment, a connection in which she saw no merit. Furthermore, since she had determined on accompanying Tish to Margate, Maidie was not needed as a companion. In fine, she would give the subject the careful thought such a step deserved . . .

"Wonderful, Phina," Fanny at last interrupted. "I had hoped that you would give us the benefit of your judgment. You are so seldom swayed by other than practical considerations."

Seraphina turned as suspicious an eye on Fanny as their brother might have done. Fanny returned her scrutiny with a limpid, wide-eyed gaze, which Seraphina, from long experience, recognized as Fanny's guilty look. However, she could see nothing seriously amiss in the plan, and in fact thought it rather a good one. A month or two was not sufficient time for any complications of an amorous nature, and Maidie showed signs of restlessness that she couldn't quite like, not to mention that ninny Calvette hovering about. A little time away from London would do the child good.

Two

Emery Clarke, eminent essayist and historian, stood outside a Kendal coaching inn awaiting the arrival of his brother-in-law's carriage. He was not a tall man—he was in fact an inch shorter than Fanny—but he was robust and ruddy and made an imposing figure, even here in the north among men who prided themselves on being the tallest and strongest in England. Kind, thoughtful eyes peered nearsightedly out at the world and its inhabitants from under the high, domed forehead which dominated his face, the nobility of its expanse emphasized by a receding hairline.

At this moment, however, Emery was frowning, gazing impatiently down the highroad. He had already been waiting two hours, and Fanny's arrival would not be hurried by the watching, but at least out of doors he could pace more comfortably.

As he stepped into the street, a post-chaise approached, bearing a gentleman who, after calling to the post boy to halt, leaned from the vehicle to greet him. "Good afternoon, Clarke. Remarkably fine day."

"Why, hello, Gilmichael. Off on a journey?"

Allan Gilmichael, Lord Enett, descended from the chaise and extended his hand. "Brief visit in Derbyshire. Duty to an old aunt."

"You will be returning to us then?"

"In a week or so. Thought I'd return by the western lakes—fish Crummock Water and have a leisurely tramp back to Krigsmere."

"Excellent fishing there."

"I'll be looking forward the while to visiting that tarn you described when we were fishing Haweswater."

"Will be a pleasure," Emery replied. Gilmichael was not one to mix with the local people, and Emery was flattered, in his quiet way, to be on terms with him.

"My pleasure, also," Allan said. "I presume you're waiting for Mrs. Clarke?"

Emery nodded. "Yes. She's been gone much too long. She's bringing our niece with her. Daughter of Fanny's brother. Perhaps you know the Worthing Bank?"

"Yes, of course. Under the sign of the morning glory."

"You must dine with us when you return. Fanny will want to meet you, and it will provide some diversion for her niece. Maidie always was a self-sufficient child, but she doesn't have any experience with country living."

"I wouldn't worry. If she's like my sister, she'll bring her Claude glass, her sketch book, a volume of Wordsworth, and sigh over the sublimity of the scenery."

"Doesn't sound like Maidie."

"Then perhaps your many visitors? They should be entertainment enough for even jaded London tastes."

"Perhaps . . ."

"Again, I must be going. Good day to you, Clarke. My regards to Mrs. Clarke. I look forward to meeting her on my return. And your niece as well."

Allan sprang back into the post-chaise, tipped his hat, and bade the boy be off.

They were soon leaving the last straggle of houses for open country, and as the horses stepped smartly along it came to him, in a moment of wry surprise, that he was studying the state of the crops with a critical eye. Only two years past he would have been staring at the countryside without seeing it, sunk in his own gloom, and certainly without one thought, Heaven forefend, to anything agricultural.

Allan Gilmichael had a probing mind and a keen intellect, neither of which he had learned to use until he became a soldier. His army superiors had judged him a man born to command, but often described him as too much the daredevil. Daredevil or not, his troops knew that even when he was ordering them into battle, their best interests were his foremost preoccupation. Fate or the Monsieurs might kill them, they often said, but never, as long as Captain Gilly was in command, a dunderhead officer.

Such force of character might have implied a settled gentleman of serious parts, but those who knew Allan well knew that such was not the case. Until the death of his elder brother, Clarence, he had been anything but settled. His peers knew him for a firm hand with the troops and a light hand with the ladies. In Spain, when not engaged in warfare, he drank with fell companions, attended bullfights, wooed Spanish señoritas and a few señoras. He had fought one duel—in Paris during the months between Bonaparte's first exile and his final defeat at Waterloo. In those tumultuous days, many a young French officer believed that honor demanded he challenge an equally young English officer in order to counter in single combat what had already been settled by armies on the battlefields of Europe. Recalled to arms at Waterloo, Allan passed his final battle accumulating glory, and emerged unscathed. He was in England, looking forward to a return to duty in Paris when Clarence, his older brother and holder of the Marquisate, died.

Unwilling though Allan might have been to assume both title and responsibility, he had no choice. He had devoted himself without cease to the tasks of learning to manage an estate that, he soon discovered to his horror, had fallen into decline under the well-meaning but inept supervision of first his father and then his older brother. To his considerable surprise he discovered that he had a knack for farming, and expected eventually to bring the land back into good heart, but at the same time he began to suffer from unaccustomed black moods. After a vexing turn up with his young sister, he had decided that both he and his family would benefit by his absence.

On an impulse he had passed himself off to those he had met in the Lakes as plain Mr. Gilmichael, rather than the new Marquis of Enett. He had the contradictory notions that ignorance of his title would protect him from intrusions on his solitude, while permitting easy intercourse with the local people; and at the same time spare him the automatic deference—even servility—that to his great dismay he found his new rank called forth. He had determined that during his Lake visit he would only acknowledge a distant relationship to the present marquis. If anyone mentioned that he resembled that gentleman rather startlingly, he would reply that "Yes, he had been told so, but having never met the marquis, couldn't say." He had not, however, been called upon yet to make any such false statement, and he now considered it a first-rate piece of foolishness leading to more foolishness, such as his sudden invention of an old aunt for Emery Clarke's benefit.

The postboy pulled the chaise to the side of the road to let pass a herd of cattle on the way to market, recalling Allan to the present. He eyed the cattle, thinking what fine looking beasts they were, even though gaunted from their journey, which in turn set his mind to the problem in husbandry that had necessitated a visit to his Derbyshire estate.

As he glumly considered his responsibilities and the dark mood that was threatening to descend on him again, the chaise was once again pulled over to permit passage for a magnificent carriage drawn by four matched bays and accompanied by liveried outriders. Allan wondered vaguely if it carried Mrs. Clarke and the banker's daughter before turning his mind again to estate problems.

Emery, meanwhile, was meeting yet another of his neighbors. He had just paced off the tenth of his short marches in front of the inn when he heard his name called. Turning, he saw approaching young Wendell Duval, would-be poet, declared radical and democrat, and Emery's distant cousin. Neither he nor Wendell was certain exactly how they were connected, although an ancient relative had tried to tell them, and would try again, should they be so unwise to ask.

It was this ancient lady, somehow related to his grandmother, and known in the family as Miss Hattie, who had recommended Wendell to Emery. Her letter introducing him had been precise in setting forth her opinion of the young poet.

Salvatore—or Wendell Duval, as he styles himself—is at present a foolish young man, for as you know, your mother's side of the family was connected to the Bassetts and through them to the Toones of Sussex. The Toones were a titled and, in their time, an honorable and wealthy family.

Emery did not know he was connected to any family of Toones, in Sussex or anywhere else, but he had had some curiosity as to why his relationship to them should indicate foolishness in a young man.

Although his connection to the Sussex Toones is tenuous at best, young Salvatore may still claim that connection. It is, in fact, a somewhat closer connection than yours, since he is related through the Cholmeleys rather than the Bassetts as well as himself bearing the name of Toone. That is, he is twice related to the Sussex Toones, as you will see by the attached genealogical diagram. But what will the Silly Boy choose to do but to call himself by the fanciful name by which I am introducing him to you. I have pointed out to him the absurdity of such a name as Wendell Duval, and that his own name, Salvatore Toone, is honest and straightforward. He asserts nonetheless that he prefers the poetic ring of Wendell Duval.

Emery rather saw the young man's point. Salvatore Toone did have a less poetic ring than Wendell Duval.

When I learned that Salvatore was in London, I invited him to call on me. On further acquaintance with the Silly Boy I have determined that although his poetry is execrable, and his politics lamentably juvenile and overwrought (as well as harking back to those abominable American and French revolutionists), there is every reason to expect that his better sense will win through in the end. He is not unreflective in habit, and I have assured myself that he is of good moral character and high principle. Despite a physical beauty that should make the most modest youth a veritable Narcissus, he seems entirely unaware of his outward appearance.

I therefore recommend to you your cousin, Salvatore Toone, calling himself Wendell Duval. He has recently come into a very modest inheritance and intends to spend a few months pursuing his Muse, after which, he has assured me, he will either be earning by his pen, or seek some honest work in this, our Earthly Vineyard.

Emery had drawn breath and forged on into the description of his relationship to Salvatore Toone—who chose to call himself Wendell Duval—but it was so complicated that his interest soon flagged. Genealogy charts had always made him yawn; he had encountered the same difficulty as a boy learning his history, for history included too many of those often obscure connections on which royal inheritance depended and over which wars were waged. It had almost turned his mind against history altogether.

Fanny had shown no more interest than he in deciphering the diagram his ancient relative had so thoughtfully provided, and so Emery had put the letter away and set his mind to finding young Wendell a residence. By good luck a cottage, only fifteen minutes walk from his own Pennelbeck Farm, was offered to let the following week, and Emery immediately secured it for such a reasonable rent that the young poet radical could live comfortably for as long as pursuit of his muse required.

Emery sighed now, on seeing Wendell approach, but nonetheless smiled and extended his hand. "Hello, cousin," he said cordially. "I didn't know that you were coming to Kendal. You could have walked along with me. Fanny comes today, you know. I've hired an equipage to carry us all home, and if you care to join us I'm sure we'll be able to find room. I'll have to see to the care for the night of her brother's coachman and horses, and no doubt a dozen outriders as well, but when that's done, we'll be on our way to Sagpaw."

"I thank you, Emery, but I prefer to return on my own two legs. I overlook no opportunity to view the waterfall by the path over the fells. It has such an abandoned beauty, and is set in such an untamed landscape that one fancies at times it possible to meet a wood nymph, or one of the Bacchantes—even Bacchus himself. But did you say that Fanny and her niece will be arriving soon?"

"Yes. Pennelbeck Farm and I have been sadly wanting our mistress. And I'm anxious to meet our niece again. I confess myself quite at a loss to understand how Fanny persuaded her parents to let her come to us, and for a whole summer."

"The young lady is a Child of Privilege, I am to understand?"

Emery, omitting to note that his own wife was the Sister of

that same Privilege, replied that he did rather believe her father was in adequate pocket, being the proprietor of a well-known bank.

"Ah, so, the Monied Interest. I have a pamphlet by Cobbett." Wendell began searching his pockets. "It deals quite harshly with the jobbers and brokers. I'm sure you'd find it interesting."

Emery held his peace as the search proceeded, but at last Wendell was forced to admit that he had perhaps left the pamphlet lying by the waterfall where he had taken it from his pocket to read again, to the music of the splashing and purling of waterfall and stream. "However," he told Emery, "I am quite familiar with it, having read it three times, and I believe I can give you an adequate summary of the salient points."

"No, no," Emery protested. "As you may imagine, I'm much too excited at the moment to lend proper attention."

"Of course. I quite understand." Wendell extended his hand again. "Well, I must be getting about my errands." He lowered his voice for his next revelation. "I'm sending a poem to the *Edinburgh Review,*" he confided. Then, lowering his voice still further, he added, "It's quite radical. A paean to democracy, in fact."

Emery, somewhat alarmed and no longer amused, said, "Do you think that's wise? I dare say it's a fine poem but. . . ."

"Oh, I've not been so foolish as to suggest that democracy be immediately instituted in England. Even I would not dare to make such a suggestion through the medium of the *Edinburgh Review;* proposals for immediate democracy must be confined at present to less august journals." A faint sarcasm edged Wendell's voice. "Rather I praise the democracy of ancient Greece. It would be too much indeed to expect that either an Arrogant Aristocracy or the Monied Interest could accept democracy without violent protest . . ."

At that moment a horn was heard, and Wendell's discourse

trailed away in the blast. The Worthing carriage was approaching the inn, and Wendell, who was not insensitive to others, despite his love of discourse, said, "I'll be going on then, cousin. I hope you will permit me the pleasure of calling soon to welcome Fanny and to pay my respects to your niece."

Emery responded that he was certain both ladies would look forward with anticipation to the call, and Wendell, with a bow, walked off down the street. In another minute the carriage was at the inn door.

Maidie's first introduction to Pennelbeck Farm was not the house itself, but the view, for the buildings—a spacious stone farmhouse and barn—were entirely screened by trees as they approached along the narrow road. She had been properly awed by the scenery on the drive from Kendal to the village of Sagpaw and then to the head of Krigsmere, but as she alighted from the chaise she could not help exclaiming at the tranquil beauty that lay before her.

The farmhouse, on a slight rise above the lake, commanded a view of a small green meadow on which several cows were at graze. A gate in the stone wall that bordered the road gave access to a path that descended into and through the meadow, and thence to a boat landing. The lake stretched away to the south, and beyond it a range of high craggy hills thrust skyward, the peaks rising purple shadowed and bare from the meadows and woods that covered the lower slopes.

"How magnificent the mountains are!" Maidie exclaimed, awestruck. She had never seen a mountain before.

"We call them fells here in the Lakes," Fanny told her.

It was nearly sunset, and the rays of the sun, just sinking behind a yet loftier western range, illuminated the windows of a house situated on a high promontory on the eastern shore.

Fanny, noticing the direction of Maidie's gaze, said, "A family named Califaxton lives there. They have a houseful of young people, all of whom I'm sure you'll be anxious to meet." She thought it the exactly right introduction—casual and offhand—of the family from among whose sons she would find a husband for Maidie and a successor for Sam.

After meeting the household staff and eating a light supper, Maidie was happy to go immediately to her room. She was too young and healthy to be seriously fatigued, but sensibly decided that if she wished to be useful on the morrow, it would be well to recruit her resources with a good night's sleep. Fanny, knowing that her niece was unaccustomed to preparing herself for bed, offered to send the housemaid to her, or to herself assist, which latter Maidie gratefully accepted.

One of the several difficulties put in the way of her visit had been Aunt Seraphina's insistence, supported by Mr. Worthing, that in the interests of propriety, as well as personal comfort, she could not do without her maid. She had been adamant in her refusal; Fanny had concurred; and Clarice, to Maidie's great relief, was left behind to minister to whatever unlucky young lady Seraphina should find to employ her.

"It's just the buttons, Aunt Fanny. I'll soon learn, for indeed, I can't have you helping me every night, or depend on your housemaids, who surely have enough to do. I want to be self-reliant. To live simply, like you do. I was wondering if there's a woman in the village who could make up some simpler dresses for me? And my hair . . . perhaps I'll cut it, like you have yours." Maidie giggled. "Oh, wouldn't Papa have a *fit!*" Then, feeling guilty at such defiance of Papa, she said, "Or just do it in a simple knot on top, secured with a ribbon."

"Well, you must remember that I have my dearest Emery to help me with buttons, so you needn't feel at all that you're imposing if you must ask my help now and then. But, yes, there is a dressmaker in the village. She makes up my own dresses—except for the two or three I wear to magnificent London events.

She has some skill, although I fear her styles are limited. There," she said as the last button was undone. "Finished."

Slipping out of her dress, Maidie drew on her night robe and sat down at the small dressing table to brush her hair. "Do you understand, Aunt Fanny? I know I should be contented, I have so much. I have the kindest and dearest parents in the world, and I've had so many advantages—but I've so often wished . . . Oh, I don't know."

"Wished what, dear?"

"Wished my life was different. I, I'm just useless!"

Fanny, startled, said, "Oh, no, my dear. You have a good mind, you're well read, young, and positively blooming with health. You've had an excellent education, so much better than most girls receive—"

"There, you see, Aunt Fan. That's just it!"

"What's just it?"

"You just said it. I've been so much luckier than most females. So I should be content. But I can't be a lawyer or a doctor, or stand for Parliament. I don't want to study theology and argue for religious and civil rights, like Mama. If I could write, like you . . . but I can't."

Fanny could not deny that there were few acceptable employments for women aside from their households, so she only said, "Well, I can assure you, you'll not feel useless here, for you'll have to do your share of the baking and ironing and gardening."

"Oh, Aunt Fan, that's *just* what I want—to be useful! Just like you say it was with Mr. Wordsworth and his sister in their cottage. Plain living and high thinking."

"Yes, dear," Fanny replied. "Plain living and high thinking."

Later, after Fanny had at last fallen into her husband's arms, and both were satisfied that the joys of reunion had been adequately expressed, Fanny observed, "You know, Emery, Maidie has been simply *suffocated!*" She sat up in bed and pulled the blankets to her chin, uncovering Emery's toes.

Emery plumped his pillow and pulled himself up beside Fanny. He cradled her head against his shoulder. "Suffocated, my dear?"

"Tish and Sam love Maidie dearly, as she does them, and on the whole they've managed not to spoil her, but really, they do keep her too closely tied to their apron strings. The child needs a taste of freedom."

"Yes, I was surprised when you wrote that Maidie would be accompanying you. How did you convince Sam and Tish to let her come?"

Fanny skipped lightly over the preliminary hurdles—in fact, hardly touched them at all. "I just let Sam arrange a leisurely schedule so his only chick wouldn't tire herself too terribly much on the journey, or be in danger of brushing elbows with the rabble. Considering our own vulgar antecedents and Sam's antipathy to aristocrats, you would think he might be a little more republican in spirit! Well, he's given up on me, but his Maidie wasn't going to racket along up here in a common public conveyance, or sleep between possibly vermin infested sheets. So we traveled in state, as you saw, and he arranged for our accommodations. And where he judged the coaching inn inadequate, he found an acquaintance to entertain us. The fact is, we spent only two nights, of the five we were on the road, in coaching inns."

Emery's sympathies were with Mr. Worthing; he had never liked Fanny's insistence on traveling by common coach, unaccompanied by a maid, no matter how much authenticity it lent her journals.

Fanny patiently listened to her husband's well-worn observations on That Subject, and then placidly continued. "The family who entertained us in Birmingham was absolutely wonderful. I'm hoping they can visit us here. Unitarians of course—Tish's connections, not Sam's. That is, not banking people. In fact, I doubt Sam knows they aren't married—officially, that is."

"I wasn't aware there was any other way to be married than officially."

"Unitarians and other religious dissenters aren't licensed to perform marriages. Did you know that? Anyway, except for the Quakers and Jews among their own congregations, only Church of England clergy can marry people. Tish is spending much of her very limited strength these days on seeking civil rights for nonconformists. I may write an article . . . it's disgraceful, really. Well, be that as it may, the people who entertained us in Birmingham must stand on their principles! So they went through a private ceremony—exchanging vows and swearing eternal fidelity—I'm sure it was wonderfully affecting—and now claim to be married in the eyes of God. In fact, they admit that even some of the Unitarians in Birmingham won't accept them. But I do hope they will visit us. They have the most delightful children!"

"Children, by Jove!" Emery put Fanny from him to frown at her. "This is worse and worse!" He pulled her against his shoulder again and kissed the top of her head. "Although, I suppose, we needn't point out to our neighbors that they aren't married— officially, that is."

Fanny turned her face up for another kiss, which she received on the tip of her nose. "That may be a difficulty. I think they rather like pointing it out. Anyway, as I was saying, even though I permitted Sam to make all our arrangements, I can't say he was easy to persuade. Right up to the absolute ultimate minute I was in the most dreadful fear that he'd change his mind. Tish, I think, understands that Maidie really does need more freedom, although she'd never be able to permit it herself. The thing is, they've taught her to be independent, without permitting her to *be* independent."

Emery yawned. "Perhaps you're right, but it's time you were asleep, my dear. That was a long journey. I suppose you have two notebooks full of your adventures?"

"Mmmmmm," Fanny murmured, and snuggled more closely into the curve of his arm.

Fanny and Emery occupied a large bedroom in the Peel tower that formed the eastern anchor for the old farmhouse. This three-storied rectangular tower with its spiral staircase and battlemented roof had once been the home of a Westmoreland landed family. When cattle raiders from Scotland approached, or one of the innumerable battles of the interminable border wars threatened, livestock was gathered into the close-by barmkin; while in the tower the ladder to the living quarters above the ground floor storage cellar was drawn up, and the house became a fortress. As peace became more prevalent in the reign of the great Elizabeth Tudor, the tower cellar was given a decent floor, a door and windows, and a wing was extended from the western face. Time passed. The barmkin became an ordinary barn and farm yard. An improving owner enlarged and remodeled the Tudor wing, and removed the last concessions to fortification by converting all the tower loopholes and slots to windows, an undertaking that required the removal of a prodigious amount of stone. The thrifty improver used the stone for building a terrace. The fortress became a spacious farmhouse.

The Clarkes had made the tower their own. A library occupied the ground floor, and in the large room above, where an entire family had once lived and worked, they too worked. This workroom, which they called their Scriptorium, housed their desks and papers. There were also scattered tables, a sofa, and comfortable chairs so that even when not working they could retire alone if the house was too full of guests. Above, under the battlemented roof, was their bedroom. The old staircase, spiraling upward, had been restored and strengthened, and provided private communication between the three floors.

There were six bedrooms in the long farmhouse wing—three large rooms on the front, and three other rooms that overlooked the kitchen roof and the farmstead behind, and by their smaller size left space for the main stairway that angled up from a central hall below. Given her choice of bedrooms, Maidie without hesitation took a corner room on the front, from which she could look out on the orchard beside the house, or across the narrow road to the lake.

Before she climbed into her bed, she went to the window and swung open the casement for one last glimpse of Krigsmere. A sliver of moon silvered the crests of the ripples raised by the slight breeze blowing over the lake. The orchard had passed its bloom, but imagination brought her the scent of apple blossom. What adventures, she wondered, awaited her here? She shivered deliciously and hugged herself, but she threw her head back and took several deep breaths before bouncing across the room and into her bed.

As she lay curled under the covers, gazing out the still open window, she spared a thought for Lord Calvette. He had been decidedly trying at their leavetaking, had become quite passionate, attempted to declare himself, promised to write her every day, and threatened to follow her north within the week. Ah, the follies of inviting a kiss. She had foiled his attempts to declare himself, she hoped with enough skill that he would realize such a declaration to be in vain, and suggested that her father would disapprove, as well as her aunt and uncle, should he write to her, and even more should he follow her north.

Lord Calvette did not occupy her mind long. Her thoughts strayed instead to the people they had met on their journey, and Fanny's talent for encouraging them to tell her the most amazing stories about themselves. Fanny had made their trip an adventure, even if her father hadn't allowed them to travel in a public coach, and she had loved every minute of it. More contented than she had been for a long time, she went to sleep.

She was up early the next morning, expecting to help with the breakfast preparations, but she found her aunt and uncle already at the table, each reading a newspaper, and their own breakfast plates cleared away.

"Oh," she said, disappointed. "I thought I was up so early! Why didn't you call me to help with breakfast?" She leaned down and kissed her aunt's cheek, and then turned to Emery. "Good morning, Uncle Emery."

Emery smiled at her. "Sit down, Maidie. No one expects you to do any work the first day you're here."

"Yes, dear, do sit down. Stella and Mrs. Eckston always prepare breakfast. And in any event, I want to show you my domain as soon as you've eaten, and if you feel rested enough, we'll go visiting this afternoon."

Emery folded his newspaper. "I should warn you, Fanny, that Wendell has already expressed his intention to pay his respects, and although I doubt he'll call today, I'm sure he'll only wait until he judges you both have had time to get settled."

"Wendell is the young poet I've told you about, Maidie," Fanny explained. "He's Emery's distant—very distant—cousin. A well-mannered young man, despite his lofty pretensions to poetry and high principles. Of course, I was only just getting acquainted with him before I left for London."

Emery smiled. There was something about Wendell that seemed to call forth smiles. "I've come to know him rather well in the month you've been gone, Fanny. When, as in Cowper's poem, 'I never heard the sweet music of speech, and started at the sound of my own,' I often invited him to join me for dinner and the evening. He strikes me as sturdy and responsible, for all his prattling. More interested in politics than poetry, I suspect. Has his cottage strewn with Cobbett's and Price's pamphlets; he quotes from old Tom Paine or Will Godwin whenever he gets a chance. But before I forget, we've another new Lakeland resident."

"Oh?" Fanny's enthusiasm was not marked. "I do detest the villa builders!"

"Our newcomer isn't planning to build, Fanny," her husband pointed out mildly. "He's only renting the old Huddleston house in Sagpaw for a few months. He's not even here at present. Visiting Derbyshire and the western lakes. Name's Gilmichael. A distant relative of the present Marquis of Enett, I believe. Was on the Peninsula with Wellington. You'll like him, Fan, and so will you, Maidie. He might be called proud, I suppose, but I haven't found him so. He's an angler. Matter of fact, I met him while fishing Haweswater. Krigsmere was too calm that day for good sport."

"Oh, well," Fanny patted her husband's hand indulgently. "If he's another of the Piscator species I'm sure we'll welcome him as is his due."

"I'm sure you will, my dear, but I doubt your hospitality will be often tried. Although conversable enough, he strikes me as desirous of solitude. Not at all like the Califaxtons, who show strong inclinations toward conviviality."

"The family across the lake in that awful house?" Maidie asked.

"No, really, Maidie." Fanny's eyes were thoughtfully focused on the sugar bowl. "We mustn't judge people by their houses. Of course, I only just met them before I left for London. Although it appears that Emery has been furthering the acquaintance . . ."

Emery nodded, eyeing Fanny. When Fanny addressed sugar bowls, he sensed mischief. "Yes, others of our neighbors whom

I sought out during my lonesome weeks without a wife. They seem pleasant, despite their crime of positioning their house in the middle of the view. There are four young men and their sister, and the parents, of course—"

"I thought the sister would make a friend for you," Fanny interrupted. "We'll certainly try our best to call on them this afternoon." Fanny sturdily ignored the faint pricking from her conscience; she had felt similar pricks so many times in her thirty-five years that she was quite hardened to them. "No one ever stands on ceremony here, you know. And Emery can manage any callers. We have so many amazingly interesting visitors in the summer—so entertaining! So we just keep open house in the afternoons. You'll see. But today we will call on the Califaxtons. One should never neglect one's neighbors."

Emery retired to the tower workroom, and when Maidie finished her breakfast Fanny led her out into the garden, without even a suggestion that dishes might need washing. "Oh, Mrs. Eckston and Stella always wash up," Fanny said carelessly.

A stiff, fresh breeze was raising small whitecaps on the surface of the lake as Fanny and Maidie finished their inspection of the gardens. Tying their bonnets more securely, they crossed the road to sit on the drystone wall and enjoy the midmorning view of the lake.

"It's only a mile and maybe a quarter long, and half as broad," Fanny said, "but if Grasmere, which is a smaller lake, was sufficient for Wordsworth's youthful muse, I'm sure Krigsmere is big enough for mine. And really, I only cared that my new home have a soul-shatteringly exquisite view. As for Emery—although not immune to the glories of nature—he wanted only good fishing."

Emery, who had come out to join them, added, "Yes, good char and trout in our lake, and some fine trout streams and tarns on the fells that aren't too far away or difficult of access. We'll be sampling some of the char tonight, for I had excellent luck this morning."

Fanny patted his hand, and smiled.

Three

Fanny and Maidie, accompanied by Emery, set out that very afternoon to call on the Califaxton family. "It's much more the thing, you know, to walk than to drive, and certainly much more healthful," Fanny remarked. "Although we could also row across the lake. That must be one of your first lessons—rowing. I'm sure you know how to walk."

They had just left Emery at the small Sagpaw inn, where he was expecting a package of books delivered, when Fanny, who had been pointing out to Maidie the few sights of the village, exclaimed, "Why, there's Wendell!"

Although an object in a window had first caught the eye of the young poet-radical, he was now staring at it blankly, unaware of anything or of anyone, having suddenly hit upon a thought inspired by an early morning reading of a pamphlet on education for the working man. Others, however, were not so unaware of him. Despite his carelessly rumpled appearance and windblown hair, he attracted the eyes of every female in sight between the ages of ten and senility.

Wendell would have liked to be languorously thin, with a pale, poetic, and possibly consumptive complexion, but he had soon discovered that a poet—at least a poet with a tendency to tan— cannot revel in scenes of nature and remain pale. He had also discovered that he was too fond of a good chop to achieve the delicate physical state his poetic ambition seemed to require, and in any event, as he sadly recognized, nature had given him a well-muscled body that would need rigorous starvation to achieve emaciation. Other than regretting that his physical appearance was out of tune with his ambition, Wendell was (as their ancient relative had written Emery) entirely free of any personal vanity or self-consciousness.

Fanny took Maidie's arm to direct her across the street. "You might as well meet Wendell now as later. He's one of the local sights, you know. And really, I was growing quite fond of the boy before I went to London. But I should warn you . . ."

Wendell turned away from the window just as Maidie and Fanny were approaching, and the abstraction faded from his eyes as his face lit with recognition and welcome. Maidie, like all others of her sex, was staggered by the sudden encounter with such a gorgeous male specimen. Although forcibly struck, she responded to the introduction with admirable self-possession, hoping meanwhile that she had not betrayed her bedazzlement. She was certain that any young man blessed with such beauty must be vain, and she was determined not to add to what must surely be either conceit or vanity.

"So you're going to the Califaxtons!" Wendell exclaimed. "I'm of half a mind to go along with you, if my company won't burden you. I don't believe I've called there for nearly a week!"

"Yes, do join us," Fanny invited. "We'll only be stopping for a few minutes. I was thinking of a walk all the way around the lake, but I don't believe Maidie is up to such a long walk yet. We really must get her a pair of sensible shoes before we let her go clambering about the fells."

"Aunt Fanny!" Maidie protested. "I'm sure it's unfair of you to make me sound like some delicate miss who never did anything but play the pianoforte and paint posies on velvet! Was I not reared according to the principles of Dr. Erasmus Darwin to enjoy health and agility of body, as well as of the mind?"

Fanny squeezed her niece's arm. "No, love, how could I possibly give Wendell such a horribly mistaken notion of my favorite niece? Painting on velvet, indeed! No, it's just that one doesn't go walking too far at first, when unaccustomed to it, and especially in such dainty footwear as you are shod in."

Wendell, trying to hold his six-foot-plus stride down to Maidie's slower pace (although Fanny, as he knew, could snap along as briskly as any well-seasoned soldier on the march), thought to tactfully mention that Miss Califaxton painted on velvet—rather well, in fact. He then fell into an amiable discourse upon the beauties that Maidie could daily expect to unfold before her dazzled eyes.

"Oh, I'm so looking forward to seeing it all! Aunt Fanny described to me the view from one of the peaks. Which one was it, Aunt?"

"Skiddaw. When you've become more accustomed to long walks we'll go up again together. Or we can hire a guide and climb about on Place Fell, or the High Street, or our own Sagfel. I've simply glorious ambitions to conquer many heights. Dorothy Wordsworth did Scafel, and she's older than I am! But one mustn't just wander alone among the fells, you know, unless one is *absolutely* certain of the way. The mists drift in unexpectedly, and one can so easily stumble over a dangerous precipice. And a wrong turning, even in broad sunlight can leave one completely lost."

"High Street?" Maidie asked, puzzled.

"A corruption of Ystryd, the rector says," Wendell replied. "It's Norse—like fell for mountain and beck for stream. In the thousand years since the Vikings invaded the lakes, we've managed to turn Ystryd into good English. Although, if one thinks about it, the appellation in English isn't inappropriate, for one can still trace the remains of the Roman Way along the High Street Ridge. One's mind inevitably turns back to the Romance of the Past—there are worthy stories here for someone who

writes in the *Waverly* vein. I've done my poor best with an Ode
to the Legions of Agricola. It was Agricola who established Roman hegemony up here in the North, you know. And the view
is superb. It fills one with awe at the grandeur of nature . . ."

"Was it the beauties of nature, Mr. Duval, that brought you
to the Lakes?" Maidie asked, having already discerned that conversation with Wendell might occasionally involve a judicious
interruption.

"No, no, you must call me Wendell. We are practically cousins, you know. But to answer your question. I've thought of
coming to the Lakes ever since I read my first poem by William
Wordsworth. Have you read him?

> Through primrose-tufts, in that sweet bower,
> The periwinkle trailed its wreaths;
> And 'tis my faith that every flower
> Enjoys the air it breathes."

"Really, Wendell," Fanny expostulated. "An aspirant to literary achievement should look for his own lines."

Wendell laughed, a hearty, fulsome laugh that pleased Maidie,
who had already begun to reassess her first impression of the
young man.

"But," he said, "I do fancy the notion of the flowers enjoying
the air they breathe. And who says it better than old Daddy
Wordsworth? I'm sure I can't. In any event, Miss Worthing—I
hope I'll be permitted after a decent interval to call you by your
given name—but as I was saying, a distant relative of mine and
Emery's, when she learned I'd conceived the notion of coming
up here, recommended me to him. And as you see, here I am."

"And," Fanny said, "here we are at our destination. And Miss
Califaxton is coming to meet us, I believe."

Prudence Califaxton, in a simple white morning dress and
carrying a parasol, was hurrying down the walk toward them.

She met them at the gate, where she welcomed Fanny home, shyly surrendered her hand to Wendell for a brief instant, and then turned to Maidie. "Mr. Clarke told us that you would be visiting, Miss Worthing, and I'm so happy to meet you. I've been so looking forward to having another girl to walk with, and—" Then, seeming suddenly to feel she had been too presumptuous in expecting Maidie to want her friendship, she stopped, a pretty blush tinting her cheek. "But please come in. My mother has also been looking forward to your return, Mrs. Clarke, and to meeting Miss Worthing."

Wendell, putting on a wistful look, asked, "And are you including me in this invitation, Miss Califaxton?"

Another quick blush touched Miss Califaxton's cheek, but she replied, with a little laugh, "Of course, Mr. Duval. You know you're always welcome."

She led the visitors into a bright drawing room, where Mrs. Califaxton sat before an easel, sketching the panorama. The easel was quickly set aside, following a few compliments from her visitors on her skill with the pencil, and the bell rung for refreshments and to inform the young Califaxton gentlemen of callers.

The first of these interesting persons to enter the room was John, who although no match for Wendell in physical beauty, was well-enough looking to attract the female eye. He was simply dressed, as befitted the informality of a lakeside retreat, but the tailoring of his jacket was flawless, and his soft white shirt of the finest material. John Califaxton was fastidious, sober, elegant, and immaculate.

He carried a book in one hand, a finger still marking his place, which caused his mother to scold him for not having left it behind—surely he didn't intend to be so unmannerly as to read while they had guests? He replied vaguely that he'd forgotten to put it down, and deposited it on a nearby table.

Mrs. Califaxton then showed signs of wanting to scold him

for being absent-minded, but Fanny intervened by offering him her hand.

"You're looking exceedingly well, John. I hope I may call you John? There are such a daunting number of Mr. Califaxtons in this household!"

"Thank you, Mrs. Clarke, I'm very well. You may call me John, of course; I would prefer it. But may I welcome you home? Did you enjoy your trip to London?"

"I always enjoy seeing my relatives there, of course, but I can't say that I enjoy London itself. A few entertainments, a few friends, a visit to a museum, some artists' galleries and a ball with Maidie, and I've had enough of dreary city life. I'm afraid I've become an absolutely confirmed provincial."

"I quite understand. I wonder now that I once was opposed to my mother's Lakeland enthusiasm. But I did want to tell you how very much I enjoyed your last article in the *Edinburgh Review* about Owen's Lannark mill. I've suggested to my father that we should be imitating his system."

"Oh, really, John!" Mrs. Califaxton interrupted. "Spending all day with your poor head in a book! I've told him, Mrs. Clarke, that too much reading not only makes one nearsighted but gives one too many ideas. And I've told his father the same, but *he* won't do anything about it! He always did encourage the boy too much in his folly."

A good part of any conversation with Mrs. Califaxton was necessarily devoted to leading her away from her family's various deficiencies. John, whose clear gaze showed no sign of nearsightedness, smiled at Fanny. He, like others of the family, accepted with admirable equanimity that their mother, although a worthy woman, was a perpetual scold.

John acknowledged Wendell with a friendly handshake, and then said, turning to Maidie, "And is this the Miss Worthing who Mr. Clarke has spoken of? We have all been anticipating your arrival."

Fanny performed the introductions, to which Mrs. Califaxton was prepared to add considerable verbiage, until cut short by the entrance of Chester Califaxton.

While Chester stood by, a hint of amusement in his eye and more than a hint of impatience, Mrs. Califaxton told Maidie and Fanny that Chester was a good-natured boy. He'd never been a Dissenter like the rest of the family—always would go his own way, including the wrong way—but it explained why his father, much as she herself disapproved, insisted on Cambridge, that citadel of Anglican power. He was twenty-four, and although both she and Mr. Califaxton were anxious to see his future decided, he at present could think of nothing more than cutting a swath through Society and gadding around.

Maidie was at a loss how to respond to such a biographical introduction, but Chester, accustomed to his mother's eccentricities, took it in stride.

His attentions to Fanny and Maidie were all that was expected, but Chester readily saw that both ladies were already pleasantly settled, Maidie by Prudence, Fanny with his mother, and good old John as pivot. There would be plenty of time later to make the acquaintance of the pretty Miss Worthing, since he was going to be stuck in this rural retreat for an indefinite interval. He had begged his father to let him at least return to Manchester, if London was so absolutely forbidden, but that curmudgeony gentleman had flatly refused, and left him in the wilderness to reflect on the evils of overspending allowances and living on tick. So he turned his attention to Wendell, engaging him in the only one of his several interests he thought Wendell might share, a discussion of the local equine stock.

Wendell, for whom a horse was a creature to carry a man from one place to another more expeditiously than his own feet, would have preferred to join Maidie and Prudence rather than discuss horses with Chester. Nonetheless, as a radical poet and pamphlet reader committed to political justice and the common people, he intended to learn all he could of local industries, which in the Lakes had much to do with agricultural and pastoral pursuits. He soon had the younger Califaxton, who had an eye for horses, lecturing on Fell ponies, the sturdy little work animals that Wendell admired in much the same spirit that he admired working people.

Maidie had taken advantage of John Califaxton's conversation with Fanny to draw Prudence aside, in order to further their acquaintance by commenting on a framed picture, a spray of violets painted on velvet, which she correctly guessed, thanks to Wendell, had been executed by Prudence. The girl was shy and self-deprecatory, but a few minutes of listening to Mrs. Califaxton had been all that Maidie needed to explain her daughter's retiring manner. She seemed a sweet girl, although with no great depth of intellect, and certainly eager to be a friend.

Maidie exerted all the skill at her command to make Prudence feel her genuine interest in her and her activities, and was eventually rewarded by sentence-long replies rather than just "Yes, Miss Worthing" and "No, Miss Worthing." Prudence was clearly longing for the companionship of another young female, surrounded as she was by brothers, and separated from her Manchester friends. So she asked if Prudence would be so kind as to show her some of the more famous lake views in the days to come, to which Prudence consented with great eagerness.

There were no restrictions, Prudence said, on well-brought-up young ladies walking alone to the village, or to visit their friends, or even to explore the paths around the lake. When Maidie exclaimed that it was wonderful to be able to anticipate such freedom, and that it would be delightful beyond anything after the confinements of London, Prudence replied eagerly, "Oh, yes, I too find it restful. One is so constantly attended in our situations, and of course, everyone thinks that a mere girl can be interrupted any time, no matter what she may be doing!"

Astonished by these symptoms of rebellion, Maidie replied,

"Yes, isn't it just the way! Well, we will walk together whenever
you want. I am completely at your disposal—as soon as Aunt
Fanny sees to more appropriate footwear for me. She tells me I
am most inappropriately shod for jauntering. Do you have any
particularly favorite walks, Miss Califaxton?"

John, on overhearing this last remark, turned to the young
women. "Prudence and I share a favorite walk up the Vale of
Pennelbeck, don't we Pru?"

As John turned his attention to Maidie and his sister, Fanny
took the opportunity to make some polite inquiries concerning
the missing Califaxton males, beginning with the head of the
family. "Mr. Califaxton is well, I hope?"

"Oh, yes, he's quite well." Mrs. Califaxton sighed. "I fear,
however, he presumes too much on a robust constitution. He
had been here with us only four days when he was required to
return to Manchester. It does seem unfair that I am left so much
alone; I sometimes wonder if we were wise to build—if perhaps
short-term rentals might not have been better. But you know
how it is with business, something always going awry! And of
course he felt it necessary that Arthur be with him."

"Then we are not to have the pleasure of Mr. Arthur's company today either?"

"No. Nor for many a day, if I'm any judge. But business
affairs must be attended to. I'm sure I am not one to speak poorly
of the source from which my comforts come—that is, I speak
of the demands of Mr. Califaxton's trading and manufacturing
interests. Although my family were gentry, I have never been
one to look down on those who engage in trade, and although
my papa objected to my marrying Mr. Califaxton, when it came
to marriage I determined to please myself."

Fanny, granddaughter of a banker who had begun life as the
son of a landless laborer, said wryly, "I admire your republican
spirit."

"Thank you. There are some who might not find that a compliment, as you are aware, Mrs. Clarke, but I do. I'm not ashamed of my opinions. I'm afraid Mr. Califaxton is not so liberal, nor Arthur either. How anyone can be a Tory and a Unitarian at one and the same time simply overwhelms the mind! Of course an elder son should be at his father's right hand, so it's well they share like views. And Lance thinks of nothing but the army. He would be off, you know, there was just no stopping him . . . no concern for the welfare of the business at all—"

"I thought Mr. Lance had sold out after the peace," Fanny interrupted. "Do you mean to say he has returned to the army?"

"Yes, indeed he has. He says he never should have sold out. He intends to make army his 'career,' as he calls it. I say it's time both he and Arthur—and John and Chester too—started thinking of the *first* career that men were designed to pursue—marrying and begetting children. Who ever heard of a woman with four grown sons over twenty-four years of age, and no grandchildren!"

Fanny, staggered by the rapid evaporation of eligible Califaxton males, remarked weakly, "I suppose then, that we shan't be seeing Mr. Lance again for some time?"

"No, he's to be posted to India, I understand. He may get a week at home before he departs. He has a friend here, you know. Mr. Allan Gilmichael. Distantly related to the present marquis." Mrs. Califaxton, for all her republican sympathies, preened delicately. "Have you met him?"

"Mr. Gilmichael? No. Emery has spoken of him. I believe Mr. Gilmichael is an angler?"

"Yes. He came here for the fishing on Lance's recommendation. The Huddleston house was just vacant. So convenient. Such a well-mannered, gentlemanly man, although between you and me, I find him rather gloomy—or perhaps I should say, to the better credit of his character, that he appears low in spirits—but whatever it might be, he is not at all disposed to be sociable. But very handsome in a dark sort of way. At first you believe his eyes are too close together, but then you see that it lends a certain distinction to his face. I was hoping he would consider himself one of the family, but he keeps to himself. It would have made our days more lively, to be sure. With Chester poking around wishing he was in London and John spending so much time with his books and preaching, they might as well not be here either. By the way, did you know John's going off to Scotland to do missionary work? Isn't that just what one could expect from too much reading?"

John had been listening with one ear to the conversation on his right, while engaging his sister and the charming Miss Worthing on his left, and wondering where in blazes were the refreshments his mother had ordered. The arrival of a tea tray and a selection of fruits at the moment his mother began another exposition on his foolishness was welcome. "I'm sure Mrs. Clarke isn't interested in my affairs, ma'am," he remarked in his habitual calm voice. "Shouldn't we perhaps all have some refreshment?"

"Yes, of course. But Scotland! Unitarianism is too difficult for the lower class of people in any event, and then to think one could convert such people as the Scots, who are already Presbyterians! It's too provoking. As I've said to him many times, reading too much is dangerous—"

"Ma'am," John said, "Mrs. Clarke is waiting for her tea."

There was a tone in John's voice, gentle as it had been, that Mrs. Califaxton had long since recognized as brooking no nonsense. He was the only one of her children she held in awe, and she thought it odd that it should be her second son who had inherited his father's force of character, even with his infernal bookishness. Lance had command, and Arthur business sense, but John. . . . Mrs. Califaxton let the thought go, and turned her mind to her duties as hostess.

The arrival of the refreshments drew the circle together again, and the conversation remained general until the Pennelbeck party rose to make their farewells.

They were no sooner outside the Califaxton gates than a discussion of the family was underway.

"One would never know, to listen to that nag of a woman," Fanny said, "that she is very good with her pencil, and her interest quite serious. And if Prudence would give up velvet, I believe she might be even better."

"What have you against painting on velvet, ma'am?" asked Wendell. "I rather admire Miss Califaxton's pretty pictures of flowers and kitty-cats. And the subjects stand out remarkably well against the soft texture and midnight shade of the velvet."

Maidie thought as little of such endeavors as her aunt, but nonetheless had liked Prudence. "She's such a sweet girl, Aunt Fanny, that soft velvet seems just the right medium, and flowers and kitty-cats just right for her subjects."

Fanny, disgusted at such philistinism, changed the subject. "How disappointing that Arthur and Lance have gone!" she exclaimed. "I had all sorts of entertainments planned for you, Maidie, and now all the Califaxtons are leaving—even John!"

"Chester remains," Wendell said, a little gloomily. He had come to rather like the older Califaxton brothers, but he thought Chester a devilish bore. "And I don't think Mrs. and Miss Califaxton have any intention of leaving soon. Poor Miss Califaxton! Chester will keep himself out of sight as much as possible, and she'll be the only one left for her mother to scold. A regular Xanthippe, that woman!"

"I hope," said Maidie, "that I'll be able to relieve Miss Califaxton now and then. She says that we may explore the paths near the lake without chaperons. We've already agreed to walk tomorrow if it's all right with you, Aunt Fanny. Mr. John Califaxton says there's a Druid circle just off the cart road up Pennelbeck Vale, and not far beyond it a spot called Melt's Crag, which he says isn't a difficult climb, but that the prospect from the height is noble."

Fanny did not like to restrict Maidie's activities so soon, but the way to Melt's Crag could be easily lost once the cart road and stream were left behind. "You and Prudence may walk anywhere you like on the paths close to the lake, but I don't think Mrs. Califaxton would permit her daughter to venture so far as Melt's Crag without one of her brothers as an escort."

"Oh, Mr. Chester Califaxton might agree to accompany us, although Miss Califaxton says he isn't at all fond of walking. She suggested that you, Mr. Duval, might enjoy an excursion to Melt's Crag also."

Wendell said that he would take great pleasure in accompanying the party, and Fanny, relieved at such immediate results to her scheming despite the absence of two of the Califaxton males, agreed that it would be a most excellent expedition for them, as soon as Maidie had acquired some sturdy walking boots. In fact, they could stop at the shoemaker's shop on their way through the village to have her measure taken, and within a week she would have her boots.

While Fanny and Maidie visited the shoemaker, Wendell made the purchases that had originally taken him to the village. He had just left the apothecary shop, where he had secured a compound guaranteed to destroy all forms and sizes of ants with one application, when he realized that he had left his other packages on the counter. He turned around to return, and as he did so, a ginger-haired gentleman stepped quickly into another shop two doors away. Wendell had seen the man once before; and at the time had thought his actions furtive. And there'd been that feeling that he was being followed the day before, when he went to Kendal. It was true that there had been an increase in crime in recent years, but it was concentrated in the cities, and here in the Lakes there were few who seriously locked their doors. He

could hardly report the man to the magistrate on the basis of a
furtive manner, but he made a note to keep a sharper eye out.

He sat down on a bench in the modest market square beside
a ruddy farmer who was also awaiting his womenfolk. The
farmer easily recognized Wendell as an Outsider, and felt it a
civic duty to give him some advice on what he should see and
do during his stay in the Lakes. On discovering that Wendell
was at least for a time a permanent resident, he moved on to
Lakeland entertainments more admired by local folk than gawk-
ing at scenery.

Wendell was of two minds about foxhunting, on which the
farmer was waxing eloquent. The shepherds and farmers insisted
that they lost an appalling number of lambs each year to foxes,
but on the other hand, he had never really liked the idea of hunting. Shooting an animal was one thing—even justifiable if killed
for food, but hounding it to exhaustion and then leaving it for
the dogs to destroy was cruel. Wendell was not a sportsman, and
the farmer's fulsome admiration for a fox that had consistently
eluded the best hounds of the Sagpaw pack not only puzzled
him, but struck him as plainly odd.

"Come join us if you're still about when the hunting season
begins," his new acquaintance invited. "We're not exclusive
here; quite democratic, if I may use the word. We follow the
hunt on foot, you know."

This latter revelation—that foxhunting in the Lakes was not
the privilege of Landed and Monied Interests—in fact, even
called democratic, softened Wendell's attitude to a small degree.
He thanked his companion, but said he thought he might not be
in the Lakes long enough to enjoy that pleasure, at which the
farmer said that he shouldn't miss the sports contest in the
autumn.

"Big fellow like you, lots of muscle—ought to be wrestling.
Wasn't bad at it myself in my youth." And if Wendell got up
toward Place Fell way and the village of Patterdale, he should

stop by the farm and have a bite to eat—stay the night even, if
he liked. Good fishing in the tarn nearby, if he happened to like
that activity—or (with a wink) needed to fill out his larder. He'd
even show him a few tricks a man ought to know about fell
wrestling. Took skill more than brute strength. "None of this
country fair stuff, where the biggest young lout in town can
challenge a broken-winded old ringster."

Wendell thanked the farmer, assuring him that should he
decide to wrestle, he would certainly need some instructing,
and went off to meet Fanny and Maidie, who he perceived
approaching.

When they reached his cottage, he urged them to stop for a
few minutes. Wendell, among other talents, was handy, and he
wanted Fanny to see the improvements they had discussed and
that he had made during her absence. Maidie thought the white-
washed stone cottage charmingly picturesque, with its lead-
paned windows and sweet-scented honeysuckle growing
lavishly over the wall, and was delighted to see the interior.

The kitchen was not large, but Wendell had added shelves for
better storage, and a worktable that fit cleverly in an alcove.
Although Fanny would have preferred he have a stove like the
one at Pennelbeck Farm, she declared the fireplace and its ap-
purtenances completely adequate. The sitting room was larger
and also boasted a fireplace, before which Wendell had placed
several comfortable old chairs and a low, rustic table. He had
shortened the legs to make it a convenient height for occupants
of the chairs, an innovation with which Fanny was delighted.
The table was nearly hidden beneath a burden of books, pamphlets, and sheets of scribbled paper, except for one corner occupied by a portable writing desk.

"And above," Wendell said, "there's a loft. The ceiling's low,
but there's a dormer wide enough for my modest pallet, and
before I set myself adrift on the River Lethe I can contemplate
the expanse of the heavens and the length of Krigsmere—" He

suddenly stopped, a puzzled expression on his face. "What's that ladder doing there?"

Fanny cast him a half-mocking look of puzzlement. "Why Wendell, dear, I believe that's how you reach your lovely loft."

"Yes, of course, but I never leave it in place during the day. See, there are hooks along that wall, for keeping it out of the way in the daytime."

"Are you sure? One does forget now and then, you know."

"No, I'm certain I hung it up. I remember doing it. Old Peggy doesn't do the loft, and she wants the ladder out of the way when she's working. But she's visiting her daughter over near Coniston this week, and I've left the ladder down. Then this morning I decided I'd better sweep up a little. I remember hanging up the ladder because I thought to myself as I was doing it that, just like Old Peg, I like it out of the way when I'm tidying the room."

"Your door wasn't locked," Maidie observed.

"No, not the front door, but the back door was. I don't expect thieves to walk in the front."

"Well, someone did," Fanny said. "Unless the back door lock is broken."

Wendell went off to check, but returned immediately to report that the back door was still locked with no sign of any attempt to force it. "He came in the front door, whoever he was. I must say, he was a nervy one!"

"Shouldn't you examine the loft to see if anything's missing up there?" Maidie asked.

"No sooner said than executed!" Wendell bolted up the ladder, and they heard him moving around above their heads. He was soon back down to report that nothing seemed disturbed.

"Shouldn't we check the kitchen again?" Fanny asked.

They all trooped into the kitchen, but they discovered no supplies missing, the pots and pans were all on their hooks, and some coins lying in plain sight on a shelf were undisturbed.

"It is exceedingly strange," Fanny mused, as they returned to the main room. "Why would anyone enter a cottage, go up in the loft, but not take anything or disturb anything?"

"Strange indeed." Wendell stirred around in the literary works on the low table, but shook his head. His small lap desk was open and he suspected that it had been searched, but he didn't want to agitate Fanny or frighten Maidie. He could investigate that matter later. "I can't tell whether any of these papers or books were moved or not. I just toss them higgely-piggely on the table. Perhaps whoever it was thought he was in imminent danger of discovery and hurried away before he could steal anything. Or more likely some boys up to some mischief. Yes, now I think of it, I'm certain it must have been some misbehaved boys. Well, I'll lock both my doors and the shutters for a few days, but I'm not going to worry about it. And don't either of you worry either. Or bother Emery with it."

Fanny stated firmly that thievery and vandalism should be reported to the authorities, and that he should make a more thorough and careful inspection. Wendell agreed, but was determined to keep his own counsel.

Four

Three youngsters were playing on the lawn at Pennelbeck Farm when Fanny and Maidie arrived home, and in the house Emery and a gentleman with a beard were in animated converse, while a pleasant, fair-haired lady listened indulgently. "Just another historian," as the gentleman introduced himself, passing through with his family on the way to Scotland, and desiring to discuss with Emery an obscure point having to do with Charles II and the Restoration.

The two historians talked late into the night, after a plain-living supper of mutton and boiled potatoes followed by a simple pudding, and so it was midnight before Emery was free, and Fanny able to unburden her stricken soul.

"So this afternoon," she related, as Emery prepared for bed, "we called on the Califaxtons, and I was mortified to the greatest degree to learn that the oldest son will be indefinitely in Manchester—something to do with business. Then the military one has rejoined the army. And John's thinking of going off to Scotland as a Unitarian missionary! I have to agree with Mrs. Califaxton there. She thinks his brain has been weakened by too much reading! That leaves Chester, who must be about Maidie's age, and unless I've sadly mistaken the case, is in any event much too youngish for her. Or irresponsible, perhaps I mean. I've lured Maidie away up here with false promises."

"No, Fan, I can't believe Maidie wanted to visit us because of the Califaxtons. She isn't the sort to be desperately campaigning for a husband."

"Maidie doesn't know anything about it. And I'll thank you not to give me away. I promised Sam and Tish four eligible men—and not one of them aristocrats. You know Sam's prejudices!"

"And how did you know they were eligible? You had only just met them before you left for London."

"I know, I know. But they were all so handsome, and well-bred and agreeable—none of them married, and the family wealthy enough that there'd be no need to fear heiress hunting."

Emery completed his toilet, carefully snuffed his candle and, joining Fanny in bed, leaned over to kiss her cheek. Fanny snuffed her own bedside candle, leading Emery to suppose she was composing herself for sleep. But just as he was drifting off, she spoke again, in a perfectly wide-awake voice.

"The angler you spoke of . . . Mr. Gilmichael. How old is he?"

"Ummm," Emery answered sleepily. "Never asked him."

"Of course you didn't. Guess."

"Oh, maybe thirty or so—perhaps a year or two younger."

"Is he morose?"

"Morose? No."

"Something weighing on his spirits?"

It struck Emery that he might have said so, had he given it any thought, but he merely grunted a sleepy, "Why?"

"I just wondered. Does he have money?"

At this question Emery surrendered. He sat up in order to stare down at Fanny with an admonitory frown. "Just what scheme are you concocting now?"

"I can't see your censorious expression in the dark, dear one, so lie back down and be comfortable. I merely wish to know if Mr. Gilmichael is beforehand with the world. These 'distant cousins of marquis' are often a bit out at the elbows and on the look-out for heiresses. On the other hand, anyone too extremely rich wouldn't suit either, you see—"

"Disabuse yourself of that dream, Fanny. Although I'd lay odds that Gilmichael is an honorable gentleman, and I can't believe that he's out at the elbows, he's not suitable for Maidie. And he clearly wishes to keep his past and his present circumstances to himself."

"Oh? How intriguing. Then how do you know his relationship to the Marquis of Enett?"

Emery, now fully and irritably awake, replied crossly, "I just know." Then, thinking to protect his angling friend from a reputation for boastfulness, he added, "Gilmichael's never mentioned it, and I'm sorry that I did, for it neither adds nor detracts from his character, which I judge to be upright and principled. It was Mrs. Califaxton, I suppose. Gilmichael's an acquaintance of the military son . . . whatshisname . . ."

"Lance, of course. A perfect name. I wonder if it influenced his choice of career?"

"Now what is going on in those stupendous Worthing intellectuals?"

"I'm ashamed of you, Emery. Isn't a lance a military implement?"

"I'm going to sleep."

After another brief silence, Fanny said, "Anyway, I needed a good argument to use to convince Sam and Tish to let Maidie come to us. They'd never have permitted it otherwise. I only care that Maidie marry someone who's worthy of her."

"Takes a lot to be worthy of a Worthing," Emery remarked.

"I'm tired of that joke," Fanny said severely. A few more minutes passed and Emery was dropping off again when Fanny said, "I must remember to warn Maidie not to mention in her letters that Wendell's politics border on the radical. Probably shouldn't mention he's a poet, either, but then his poetry is so bad . . . What do you think, Emery?"

Emery preserved his silence, and Fanny, with a smile, subsided.

A few suspicious thoughts had crossed Maidie's mind when Fanny lamented the missing Califaxton males, but it would never have occurred to her, even on deep reflection, that her favorite aunt had used the lure of four eligible young men to wheedle her parents. In fact, the following days were so filled with activity and new people and experiences that she had little time for reflection on any subject.

They went to bed at odd hours and arose when they felt like it. Sometimes Maidie was called from her bed to watch a sunrise, or they sat by starlight in the quiet, fragrant orchard, talking until the early morning hours. There was her new friendship with Prudence Califaxton and Emery's cousin, Wendell. And there were the visitors.

Fanny and Emery's mornings and early afternoons were reserved for their writing. A light luncheon two or three hours after midday served as their dinner, and at four o'clock they threw their teatime open to all comers. High thinking—politics, political economy, literature, any subject of the day—but also gossip and nonsense occupied the guests as they drank tea, or coffee or chocolate, and ate whatever plain-living consumables the household had on hand that day. Neighbors and local people came, friends from many parts, and the trippers, the sightseeing travelers who were also eager to meet the literary folk who had settled in the Lake District—among them Fanny and Emery, the Wordsworths at Rydal Water, and the Southeys at Keswick. Then perhaps the trippers would be on to Scotland, where Walter Scott held open house at Abbotsford.

The only meal taken at any regular hour was supper, at nine

in the evening. As time went on, Wendell was expected to join them. Fanny thought he needed mothering, and within a week his presence was taken for granted. After their supper they read aloud, recited poetry, discussed history or literature, or whatever subject came to mind. It was Wendell and Maidie's duty to wash up afterward, since Fanny did not believe in keeping servants late just to cater to their employers' evening activities.

As Fanny had promised, Maidie was also given tasks to do. She made her own bed and tidied her room. She helped in the flower and vegetable gardens, was learning to iron her own dresses, had made gingerbread, and would soon begin instruction in bread baking. For all that there were chores she was expected to do, and for all that schedules and routines were largely ignored, she was beginning to wonder about plain living, for life at Pennelbeck Farm was very comfortable indeed. She had hours of leisure in which to explore her surroundings and to pursue her friendship with Prudence Califaxton. But although she might doubt plain living, Wendell certainly gave her to believe that at least one among them indulged in high thinking.

Wendell took to rambling the lake paths and lower fells with Prudence and Maidie, sadly neglecting his creative duties, but he never forgot to carry a notebook and a stub of pencil in his pocket, and often stopped to record in verse a particularly delicious scene. He had a habit of carrying radical pamphlets stuffed in his pockets as well, which he read to them, and which sometimes led to spirited disagreements, particularly on the occasions when Chester Califaxton accompanied them.

Prudence carried a sketch pad, for besides painting flowers and kittens on velvet she also drew timid landscapes. Maidie, who couldn't draw, and who had never willingly written a poem in her life, nonetheless carried a notebook to record impressions. She would have felt neglectful had she failed to do so.

Maidie was hard-pressed in her letters to her mama and papa to describe all the beauties, they were so many and varied; and

as the days passed, more of her paragraphs were devoted to their
many activities and fewer to nature's glories. One splendid rainstorm which elicited a lengthy poem from Wendell's pen, from
Maidie's resulted only in a description of Wendell (imitating Mr.
Wordsworth) standing under an umbrella for an hour or more
contemplating the downpour and fashioning lyric phrases to describe it—and suffering a heavy head cold as a consequence.
He had recited his "Rainy Day on Krigsmere" to them as soon
as he was sufficiently recovered to pronounce his nasal conso-
nants, but Maidie didn't think it worth wasting ink to transcribe.
Mindful of her father's distaste for poets, she assured her parents
that Wendell wasn't *much* of a poet. And she felt quite certain,
she added, that Mr. Wordsworth, although she had not yet had
the pleasure of meeting him, did not use a *leaky* umbrella.

Busy as life was at Pennelbeck Farm, one fine morning three
weeks after Maidie's arrival, she found herself without a single
chore to do or guest to entertain. The morning was brilliant after
two days of heavy rain, and a brisk breeze, with nearly twelve
hours of uninterrupted sunshine the previous day, had dried the
paths—all of which together demanded a walk to some local
beauty spot.

She climbed the spiral stair to peek into the Scriptorium on
the chance that her aunt might also want exercise, but Fanny's
creative forces were in full spate. Her hair showed signs of the
tousling it always received when she was composing vigorous
prose, and she was barefoot and still wearing her wrapper. She
didn't turn when Maidie opened the door, but continued to scrib-
ble, muttering to herself. Maidie quietly descended again.

Her next thought was Wendell and Prudence, but the destina-
tion she had determined on, an outcropping of rock called the
Giant's Head from which to enjoy a favorite morning view of
Krigsmere, was in the opposite direction. She was also reluctant,

after the sunny tranquility of the quiet house and a solitary breakfast, to inject Wendell's discoursing into the peace of the morning. She ran up to her room to change into a simpler dress and
her walking boots, and to find a small volume of Wordsworth's
poems; paused to tell Mrs. Eckston in the kitchen her destination
and to ask for some gingerbread to carry with her; then opened
the door to bird song and sunshine and a heart bursting with
Wordsworthian sentiment.

The walk along the lake, after the roadway was left behind,
was a lightly shaded path under sycamores, ashes, and oaks
where wild foxgloves bloomed in profusion. She heard the sound
of the waterfall before she reached the path that led upward to
the Giant's Head, and was tempted for a moment to continue on
to its foot. The fall, called Maiden Force, tumbled from a cleft
by the side of the Giant's Head. At the foot was a sylvan spot
of springy turf, and of ferns among the mossy rocks, where
Maidie liked fancifully to imagine the nymphs and Bacchantes
who Wendell claimed should be playing in such woodland
scenes. But if she stopped to enjoy the waterfall, she would miss
the best view of the lake from above, so she turned instead onto
the path that led to the Giant's Head.

She was warm, but not at all tired after scrambling up the
rocks and onto the immense outcrop that fancy had named the
Giant's Head. She found a spot where she could dangle her legs
and enjoy the view. Maiden Beck sparkled and gurgled through
the rocky cleft that separated the Giant's Head from another
great boulder beyond, and from below came the splashing of its
fall. Krigsmere lay before her, calm and shimmering.

The sun was warm on her bare head. It was one of the free-
doms she indulged, for she loved the feel of the wind on her
cheek and in her hair. What did it matter if she tanned and got
a few more freckles? A bird sailed over her head, and in the trees
behind her a rook cawed. She drew a deep breath and decided

that she chose to believe, with Wendell and Wordsworth, that the trees and flowers were also enjoying the air they breathed.

Eventually she took the small volume of poems from her pocket, and from another pocket a piece of gingerbread. The bread was nearly a week old, and hard, but the ginger and molasses flavors were sharp and sweet. When she finished she was thirsty, and thought to follow the beck for a short distance upstream until she found a place where she could scoop up a drink of water. She replaced the Wordsworth in her pocket, and with a last look at the lake, started along the path that edged the beck.

She drank at a quiet pool where the stream emerged from a narrow ghyll in the wall of rock, but the path, rock-strewn and cramped between the stream and the side of the ravine, continued on beside it. She had never explored beyond the Giant's Head, and she had been warned not to wander in the heights without a companion familiar with the fells, but, she reasoned, if she followed the beck there was no danger of getting lost.

Maidie had been walking upstream for nearly twenty minutes, climbing gradually, and was beginning to feel hot as the sun, now approaching zenith, beat down on stone and scree. The beck, running clear over a rocky, pebbly bottom, descended through the ghyll in easy stages, purling softly over the level stretches and foaming over the shallow rapids. She stopped to sprinkle some water over her head, and then dipped her handkerchief in the stream to wipe her face and neck. She pushed her hair back, then tried to tie it more securely, while vowing that at the first opportunity she would cut it like Fanny's, no matter what Papa might say. In two places she had to climb over old rock slides, and the path seemed almost to disappear ahead of her, but it was apparent that others had passed the same way, and she did not hesitate to go on. She thought she could hear the sound of another waterfall ahead. She had just passed a patch of fallen rock when the ghyll twisted to her left. And there in front of her was the fall, only four or five feet in height, where the beck dropped over a broad ledge of rock.

Maidie clambered up over the great boulders tumbled by the side of the waterfall, following the faint suggestions of a pathway, and found herself beside a tree-shaded pool, dammed behind the same lip of rock. The sides of the ravine fell away sharply on both her right and left, and before her lay a pretty little valley. She was so entranced that she did not notice the exasperated gentleman who stood glaring at her from a few yards away on the other, and deeply shaded side of the tarn, until he called to her peremptorily to move back.

Startled, her foot slipped on the loose stones scattered over and among the larger boulders. Unable to save herself, she sat down suddenly and hard.

"Now your damned blundering has frightened the trout for the rest of the day!"

Her first impression was of a dark, glowering visage. But whether he was as large and overwhelming as she later remembered she couldn't tell, because he was standing nearly up to his hips in the water. She scrambled to her feet, her heart hammering on her ribs, for he looked quite dangerous.

Once again on secure footing and her heartbeat slowing, she said indignantly, "I'm sure I'm very sorry, but I didn't know there was a rule that one must go about the fells on tiptoe!" She stooped to wring out the hem of her skirt, which had been wet in a pool of water captured in a slight depression in a boulder. The uncouth villain hadn't even asked if she was hurt!

He was now climbing out of the water, and Maidie was considering precipitate flight, when he lay his fishing rod on the grass, sat down, and began to take off his wading boots. "I haven't found such trout for sport since I've been here, and then some stupid girl . . ." he muttered loudly.

In the clear still air his stage-voice muttering was perfectly audible on Maidie's side of the pool. "Well," she replied haughtily, "if it was only sport you were enjoying, I may presume that I have not deprived you of your dinner, and my conscience need not bother me in the *slightest!*"

The sporting gentleman stared at her from under lowered brows. "Not that it's any of your business, but I eat what I catch."

Maidie would have liked to sit down in the shade and wash her hand, which she was certain from the sting had been scraped in her fall, and calmly consider if she had any serious injuries, but the sudden encounter with such a hateful man had unnerved her. He made no move, continuing to sit comfortably in cool shade, glowering across the pool at her, while she stood in the hot sun. No one, neither Emery nor Fanny, nor even Mrs. Califaxton, had ever warned her of danger from strangers. Restrictions—even Fanny's restrictions on her own wanderings alone, had nothing to do with strangers, only with losing one's way or injuring oneself in an accidental fall.

The man's better nature finally seeming to get the upper hand, he asked, "Did you hurt yourself?"

"No. No thanks to you."

"I shouldn't expect you to thank me."

"A gentleman would apologize."

"That I will do. I apologize."

"*Sincerely* apologize."

"I *sincerely* apologize."

"Thank you."

That seemed to be the end of the conversation, at least as far as the man was concerned. As she stared at him, uncertain whether to stay or to retreat, he showed signs of getting once again to his feet. Her course was immediately decided. "Then I bid you good day, sir." An impish impulse seized her, and she bobbed a curtsy in the best manner of her former maid, Clarice. "And it's truly turrible sorry I am that I disturbed the sporting gennelman's fish." Then she turned and, at a leisurely pace and

with admirable dignity, climbed through the pile of boulders to
begin her return journey.

When she was several yards into the narrow ghyll she risked
a glance over her shoulder, but there was nothing behind her but
an empty path. When she had gone several more yards she
stopped again to look back and to listen for sounds of pursuit,
but there was only the sound of the beck. All was empty and
silent as before. Confident that she was not followed, she exam-
ined her hand, washed her face again and once more dripped
water over her head. She wished that she had brought a bonnet.

As a matter of fact, there were four sizable trout in Allan
Gilmichael's fishing basket, more than sufficient for the *al
fresco* luncheon he planned to enjoy. Also as a matter of fact,
he had just decided, before the girl so suddenly appeared, to call
it a day. He had discovered the tarn exactly as Maidie had. He
often fished it and the beck above, and then he would explore
the valley and the surrounding heights, making the acquaintance
of shepherds and visiting the owners of the one farm in the little
valley.

He realized that it had been disgracefully discourteous and
also unfair to be so rude to the girl who had intruded on his
solitude, but he was too out of sorts to admit it. He was also too
out of sorts to admit that her saucy departure had amused him.
As he cleaned his fish he wondered who she was. She had been
wearing stout boots and a simple, country dress, but her voice
was well modulated, and her accent, even in her burlesque departure, was properly English. He at last allowed himself a small
smile. On the other hand, the daughter of a family of lake-loving
gentry would not be permitted to roam alone so freely. She
couldn't have been more than eighteen or nineteen. Nor had she
been wearing a bonnet. His impression was that well-brought
up girls were not permitted to step out of their doors without

bonnets or parasols; he was quite certain that his own sister—the exasperating baggage—was so prohibited. It had aroused his curiosity, though, this sudden encounter in what he had come to think of as his own private valley.

It was nearly two years since Allan's curiosity or interest had been much aroused. Two years, he thought, two years since Clarence died. He had come to the Lakes to relieve both his family and himself of his ill-humor, but he now knew that he had needed to make his terms with grief, and death. And with his future. Solitude had seemed his greatest need; fishing was his distraction.

He no longer compulsively reviewed those few moments in which his brother died. He had known that it was deliberate self-punishment to do so, and had made an effort to turn his thoughts to other things. And Heaven knew that there were enough of those to occupy his mind! But sometimes, when a trivial incident tripped the latchstrings of memory, such as that girl falling on the rocks, he would suddenly be lost in the past, with neither the consciousness nor volition to halt yet another review of that fateful day.

He had been at Thresseley, on a short leave from duty, and debating in a leisurely fashion his future while enjoying all the pleasures of his childhood home . . .

His older brother Clarence, and Eunice, Clarence's young wife, had not long before fallen in love with a starveling puppy of unknown antecedents. Allan was amused by the dog that they had taken to their hearts, and amused likewise by their doting affection for what was, to all other eyes, a perfectly ordinary beast, so undignified in his great long-legged ungainliness that although he had been given a proper name as a puppy, he was known only as Clown.

On the day that still haunted his thoughts, Clarence, returning from a two day inspection of his properties, was met at the head of the long flight of steps leading to the terrace by Eunice, Allan, and an ecstatic Clown. The dog, as he had been encouraged to do when still a puppy, came leaping to Clarence's arms to be petted and fondled. But Clown was no longer a puppy, and his brother's attention had been at that moment distracted. Clarence made a ridiculously ungainly attempt to save himself before he fell backward on the stone steps.

Allan, the soldier, had known immediately. On seeing the truth in his eyes, Eunice struck at Clown, hitting him again and again, screaming hysterically. Allan was certain, remembering, that the dog knew what he had done, for he lay—not cowering, but as though simply accepting his punishment—beneath the blows. Allan grasped Eunice and pulled her away. Clown crawled to his master's body and whined his misery. Eunice collapsed in Allan's arms.

It fell to Allan to make all those arrangements that accompany death, to hold together the grief-stricken family and the shocked servants and tenants. Eunice's grief was embittered by shame— shame for having struck a dumb animal that had intended only to show its love for its master. The dog's devotion to his mistress was the more intense for the loss of Clarence, and he refused to be parted from her. Clown would rise often, to put his head in her lap and, whimpering, look into her eyes.

That a dog should grieve and beg forgiveness, and that it should so affect them all, was as macabre and horribly ridiculous as the memory of Clarence's arms windmilling uselessly in the air as he tried to regain his balance—robbed of dignity in the final moment of his life. It was more than they could bear, until Allan in desperation came near to doing away with the animal. He was stopped by his sister's entreaties from an act he knew he would regret even at the moment he contemplated it. Like Eunice, he had wanted to punish the dog.

For Allan, his elder brother's death meant that he was suddenly thrust, without expectation, into a role for which he had neither training nor desire. He had wondered, sometimes, if years of campaigning with Wellington had spoiled him for the unexciting pursuits of peace. Spoiled or not, he had no choice. But once the urgent affairs of the estate were settled, and he had full grasp of their direction, when the other members of his family seemed to be picking up their lives and Eunice gradually achieving some peace of mind, he had at last felt free to leave for a time his responsibilities and come to terms with himself.

His recent short visit to Thresseley had not been happy. Eunice was already showing signs of embracing a sterile and self-sacrificing widowhood that must be countered, and his unmanageable sister Julia, now nineteen, was still sulking over his refusal the year past to permit her a season so soon after Clarence's death . . . Allan had seen in the war how death and pain could afflict the mind; he believed Julie was refusing to admit that Clarence was gone, for she had loved her eldest brother devotedly. His mother, like Eunice, should be going again into society; but both had refused to take Julie to London for the season, which, unless he prevailed against their stubborn and self-imposed seclusion, meant that he would be required to open Enett House himself and find a companion for her. But not until the little season in the fall. Selfish (as Julie charged) or not, the spring and summer were his.

For the present, at least, he had again put his responsibilities aside. He was still angry with Julie, with Eunice and his mother, but what he most desperately needed was more time away from them in order to make his own peace with Clarence's death and with the changed circumstances of his life.

Both he and Clarence were dedicated anglers, and they had enjoyed many holidays together in the Lakes. The week before he left with the Regiment for the Peninsula they had shared a final holiday at an inn near Crummock Water. They both had also a taste for the new poetry, which led them to call on Mr.

William Wordsworth and his wife—and Miss Dorothy
Wordsworth, his curious, unworldly sister. The memory of that
week had led Allan back to the Lakes. He rented a modest house
just beyond the village of Sagpaw, thanks to a chance encounter
with an old army acquaintance, Lance Califaxton. He and Califaxton had never been close friends, but they liked and respected
each other, and Califaxton had a ready sympathy with his need
for solitude. Lance had given his family to understand that he
was not to be teased into social engagements.

Lance, mildly amused by the charade, had been willing to
pass Allan off as a distant relative of the present marquis, agreeing that a modest mister before his surname would guarantee
him such acceptance as he might crave among the local gentry
(unlikely circumstance), while protecting him from the social
importunities of the ambitious. Foolish he now thought it, but
he could not deceive himself. He was still pretending that the
title was not his. In his own way no different from Julie, or
Eunice, or his mother.

He had just returned from the western lakes, where he had
revisited the inn on Crummock Water at which he and Clarence
stayed so long ago. He fished the lake and nearby becks,
tramped among the fells, and climbed Scafel with a shepherd
for companion. The latter had remarked on the oddity of anyone climbing a mountain for entertainment, although it was
said that one of Those Poets had climbed it once. And that
wild-eyed Gypsy woman, old Willum Wudsworth's sister, had
also gone up Scafel it was said, but then Those Poets and their
lot were always tramping around, daytime or nighttime—it
didn't matter to them.

And then Allan had puzzled his shepherd companion even
more by climbing to the highest spot he could reach and shouting
into the wind, *"Damn you, Clarence Gilmichael!"*

He had made his way back to Krigsmere in leisurely wanderings from inn to inn. He had, as he had hoped, found a measure of solace in the solitudes of Lakeland, and memories of Clarence's death had ceased to hurt so intensely. Nonetheless, rebellion still smoldered in his soul, and annoyance with his family hovered at the forefront of his mind. It made him testy with intruding girls and unhappy with himself.

As his fish roasted over the fire, Allan stripped off his clothes and stepped into the tarn. It deepened sufficiently that he could swim several strokes before reaching the other side. The water was cold and refreshing, and the current was strong enough to require exertion to breast it. He swam to the head of the pool and then allowed himself to be carried with the current to the lip of the fall, a mildly foolhardy business that he repeated several times. He climbed out of the water in better humor, and hungrier than ever for his trout.

When Fanny emerged from the grip of her muse, she learned from Mrs. Eckston that Maidie had been gone some four hours. Worried, she then sought Emery, who she finally discovered sitting on the stone wall overlooking the meadow and discussing some undoubtedly abstruse subject with Wendell.

"Emery!" Fanny called as she approached them. "What are you doing out here? Hello, Wendell," she added offhandedly.

"Hello." Wendell smiled at her, but in light of her glare at Emery, decided to keep his tongue between his teeth.

"Yes, Fanny. Come sit down. And why are you glaring at me?"

Fanny sat down on the wall and swung her legs over. Settling her skirts, she said, "Because I couldn't find you anywhere and I'm terribly worried about Maidie. She went to the Giant's Head and isn't home yet and it's been over four hours."

"She'll be all right. She's probably with Prudence and Chester."

"No, she went alone, Mrs. Eckston says. I do think someone ought to go looking for her." Fanny, like many another, was discovering that it is not always easy to match conviction with action; although she was determined to give Maidie freedom, she couldn't help worrying. Four hours at the Giant's Head was too long.

"Maidie can take care of herself," Emery said absently, his mind complacently occupied with the beauty of his new heifer, which was grazing contentedly among his other beauties.

Wendell, who had been longing to do something more active than sitting on a wall looking at cows, spoke up. "I'll walk along to the Giant's Head, if you like. But I don't think you need to worry."

"Oh, would you, dear? But don't let her think that we're worrying about her."

"I'm not worried," Emery said.

Wendell, hoping a spat wasn't brewing, stood up and, assuring Fanny that he would pretend to have met Maidie *quite* by accident, went whistling on his way.

Wendell agreed with Emery that Maidie was capable of looking after herself—unlike Prudence Califaxton, who really needed someone to take care of her—but the Ladder-Moving Intruder, whom he suspected was one and the same as the Furtive Ginger-Haired Stranger, had left him uneasy.

He'd had a face to face encounter with the stranger—he was certain of it—only yesterday, which heightened his mild anxiety for Maidie's safety. It had been such a sun-washed morning that wet underfoot though it was, he had determined on a climb, and after donning a pair of sturdy boots, had filled his pockets with paper and a pencil and set out for the long ridge called the High Street. It was a lengthy climb over two ranges of fells, and he stopped frequently to jot down his impressions of the changing scenery. His purpose was to trace the remains of the Roman fortifications along the High Street ridge, and to try to imagine the Romans who once marched that way. He was considering an ambitious poetic effort, recalling in a series of heroic verses the Celts, the Romans, the Norsemen, and the Normans who had left their impress on the Lakes, to end with a few rousing verses on modern shepherds and farmers.

A secondary purpose was to look over the natural arena where shepherds carried on their wrestling and fell racing contests. A natural athlete himself, he enjoyed feats of physical skill, and had been considering whether to take up the suggestion of the farmer he'd met in the Sagpaw market square, and enter a wrestling contest.

Although the morning had been sunny, he was caught in a cold swirling mist on the High Street—one of the normal hazards of fell walking. He perched on a fragment of Roman wall, hoping the mist would blow away soon, and was trying to jot down an occasional poetic line in his notebook, when a man came puffing along the path. He didn't have ginger hair—at least what little was visible under his cap didn't seem to be ginger-colored—but there was something familiar about him, something reminiscent of the Stranger. The man had saluted him, politely passed the time of day and then continued down the path.

Pondering the incident, Wendell nearly forgot he was looking for Maidie. He was so profoundly cogitating on the mystery that he even failed to notice the wild foxgloves along the lakeside path—and consequently was severely startled when Maidie suddenly appeared around a boulder-screened bend.

"Maidie! What the devil are you doing sneaking up on a fellow?"

Maidie's first impulse was to snap back at him, but her second impulse was to immediately relate her exciting encounter with the hateful sportsman who seemed to think he owned the fells, and the streams and ponds besides, giving Wendell to think for a moment that the ginger-haired stranger had once again shown

himself. Maidie was quite definite that the sporting gentleman's
hair had not been ginger-colored, although what color it actually
was, she couldn't say. Anyway, Wendell reflected, he had last
seen Mr. Ginger-hair apparently on his way elsewhere. A few
minute's further reflection then suggested that the sporting gentleman might be Mr. Allan Gilmichael, who had occasionally
called on Emery when Fanny was in London and bored on with
him about fishing—both being dedicated Waltonians. Wendell
had twice been subjected to their angler's enthusiasm, and both
times he had made his escape as soon as courtesy permitted.

"Thirty minutes," he told Maidie, "in serious discussion of
the construction of an artificial fly, using the most amazing ma-
terials, and another half hour debating the best insect for a specific season—nay, a specific hour of a specific day—to get the
trout to rise."

"Oh, well. In my father's house, it's often the ins and outs of
banking, so both my mother and I know a great deal more about
the subject than we would wish."

Maidie's mention of her Monied Parent had gone by Wendell
without stimulating so much as one fleeting thought pertaining
to the Rapacious Monied Interest. He had come to accept that
both Maidie and Prudence Califaxton were Daughters of Privilege. Although Wendell often vowed that he would never put his
foot in a rich man's counting house, nor his feet under a lord's
table, his radical politics tended to be more theoretical than not
when it came to his social life.

"It's easy to see that you know nothing of sportsmen," Wendell told Maidie scornfully. "I sat with a farmer in the market
square—waiting for you and Fanny the day we all visited the
Califaxtons. He desired to discuss foxhunting in soporific detail,
including the personality of every hound in the Sagpaw pack,
and the characteristics of every fox that ever lived or died in the
county."

"Who is this Mr. Gilmichael, besides being a sportsman?"

Maidie asked, more interested in her recent encounter than Wendell's opinions on fox hunting.

"Well. He was military—a captain. Same regiment as Lance Califaxton, who says Gilmichael would have been a general one day if he'd chosen to stay in the army. On the Peninsula with Wellington; on his staff in Paris before Bonaparte got loose from Elba, fought at Waterloo, back in Paris again with the Army of Occupation—"

"What's all that to say to anything?"

"You wanted to know who he was, so I'm telling you what I know. Distantly related to a marquis, Lord Somebody or Other."

"He sounds very dull. As well as lacking manners. You may forget him with my approval. I assure you I shall."

After leaving Maidie, Wendell returned to his cottage and then strolled into the village to enquire for his mail. Then it seemed an excellent idea to have his supper at the inn, since there were a number of good fellows in the tap room with whom he could discuss wrestling.

He had had an uncomfortable feeling when he left the post office that he was being followed, and a feeling of being watched persisted as he sat in the tap room. It was an advanced hour of the night when he left the inn, and on sudden impulse he rounded a corner and then waited quietly for a pursuer to appear, but no one came past except the night watch, who greeted him amiably and passed on, leaving Wendell himself feeling like the guilty lurker.

Once well out of the village and on the road leading to his cottage, he turned around suddenly, hoping to catch someone dodging behind a tree, but the road was empty behind him. Subsequent repetitions were equally unsuccessful. Or was there a shadow among the trees? He was forced to conclude that the stranger was beginning to prey on his nerves, an idea he didn't like. Was his unease simply the product of an over-active imagination, as he suspected his cousin Emery might think?

He lay wakeful in his bed considering what to do. Await developments? Accost the stranger should he see him again and force an explanation?

When he awoke the following morning he was no nearer to a conclusion than he had been when he went to sleep. But the jottings from his climb to the High Street needed organizing, and there was a new copy of Cobbett's *Political Register.* Wendell sat down to his breakfast with the *Register* propped up against the milk jug, determined to put the whole business out of his mind.

Five

As it happened, Maidie found no opportunity for relating her adventure, other than that she had wandered up the ravine behind the Giant's Head. Fanny was resting when she returned, and wished only to know she was safe. Emery had gone to Kendal to see a man about a horse, and would not be back until the following day. Then there were callers for tea, among them two ladies, admirers of Fanny, who were asked to stay to supper before they proceeded on to the Sagpaw Inn. By the time they at last departed it was so late that Fanny said she could describe the rest of her adventure in the morning.

The next day when Maidie came down to breakfast, prepared again to recount her adventure, she found Fanny lying on a sofa, looking indisposed. "Why Aunt Fanny, whatever is the matter?" she asked. "You look so unwell. Can I get you anything?"

Fanny had begun to suspect that an unprecedented and unexpected event had occurred. She and Emery had given up hope, after five years of a childless marriage, of ever becoming parents. In the subsequent five years they had made a comfortable adjustment to their childless state—such a comfortable adjustment that she had hoped that her suspicions were not warranted. However, a tendency to feel slightly unwell in the mornings had confirmed her belief that she was, indeed, pregnant. And now to begin suffering this terrible morning sickness, as though she were some idle Society Lady, rather than a boundingly healthy woman who could walk countless miles in a day! It didn't bear thinking about! Nor did it help that Emery was actually, after his first surprise, beginning to look pleased, and could hardly be restrained from announcing the matter to all and sundry.

Thus it was in no good mood that Fanny looked up at Maidie and said, in an exasperated voice. "I'm afraid nothing anyone can do can help." Then, acknowledging the serious concern in her niece's expression, she decided that, no matter how rebellious she felt, what could no longer be denied might as well be publicized. She sighed. "Forgive me, my dear. The truth is that I am increasing." Maidie's ecstatic response did not make her feel better. Nevertheless, she rallied her forces and said teasingly, "You will now have to do more of the gardening and baking, and I fear that you will soon rather be in London."

Maidie denied it stoutly, and after a time Fanny felt well enough to go to the breakfast room, but she found it necessary to hastily depart again when Maidie cracked a soft-boiled egg.

In her excitement over Fanny's news, and with Fanny feeling so ill, and then Emery returning only in time to change for tea, Maidie forgot to tell anyone about her encounter with a stranger at the tarn above the Giant's Head.

Allan Gilmichael, that same day, prepared to visit his fellow angler, Emery Clarke. Mr. Clarke's wife had returned during his absence in Derbyshire and the western lakes, and courtesy required he pay a call. He had read some of Fanny's essays, and expected to find her a sensible woman; he was also privy to the general neighborhood knowledge (although from what source he couldn't have said) that when Mrs. Clarke was at home visitors were welcome to share their early tea.

Allan was preceded in the large front parlor by Wendell, and by Prudence and John Califaxton. John was not generally given to making calls, preferring to spend his time with his books in preparation for his missionary work, but he had come across a particularly well-reasoned theological article in the *Monthly Repository* by a Mrs. Letitia Worthing, and was mildly interested in discovering if she was related to Maidie. It seemed possible, since Maidie had mentioned attending services at the Essex Street Chapel in London, a Unitarian congregation. He had also a curious incident to report to Wendell. He hoped he could manage, under the cover of the general conversation, to arrange a private interview with him as soon as opportunity permitted. The incident had rather worried him, and the sooner he could inform Wendell of it, the better.

He had consequently, much to Prudence's surprise, proposed that they call upon the Clarkes, supposing it likely that he would meet Wendell there as well as Maidie, and could bag his two birds at one swoop. As it happened, Wendell was strolling up and down in his garden composing when they passed his gate. At the prospect of a walk in their company, he immediately lost interest in his poetic paean to a shepherd's faithful dog, and announced that he would accompany them.

When Allan, a half hour later, was shown into the parlor where several guests were already gathered, he recognized Emery Clarke's young cousin, Wendell Duval, seated by Prudence Califaxton. Her brother John stood by the window conversing with Emery. Mrs. Clarke was not present, and on asking after her in order to pay his respects was told that she was unwell and would not be joining them that afternoon, but that her niece would be coming down presently.

Emery had been pointing out to John the new heifer grazing among the cows in the meadow by the lake. He had purchased her only days before and was proud of her, for he felt he was developing a true eye for cowflesh. When Allan joined them, Emery exclaimed, "Welcome back, Gilmichael. I didn't know you were returned." Allan shook hands with both Emery and

John, after which Emery thought it necessary to point out the new heifer to him also. The three men were engaged in a discussion of bovine attributes when Maidie came into the room.

She was greeting Prudence Califaxton when Allan turned from the window; he knew immediately that this was the girl he had encountered the day before, and that she was also, undoubtedly, the niece of whom Emery Clarke had spoken. She had not yet recognized him, with the light of the window behind him, but the minute she turned her attention from Miss Califaxton and that young cousin of Emery's, she would know him immediately for the surly and ungentlemanly fellow at the tarn. He suffered a quick stab of shame, remembering his churlish behavior. But what, he wondered, were the Clarkes thinking of to let such a young girl venture so far afield by herself? Only half attending to Emery and John, he watched her as she moved among the guests. An elegant little chit, he thought, and remembering the stout boots and country attire of their first encounter, he smiled to himself.

Maidie spoke to Wendell and Prudence, greeted the rector and a young woman who proved to be his granddaughter, drew a shy young man forward to meet them, and then approached her Uncle Emery, who was speaking to John and a guest she didn't recognize. His back was to the window and so his face was shadowed, but he did not in any event look familiar. However, as the strange gentleman stepped forward to be introduced she immediately saw that she was due for another encounter with the sporting gentleman. Her eyes widened in surprise, but she greeted John placidly, and then, resigned to exposure, waited for the introduction. She could scarcely hope that the sporting gentleman would be reticent about their encounter at the pool.

She was correct. Allan had no intention of reticence. A young girl shouldn't be allowed to wander about alone like that, and he felt certain that neither her aunt nor her uncle had known, or would have permitted it. After the introduction, he addressed Emery, ignoring what was obviously the girl's attempt to convey a message to him by pretending she had never seen him before. "Miss Worthing and I have met. And I'm afraid I owe her an apology, for I was, I'm ashamed to say, guilty of inexcusable discourtesy on our first meeting." He then favored Maidie with a smile. He was surprised when she neither blushed at what he suspected was a revelation of a misdeed, nor made any attempt to dispute his confession of previous discourtesy. Her level gaze did not waver; her chin merely came up a fraction, and her eyebrows rose slightly, slanting up even more at the corners, clearly indicating that she was waiting for the forthcoming apology.

Maidie longed to smile, for she was certain that she had made the vile sporting gentleman uncomfortable, and she certainly agreed that he had been discourteous. John Califaxton, observing, did smile, but Emery, who was suddenly called upon to respond, said in a bewildered tone, "Oh, you've met before?"

Although annoyed at being bested by a chit the age of his sister, and determined not to let the circumstances, or rather, the location of their meeting pass, Allan nonetheless delivered a graceful apology. "We met under adverse circumstances, I'm afraid. I was fishing the tarn above the Giant's Head, where your niece happened upon me and, unaware that there was a fisherman nearby, loosed a rock in passing along the path." He turned to Maidie. With a slight bow, he added, "However, I do not intend to make that an excuse for what was inexcusable rudeness. I hope you will accept my sincere apologies, Miss Worthing, and that we may meet henceforth without rancor. I assure you that I desire your forgiveness very much."

Maidie considered this to be buttering the bread a bit too thickly, but she beamed benevolently upon him, and spread some butter of her own. "Of course, Mr. Gilmichael, I'll forgive you. And now I must ask you to forgive me for having been so clumsy.

I'll certainly take more care should I happen on you again at your sport."

"I am relieved, Miss Worthing." What a saucy baggage she was!

"If you'll permit me to interrupt this exchange of apologies," John said, "I've been wondering, Maidie, if you are related to a Mrs. Letitia Worthing?"

"Why, yes, she's my mother."

"I wondered if that might not be the case. I've just read an article of considerable interest in the *Repository* which she authored."

Allan drifted off to speak with Prudence and to enquire after her mother and her soldier brother, Lance, while Emery settled into a theological discussion with John. So the girl had a scribbling mother, as well as a scribbling aunt. No wonder she was so forward! Even as he conversed with Prudence, and then with an elderly gentleman who proved to be the rector of the local parish, he was aware of her. It was not until the tea tray arrived, with Maidie presiding very competently, that he had an opportunity to speak to her again. He waited until the other guests were served before approaching her.

"I hope, Miss Worthing, that you did not suffer any ill effects from your fall yesterday."

"No, I'm perfectly well, thank you."

"No bruises?"

"Only bruised dignity, sir, and I think it unkind of you to remind me."

He thought she might at least have been grateful that he hadn't mentioned her fall in public. He bowed. "Once again, Miss Worthing, my apologies."

Maidie dipped her head slightly in acknowledgement. "One lump of sugar or two?"

"It's not been my impression, Miss Worthing, at least to date, that you are in the habit of handing out sugar." At Maidie's quick glance upward, he smiled blandly, "But no matter, I take only cream in my tea."

Maidie added the cream and handed him the cup, hoping sincerely that he would go away, especially since no adequate reply to that vile remark came promptly to mind.

Allan was not done with the foolhardy young lady, however. She had undoubtedly been a very naughty child, and her present behavior suggested she had not outgrown it. He sipped his tea slowly, still at her side, noting with amusement that she was busily rearranging tea things that needed no moving. At last he remarked, "I have a feeling, just a feeling, mind you, that you haven't mentioned to your uncle and aunt that you had wandered so far from the lake paths alone."

"I haven't been forbidden to walk alone wherever there is no danger of getting lost." Maidie would not for her life have cravenly explained that she had not yet had an opportunity to reveal the full story of her walk, but that she had always meant to do so. It would have sounded simply too childish.

"Nonetheless, the very fact that you didn't reveal where you had been yesterday suggests to me that you know very well that you shouldn't have been there."

This brought Maidie close to losing her temper. Who was he to lecture her on what she should and shouldn't do?

"I don't believe that the matter is of any concern to you, Mr. Gilmichael, nor that it should be. You have very neatly informed my uncle, and if he and my aunt choose to reprimand me, I will consider myself corrected, and I will respect whatever restrictions they impose hereafter and obey them as their due. But I can only consider you a tattle-tale, and your warnings as meddlesome."

Taken aback, his expression settled into carved stone. "My apologies again, Miss Worthing. I spoke only with your own safety in mind, not with an intent to meddle. Your fall yesterday on the rocks should make it clear to you how easy it is to injure oneself when climbing on the fells."

Leaving Maidie fuming, Allan stalked off. He refused to admit to tattling, an activity he associated with girls' schools, but he did have to admit that he had treated the saucy chit as though she were his younger sister. Whatever had happened to the devil-may-care young officer he once had been, who could set aside the responsibilities of command to dance and flirt a night away? In former days he had never thought it his duty to correct the conduct of chance-met girls. He carried his tea to a seat by the elderly rector's granddaughter, who, after receiving an elaborate compliment, blushed and giggled as a proper girl should.

John Califaxton, noticing Wendell for a moment disengaged, approached him, and after a few general observations, said in a low voice, "I'd like an opportunity to discuss something with you that has given me some cause for concern."

Wendell, off his guard, blurted, "If it's about your sister—"

"No, it's nothing about my sister. Should there be something?"

"No, no," Wendell replied quickly. "It's just that Miss Califaxton and I were discussing an excursion to the Druid's Circle with Miss Worthing. I thought perhaps—it's rather far . . ."

"Not so very far, and no danger of getting yourself lost if you don't try for Melt's Crag. But I approached you because I'd like to make an appointment to see you privately. As I said, something has occurred that has caused me some concern, and that I think you should be aware of. Could I perhaps call on you this evening?"

Wendell, considerably puzzled, consented, at which John pointedly changed the subject.

Wendell excused himself from supper with Maidie and the Clarkes, and after a simple meal in his own kitchen made ready to receive John Califaxton. He opened a new packet of China tea and put the teakettle on the hob, then laid a small fire in the fireplace in the main room. The nights were usually chill in the Lakes, and although he had found a battered old carpet at a country auction to cover the stone floor, it was only a partial solution to the cold and damp.

As he prepared for John's call he worried about the reason for it. He'd nearly given himself away by jumping to the conclusion that he wished to discuss Prudence. Wendell shook his head. He had been known among his whist-playing university companions for his cool imperturbability at cards, and he had always flattered himself that it was a characteristic he could call into play in other situations in life—and then to burst out like a guilty schoolboy! But what other matter could John Califaxton, of all people, care to discuss with him, or feel he should know? The Ladder-Moving Intruder and the Ginger-Haired Stranger came naturally to mind, but that John should know anything having to do with them seemed unlikely.

John's knock came promptly at 8:30. Wendell seated him comfortably before the fire, and went off to the kitchen to get the tea things. Left to himself, John glanced over the literature on the low table before the fire. He could choose from copies of Cobbett's *Political Register* or reprints of speeches by several other well-known radicals; copies of the *Examiner* or *Edinburgh Review;* Byron's *Manfred* or a volume of Horace; recent newspapers or a biography of Chaucer. Scattered among this diverse collection of literature were sheets of paper on which were scribbled and marked-up attempts at what John guessed from the arrangement of the lines might be poetry, although he was too polite to pick one up to verify his conjecture. He chose the Horace and glanced through the pages, picking out a familiar line here and there, until his host returned with the tea tray.

Wendell pushed books, pamphlets, and papers aside to accommodate the tea things, and then brought a bottle of brandy and two glasses from a chest which stood along the wall. "Perhaps you'd like brandy instead. I'm sorry I forgot to offer earlier."

"No, no. Tea will do nicely. Perhaps later I'll have a glass of brandy against my return home." Accepting his cup of tea, he leaned back in his chair, and said, "I know you must be curious about this visit, so I shan't waste words. What I want to discuss is a person who approached me yesterday. I am convinced he was, of all things, wearing a wig to cover his own hair. In any event, in the course of a general conversation he asked some questions about you."

"About me?"

"The man tried to be subtle and indirect, but there is no doubt in my mind that he was interested in you, your political opinions and personal life."

"But why should anyone be making enquiries about me?" Wendell asked, more in a spirit of speculation than in disbelief or surprise, for here was the proof that his suspicions had not been mere fantasy.

"I can't answer that with any certainty, of course, but I have understood from conversations with you—and from some of the literature I see spread out here before us—that your political views are radical. I believe also you have mentioned some radical verse . . . ?"

Wendell's face was unreadable. "And what of that?"

Before John could reply, they were surprised by a knock at the door. They stared at each other for a questioning second before Wendell rose to answer the knock. They were even more surprised to discover Allan Gilmichael.

"Good evening." Allan smiled disarmingly. Then, catching sight of John, he said, "Oh, sorry. Didn't mean to intrude. I'll call another time."

Wendell was incapable of telling a gentleman of Mr.

Gilmichael's exalted category to go away, even had he desired to do so. Not that he was impressed by the wealth the man obviously enjoyed. It was the authority of his manner that left him feeling so uncomfortably green.

As Wendell ushered Allan in, John rose and held out his hand. "Good evening, Allan. I believe I will be welcoming your assistance, for I suspect you may be here on the same matter that I am." Whether or not he had been approached also by the curious gentleman in the peculiar wig, he could at least add his counsel, John thought. His brother Lance spoke very highly of Allan Gilmichael's character and judgment, and he had found reason only to agree.

There was more ado getting the new caller seated and supplied with tea, but that accomplished, John returned to the subject of his visit. Addressing Allan, he said, "I've been telling Wendell about a gentleman who's been asking questions about him, and I mean to suggest that the man may be a government spy."

"A *spy!*" Wendell exclaimed. Just as he had expected!

"A spy?" Allan asked.

"Or perhaps more accurately, a government agent. But I presume then," John said to Allan, "that you haven't been visited by the stranger in the ridiculous wig?"

Allan laughed. "Yes, and ridiculous it certainly was. But I didn't take him for a government agent. I had the impression he was on some kind of personal investigation of Mr. Duval."

He did not add that the stranger in the wig had addressed him as your lordship. He had given the man to understand that one word of his title among the local inhabitants and he would see that he was roasted over a hot fire, sent in irons to New South Wales, pursued to the ends of the earth, and any other such dire possibilities that might occur to him. He was confident that he had sufficiently impressed the man with these extravagant warnings that his secret was safe. And he hadn't liked at all the stranger's attempt at prying questions about his acquaintances in the neighborhood, even though it had been obvious that it was young Duval who was the focus of his interest. He had ordered the fellow off the premises.

"Have you applied for any large loans from anyone, Mr. Duval? Or for a position of some sort requiring a sterling character?"

"No, of course not. I have no need for either. Wealth and sinecures corrupt the soul."

John with difficulty repressed a smile. "Let me explain why I suspect that the man may be a government agent. Although I should emphasize that this is only speculation." He placed his tea cup on the table, and absentmindedly squared up a stack of loosely piled papers before he continued. "You are aware, of course, that this government is not tolerant of radical views."

"How can one not be aware?" Wendell asked. "Honest workers hung for treason—known informers rewarded!"

"Yes, the Luddite scare, and the recent strikes among industrial workers have added fuel to the fears. I've heard also that the government has stationed something like twenty-six thousand troops in the industrial counties."

"Twenty-six thousand?" Allan did not like to say that he had put little thought into political affairs in the last two years—how could he without hinting at his identity or exposing himself as unthinking? He believed himself to be a man of traditional views, yet even in these disturbed times he had no fear of revolution. He couldn't say why, but he thought perhaps because of his experience commanding the common soldiers, which had made him believe that the ordinary people had no wish to overthrow king and established church—that they only asked for decency. Certainly he was not impressed with the current government or its conduct of affairs, and certainly the Regent was not one to command unquestioning respect. But could the stranger indeed be a government spy? No, he found it hard to credit.

"Twenty-six thousand is the number I have heard," John said, "but of course it may be less, or more. I do know certainly that Parliament is considering new laws to make it easier to prosecute so-called political offenders. As you know, I am Unitarian, and those of my church are working for the civil rights of Catholics and of Dissenters—Congregationals, Baptists, Presbyterians—as well as Unitarians. Unitarians have been victims of calumnies and of violence. We have even been accused of treason for opposing the Church of England's control of matters that are purely civil. If such an effort can be expended on us, who are so few in number, and so powerless, consider what the government will undertake against those it believes are more dangerous."

"Yes!" Wendell leaped to his feet and launched into a passionate defense of democracy and workers' rights, culminating his oration by snatching up a copy of Wordsworth's *Excursion,* waving it in front of his hearers' eyes, and then disdainfully casting it onto the heap of pamphlets in the middle of the table. "And Wordsworth! Accepts a government sinecure! Writes as though he understands the common people!"

"Well," John said soothingly. "Some men grow more conservative as they grow older and accumulate responsibilities. Mr. Wordsworth must support a very large household, you know."

"And what has that to say to anything?"

"Indeed disappointing in such a great poet," Allan remarked diplomatically. "But to return to the matter at hand, Mr. Duval. Let me just add my counsel to John's. It would be more prudent at the moment to keep political opinions to oneself."

"I must fight for what's right," Wendell said stubbornly.

"Yes indeed, so must we all, if we are men of honor. But John speaks from experience."

"You do not agree with Tom Paine, then—that moderation in principle is always a vice?"

John intervened. "I believe Allan's counsel is sound, Wendell. But do sit down. My mother tells me that when you last called you had just published an ode to South American freedom fighters, supporting their revolt. The men who control our government may in fact be pleased that Spain's empire will be weakened by these revolts, but they have a horror of republican governments, which the revolted colonies propose to establish. Reasoned argument for reform at home, without attacking the government directly, will be more effective in the long run. I'm sure that the poet Shelley, whom I've heard you speak of, shares many of your opinions, but voices them somewhat more prudently."

"Shelley is anything but prudent, either in his private life or his poetry. I've known him for years. But that's nothing to the purpose."

"Ah, well," John said wryly. "I am not a student of poetry, nor have I an interest in poets' affairs."

Despite his propensity for discourse, Wendell was capable of keeping his own counsel. It was now clear to him that the Ginger-Haired Stranger, the Ladder-Moving Intruder, and the government spy were one and the same. He would deal with the man, and face to face, but he needed time to consider, and he did not need the advice or assistance of either John Califaxton or Mr. Allan Gilmichael. Their counsel of caution made it abundantly clear that they preferred he apply a gag to his pen and to his voice, and would object to any direct action. In fact, they were treating him very much like an erring schoolboy.

"Very well," he said, "for the time being I'll not attempt to publish any poems except those dealing with Nature. But I will state here and now that I will not change my position."

"We aren't asking you to change your position. Not at all. John and I are merely suggesting discretion."

John echoed Allan and then added, "It might be wise to confine the exposition of those opinions to our small circle—to me, to Mr. and Mrs. Clarke. Incidentally, I presumed you wouldn't want to worry your cousin about this."

"I thought it unlikely our bewigged investigator had approached him," Allan said, "which is why I came directly to you, Mr. Duval."

Wendell understood that his visitors were implying that his radical statements might implicate Emery, and nodded. "Of course I'd rather that my cousin not be worried."

"Well, then," John said. "That's settled." He picked up the biography of Chaucer. "Godwin, hmmm? I didn't know he wrote anything other than novels and political works."

"That's Emery's. Thinks Godwin's approach to biography admirable and revolutionary." Wendell grinned at his guests. "And anything revolutionary, as you know, will catch my interest."

Wendell then suggested brandy, and the three gentlemen settled back to discuss literature and poetry, politics being a subject they all thought better for the moment forgotten.

Later, as Allan took another glass of brandy beside his own fire, he reviewed again the case of the suspected spy, if such the man was. At the urging of Lord Blout, a long-time friend of his father's, he had taken his seat in Parliament, and although he had not yet attended many sessions, he was aware of the existence of government spies, the Secret Parliamentary Committees, and of the general fear of revolution that John Califaxton had described. That the stranger in the wig had been able to identify him as a peer did suggest that the man was a government agent. On the other hand, a Bow Street Runner, making some other kind of investigation of young Duval, should have the wit to know who his informants were.

He regretted now that he had so summarily dismissed the fellow without attempting to learn for whom he was spying, if indeed he was spying. Perhaps he should write to Lord Blout to discover if a young man named Wendell Duval was under suspicion. If he was, it must be through some mistake; he judged Duval's radicalism to be no more than an imitation of his current political heroes, just as his poetry was no doubt an imitation of his current literary heroes, and he would probably put both aside with a few more years of experience.

Allan was not one for postponing a chore. He went to his desk, lit another candle, and sat down to begin composing his enquiry to his father's old friend. He then turned to one of the books he had borrowed from Wendell, choosing Emery Clarke's biography of Chaucer rather than the free-thinking writer the young man had recommended.

Wendell, meanwhile, comfortably reposed in his bed, his hands behind his head and his eyes thoughtfully resting on the low ceiling above, was coming to his own, rather more momentous decisions. First off, the spy had to be dealt with. Wendell had no doubt that the government had assigned a spy to discover whether he was stirring up discontent among the citizenry, and he intended to find out who the man was and expose him and his employers. England was supposed to be a free country, wasn't it?

And he had a second decision to make, of at least equal importance. No, of greater importance, for jail was no more than a consequence of tyranny and could be endured. But love . . . The fact was that Cupid's arrow had pierced Wendell's heart. How deeply it had pierced had been borne in upon him that afternoon, when his first thought had been that Prudence Califaxton was the "matter of some concern" that her brother wished to discuss with him. Wendell dwelt for a few moments on her golden hair, her sea-green eyes, her rosy cheeks, the sweet curve of her delicious lips. His thoughts for a time wandered to dreams of planting kisses on those delicious lips.

He was certain that Prudence was not indifferent to him, but had she come to love him? Could he hope? Her family would object; would think they had not known each other long enough; that they were both too young (the working people married even younger, he would tell them); that his politics were too radical. Even though Mrs. Califaxton had republican sympathies, Mr. Califaxton was a known Tory.

He cared not a farthing if her father refused her a dowry and cut her out of his will; he would not be tainted by accepting so much as a shilling of Califaxton money, gained as it was from exploitation of the working people. His competence might be small, but he had prospects. His education was excellent. He'd give up poetry, of course. But would Prudence wait for him while he qualified himself for the bar? Or established himself as a journalist? Could he ask her to endure the slings and arrows that would come his way when he stood for Parliament as a radical and reformer? And if her family cast her off forever, could Prudence bear that? Could he ask it of her? Well, the first step was to discover whether he could hope. If not, then he would join the Freedom Fighters in South America.

He needed an ally, and Maidie Worthing was exactly the one to take into his confidence. She liked Prudence and Prudence liked her. She was independent-minded and she could take care of herself. Wendell's sharp eyes had not missed the exchange at the tea table with Allan Gilmichael, and although he hadn't heard what was said, the gentleman was obviously routed. Wendell could give credit where credit was due; Maidie hadn't been awed by Gilmichael's formidable air of consequence—as, truth to tell, he had been. Although since this evening, seeing that the man could unbend and talk about something other than artificial flies, he believed him to be perhaps more amiable than he had thought. Yes, Maidie was the one to confide in.

John Califaxton, unlike Allan and Wendell, was already asleep, the candle by his bed burned to the socket and the book he'd been reading still open on his chest. As the candle guttered, he awoke briefly, closed the book and lay it aside, blew out the flickering flame, snuffed the wick with his fingers, and sank back into virtuous slumber.

Six

Wendell was up early, and after a hasty breakfast was off hotfoot to make his proposals to Maidie. He found Fanny in the dining parlor, gloomily contemplating a cup of tea and a piece of dry toast. In response to Wendell's query after her health, she replied that she was feeling better, and in response to his inquiry after Maidie, she waved her hand listlessly in the general direction of the kitchen.

It was baking day at Pennelbeck Farm. The kitchen was hot, even with Fanny's modern stove, and Maidie, looking flushed and very hot herself, was up to her elbows in flour. She was wrapped in an apron, and wore a kerchief on her head, tied Gypsy fashion, from under which a few wisps of hair had escaped to curl damply around her face. She brushed at one of the escaped wisps as Wendell entered, adding a streak of flour to her cheek.

"Tomorrow," she said, "I'm going to cut my hair!"

The young maid Stella wiped her hands on her apron. "I'll tie your kerchief up again for you, Miss Maidie, real tight and nice. But first let me get your hair up better. I declare, I don't know why you won't let me do it up for you in the morning. It's plain as can be that you don't know how to manage it."

"I'm going to have it cut, first thing tomorrow morning," Maidie replied grimly.

As Stella worked at securing Maidie's abundant hair in a

tighter knot in order to confine it better under the kerchief, she said, "You shouldn't cut such pretty hair. You should get a cap, Miss Maidie, for the kitchen. Like the one I wear."

"Thank you. Perhaps I will," Maidie said. And then, seeing Wendell, she said crossly, "And what are you grinning about?"

"Nothing. Nothing at all. It's just a . . . a . . . smile of greeting. But you look absolutely feverish. It's the temperature of an ironworks in here!" Wendell picked up a newspaper from a chair, and began fanning himself.

"Yes, and you'll look feverish, too, if you stay here much longer."

Wendell lowered his voice slightly, with an eye on Stella and the housekeeper, Mrs. Eckston, who were working at another table. "I'd like to talk to you about something. Need your help. Can you come outside a minute?"

"No, not now. Bread must be kneaded for thirty minutes, Mrs. Eckston says, and I've only been kneading for ten. It sticks to one's hands so! And one must keep sprinkling flour—but not too *much* flour! Although Mrs. Eckston says that soon it'll be smooth as satin. Oh! I stopped when Stella was tying my kerchief! Mrs. Eckston, does it matter that I stopped kneading while Stella was tying my kerchief?"

Mrs. Eckston, smiling to herself, said, "No, Miss Maidie. Not if you don't stop for more than a minute or two."

Maidie, back at work kneading the bread, asked Wendell, "Will whatever it is you have to say take longer than a minute or two?"

"I'm afraid so. When will you finish?"

"I'm making gingerbread, too, but the bread has to be set to rise first . . ."

"How about between the bread and the gingerbread?" Wendell had no time for housewifely chatter.

Maidie brushed at another wisp of hair that had already escaped her newly tied kerchief. "I suppose I may."

"I'll wait, then. Where's Emery? Fanny didn't look up to the mark today. She didn't seem to want company."

"No, she's been unwell. Uncle Emery's in the barn."

Maidie forgot that it was necessary to mold the dough into loaves before she set it to rise. And Mrs. Eckston, with apologies, made her first chop the dough four hundred strokes with a knife to make up for her inexpert kneading, and then she couldn't seem to get her loaves to look like Mrs. Eckston's. She was therefore just setting the last pan to rise when Wendell returned, accompanied this time by Emery and Allan Gilmichael.

"Mrs. Eckston," Emery said, as they entered. "We're looking for a nice cool glass of buttermilk. Do you have any on hand? Is Maidie here? Oh, there you are, Maidie. How did the bread turn out?"

"It isn't finished yet, Uncle Emery."

Mrs. Eckston, bustling off to bring the buttermilk, stopped to pat Maidie's shoulder. "It's going to turn out just fine. She's done herself proud for a beginner. I've trained lots of girls in my time, and I taught Mrs. Fanny herself, you'll remember, sir, and I can't say that any of them—even Mrs. Fanny, God bless her—did as good the first times as Miss Maidie."

"Well done, Maidie!" Emery beamed. "There's a good deal of philosophy as well as skill goes into bread making."

Maidie, hot and floury, gave Mrs. Eckston's cheek an impulsive kiss. "She's just such a wonderfully patient teacher!"

Embarrassed, Mrs. Eckston flustered, "Now you all just go on in to the dining parlor and I'll bring the buttermilk. You, too, Miss Maidie—plenty of time before you mix up the gingerbread. Stella, you get glasses for the gentlemen and Miss Maidie."

Maidie began dusting at her apron, raising a small cloud of flour. "But I should clean the table and the kneading trough. I haven't forgotten that that's part of baking, too."

"No, you run along. Time enough another day to learn about cleaning up."

Maidie could no longer avoid acknowledging the odious sporting gentleman. "Good morning, Mr. Gilmichael. Has my uncle been showing you his cows?"

"Yes. He has a nice little herd."

"Afraid I dragooned him, Maidie. We're off soon to one of the tarns he hasn't discovered yet. It's quite a scramble, and hard to find, but some of the best fishing in the Lakes. We've asked Wendell to join us, but he says you're all going to Blea How this afternoon." Emery slapped Wendell on the shoulder. He was in fine fettle this morning, having just completed a difficult chapter of his history, and on top of it bursting as he was with the secret of a descendent in the offing. "Stella, while we're having our buttermilk, you might pack us up a little cheese and perhaps some of those biscuits Mrs. Eckston makes."

Allan, who had been thinking how enchanting Emery Clarke's impertinent young niece looked in kerchief and apron, with flour streaked across her cheek, said, "I hope you will join us, Miss Worthing, as your teacher suggests. Rest and refreshment surely are called for after such hard, hot work. I'm only sorry your bread isn't ready for sampling. I wish my young sister would take an interest in such useful accomplishments." Why, he wondered, did he feel this desire to spar with the girl?

Maidie's chin tilted up just the fraction of an inch, and he knew why.

"Thank you," she said, "but I'm really not thirsty. And if I'm to finish in good time I must tend to my work, or there will be no walk to Blea How this afternoon. Prudence is most particularly anxious to begin a sketch of the view." She shot Wendell a quick glance. "I'll just rest a few minutes on the bench in the orchard. If you will all excuse me?"

"It is indeed a splendid prospect from Blea How," Wendell remarked. "Always stimulating to the poetic urge. I never tire of it myself."

Allan, who had seen the look exchanged between Wendell

and Maidie, refrained from delivering an opinion on the inspirational qualities of Blea How. A more interesting speculation was what was going forward between these two young people. "So," he thought, "the girl is carrying on a flirtation with young Duval!"

"Run along then, child," Emery said. "And here's Mrs. Eckston with the buttermilk. Gentlemen, will you join me?"

Wendell downed his buttermilk as hastily as seemed fit, and then said, "I say, Emery, I forgot I've a message for Maidie from Miss Califaxton. Something to do with our excursion to Blea How." Wendell waved his hand vaguely to indicate that it wasn't of any great importance. "So I'll be going along as soon as I've seen Maidie. Phoebus already rides high in the sky, and I've my sonnet to finish. Uh, my thanks, Emery, for the cooling draught. Pure ambrosia. Nectar of the gods on a day like this. Good to see you again, Mr. Gilmichael." With which, and a quick bow to Allan, he was off to the orchard to lay his proposals at Maidie's feet.

Wendell hoped ardently that Prudence's irritating brother Chester would not choose to join them today. He never seemed to decide until the last minute. Fact was, fellow had discovered that Maidie was not susceptible to his charm, which seemed to have quenched an early interest in their excursions. Maidie's indifference was a demonstration of her good sense, Wendell thought. Nor was Chester susceptible to Nature. He was never behindhand in expressing the opinion that poetry about trees and flowers and views was an utter bore, and political discussions even more fatiguing. Which could not recommend him to any man of either sense or sensibility. But if the irritating fellow should come along . . . If Maidie could just get him out of the way . . . Brothers were inhibiting influences at the launching of courtships, particularly when they were likely to disapprove the suitor, as he had no doubt Chester would.

To Wendell's surprise, Maidie was not as enthusiastic about

his intention to immediately declare his love to Prudence as he had supposed she would be. When he had completed his hurried presentation, including Maidie's role in the drama, she was regarding him with a disapproving frown.

"The proper place to make a declaration is in Prudence's drawing room," she said severely. "After you've spoken to her papa. Or at least to John if you can't wait until Mr. Califaxton returns. Really, Wendell, I'm ashamed of you!"

"Well, I thought you'd show some little interest in the business, at least! I thought all women were romantic." Then immediately forgetting his disappointment at Maidie's lack of enthusiasm, overcome as he was by his own, he blurted, "Do you think she cares for me? Has she ever said anything to you?"

Maidie searched a moment for the proper response to Wendell's eager question. "She seems to like you well enough," she observed cautiously.

"No more than that?" Wendell jumped to his feet and began to pace back and forth in front of her. "Not even a hint that she might favor me, just a little?"

Maidie suddenly laughed. "Don't look so despairing. If I didn't guess that *your* heart was burning with this passion, how should I divine Prudence's feelings? Especially since she's such a sweet, tranquil girl—not given at all to drama, to which you, Wendell, are most uncommonly prone."

Wendell sat down again. He kicked at a stone that rested near his foot. "Please, Maidie, just listen a minute." He then launched into a catalog of all the objections that a wealthy family such as the Califaxtons would have to a young man of his political persuasions and modest prospects. He realized that he'd have to settle on a respectable profession, but he was prepared for sacrifice. He knew they were young, but so were Romeo and Juliet! And he would wait . . . not forever, of course. But he couldn't change his politics. He was likely one day to stand for Parliament, on a reform ticket . . . "Now don't laugh!" he exclaimed, on suddenly realizing that he had been so carried away that he had revealed one of his secret dreams.

"I wouldn't think of laughing. It's a wonderful, worthy ambition."

Wendell seized Maidie's hand, and lapsing into the vernacular, said, "You're top of the trees, Maidie. A real trump! If I'd ever had a sister, I'd have wanted her to be like you. You're the best, Maidie."

"Thank you. And . . . and I shouldn't have minded at all having a brother like you, Wendell—but it still doesn't alter the fact that you're asking me to do something wrong."

"No, Maidie, listen! If Prudence tells me there's no hope at all that she could ever love me, I shall go away." Wendell leaped to his feet again, assuming a heroic stance. "I will not force myself upon her." He raised his right hand. "I swear to you." He sat down again, his head bowed. "I know it's perhaps too much to hope that a girl like Prudence could accept someone like me."

"You'd go away?" Maidie asked. "Where?"

"To South America to fight for freedom!"

She stifled an urge to giggle. Although she doubted that Wendell would take flight to South America, and although he was perfectly ridiculous in his ardor, she didn't question his sincerity or his honor. Another emotion—a faint subterranean stirring in the subsoil of her psyche—determined the case. It was as Wendell said, she later told herself: one is always sympathetic with lovers.

Wendell launched into an even more impassioned description of all the possible reasons why Prudence would refuse even to assure him he might hope, with a recapitulation of all the objections the Califaxtons would raise in the unlikely event she should permit him to hope, and at last ended with a gloomy, "And Wendell isn't even my name! They'll think I've something to hide because I've been using a false name all this time. I suppose that's one reason I'm spied upon. It makes my political beliefs seem even more dangerous, and—"

"False name? Spy? What ever are you talking about?"

"Emery and Fanny never told you?"

"Told me what?"

"That my real name is Salvatore Toone?"

"Salvadory Toone?"

"Salvatore. Sal-va-tor-ay. I'm told my mother was a great admirer of an Italian opera singer . . ."

"T-t-toone, did you say?" Maidie put her hands over her mouth to again stifle a disgraceful attack of giggles.

Wendell was once again on his feet. He clutched his hair with both hands, pacing back and forth with agitated steps. "It's not funny! I knew. *I knew!*" He gesticulated wildly. "I *knew* if I explained my name this would happen! Why was I born a Toone? More eccentrics and madmen in my family than a flytrap has flies!"

Maidie wiped her eyes. "I'm sorry, Wendell. Do sit down again."

But Wendell was too agitated to sit down. "I'm cursed! Cursed! And now I've a government agent spying on me!"

"Do calm yourself. You're imagining things." Then, as her own imagination took a leap, her eyes widened. "Have you done something? Is that why you've changed your name?"

A whole novel opened before Wendell's eyes. He would capture Maidie's imagination, her sense of justice—but he'd need a little time to think up the plot. He threw himself on his knees before her and clasped his hands in supplication. "Nothing. I *swear,* I've done nothing wrong. Please, I beg you, help a desperate man!"

"Get up, foolish boy. If anyone should see you, they'd think you were making me an offer."

Wendell arose and energetically brushed the knees of his trousers before sitting down again. "I'll tell you another time about

changing my name. But I'll want your help with the spy. But
don't tell Emery."

"But shouldn't he be the one to help you? You're his cousin,
and I'm sure . . ."

"No. I won't involve Emery. Too dangerous for him. You see,
I'm certain the spy's following me, and that he's the one who
moved the ladder while searching my cottage. Remember? Then
I learned that he's been asking questions about me—of both
John Califaxton and Mr. Gilmichael—perhaps others. They've
been to warn me. But they think I only have to keep quiet about
my political views. They think, you see, that I'm just going
through a schoolboy fascination with radical ideas."

Puzzled, and secretly in agreement with the two gentlemen,
Maidie asked, "But how can I help you?" It all suddenly seemed
so ridiculous that she added, "A spy. Of all things! I still don't
believe it."

"You just keep your eyes open this afternoon. Ten to one he
follows us."

Maidie was still considering Wendell disbelievingly. "And
just what does this spy look like? How will I recognize him?"

"I can't tell you that. He wears disguises. I met him up on
the High Street. I was sitting on a section of the old Roman wall,
and he came walking by, and in a great hurry. I expect he thought
I was still ahead of him, and was afraid of losing me in the mist.
And because of the disguise and the mist—could hardly see my
hand before my face—I didn't recognize him, even though I
thought he looked familiar. When I first noticed him he had
ginger-colored hair. And he was wearing a wig when he spoke
to John Califaxton and to Mr. Gilmichael. So keep a close watch
this afternoon. I'll need your help later, when the time comes to
deal with him."

"Well, so I am to watch for a strange man who keeps changing
his wig. But I still don't see how I can possibly help you deal
with a spy."

"I'm going to catch him."

"Catch him?"

"Yes, and force him to tell me who has set him on me." Then, remembering that he had intended to make Maidie think he was fleeing from an injustice, he added darkly, "I may have to flee again."

Maidie had not been brought up in a banker's household and by rational principles to believe everything she was told. She regarded him thoughtfully. "Well, you can tell me your plans for the spy later and then we'll see. I must get back to the kitchen now."

"This afternoon? You'll help with Prudence?"

"Can you assure me that you are not being spied upon for anything that would make you ineligible to address a girl like Prudence?"

Wendell began to repent his suggestion of some dark drama. "I swear it, Maidie. Again and again. There's nothing."

And so she gave him her promise.

Maidie, freshly bathed, in a clean but practical dress, and wearing her walking boots, sat on a bench in the garden watching the rowboat cross the lake from the Califaxton boat landing. Chester was at the oars. She sighed. That meant that she would have to find some means of luring him out of earshot of Wendell and Prudence. It was only now occurring to her that Chester might feel that it would be improper to walk off with her, leaving his young sister alone with Wendell. Perhaps she could find means to send Chester after something, while she stayed near the lovers, but at a discreet distance. She should have counseled patience—that Wendell's declaration await a more convenient time and place. In fact, she mused, feeling the weight of twenty-three years which felt more like thirty-three, she shouldn't be participating in any of Wendell's foolishness, and particularly in any foolishness involving a spy! The potential difficulties facing Prudence and Wendell appealed to her egalitarian principles, and, she supposed, it was romantic. But . . . well, her promise was given.

Still considering the various problems Wendell had placed in her lap, she walked down to the boat landing to greet the brother and sister.

Chester held the rowboat while Maidie took the picnic basket and other paraphernalia that Prudence handed her. Wendell hailed them from the road just as they were gathering it all up, and so they set off, somewhat overburdened, for Blea How. Wendell walked beside Prudence, conversing with her so casually—even with restraint—that Maidie, following behind with Chester, thought it small wonder she hadn't suspected anything between them.

Chester was much more loquacious. He was in low spirits, he told her at some length, for his father had once again refused him permission to return to Manchester, and advised him not even to think about London. "Frightful bore," Chester said gloomily, "loafing about up here."

"Why don't you try to find something worthwhile to do?" Maidie asked unsympathetically. "If you set yourself to some occupation, something to improve your mind, you wouldn't find it so boring. And your father might be sooner to relent."

"What a lecturer you are! As bad as *mon père*," Chester said, more cheerfully. "No, never did have any taste for the books. Old John's the scholar in the family. Never had a taste for business or the army either. Like horses, but a man can't spend all his time with a horse."

"You could try to learn something about the Lakes."

"What? I'm not like you three. Don't see anything in hills and rocks."

"There's the history of the Lakes. The Romans and so on. And natural history—mineralogy, botany, entomology . . ."

"Might have liked that, but not much chance at Cambridge. Stuffy old dons think science anti-religious, you know. 'Course I'm never going to be a clergyman, so ain't sure why I was even there. Waste of time, as I told *mon père*. Might not choose to follow m'family's dissenting ways, but didn't mean I wanted to be stuck in university."

"You could always study things like botany on your own."

"Too lazy," Chester said, with a sly sideways glance that caused Maidie to laugh in spite of herself.

"I suppose you'll have equally ready objections to any other suggestions I might make, so I will desist. I leave all further conversational initiative to you."

Prudence, who was finding Wendell unusually quiet, had been listening to the conversation behind her with growing amusement. No one could best Chester on the subject of avoiding useful activity. "It's no use, Maidie," she said over her shoulder. "You are wise to give up the effort."

"Perhaps he'll find something to interest him when we get to Blea How," Wendell said, coming to life again. "While Miss Califaxton finishes her sketching, you can show him the ruined cottage, Maidie. You know, where the ghost is supposed to appear every second of February."

"Perplexing why a ghost should choose the second of February," Chester remarked, and Wendell was gratified with the thought that he might have hit on the means to get Prudence's bothersome brother from underfoot.

When the time came, however, Chester was clearly reluctant to leave his sister alone with an unrelated male, no matter how good friends they all were. Maidie had managed to maneuver him a little apart from the other two, although barely out of hearing, and when she suggested they explore the ruined cottage, he replied that since it wasn't the second of February and no ghost would be around he couldn't see anything of interest in such an expedition. "Seen plenty of ruined cottages," he pronounced flatly.

"But it's so picturesque!"

"Seen plenty of picturesque ruined cottages, too."

Maidie let a few minutes pass, and then suggested he accompany her to the crest of the hill to look at the view. If as she suspected he was reluctant to leave Wendell and Prudence alone together, he could at least keep an eye on the two of them from a higher vantage point, with no danger of overhearing any impassioned statements.

"Haven't any interest in views," Chester said. "You know that, Maidie."

"Would you mind accompanying me in case I should need some assistance? It's a steep climb."

"Don't want to be ungallant, but you never need assistance. Ask Wendell to go. He's the one likes a view."

"Yes, but he's composing, can't you see?"

Wendell had thoughtfully brought out his notebook, and periodically, following contemplation of some distant point, jotted something in it. He now rumpled his hair, moved his lips while his unseeing eyes gazed at what ecstasy they were not to know, and then furiously scribbled several lines. Prudence seemed absorbed in her landscape sketch.

Chester shook his head. "What a hum!" He lowered his voice. "Fellow's poetry's terrible, you know."

Maidie looked at him in surprise. "How do you know? Have you read any of his work?"

Chester looked ashamed. "Shouldn't have mentioned it."

"Where have you read any of Wendell's poetry?" She didn't think much of Wendell's poetry either, but he was practically her cousin. And she couldn't believe that Chester read the cheap radical papers that were the only publications that so far had accepted Wendell's efforts. "Where?" she persisted. "Tell me."

Chester was now looking uncomfortable. "Shhh, don't speak

so loudly." He glanced uneasily in the direction of Wendell and his sister. "Prudence had some," he mumbled. Then, with another guilty glance at the other two, he said, "Don't tell her, though. Doesn't know I saw them."

Maidie stood up. "Come with me." She pointed imperiously to the crest of the how. "I want to see the view. And I also am going to give you a lecture, in a firm—and probably loud—voice. So it's either up there or right here."

An abashed Chester rose to follow, but he was not ready to admit guilt. "Can't let you go off by yourself. But as for a lecture, it wasn't anything, you know, just some bad stuff about shepherds and sheep dogs, and silly nonsense like that. Fellow doesn't even know how to rhyme. Prose gone mad, I'd say."

"You are an authority on poetry?"

"Know what I like."

They had come to the steepest part of the climb and found it necessary to save their breath for their upward advance. But when they reached the top, Chester, panting lightly, said defiantly, "And that was Pope I was quoting—'prose gone mad.' " He frowned. "Or perhaps it's 'prose run mad.' Yes, that's it. 'Prose *run* mad.' I didn't waste all my time at Cambridge. Can quote Milton, too, if you like."

"Well, I'm certainly gratified that your Cambridge years weren't wasted, but you must know that you shouldn't have been reading Wendell's poetry without permission! He gave the poems to Prudence to read because she's sensitive and—"

"Fellow's sweet on her, you know."

Maidie stared at him. "Why . . . I . . . how . . . wh-what makes you ever think so? Why, how ridiculous!"

Chester, although recognizing that he had now gained the upper hand, had had no intention of hurting Maidie. "Hope you ain't sweet on the fellow yourself. Didn't mean to spring it on you like that. Know you think a lot of him."

Maidie sat down on the grass. "No, I'm not sweet on him. He's practically my cousin."

"Wouldn't have wanted to do any harm, you know."

"Do you object that he's . . . um . . . sweet on Prudence?"

"He's a good enough fellow. But he's young."

"He's almost 24."

"Well, then, he's young," Chester said, with undeniable logic. He sat down beside her. "Wouldn't want him getting too interested in my sister until he settles into something steady. But I don't object to him."

Maidie observed her companion with mild surprise. "You're a strange one to talk about settling into something."

"Oh, I'm not so good for nothing as you all think, just because I want a little time to sow some wild oats. Man's settled down a long time, you know. Ain't nothing to interest me here, but something will come along." He turned suddenly to Maidie and said, "I know it. Feel it. *Here.*" He thumped his chest, adding a Wendellian touch of drama. "Did you ever get the notion that you were just on the edge of something, but you didn't really know what it was? Kind of expecting something? Got that feeling. Don't know what it is, but something." Seeing Maidie's astounded stare, he said in an embarrassed voice, "I guess you haven't. Sorry. Must have sounded silly."

"Oh, no, not at all!" Maidie exclaimed. "I think it's wonderful! You have anticipation of something!" Chester's notion could hardly be classified as an ambition, like Wendell's desire to become a politician, but his confidence in something that he would eventually settle down to was almost like ambition. She liked Chester the better for it, but nonetheless, he shouldn't have been reading poems that Wendell had intended only for Prudence.

"Nonetheless—" she began, but Chester interrupted with a surprised, "I say, who's that fellow lurking about down there?"

Maidie, after a startled glance at Chester, began scanning the hillside below. "Where?"

Chester pointed. "See that wall of rock, behind Pru and Duval. To the left as you face it. Now, there's that tangle of dwarf oak at the foot. He's in there. Stretched out flat. And he's close enough, if he has good ears, that he can hear what Pru and Duval are saying. Upon my word, I believe the fellow is spying on them!"

"I don't see . . . oh!"

"You see him, d'you?"

"Yes!"

"The blackguard!" Chester exclaimed. "Spying on a private conversation! I'm going down there—"

"No!" Maidie caught his coattails. "Wait. As soon as we move he'll be alerted. You can't get down the hill in time."

"Let go my coattails." Chester sank back. "Guess you're right. I'll shout at Duval—scare Pru into fits, but she'll get over it. Ain't missish, my sister, if I do say so. And I'll take off running. You keep your eye on him. He'll realize he's caught when I shout, so you watch and point the way he goes. It'll either be into that grove, the way we all came up, or over the rocks."

There was no time for Maidie to debate pros and cons. Chester gathered himself, prepared to come to his feet running. They both scanned the undergrowth in order to place the man accurately.

"I don't see him," Maidie said. "Can you?"

They at that moment caught a movement. The brush at the point where the rock face had sheared away into a fall of boulders swayed slightly, and then was still.

"He got away! Well, if I'm not some kind of fool! It must have alerted him when I started to get up. Caught the movement. No chance now, worse luck. Who do you think the fellow was anyway?"

* * *

Below them, Wendell had been seizing his opportunity to figuratively throw himself at Prudence's feet. He apologized for addressing her before speaking to her father, stated his high regard for her, and before she had an opportunity to tell him whether she reciprocated his regard or not, began to list all the disadvantages that she would suffer should she make him the happiest man on earth by allowing him to hope.

"Oh, please, Mr. Duval," Prudence at last interrupted him to beg, *"do* let me speak! You haven't given me a chance to speak."

Wendell's heart sank. She wanted to stop him before he said anything further—she was trying to save his pride. "I beg you to pardon me, Prudence—Miss Califaxton—I know I've been presumptuous. I should never have addressed you. Please forget what I've said! It will never be mentioned again. I'm going away—"

"Wendell!!!"

Wendell stared open-mouthed at his beloved. He had never dreamed his gentle Prudence could speak so forcefully.

Prudence faced him, her face grave. "Forgive me for speaking to you so, but you made me a proposal, and then didn't permit me to answer. In fact, you answered for me. I really would prefer to speak for myself."

Wendell gave up all pretense that they were engaged in an ordinary conversation, whatever Chester might think if he looked down on them from up there on the hilltop. He took Prudence's hands. His portfolio and notebook tumbled unnoticed to the ground. "Forgive me. Only do not torture me. Quickly, speak, I am at your mercy."

Prudence smiled shyly at her impetuous lover. She withdrew her hands from his clasp, conscious of her brother, still in sight on the crest of the hill, but she reached out to lightly touch his cheek before folding her hands demurely in her lap. "You may hope," she said, and then, having expended all the boldness in her power, she lowered her lashes over her sea-green eyes.

Gazing at her with ecstatic devotion, Wendell took off into a flight of elevated declarations of love, which, once he brought himself to a halt, elicited from Prudence a shy admission of having fallen in love with him at very first sight.

It was not the time for a discussion of ways and means; that could come later, when they had both had time to absorb this momentous event. Nonetheless, there was one practical matter that had to be discussed; the awful moment had come for him to make his most terrible confession. How could he ask a woman to accept such a name as his? One thing he *wouldn't* do, though, was confess again that he was named after an opera singer! He almost wished that Maidie and Chester would show signs of returning, but they seemed to be deep in some kind of discussion. So, without further preliminary, he said, "My name, Prudence, is Salvatore, Sal-va-tor-ay Toone."

The sudden shift of ground took Prudence by surprise. "I, I don't understand." She drew away from him ever so slightly.

"Oh, I know it's ridiculous, but you have to know. My real name is Salvatore Toone—Wendell Duval is just a name I made up because I like the sound of it."

"But," Prudence was still attempting to adjust to the new ground. "I don't understand. Why should you use a false name?"

Wendell abandoned any idea he might have had of pretending to a dramatic explanation. "I've always hated my name. You can't imagine all the ways my schoolfellows had to make fun of it—especially after they learned that Salvatore means savior in English—and how they were always telling me I was out of tune and other abominable puns on my surname, so I just thought to give myself another. That's all. Do you think me terribly foolish?"

"No, of course not," Prudence replied. "But, indeed, I don't care what your name is. I esteem you for yourself." She was too shy to declare herself yet again and say forthrightly that she loved a very passionate and handsome young man—not a name.

Signs of activity on the hill above warned them that they must try to act as though nothing unusual had passed during their companions' absence. "We must talk again, my sweetheart." Wendell said. "But until then, I think it best that we say nothing to your family."

"Whatever you think best, dear," Prudence replied, with a happy smile. She felt daring beyond anything at using the endearment. "But I'd like to tell Maidie. If you don't mind, of course."

This statement reminded Wendell that Maidie had known of his love before Prudence herself. "No, of course not," he assured her. Now he'd have to find an opportunity to tell Maidie that she should seem surprised when Prudence broke the news. Whoever had set the spy on him, he thought, was certainly deluded. He might have iron nerves at a whist table, but he had no talent for conspiracy, even in such a simple matter as declaring himself to the woman he adored.

Thus reminded of the suspicious stranger, Wendell realized that he had seen no sign of the spy that afternoon.

Almost the moment the thought came to him he learned that the spy had not deserted him. Chester and Maidie were descending from the crest of the how, Chester obviously anxious to hurry Maidie in her descent. "I say, Duval," he called, "there was a man lurking in the underbrush behind you. Did you see him? Hear him?"

"Behind us? No, I . . . we were talking . . . we . . ." Wendell for once was speechless. The spy had been within a few feet of him, and he'd not known? How many other times? He must have heard everything! What other times had he been listening under windows, or behind trees?

Chester was poking at the brush. "Yes, here's where he was.

I sighted on this broken oak branch . . . Look, he wiggled in on his stomach. The blackguard was spying on you and Pru!"

"Spying!" Prudence said, her disbelief patent. Prudence had had experience with brothers; and with Chester particularly, who was especially prone to telling her extravagant tales. "When will you *grow up,* Chester?" she asked impatiently.

"No, God's truth. Ask Maidie. Wasn't there a man in the brush, Maidie?"

"Yes, there was, there really was, and he certainly could have heard whatever the two of you were saying if that was his intent."

Wendell smote his brow. "And he was within my grasp!"

Seven

"Whatever could the scoundrel have meant?" Chester asked. "Can you think of any reason why some fellow would want to spy on you and Pru?"

"Because of my politics, of course!"

"Your politics? What stuff!"

"How would you know? You never even read newspapers. The most casual perusal of which would inform you that it's risking prosecution to demand political justice—to take up argument in favor of manhood suffrage as I have, or to voice sympathy with the poor and the working people when they demand higher wages and the right to combine—"

Prudence sat down suddenly, her hand to her breast. "P-prosecution?"

"Now look what you've done! Scared my sister," Chester accused. Nonetheless, he fixed an annoyed eye on Prudence, and said impatiently, "Don't be a gudgeon, Pru. Fellow doesn't know what he's talking about."

Maidie, with fresh in her mind the hint that Wendell was spied upon for some honorable but mysteriously prohibited act, in a tone quite as accusatory as Chester's, said, "Have you been organizing public meetings, Wendell? Aunt Fanny says you *know* that it's been forbidden by the government."

Wendell rounded on her. "Forbidden by the government!

What right has the government to forbid meetings of honest workmen who—"

Prudence scrambled to her feet. "Shame on you all for scolding Mr. Duval!" She faced her surprised companions with uncharacteristic belligerence. "Of course he must organize public meetings if his conscience tells him it's right! But now we have to think what to do about that man. Listening to private conversations! Why, that is . . . is *quite* as wrong as . . . as organizing public meetings! It's not even gentlemanly!"

Maidie couldn't think that Prudence had any notion of why the government might look unfavorably on public meetings. Her defense could more credibly be set down to love. Resisting a smile, she put her arm around the girl. "Pru's right. We should be thinking how to help Wendell rather than scolding him."

"I don't need help," Wendell said sulkily. "I'll catch the fellow by myself."

"Damme but you try a man's patience!" Chester exclaimed. "We can't do anything unless you explain what the devil that impertinent hedgebird wants with you."

"Yes, yes," Prudence and Maidie echoed.

"Well . . ."

"Do tell us, please, Mr. Duval," Prudence pleaded.

Softened, Wendell said, "Well, it's just that there isn't anything more to tell. I've made no secret of my political opinions, and it shouldn't be any surprise to anyone who has the barest interest in affairs"—he gave Chester a withering glance—"that progressive opinions such as mine, based in the conviction of the perfectibility and democratical regeneration of humanity, are considered dangerous by those in power. It's as Godwin says, the immediate *object* of government is security, and the *means* employed is restriction on individual independence and liberty!"

"Then what's to do except keep your opinions to yourself?" Chester asked practically.

"Oh, no, that would be very wrong!" Maidie exclaimed.

"Even if it lands him in jail? Like that fellow Cobbett he's always running on about?" Chester asked. "Just good sense to keep one's opinions to oneself. After all, I've got nothing against common people—ain't any dukes or princes in my family. But you can't just let uneducated people go around voting and such."

"Well, then," Maidie flung in, "the common people must be educated!"

"And," Chester continued, with what he considered inexorable logic, "it just stands to reason that the man who owns the factory knows how much he can afford to pay the laborers."

"Oh *do* be quiet, Chester," Prudence said, stamping her foot. "Who needs your . . . your moldy old opinions?"

Chester goggled at his gentle sister. "Moldy old opinions?" he asked in a deeply offended voice. "Let me tell you, Pru—"

Maidie interposed. "Really, we're all being foolish. This isn't the time to argue about politics. We should give Wendell time to decide what course of action to take, and then if he wants to confide in us, we should try to give him sensible counsel, and if he wants our help, we'll give it."

"Yes! That's just what we should do!" Prudence echoed.

"So come, you two, help Prudence and me collect our things. We'll talk more as we walk home."

The remains of the picnic were put away in the basket, the camp stools folded up, sketch books closed, and pencils and paints returned to their boxes. Then they set off down the hill to the road that would lead them back to Pennelbeck Farm.

When at last the brother and sister were well out into the lake, Wendell gave them a final wave and said, "Come on, Maidie. I'll walk up to the house with you." The animated discussion of the spy had consumed every minute of their return from Blea How, which had prevented Prudence from finding an opportunity to confide her secret to Maidie, a circumstance that Wendell considered fortunate. Couldn't have Pru thinking he'd revealed his love to someone else before speaking to her. She might be jealous, he thought, with a self-satisfied smirk.

As soon as they were out of sight among the garden shrubbery, he burst out, "Well, she accepted me! And it didn't signify a tittle that I bear such a foolish name—or that my politics are radical. I'm the happiest man on earth! Congratulate me, Maidie." After Maidie had responded to this demand to Wendell's satisfaction, he cautioned, "Prudence wants to tell you herself, so don't let on that you knew anything about it."

Maidie began to laugh. "Oh, Wendell, Chester already guessed."

"What? That hare-brain? How does he know? You didn't . . ."

"No. Of course not! How could you think such a thing?"

They sat down on a bench to discuss Wendell's suit in detail, the complications arising from Chester's sharp eyes, and to go over again all they had already said of the spy. Should Wendell approach John Califaxton for permission to address Prudence, or wait until her father returned? Maidie insisted he should declare his suit to John, now that Chester suspected the truth. Wendell disagreed. And what to do about the spy—how to trap him—should they include Chester in the scheme? Prudence? Maidie felt that capturing spies was not appropriate for a girl of seventeen. Wendell agreed, but now that Chester knew about the spy, and would lend his assistance, was it really appropriate for Maidie herself to undertake such a dangerous mission?

With the undeniable proof of the spy's existence, and a confession by Wendell that his political crimes were limited to publishing radical poetry and speaking freely with local people on subjects unpopular with government authorities, Maidie was determined to assist in the exposure of the spy.

"I want to be consulted on any plan you devise," she demanded.

"Well, I've to meet a wrestler over near Patterdale tomorrow.

It's all arranged. But I'll have a plan ready by the day after to-morrow."

"If you think catching your spy can wait, why should I de-mur?"

And finally, would the spy have a gun? Wendell thought not. "Government spies don't make arrests themselves," he observed knowledgeably. "They make reports. The government and the courts do the unsavory work of repression."

Emery and Allan Gilmichael came upon them as the shadows stretched long across the grass and the lake darkened to blue-grey in the encroaching twilight. The two men had the look, as Fanny would have said, of happy Waltonians after a day of good fishing. The sport, and their success, had justified their long walk to the mountain tarn. They had been given an excellent luncheon by a farmer's wife; had discussed exhaustively the mer-its and talents of the Duke of Wellington and Napoleon Bona-parte as strategists, tacticians, and commanders; and had put their minds to solutions for the problems of the times, as well as spending several hours in companionable silence. It had been such a pleasant day that Allan had been prevailed upon to share the Clarkes' plain living supper.

"Well," Emery said, after they greeted Maidie and Wendell. "It looks like Fanny had to carry on alone if we had any visitors this afternoon, for I see you still have your walking boots on, Maidie. Where was your excursion today?"

"We went to Blea How with Prudence and Chester Califaxton."

"Oh, yes. Good views from up there. Well, Wendell, are you joining us for supper, too?"

"No, I'll be going on. I've a poem taking shape." He pointed to his breast. "Here. Before Erato—no, no, not Erato—uh . . . who's the other muse?"

"Perhaps Caliope or Euterpe?" Allan suggested.

"Yes, Euterpe, muse of lyric poetry. Exactly. Anyway, before she abandons me." Wendell was anxious to make his departure. He suspected that Gilmichael was secretly amused by his fumbling. He knew perfectly well which muses Caliope and Euterpe were; but he'd done it again—almost let his cat out of the bag by naming the muse of love poetry. Feeling sullen, and anxious to depart, he couldn't resist a poetic parting shot. "So, as Blake says, admittedly in another context, 'Through evening shades I haste away, To close the Labours of my day.' "

Love was turning him into a fool, he thought crossly, as he turned his steps toward his cottage. True, Cupid's shaft had made fools of more than one of the ancients, not omitting a number of the gods themselves. But why had he used that pretentious quote from Blake? There were times when he felt like Pope's bookful blockhead, with loads of learned lumber in his head. He firmly resolved to be less learned, and then, resolution taken, submitted to Cupid's call by turning his thoughts to the love lyric aborning.

Allan, blissfully unaware of Cupid's mischievous presence in the neighborhood, enjoyed his supper, the conversation, and the company. Fanny was feeling well; Maidie again looked enchanting, although she challenged his political statements (undoubtedly the influence of young Duval); and Emery, in top form, told them anecdotes of the Wars of the Roses.

"Uncle Emery," Maidie said, "I think perhaps I'm at last beginning to understand what the Wars of the Roses were about. I'm sure both of you gentlemen were required to study them to distraction when you were schoolboys, and have firmly fixed in your minds which was which, but I could never keep the contenders straight once I put my history book down—white rose, red rose . . ."

"Very simple, my dear. You should have asked me before. You see, as red and York are the shorter words, and white and Lancaster the longer, you simply remember: short color, long name—a schema. Where's some paper, Fanny? If one draws—"

"But Uncle Emery, one must remember York and Lancaster for your schema to work."

"I think she has you at a standstill there, Clarke," Allan remarked.

"But my own failings aside," Maidie said to Allan, "when I listen to Uncle Emery talk about history I wonder why so many people think it dull! He taught me to love history, bad as I am at remembering details. If it hadn't been for him, I should think it as tiresome as Catherine Morland did."

Allan raised his eyebrows. "And what is that, and who is Catherine Morland?"

"What? You haven't read Miss Austen's novel, *Northanger Abbey?* Well, it's just been published recently, so I suppose you can be forgiven. Catherine Morland is the heroine of the novel. Wait, I'll get the book and read it to you."

As Maidie hurried off to the library, Fanny explained, "It's one of Miss Jane Austen's novels, published posthumously. She wrote it—oh—years ago, when Gothic romances were the rage, as a sort of satire—and her brother, I believe, saw to its recent publication."

"I don't think I've ever heard of her," Allan said. "In truth, I can't remember when I last read a novel."

Maidie had entered the room in time to hear this last remark. "Oh, you're missing so much fun!" she exclaimed. "I do feel so sorry for people who don't read novels."

"Now, Maidie," Fanny scolded, "people have different tastes and interests, just as they have different talents."

Maidie made a brief curtsy in Allan's direction before reseating herself. "Forgive me, sir. Aunt Fanny is right and I apologize. But here's what Catherine Morland thought about history: 'The quarrels of popes and kings, with wars or pestilences in every page; the men all so good for nothing, and hardly any women at all—it is very tiresome . . .' "

Allan laughed heartily. "If that's an example of this Miss Austen's work, I humbly accept your judgment, Miss Worthing, that I have been missing the fun. Will you lend it to me?"

"Of course. But you must remember that it's one of her very first novels. Her later ones are even better."

"Will I stand higher in your estimation, Miss Worthing, if I tell you that I do read poetry?" he asked as he rose to take the book from her.

Maidie's eyes widened innocently. Fanny could not have done better. "Why, Mr. Gilmichael," she said, "I didn't say that you stood *lower* in my estimation for *not* reading novels. I said only that you were missing the fun."

Allan, looking down at her, noted the very slight tightening at the corners of her mouth that suggested a smile—possibly even a laugh—held in check. Damn the girl, she was challenging him again. "I am again relieved," he said, returning to his seat. He crossed his legs nonchalantly and remarked, "Perhaps in exchange for Miss Austen I can give you Blake, Miss Worthing. You do read poetry, do you not?"

"Not often, I'm afraid, although I hesitate to confess it, for you will surely tell me that you're sorry I should be missing so much . . . so much . . ."

"Precisely."

Emery was frowning. "Blake, hmm? Very strange poet. Hadn't ever heard of him until that painter last summer. You remember, Fanny. Couldn't recommend him enough."

"Yes, very strange," Allan agreed. "I'm sure, Miss Worthing, you will find Blake interesting."

"Does he write things like 'John Gilpin's Ride'? That's my *very* favorite poem! 'Away went Gilpin, neck or nought . . .' "

"Maidie!" Fanny frowned at her niece. "What has gotten into

you? It's a diverting poem, but there are many others by Cowper that you—"

Allan had not taken his eyes from the girl, but her gaze had not faltered, nor her air of innocence. "Your niece is teasing me, Mrs. Clarke."

Maidie laughed outright. "But I do love John Gilpin and his good wife! Although it's true I was teasing. I'm sure that just as soon as you are gone, Mr. Gilmichael, Aunt Fanny will scold me for being so terribly ill bred. But I'll read Blake with interest, and hope I'll find as much pleasure in his poetry as I hope you'll find in Miss Austen's novel."

Gracefully said, he thought. Young as she was, she was too much for that green young calf, Duval.

An hour later, he discovered it was nearly midnight, and with apologies for overstaying his welcome, which were vigorously rejected by all, he took his leave. At the garden gate he stood for a few moments with Emery, looking out over the lake.

"I hope I haven't erred, forcing Blake on Miss Worthing," Allan said, conscious that Blake had sprung to mind because of that ridiculous quote by Duval. "She seems remarkably well read for one so young, but even so, I'm not sure that Blake is appropriate for a young girl."

"Who, Maidie? At twenty-three she's certainly old enough to be reading whatever she chooses, and in any event, she's been reading the most improbable literature since she was a child. She was a smart little thing, and her mother had progressive notions about her education. She read books ordinarily kept from girls. She was reading Fielding's novels at thirteen. Didn't understand the half of it—all that rollicking around in feather-beds—but, well, she's turned out very well. Her father saw that she had what you might call a more proper education, although I don't think it really took hold. And probably just as well."

Walking home in the moonlight, Allan had something new to ponder. She looked so young. . . . He suddenly laughed aloud.

He'd enjoyed the sparring, but now he knew she was a woman, and not just out of the schoolroom, he would enjoy it even more. He always preferred even matches. Although he had to admit that if an Olympian judge were keeping score he would probably be judged the one lagging behind. But no more. "Sword un-sheathed from now on, Miss Worthing," he announced to the air and the gods of the night.

Cupid laughed.

Although he had planned a ramble on the fells, and perhaps a climb of one of the peaks, Allan decided that duty required he postpone that pleasure in order to deliver the promised copy of Blake to Miss Worthing. Thus it was that the following afternoon he found himself again entering the Clarkes' drawing room. He saw Maidie at once. She was politely listening to a young man who seemed to be waxing eloquent—without a doubt on some radical subject or other. As though she knew his eyes were on her, she looked up and their eyes met. She smiled.

Maidie held out her hand to Allan as he crossed the room to her. "Good afternoon, Mr. Gilmichael. I see you have brought me the promised poetry. Such courtesy and promptitude! I do hope, however, that I shan't be called upon to give a learned opinion as quickly as you have been to bring me the book."

He bowed over her hand. "Not at all, Miss Worthing. Blake is not a poet for instant review."

"But let me make you known to Mr. Trawley. He's stopping with us for the night before continuing on to Mr. Clarkson's, who as you no doubt know has these many years been advocating the abolition of slavery in our West Indian plantations. Mr. Gilmichael is an enthusiastic angler, Mr. Trawley, like Uncle Emery, and he also reads poetry, but I can't say whether he's ever given so much as a thought to the evils of slavery."

The young clergyman bowed. "I would have all people of

good will join those of us who abhor slavery, but there is such great need for reform in England today that one knows not where to begin. Or where to draw the line. Miss Worthing has just been listening to a proponent of this man Bentham on Parliamentary Reform. Seems the fellow not only recommends universal manhood suffrage, but he has claimed, at least in private conversation, that women should have the vote as well!"

Allan looked at Maidie questioningly. "Oh, quite shocking, I should think. Surely women are too much heart and not enough head to be allowed in councils of state, and are too delicate altogether for political tumult. But perhaps Miss Worthing agrees that women have sufficient intellect to exercise the vote?"

"Certainly enough intellect to recognize our own interests! No, Mr. Gilmichael, when one is taught by a mother who writes serious works on religious doctrine, and an aunt who writes shocking essays on industrial conditions—"

"Ah, Miss Worthing," Allan interrupted. "You are about to draw a false conclusion. A *few* women of intellect one might rather suppose are the exceptions that test the rule."

"Perhaps. Although I've never been able to make sense of that old saying. Be that as it may, I can't believe that the only women of intellect are those who inhabit my small circle of family and acquaintance."

"But, in fact, our discussion is moot by definition. The principle on which the vote is awarded is property, not intellectual capacity. Half the Parliament and at least a third of the Ministry would lose political power tomorrow if brains were the qualification."

The Reverend Mr. Trawley, relegated to the sidelines during this exchange, decided to assert himself. "You are correct, Mr. Gilmichael. It is property that weds the citizen to the interests of his nation."

Maidie, at this turn of the conversation, realizing that the clergyman was serious, whereas Allan was not, suddenly found herself argumentative. "Property!" she burst out. "My father owns substantial property. True, it's not landed property—he disdains to purchase a country estate. But even should he do so, he would be unable to take a seat in Parliament because he's a Dissenter. And not even an ordinary Dissenter, but a Unitarian, which as you know, Mr. Trawley, is the worst kind, many times worse than a Congregational or Methodist . . . as bad as a Catholic."

The conversation suddenly striking close to home, the young clergyman said in a shocked voice, "Surely you're not about to suggest disestablishment! Society in general requires the guiding hand, the universal principle if you will, of an established religion. Especially when that religion is interwoven so closely with the Constitution. And surely you must admit that the English Church is tolerant." And in any event, he hadn't been the first one to mention property, so why was she kicking up at him?

Allan sympathized more with what he considered Maidie's over-excited outburst than with the stiff-rumped young clergyman, and decided to lend her a hand. "I've a neighbor, a Baptist. One of our progressive farmers. I know him well. He objects strongly to paying a tithe to support the Church of England when he's a Baptist, after all. Can't say I enjoy paying a tithe myself, and I have no doctrinal dispute with the established church."

"A Baptist?" Mr. Trawley's clerical brows drew down in a frown. "I'm afraid I have no great opinion of Baptists."

"Then I'm sure you have no great opinion of Unitarians, either," Maidie said. "Which proves," she continued, turning to Allan, "that we must either enter into a spirited engagement like those who are gathered around Aunt Fanny, or that we should ask Mr. Trawley his opinion of the Lakes. I suggest the latter, for I am still new enough to the beauties of the landscape that I can bore on about it quite shockingly."

"I, too, Miss Worthing. But I would be disappointed in myself should I ever become blind to the beauties of any world I inhabit."

Maidie smiled up at Allan before turning to Mr. Trawley. "So you must tell us, sir, of your experience in this Lake country. Has it opened your eyes to the picturesque? To nature? Do you now understand Mr. Wordsworth's poems better?"

"So many questions, Miss Worthing!" Mr. Trawley exclaimed, as he hurriedly tried to remember a scene that had impressed itself in any way upon him sufficiently to demonstrate a superior appreciation for nature. Since nothing came to his mind's eye, he was fortunate that their small group was interrupted at that moment by Mr. Emery Clarke, desiring to introduce him to another advocate of abolition.

"Well, Miss Worthing," Allan said, as the clergyman withdrew, "why the retreat from controversy? I had begun to think that you gloried in it."

"Because I felt myself growing heated, and furthermore thought that Wendell was coming to join us, and *he* positively glories in an unguarded tongue, as you must know. But I see he's been drawn into Aunt Fanny's contesting circle. I declare, I believe he would *enjoy* going to prison for sedition."

Allan rather thought she was right. "One of his heroes, that fellow Cobbett, went to jail on charges of sedition, and I understand lived quite comfortably. Perhaps Duval emulates him in politics as he emulates Wordsworth in poetry." The minute the final statement was out of his mouth, he rebuked himself for such an unworthy insinuation. He might think young Duval a callow, hero-worshiping schoolboy, but he had no right to diminish him in Miss Worthing's opinion.

"Yes, but Cobbett had no desire to repeat the experience," Maidie was observing, "and when the most recent gagging acts were passed, he fled to America rather than go to jail again. That's what I should do if I faced arrest—flee to America!"

Allan looked down at her, amused. "I find it difficult to believe you would ever come to such straits."

"And why shouldn't I? I have long desired to do something

useful, and perhaps I shall invade the strongholds of masculine power and demand my rights as a thinking woman—the right, as Mr. Bentham says, to speak to the governors of the nation about what pertains to my own happiness and that of other women. I'll demand the vote, shout the cause from the housetops, and insist on a seat in the House of Commons. Do you think that would be enough?"

"If you get up on any housetops I'd say it will more likely get you committed to Bedlam."

"Perhaps you're right. Then I will write political pamphlets under a masculine pseudonym, demanding that the common people receive a living wage and a basic education free of sectarian religious instruction, as Mr. Lancaster proposes."

Allan was so displeased that the views she expressed seemed to echo those of that radical greenhorn, Duval, that he found himself pursuing the same unworthy course he had just rebuked himself for. "I am amazed at your fund of political knowledge! I suppose young Duval is responsible?"

Maidie's chin came up, and her eye kindled. "Were I not aware of your good breeding, sir, I should be required to bristle at that remark. However, I'm sure you had no intention of suggesting that I, a *female,* am unable to think for myself. Surely an inadvertence! Now if you'll excuse me, I've been neglecting my duty to other guests."

She walked off, apparently unconcerned with the duty of finding him another human to converse with, and furthermore ignoring the book of poetry he still held in his hand.

Maidie, fuming, offered to replace Fanny at the tea table, leaving her aunt free to devote herself soul and body to a spirited discussion of Robert Owen's ideas for a national system of education, while simultaneously clearing the way for those guests thirsting for tea, but not for an argument. Maidie hoped Mr. Gilmichael would take his odious Blake and go home, but a few moment's reflection soon revealed that she didn't want him to go home at all, and left her wondering as well what had nettled her so. Why had their bantering exchange so suddenly soured? She was relieved when a correspondent for the *Times,* and a great friend of Emery's, requested a cup of coffee and then remained to chat with her. It helped her resist a nearly ungovernable compulsion to watch the detestable man as he moved around the room.

Allan had, in fact, considered stalking out of the room, and out the door. On soberer second thought, however, he reminded himself that Maidie was young and inexperienced, and he was too mature and sober to allow himself to be angered. He could forgive such a young and inexperienced girl for taking as her own the radical opinions of her relatives and of young Duval. A twenty-three-year-old girl, of course, but still a girl. She undoubtedly was unaware of any practical considerations in such matters as the suffrage, but her sentiments were to her honor. A shame she couldn't have chosen John Califaxton for a flirt; Califaxton was of her own religion, and a much more sober and sensible fellow than young Duval. And it was really rather charming that she had such compassion and tender feeling for distressed humanity. Very properly feminine. But who the deuce was Bentham? Or Lancaster for that matter?

When he saw the fellow who had been occupying her attention at the tea table for such an unconscionably long time walk off, he approached to ask for a cup of tea and to offer an apology.

But there was no militancy in Maidie's eye when she looked up at him; only pleasant enquiry. "Would you care for a cup of tea, sir? Or perhaps coffee or chocolate?"

"Tea, please, with milk. I'm not partial to sugar, you will perhaps remember."

She smiled. "I do remember, and it's just as well, if you and I are to be on speaking terms, is it not?"

He looked down at her speculatively, and to his own astonishment replied, "Sugar soon cloys, and the system rebels, but an artful sweetness . . . I can't believe could ever tire the appetite."

Her eyes widened, her lips parted, and a faint blush touched her cheek as she stared up at him. As he looked down into the grey, dark-lashed eyes, he felt his own cheeks reddening. What had led him to deliver such a foppish gallantry?

Maidie applied herself to pouring his tea, while desperately searching for some reply. The despicable man had left her bereft of words again! She had been in the world for years, and was perfectly conversant with the conventions of flirtation, so why was she so unbalanced? It was mortifying past endurance! She handed Allan the teacup, and turned to a petitioner for coffee. She heartily hoped that Mr. Gilmichael would take his poetry and go away.

Allan was no less anxious to escape than Maidie to have him go. Sparring with the chit was one thing; gallantries such as he had just uttered were another. She would think he was attempting a flirtation, and that he had no intention of. He quickly downed his tea and after a moment with Emery and a farewell to Fanny, with whom he left his copy of Blake, was on his way.

Eight

Emery and Maidie were at breakfast the following morning when Mrs. Eckston entered with the morning's letters on a tray, and a worried expression on her face. "Last night's post. And an express just come from London. From Mr. Worthing."

With a nervous glance at Maidie, Emery took the letter and broke the seal. She watched him with alarm as he hastily scanned the contents.

Emery's laugh broke the tension. "Well, uncivil of your father to frighten us, when an ordinary letter would have done. But the news will delight you as much as it does me. Sam says he and your mother come next week for a short visit. And Seraphina will accompany them."

"Then they are well." Although assured that the express bore no ill tidings, Maidie's mood sank. "How long do they stay?"

"Six or seven days, Sam says."

"And Mama comes too? I hope it won't be too much for her. Such a long trip."

"No, not so long. Tish is already in Manchester, visiting some of her Unitarian friends. After their few days with us, she and Seraphina will join them at their estate on the Wales Coast for a visit of several weeks. But here, you may read the letter for yourself. I'll just glance at these others before I go to tell Fanny."

Emery sorted hurriedly through the mail, murmuring to himself. "Ah, *Edinburgh Review* . . . must want Fanny to do another article. My publisher. Tend to that later. Advertisement. Hmmm. Charles Lamb. Well, let's see what he has to say."

He broke the seal, and began reading. Suddenly, he struck the table with the flat of his hand. "Of all the *damnable!*"

Maidie looked up, startled. "Why, what is it, Uncle Emery?"

"Letter from Charles Lamb in London. Says Robert Moon's been charged with sedition for publishing a pamphlet criticizing the government. The author—writing anonymously—says the era of monarchy is past, and that the governing privileges of the nobility and the Anglican Church should be"—he glanced again at the letter—"stripped from them."

Maidie frowned. These were opinions she was accustomed to hearing every day. "My mother's written many articles recommending that the civil functions the Anglican church performs should be the exclusive responsibility of the civil government. And you and Aunt Fanny also. And . . ." She paused. Should she tell her uncle about the man spying on Wendell? She compromised. "The opinions of the anonymous author sound very much like Wendell's."

"And very much like what Tom Paine was writing fifty years past," Emery said dryly. "Helped set off the rebellion in America, and still sets our king and ministers on their ears. One must believe that Robert Moon was chosen as an example to others."

"Is that what you and Aunt Fanny think also?"

"Fanny and I may have radical opinions, but we live and write like respectable Whigs. You needn't worry about us. As for Wendell—I'm assured he's not agitating among the working people. And I'm reasonably certain that he's not had more than one or two of his 'paeans to democracy' published. I suspect that even the radical sheets find his poetry too . . . too . . ."

"Dreadful?"

"For want of a stronger word. But there's no need for you to worry your head about it, Maidie."

"And why should I not worry my head? I shall consider myself ill-used indeed if you insist on shielding me from the world as it is."

"Forgive me, my dear. I'm afraid I sometimes forget you are no longer the inquisitive thirteen-year-old I first met ten years ago."

"You were not very successful at avoiding my questions then. And I am now nearly twice as old and more than twice as determined."

"Well," Emery conceded, "if it's particulars you demand. The government last year made yet another effort to silence the press, and the attack on the Regent's carriage in January gave them the excuse needed. Several journalists have been charged with blasphemous libel or sedition or both. Publishers the government suspects of radical tendency have been required to pay anticipatory fines as security for good conduct, which many are unable to pay, and so are jailed without a trial. Moon, however, has been charged, and will go before a jury. Charles Lamb, Leigh Hunt, and others are getting up a subscription to help him with his defense."

"I'd like to subscribe ten pounds, Uncle. Papa was so generous when he provided me with funds for this visit that I have an embarrassment of riches."

"Of course, Maidie," Emery said with a smile.

She bridled at the indulgence in his tone, but held her tongue. She was twenty-three years old and mistress of her own money and her own opinions! Did one's elders never recognize that children became adults?

Emery gathered his letters and those for Fanny, and rose. "I'll take Fanny Sam's letter, if you've finished it. What do you young people do today?"

Maidie answered noncommittally, as she handed him the letter. "Perhaps I'll call on Prudence."

When he was gone she helped herself to a second slice of

bread (of her own making) with which to finish her now cold coffee. She gazed out the window, considering the news. The reason for her father's visit, she was certain, was that he was unreconciled to her absence. And *why* would he bring Aunt Seraphina but for support? She would find all sorts of objections to Aunt Fanny's household! But there were other events for mulling over, and soon her thoughts strayed to Wendell's note, delivered late the evening before by a rosy cheeked urchin, suggesting she call on Prudence this afternoon. Had Wendell devised a plan?

Fanny, when Emery brought her the news of their prospective visitors, exclaimed, "How absolutely appalling!" She sat up in her bed to read the letter, which after a single paragraph set her blood simply aflame. She crumpled it and flung it across the room. "Bringing Seraphina! How *could* he? And you know that he will want to take Maidie home with him, even though he did faithfully promise her to me for the summer!"

"You are ungenerous, Fanny. It's just that they all miss the child."

"Well, I suppose," Fanny conceded ungraciously. She picked up another of her letters, but added, with an ominous narrowing of her eyes, "I know my brother. He wants to reassure himself that there is positively no risk from poets, or a democrat, or— heaven forbid—an aristocrat! At least we needn't worry about the latter, but we must warn Wendell to keep his opinions to himself!" Fanny's face brightened, as plans began forming in her fertile brain. "Do you suppose that we could invite the Wordsworths, and perhaps the Southeys, to visit while Sam is here? They've become such deplorably depressing Tories—one would never dream that they had ever had a radical thought in their heads! And we must certainly see that the Califaxtons are included in any social events. Mrs. Califaxton told me yesterday that Mr. Califaxton *père* will be with them again soon. Of course I've not noticed that either John or Chester is developing the

slightest *tendress* for Maidie, or she for them, more's the pity . . .
but perhaps I could suggest—"

"No, Fanny! No scheming. And no lying. Invite the Califaxtons, of course. They are our neighbors. Even the Wordsworths
and Southeys, for we do see them on occasion. I'll willingly
recommend to Wendell that he moderate his opinions while in
their presence. But no scheming. Do you hear?"

"Yes, Emery," Fanny murmured, turning over and burrowing
into her pillow. "Now go away and let me be miserable."

Emery patted her shoulder, kissed her cheek, and left. He
could discuss the letter from the *Edinburgh Review* and the subscription for Robert Moon later.

"We'll trap the spy in a valley up on the fells," Wendell enthusiastically explained to his listeners. "Actually it's little more
than a wide ghyll—perfect for setting a trap—because the path
that leads into it is also the only way out. Sheep go in to drink
and browse, and local people fish the beck, but it's not much
frequented. I'll lead him in—"

Chester had already divined the rest of the plan. "And Maidie
and I will block the exit. Suppose he's carrying a popper. What
then?"

Wendell was injured to the quick. "Well, I certainly don't
expect you to risk your lives! You would simply give way. Otherwise, you just shout and I come running."

"What is a popper?" Prudence asked, and then had to be re-
assured that it was most unlikely that the man would carry a
pistol. His job was to *spy,* Wendell explained, with a patience
he had not shown Chester. As he had told Maidie, spies were
not expected to bag their men, only to report on them.

Prudence shuddered. She could be a lioness in defense of
Wendell's right to riot, rumpus, blasphemy, or sedition, but she
readily admitted that she was too fainthearted to physically con-

front anyone, let alone an Agent of Government, who she unreasonably imagined not as a simple man afoot, but as a mounted dragoon in full panoply. She did, however, have courage enough to suggest timidly that Wendell's plan might be unwise. It was a suggestion that was the more courageous for the enchanted glow in which she had floated since learning that such a magnificently handsome and brave young gentleman as Wendell Duval—or Salvatore Toone—whichever—she didn't care—could love her.

Prudence was not only timid, but as Chester pointed out, she was a girl. And he objected on the same grounds to Maidie's participation in what he persisted in characterizing as a hazardous venture, adding bluntly, "Girls can't climb."

Wendell brushed both objections aside. "Maidie's a trump. Just like Fanny—I'd wager they could outclimb both of us if they didn't have those skirts in the way!"

Chester considered this observation both vulgar and improper, and said so. Maidie thanked him for his concern for her delicacy, but she was certain she could make the climb, and was in fact eager to do so.

Chester was forced to agree that her skill and endurance were adequate, despite her skirts, but nonetheless couldn't think it proper. That it also might not be proper for her to go climbing unchaperoned on lonely fells with him, an unrelated gentleman, she brushed aside with the observation that life was more informal in the Lakes.

Nonetheless, Chester had discovered a difficulty. Fanny certainly would not permit Maidie to leave the house accompanied only by Chester, and on what might prove to be an all day affair, should they adopt Wendell's plan. Therefore, Prudence would be required to set out from Pennelbeck Farm with them. But where could she spend the time between their departure and return?

They all turned to Prudence, who had been quietly bent over her embroidery. "I could wait for you somewhere," she said.

"Not alone, you won't," Chester stated flatly.

"I should think not!" Wendell exclaimed, shocked at the very idea of his beloved sitting alone for hours on some cold and lonely rock.

"No indeed!" Maidie echoed, certain that Prudence would never have the fortitude for a long, solitary vigil. "We must think of where we'll tell Aunt Fanny we're going, and then we can decide where Prudence will wait for us."

They all turned to Wendell.

"We start climbing from the Pennelbeck Vale road, so something in that direction."

"Well, it's up to you to figure it out," Chester said irritably. "You're the one who's been all over the fells."

To everyone's surprise, including her doting lover, it was Prudence who solved this final problem. "You might say that we're going to Windermere by Higg Pike Pass. John and I have easily walked there from Krigsmere, many times. I can wait at Mary Bell's cottage. I've been teaching her little girl to embroider, and have been there often."

Chester, while agreeing that Prudence had hit upon a solution, was wondering why he was even thinking about such a fool scheme. Yet, while in no way approving Wendell's politics, he had a vague notion that it wasn't quite the thing for the government to pursue people—even those who held beef-witted opinions. Although he wasn't convinced that the spy was interested in Wendell's politics. After all, Duval was an insignificant fellow—didn't even write incendiary broadsides, just ludicrous poetry. In fact, in Chester's opinion he deserved to be thrown in jail more for his poetry than his politics. Still, it was dashed curious that anyone should spy on him . . . and in any event, Chester thought resignedly, chasing a spy would give him something to do while his father had him rusticated.

The exercise of devising strategy had also set under-used gears in motion in Chester's head. "But why," he asked Wendell, "would the fellow dog your every step? You say he talked to m'brother and to Gilmichael, and who knows how many others; he's been following you for weeks. Should have enough on you now to satisfy whoever's paying him. Why follow you all the way up on the fells? Too much of a scramble, if you ask me."

"You saw yourself that he was following me only two days ago, so why would he not follow me tomorrow?"

Chester subsided in the face of this logic, but soon found another objection. "Clear path up there?" he asked.

"Well . . . no. But it's easy to find."

Chester strongly felt that in that case a preliminary reconnaissance was in order. "Fellow can get lost on the fells, or tumble off a cliff. Should know where we're going. Wouldn't want Maidie to take a fall. Or myself either."

Wendell objected, not entirely consistently, that if they took time for a reconnaissance, the spy might choose to deliver his report before the trap could be sprung, and if so they would never find out who he was spying for. He assured Chester again that the valley was easy to find, and the route not at all dangerous.

"If it's not dangerous, and if it's so easy, why ain't there a regular path?"

"It's the very deuce, Califaxton, how many impediments you can put in a fellow's way! I'll draw a map—and in such detail even a blockhead would be able to follow it."

"Blockhead! Why . . ."

Maidie and Prudence intervened again to restore amity, and Wendell, very much on his dignity, declared himself ready to repair to his cottage where, uninhibited by petty carping, he would produce a map.

"I'll be there this afternoon," Chester warned as Wendell departed. "Want to look it over. Dashed if I'm setting off tomorrow without some idea of where I'm going and how I'm to get there."

Maidie spent the afternoon gardening and pondering the project. She had kept her own reservations about the enterprise to herself, but as she pulled weeds, she gave herself over to deep thought. Trapping the spy in the valley Wendell had described would take them to the higher fells, where she had never been, and in fact had no permission to go. Nor could she quite convince herself that trapping a man who might be dangerous, and in an isolated valley so far from any assistance, was either wise or prudent. She had briefly considered suggesting that they wait in order to consult her father. Because of his considerable acquaintance among persons connected with Government, he might know someone who could discover what was afoot. But it would surely make Papa nervous, and might be just the argument he needed if he had decided to command her to return to London. As though anything could happen to her here, where people seldom locked their doors at night, and gently bred girls were permitted to walk about alone!

And it was so very wrong for anyone to spy on Wendell! Although her aunt and uncle were more circumspect in expressing their political opinions than Wendell—as Uncle Emery had assured her—it came out to almost the same thing. And if Wendell was in danger, so could they be. And even her own mother. Should she not, then, take some action?

Chester arrived at Wendell's cottage as promised to collect the map, of which Wendell declared himself excessively proud. It showed every landmark that he could recall along the way, and as a final touch, he had added a rough estimate of the time required to pass from one landmark to another.

Chester allowed that it was a good enough map, and after reviewing it, put it away in his pocket. Then there was nothing for him to do but wait for the morrow and hope it wouldn't rain. "Never did like to wait for something I've set my mind to. Ain't like you, Duval—happy to spend all my time with some dull political work."

"You are mistaken," Wendell said loftily. "I do not spend all my time reading political works. I am studying fell wrestling techniques; I write poetry; I walk on the fells and explore the lakes; I am gathering information on the history and people of the region—which if you had any ambition would keep you from the *ennui* you complain about. Furthermore, I am not bad at carpentry, for as you would know, if you troubled to read Rousseau—"

"Just so. But the improving lay ain't for me. I don't want improving, and even if I did, wouldn't do it. Bit of a bore, I say."

Wendell, nettled, replied with some heat, "I also happen to play a good hand of whist!"

"Play whist, do you?" Chester's eyes brightened. "Well, why ain't you ever said so? Old John and I've both been wishing for a game. M'mother doesn't play, and Pru's too soft-hearted. Thinks it's cruel to beat people."

Wendell, despite himself, was tempted. He hadn't come to the Lakes to engage in frivolous pursuits, but on the other hand, it had been a considerable time since he'd pitted his skill at cards against an opponent. "Who could we get for a fourth?" he asked. It was almost as if his mouth had operated independently of his brain.

"Before m'brother Lance left to join his troop, we had some good goes with Gilmichael. How about him?"

A knock interrupted the discussion, and brought Old Peg, Wendell's ancient housekeeper, from the kitchen to open the door.

"Well, speak of the Devil!" Chester ejaculated in surprise.

"And how have I been figuring in your discussions?" Allan asked, shaking his head at Old Peg, who was trying to separate him from his hat. "No thank you," he told her, "I only stopped to return these two books and to borrow some others. And to leave a message for your young master."

Old Peg turned her attention to the burden he was carrying.

"I just met your cousin Emery," Allan told Wendell as he surrendered the books. "He's on an overnight errand to Keswick. Seems he forgot to tell you that Fanny is expecting you for supper tonight."

Wendell observed that Emery did not like to leave Fanny, although he couldn't think why, since she was the most capable woman he knew, even if she was increasing.

"Don't say?" Chester said.

Allan and Old Peg, both more circumspect, said nothing.

"May I invite you to sit with us a few minutes to take some refreshment?" Wendell asked, unaware that he had just spread some interesting news.

When refreshments were refused, Chester spoke up to propose an evening of whist. "John and I've been wanting a game, and we've just been discussing it, Duval and I. Like you to join us tonight, if you could see your way clear."

Allan was surprised by the invitation, but he liked John Califaxton's company, and the two young men were supportable. Duval was always interesting, with his outrageous opinions, and the youngest of the male Califaxtons was another of the numerous youth the universities seemed to turn out like so many bolts of cloth. His very predictability was diverting. And Allan did in fact enjoy whist.

"It will be my pleasure," he said.

He had been regretting that he might have given Maidie cause to suspect an interest that he did not feel, and had determined to return to solitary and/or strictly manly pursuits. Books were satisfactory entertainment for rainy days (no more afternoons at the Clarkes) and for lonely evenings (certainly enough of those). He had enjoyed reading Maidie's *Northanger Abbey* and, remembering that she pronounced it not as good as other of Miss Austen's novels, had subscribed himself in the Sagpaw circulating library, thus securing a copy of *Mansfield Park,* which he read with even more enjoyment.

There was always his political education to attend to, in anticipation of his Parliamentary duties. Although the two most readily available private libraries had a pronounced tilt toward the freethinking and radical, they were of more use for his education than the library in Sagpaw. His desire to avoid Miss Worthing had sent him to Wendell's library rather than the Clarkes', whence he now returned to his lodging, carrying a volume of William Godwin's *Political Justice,* Mr. Bentham's treatise advocating manhood suffrage and representative government, another treatise on education by the Lancaster fellow, and an armful of pamphlets. That he departed with no more literature had not been due to any deficiency in the supply or any lack of generous urging, but rather his protest that he hadn't brought a wheelbarrow.

The evening at whist, from which Allan had expected only a few hours diversion before returning to his new supply of radical literature, yielded a surprise—a glimpse of a different and unexpected Wendell Duval. At cards the pontificating poet showed himself to be another man altogether—calculating, cool, anything but loquacious. And formidable. The Califaxtons were certainly worthy opponents; Chester played with lighthearted conviction and John with detached competence, but for sheer skill neither they nor he could hold a candle to Duval. The fellow might be a greenhorn at politics, and as terrible a poet as Emery Clarke had in confidence said he was, but at the card table he was an experienced professional.

"Well, Duval," Allan remarked at the end of a final rubber, and as John toted up the losses he and Chester had sustained,

"I must give you the credit for our success tonight. With apologies to the Califaxtons, I don't believe I've ever had the good fortune to be partnered by such a keen-witted player."

"Sure you ain't a card sharper, Duval?" Chester asked, only half joking.

John frowned at Chester, but Wendell, who had colored at Allan's compliment, held his peace. "I've been playing cards since I was seven. My father was a serious player, and wouldn't have missed his weekly whist game for the world. He taught me to fill in when a fourth was lacking. One gets to know cards when one begins so young."

Mrs. Califaxton sent a footman at eleven o'clock to enquire when the gentlemen wished their supper served, and soon the card players were helping themselves to Welsh rabbit and ale, followed by a crisp salad, and finally by coffee and brandy.

Well fed and in mellow mood, they found several interesting subjects to discuss, until Wendell, with a start, consulted his watch and discovered the hour to be well advanced. "Must be off," he exclaimed, rising abruptly. "I forgot Chester and I are accompanying Miss Califaxton and Miss Worthing to Windermere tomorrow."

"Right," Chester agreed, forgetting that he was a host. "Don't want to be too tired to go the distance."

"I'll be leaving, too," Allan said, also rising. "Enjoyable evening."

"I'll see the gentlemen out," John told the sleepy footman stationed outside the door.

As Allan reviewed the evening he began to wonder if Duval's naive political radicalism was as calculating as his card playing, although he couldn't think what his motive might be for any such playacting. He rather liked the young man, and would not have been pleased to learn that he was avoiding a gambling debt, or—more likely, in light of his skill—that he was a fledgling Captain Sharp on the run from a vengeful victim. Was it possible, even, that the enquiries about Wendell by the man in the wig had something to do with card sharping? It had now been three days since his letter to Lord Blout inquiring about Duval. He should be hearing soon. If Miss Worthing's flirtation with the fellow was more serious than he thought, disillusion and hurt were in store for her. He couldn't contemplate it with complacency. She was young enough still to be vulnerable . . .

Several moments later, realizing with some dismay that he had been dwelling on Miss Worthing's charms at the expense of his night's sleep, he consciously blanked his mind of thought, and was soon slumbering peacefully. It was an accomplishment that had served him well on the Peninsula.

As coincidence would have it, the awaited reply from Lord Blout to his inquiry concerning Wendell, sent express, lay by Allan's breakfast plate. His lordship stated his pleasure at being able to serve his old friend's son, and assured him that he had been unable to discover that anyone named Wendell Duval was under suspicion for seditious activities, at least as far as the secret Parliamentary investigating committee on sedition was concerned, nor was there any Duval on the Ministerial list of suspects. Whether he was considered a dangerous person by the Lord-lieutenant of Westmoreland County was not known.

"As I thought," Allan muttered to himself. He would stop at Duval's cottage after breakfast and tell him that whoever the spy might have been, he was not an agent of the government. . . . And he would watch closely for any consciousness that might indicate some other guilt. It then struck him that the amiable Blout could make enquiries of Bow Street. Responding promptly to the thought, he sat down to write a second letter to his father's friend asking him, after due apology for the further imposition, to make the proper inquiries.

He could now forget the whole business, he reflected with some relief. As it was, he had probably done more to identify the spy—or, more properly, investigator—than was called for. He handed the letter to his valet, and asked him to see to the posting, then turned his attention to the newspaper and his coffee. He then collected his fishing gear, and set out for the fells above Krigsmere, taking the road past Wendell's cottage rather than his accustomed path around the southern shores of the lake.

When he knocked at Duval's door, it was Old Peg who answered, to tell him that Mr. Wendell had just gone away for one of his walks. Always walking around, he was, just like that Mr. Wordsworth. Least he didn't read a book whiles walking, like she'd heard that Mr. Southey in Keswick did. Dangerous business, it was, not keeping an eye on your way.

Allan agreed that it did seem dangerous, asked for a pencil and paper, and scribbled a note describing Lord Blout's information, which he entrusted to Old Peg's hands. He then walked on, light of spirit, duty done. A good breeze encouraged him to think that he might make a very good catch—the trout would certainly be rising.

Nine

Maidie and Chester stopped to puzzle again over Wendell's map. The sun was high, and Chester, wiping his brow with his handkerchief, declared he'd almost rather have rain.

They had made a late start—first Chester had misplaced the map, then Mrs. Califaxton required that Prudence sew up a rent in a slip-cover, which she simply hadn't time to do herself, what with the rector expected that afternoon to discuss a local charity.

When they had at last arrived at the Bell cottage, where Prudence was to wait for their return, Mr. Bell greeted them with surprise. His wife had understood from Miss Califaxton's note that she would be visiting the following day. But, he hastily assured them, the missus would be home soon—had only run up to the Baddock farm for some fresh eggs, and if she didn't talk forever would be back before they knew it. Yes, little Ellen—and the maid, too, for that matter, had gone with her.

They waited nearly a half hour, with Chester every minute in a fidget; he refused to leave Prudence in a house where there was not one female to protect her reputation. Maidie's patience was equally tried, as much with Chester as with the passing of precious time.

When they did at last set off, she was worrying because of the surprise with which Mrs. Bell greeted the news that she was leaving with Chester rather than keeping Prudence company. "We're meeting my cousin," Maidie explained. "He's waiting for us just above the bridge, where he's gone to think about a poem."

Mrs. Bell's expression remained skeptical.

Prudence stepped outside to wave them off, and Maidie whispered to her to please impress on Mrs. Bell's mind that they would be meeting Wendell directly, and most *particularly* that Wendell was her cousin. She was already entertaining uncomfortable doubts about the venture, not to mention the lies they had told about their destination and purpose. She couldn't remember when, since reaching the age of responsibility, she had ever told a lie except in the interests of social delicacy.

By the time they reached the cairn that marked the beginning of the final stage of their climb, she was sincerely regretting her ready acceptance of Wendell's scheme.

She was soon regretting it even more sincerely. They had easily identified the earlier landmarks on Wendell's map, but after climbing for nearly an hour beyond the cairn they were certain that they had taken a wrong turn.

"Tell you what," Chester said, "I'll just retrace our steps and check everything I see against this map. We know we were on the correct path when we turned left at the cairn—couldn't be a better description of that than Duval gave us. But somewhere past it we must have gone wrong. He says only about twenty minutes to a small tarn, where we're supposed to strike off— more or less straight up the mountainside—toward the foot of the valley. And we've been walking"—he consulted his watch— "for forty-five minutes."

"Maybe Wendell was wrong about the time. There hasn't been another path to choose."

"Well, I'm going back. We passed a crag I think I can climb, and where I can get a good look at the lay of the land. Won't take long. You sit tight."

"No, I'll go back with you. If we're wrong we'll just lose time."

"Tell you what. You watch till I'm just out of sight. Then you keep your eyes on that spot, and if you have to come down again I'll wave and whistle soon as I can see you sitting here. Must be able to see for over a hundred yards—hardest was that bed of boulders and the climb up the slippery grass afterward. Won't take me long to get back up to you. But you watch sharp."

When Maidie showed signs of further argument, Chester added, "Hate to say this, but you ain't as good a climber as I am."

Maidie opened her mouth to contest this canard, but Chester bore on. "Skirts ain't for climbing mountains. Said that before."

"Wendell said that."

"Comes to the same thing. You just sit here. Now, let's see that map."

"Take the map with you. It won't be any use to me."

Maidie sat down on a large boulder to wait. It wasn't a comfortable boulder, and in a short time she noticed that clouds were gathering above her on Sagfel Peak. She began to worry when she estimated that fifteen minutes had passed since Chester disappeared from view; she was certain that the crag from which he intended to survey their route was not far beyond. Meanwhile, she kept a nervous eye on the gathering clouds, which were now sliding ominously down the mountainside. Within minutes she was enveloped in mist.

They had climbed so high that, once the sun was obscured, it was uncomfortably cold. She wrapped herself in the shawl she had tied around her waist, hugging it close in an effort to keep warm. As her discomfort increased, so did her impatience. Perhaps something had happened to Chester. Scree along the lip of a shallow ravine not far above the crag had been particularly perilous. It then occurred to her that Wendell, although men-

tioning a ravine, had said nothing about scree. Surely he would
have pointed out anything that might have been dangerous! So
they must have taken a wrong turn! Caution was required on
uncertain footing at any time, but especially on a downward
path, and Chester would surely be hurrying . . .

She was certain that they had made a wrong turning, and as
her uneasiness increased, so did the conviction that she could
detect a brightness beyond the swirling mist that suggested it
would soon lift or pass on. Mists and showers, as Maidie now
knew from experience, could come and go with amazing sud-
denness on the fells. It was not difficult to persuade herself that
she ought to begin a cautious descent.

Maidie proceeded slowly, stepping carefully, expecting every
minute to be out of the mist. After what seemed sufficient time
to have reached the point at which she'd seen Chester disappear,
she stopped and called. Her voice sounded muffled. There was
no answer. Now what to do? Continue on? She stood still for a
moment, uncertain; then moved cautiously forward. What
seemed to Maidie an interminable time had passed when, even
more abruptly than it had enveloped her, the mist dissipated,
breaking into long strands that floated along the ground to burn
away in the sun.

She looked around for a familiar object or a familiar peak,
but no matter which way she looked she could recognize nothing. She realized that she didn't know which way to go, and that
she had committed the inexcusable—attempting to negotiate an
unfamiliar and indistinct path in a mist. She had properly lost
herself, just as she had been warned she might.

The wisest thing to do was to stay exactly where she was. She
called several times, but received no answering hale. She sat
down, but the grass was damp, so she got to her feet again. Her
worry about Chester's safety mounted ever more forcefully until,
unable to contain her impatience, she decided she should try to
return to Pennelbeck Vale where she would find help to rescue

him. She might even come upon him . . . be able to give him aid herself—and if not, at least he would have the comfort of knowing that help would soon be on the way. Now that the mist was gone, she could perceive that she was on a level upland, with a great shoulder of the mountain behind her. She could not see Sagfel Peak, which she thought she would recognize, but nonetheless, she was certain she knew the direction. The sun was well past the zenith, and the short shadows told her which way was homeward. That there might be barriers to negotiate she did not consider.

As the sun warmed the top of her head, she realized she had left her bonnet on the boulder where she had waited for Chester. She shrugged and continued on until she came to the edge of a ghyll she was certain she had never seen. They had skirted two small ravines and crossed a stone bridge over a beck as they climbed, but this ghyll was deep and steep sided, slanting at an angle across the face of the slope. The stream in its depths—as she ascertained by peering cautiously over the edge—seemed to be no more than a mere trickle. Nonetheless, streams run downhill, which was most certainly the way she should go.

Maidie followed along the badly eroded edge of the ghyll as rapidly as she thought safe, but after a time, how long she couldn't have said, she was brought up short by another, broader and deeper ghyll into which the smaller opened. She could readily see that the larger ghyll was even more impossible to contemplate crossing than the first. Although she thought she could scramble down, she doubted she would be able to ascend the other side. She was trapped in the angle between them.

That she would need to retrace her steps was so discouraging she could easily have cried. Unwelcome tales of disaster came unbidden to mind: a young dalesman lying for an age at the bottom of some bottomless ghyll with broken leg and head; a stranger, never identified, who stumbled to his death over a precipice . . .

She scolded herself out of such missish occupation in short order; such indulgence would do her no good at all!

On calmer reflection it occurred to her that she must have passed the head of this larger ghyll in the mist. Maidie repressed a shudder at what could have been a calamitous fall, and then put it sternly from her mind. At least she now knew how to find her way back. All she had to do was follow the larger ghyll back to its source. Perhaps she would even be able to identify the boulder on which she had been waiting. But in whatever event, she would be closer to the place where Chester had left her.

As she walked she spared a thought for Wendell, who would wait for them in vain. Surely by now he would have realized that somewhere they had gone astray. Perhaps he was even now searching for them. She smiled as she thought what a chase the spy would be having—following Wendell as he searched the mountainside.

The bank of the great ravine was more badly eroded than the first, so that she had to step even more cautiously. Eventually she passed a jumble of rock that had tumbled and rolled from a lone crag looming before her, and within a few more minutes was at the head of the ghyll. She ascended several more yards before cautiously rounding it, and found herself on a hidden plateau, covered with mounded grasses, patches of bracken, and rocky outcrops. Across the plateau, she saw a man walking.

Maidie's relief nearly made her knees give way, and then she felt an unjustified surge of anger. "Chester! *Chester!*" she shouted, starting to run. She forgot entirely another rule of fell walking, particularly on unfamiliar terrain, and failed to watch her feet. She stumbled into a depression hidden by hummocks of matted grasses, lost her footing and fell flat. Scrambling up, disoriented, she saw the man running toward her. It wasn't Chester. She buried her face in her hands.

Allan threw himself into the grassy depression. He caught her close and pulled her head against his chest. "Are you hurt?" He was out of breath from the sudden spurt of effort, and also because his heart had taken a great lurch when he saw her go head over heels and disappear. He had thought she had fallen into a ravine or down an old mine shaft.

"No," she replied in a small voice, muffled against his chest. "But I think I'm lost."

He felt weak with relief, and pressed her closer, stroking her hair soothingly and murmuring comforting words. The shallow, basin-like depression into which she had fallen had perhaps at one time held a small pond that had dried up due to a shift in a watercourse or the failure of a spring. But it could have been a mine shaft or a ravine, or even a dry streambed full of rocks. Another surge of relief swept over him, and then the quick flash of memory . . . his brother falling. . . . He was suddenly angry; she was reckless and self-willed, wandering around alone on the fells. But before he could act on the anger, Maidie drew away from him.

"Thank you," she said calmly. "For just a moment I lost courage. I'm afraid something has happened to Chester."

Oh yes, she had called him Chester. "Were you up here by yourself with young Califaxton? What were you doing? Why? You've been warned how easy it is to lose one's way."

"We were meeting Wendell, but we must have gone wrong somewhere." She stooped to brush off her skirt and pick up her shawl. "Then Chester went back to see if we'd made a wrong turn, but when he didn't come back I began to worry, and then I must have lost my way again, because I've never seen this place before. Or I don't think I have."

Allan, his emotions still rocking choppily between his anger and his fear, settled on annoyance. "And just why were you up here?"

"Oh, we were just walking. But we must look for Chester. Really we must. Immediately!"

"So I'm to help you look for Chester?"

Maidie stared at him. "Well, of course. Aren't you?"

Allan sighed. He supposed he was. "Only because there's the possibility he's fallen and is hurt. But you both deserve a good scold."

"I choose to ignore the latter remark, which is unworthy of a gentleman. Do you know where we are?"

"It may be unworthy of a gentleman, but certainly worthy of an older and wiser head."

"Don't bother to rip up at me, because it won't do any good at all. *Do* you know where we are?"

"I know where I am. However, I don't know where you were, or where you were going. This certainly isn't the route to Windermere."

Maidie eyed him. "Windermere?"

"We'll discuss that later. Sit down, and describe to me exactly your route—as best you can—until Chester left you. Meanwhile, you might like to put your hair up again."

Maidie's hands flew to her hair. That morning, before setting out on their adventure, she had tied it up with a ribbon, and then pinned it, with a plentitude of pins, into an inexpert knot on the crown of her head. Undoubtedly half the pins were scattered across the countryside and lost forever in the grass, for the knot was nearly undone, with a few locks straggling down her back and the rest only partially pinned up. In exasperation, she pulled all the remaining pins out. Her hair, still bound loosely by the ribbon, fell in a cascade. Allan, watching, was reminded of the soft feel of it under his hand as he'd held her against his chest. He ignored the quick tug at his heart and firmly quelled an impulse to take her in his arms again.

"I *will* cut my hair!" she declared emphatically as she sat down beside him.

"My dear child, I have not suggested that you not cut your hair. Now, while you do it up again, let's see what plan we can devise to discover Chester. You say that you were supposed to wait for him. Just how long exactly did you wait?"

Maidie ignored the condescension in his address. She pulled the ribbon off. "Oh, at least half an hour altogether."

Her face was screened from Allan by her hair as she bent over the ribbon and attempted to unknot it, but he thought he detected a note of defiance in her tone, and was certain that it had been a much shorter time. Califaxton had probably gone back, found her not there, and was now desperately scouring the mountainside looking for her, no doubt getting himself lost as well.

"All right, tell me where you were going and describe your route, so I'll have an idea where we should start looking for Chester."

"Well, we started at the cairn above Pennelbeck Vale that marks one of the routes to Melt's Crag. But we weren't going to the Crag. We were coming up Sagfel to . . . to . . . Which way is Sagfel Peak?"

Allan pointed. "That way."

"Then I guess it would be north. Yes, north of here, I imagine, because Wendell said nothing about that monstrous ghyll I followed up to this plateau. He said there was a pretty little valley."

"The deep ravine is Fiers Ghyll."

"Fearful Ghyll, if I were naming it." As she spoke, Maidie was trying to tie her hair up again, but she was not adept, and the wind, which seemed to have risen just to plague her, did not make the task easier.

"Here," Allan said. "Let me help you. What a bother you are, Miss Worthing!"

Maidie rounded on him, prepared to make a blistering response, but the laughter in his eyes stopped her, and she smiled instead. "But I am giving you the opportunity to accumulate good deeds, which I'm sure you'll need when, as Wendell would have it, you haste away, to close the Labors of your day."

"Turn around," he said. He gathered up her hair, again enjoying its silky texture. "You've been reading my Blake? 'The Door of Death I open found And the Worm Weaving in the Ground . . .' "

" 'Thou'rt my Mother from the Womb . . .' It's strange—although I don't understand them, I go back to the same verses over and over again. Wendell thinks Blake is morbid, but I don't. Do you?"

"No, I don't think he's morbid. Now, can you tie the ribbon, or shall I?"

"I'll do it."

Her fingers touched his as she tied the ribbon, and the mood between them took on a quality more intimate than the confederacy of rescuer and rescued. He dropped his hand quickly, and Maidie, turning businesslike, launched into an even more detailed description of the day's wanderings.

He arose, and reached down to help her up. "I still don't know why you were going where you were. I think I know the valley you speak of—hardly more than a long, wide ghyll if I remember. You must have turned left rather than right at the cairn."

"But Wendell made a map for us!"

"Then his map was at fault, or you read it wrong. Mapping is something of an art; one needs a good sense of terrain."

Maidie saw no reason to defend Wendell's mapping ability. "You are no doubt right," she conceded.

"Why wasn't Duval with you?"

"Oh. You know Wendell."

Her eyes had widened slightly, and her chin tilted up. He knew that look. Challenge. "Well," he said, "the first thing is to recover my fishing gear and basket of fish. Then we'll retrace your steps. I think I know where you were going, and where you went amiss."

He would explore this odd business later; right now the task at hand was to find young Califaxton and get them all three off the mountain before nightfall.

It was not as easy as he had supposed. He was not familiar with the northern reach of the range, and had never crossed this particular section of ravines, crags, knolls, and small plateaus. Nonetheless, he had sufficient experience judging unfamiliar terrain that he had confidently chosen what appeared to be the most logical route; yet within half an hour they found themselves confronted by a sheer drop, requiring that they retrace their steps. His second evaluation of the terrain was more prosperous. Although they encountered several shallow ravines across their way, as well as drystone walls marking sheep ranges, these presented no insuperable obstacles. Allan nonetheless began to wonder how Maidie, walking in a mist, could have avoided a fall.

"I watched my feet. I just forgot to be careful when I saw you and thought you were Chester."

When Maidie complained of thirst, they stopped by a clear-running beck where they drank from their cupped hands.

"What an undignified way to drink!" Maidie exclaimed as she wiped her dripping chin with her handkerchief.

Allan, more successful with this primitive method, seated himself on a large boulder. "You know, my dear, that we can't take the time to search for Chester. I fear that my miscalculation of the best route has delayed us too long. Will you agree that the wisest course is to descend as quickly as it is safe to do so? Surely you have been missed by now."

"We weren't expected until late."

Allan decided to let investigation of this odd affair again pass. "Sit down, Miss Worthing. Now, could we assume that Califaxton may have searched for you, and not finding you have got up a search party?"

Maidie, declining his invitation to be seated, gave the proposition serious consideration as she studied the mountainside below them. "I confess that between us we have lost so much time . . . oh, of course you are right!"

"Good girl! Now—"

"Whom are you addressing, Mr. Gilmichael?" She turned to face him, her brows raised in inquiry.

"Forgive me, Miss Worthing. I remind myself that you are not my little sister."

"Indeed, I am not!"

"No, you are not." A second passed as blue eyes stared into grey, before he realized he was about to embrace a young woman who was not only depending on him for a safe return to the arms of her family, but who was quite literally at his mercy. "I think . . ." he cleared his throat, "I think, however, that we should take time to eat a luncheon."

"A luncheon?" Maidie asked in a dazed voice.

"Or call it teatime. Your aunt and uncle will already be receiving callers." He strove to make their situation matter of fact. "The day wears on, and you must be as hungry as I. We can't spare much time, but since I have several excellent trout in my basket, and we have another two hours before we can reach the lower meadows, we may as well be comfortable."

Maidie, striving also for normalcy, replied, "Oh, yes! I am hungry! I just didn't want to say so, for then you would think me a terrible one to be lost with."

"What makes you think we're lost?"

"Are we?"

"No. Now, let's make a fire and I'll cook the trout."

With handfuls of dry grasses and dead bracken from the sheltered bank that overhung one side of the beck, Allan with some difficulty made a small and fitful fire. "But good enough," he told Maidie, "to cook my trout to a lady's taste. Now, while I play the chef, you may find a flat rock that I can lay the fish out on when it's ready." As she set off, he cautioned, "Wash it in the beck."

"Well, of course," she replied. "Do you think so poorly of my housewifely skills?"

"No, I've seen you in a kitchen," he replied, as he turned his attention to his fire, and then wondered why the devil such a simple remark should imply intimacy.

With the several grilled fish on the rock between them they picked flesh from bones with their fingers. "Do you suppose this is the way plates were invented?" Maidie asked. "Although I'm not certain that laying food on a flat rock could be called *invention*." When Allan agreed that it was inventive, but not invention, Maidie asked, "What do you suppose life was like, before all the many convenient things we enjoy were invented? Because, after all, someone had to invent them."

"I've read that South Sea Islanders use the leaves of the banana plant for plates, make cups from coco shells, and carve large bowls that look like canoes for serving dishes."

"It sounds such fun! Did you ever wish to live in another time?"

"Another place, yes . . . but not another time."

They spoke of the Vikings and Romans who once walked the very ground on which they now sat. They talked of the fells and lakes, and that the scene before them—although bare and sparse, unlike the softer and greener valleys—had a wild and strange beauty. He told her of his walks among the western fells, and his love of the heights.

"That was the best luncheon I've ever had," Maidie said, as she finished the last sliver of fish.

"Food is always best when one is hungry, and fresh-caught fish cooked and eaten in the open air is food for the gods."

"Hunger is better than a French cook, Fielding says. The first people must have licked their fingers, don't you think?" Maidie asked, as she licked her own.

"Probably the Vikings, too, although perhaps not the very best people among the Romans."

"Would you have thought me a terrible companion to be lost with?" Maidie asked, irrelevantly.

For a moment he didn't answer. "I think you are a very sensible, agreeable . . . and amiable . . . young woman to be lost with," he said finally.

"Thank you." Maidie favored him with a confiding smile. "Truly, Mr. Gilmichael, if I didn't know that everybody must be terribly worried about me, and if I weren't so worried about Chester, this would be an exciting and enjoyable experience. Now I think I should wash my hands." Another thought occurred to her. She determined not to blush, and said, "I would like to excuse myself for a few moments," trusting to his delicacy to understand her meaning. Certainly he must have the same needs, she thought. "I'll . . . I'll step behind that boulder over there."

Allan, who had had the same thought and had been wondering how to phrase the suggestion in a way that would not embarrass her, pointed to another, more distant boulder. "I shall wait for you there."

He had stamped out the fire, disposed of the fish bones, and was waiting stretched out at his leisure, thinking admiringly of Maidie's straightforward approach to life. He hadn't seen a blush, heard a giggle, or witnessed a vapor since they met. He watched her walk toward him, after washing her face and hands in the beck, her head up and her step firm. The idea that he was more than capable of challenging such a young spark as Duval for her affections came to him unexpectedly. That Duval might not have found his way firmly into Maidie's heart reminded him of the mystery of her presence on the mountain. He didn't want to break their companionable mood, but he did need to discover just what Maidie had been doing with Chester Califaxton. Or at least he thought he did.

He held his tongue, however, until they were walking once again side by side. He was determined to speak diplomatically. "Miss Worthing," he began.

"Mr. Gilmichael?"

He ignored the teasing tone; he was determined that she not succeed in that ploy again. "Do you think you could find it in your heart to tell me just what you were doing up here, and why you and Califaxton weren't with Duval? They told John Califaxton and me last night that they were walking with you and Prudence Califaxton to Windermere today, and by the road across Higg Pike Pass. Clearly that is not where you were going. I might also ask, where is Miss Califaxton?"

Maidie turned her attention to picking her way through a patch of clumped heather, considering. She'd long since decided that she had been engaged in a folly of extraordinary dimension, with consequences on which she was determined not to dwell, at least at the moment. But on the other hand, they couldn't have reported the spy to the authorities, if he was an agent of those very authorities. Attempting to confront him had not been foolish, only the way they had planned to do it. She returned to Allan's question. Everyone would know all by the time this day's adventure was over, so what harm in telling him the whole?

"Well?" Allan encouraged. "Can you tell me? If there is some point of honor impeding a confession—no, I beg pardon—revelation." He would not play the older brother again.

Maidie made her decision. "Well, you see, there's a man spying on Wendell because of his political views."

He barely restrained himself from reverting to an extreme

case of older brother. He drew a deep breath before speaking. "My dear, no one is spying on Wendell for his political views. I just had a letter from Lord—well, let's just say a person in the House of Lords—"

Maidie had stopped abruptly. "You had a letter? From a *lord?* About *Wendell?*" She stared at him, unbelieving. "I don't understand."

He sighed. "A friend of my father. They went to school together. So I presumed on that old friendship to ask him if a person named Wendell Duval is being investigated by a Parliamentary committee, or by the Home Office. I received the reply this morning; no one has ever heard of Wendell Duval. You understand, friend of my father. I can't tell you who . . ."

"But that's because Wendell's name isn't Wendell!"

"Wendell's name isn't Wendell?"

"No. No, it's Salvatore Toone. He doesn't like his name, so he's been calling himself Wendell Duval."

Allan clutched his hair, and then gazed up at the sky with both hands raised. "Why did I ever come here?" He sighed again, and resumed walking. "The next time I go fishing, I'm going to Scotland."

"Well, you just go to Scotland. But someone *is* spying on Wendell!"

They trod on without speaking, both pondering a number of questions. At last Allan said, "Maybe I won't go to Scotland. It's much more interesting here, and I don't believe the fishing's any better, no matter what anyone may say. Tell me about the spy."

After a moment of hesitation, Maidie replied, a little sharply. "Very well. But only if you credit me, and Wendell, with at least a modicum of sense."

"I apologize, Miss Worthing."

"I know it's difficult to believe in spies, especially in peace time. I mean, I suppose there are always secret agents when countries are at war . . . But you must know that Chester and I actually saw him spying on Wendell, and only four days ago. The very day, in fact, when Uncle Emery was showing you his cows."

"Yes, I remember." But it was not Emery's prized herd that came to his mind, but Maidie, a sheen of sweat on her forehead and wisps of hair escaping her kerchief.

She was silent for the barest moment, as she hastily reviewed the rights and wrongs of revelation, before she began, somewhat hesitantly, to relate all that she knew, all that she suspected, and the whole of their plan to trap and confront the spy. "It was a foolish plan, but indeed, Mr. Gilmichael, there *is* a spy. Now perhaps you can tell me what *you* know about him, since you went to the trouble of writing to your father's friend."

Allan readily recounted his visit from the man in the red wig. "Not a very clever fellow. Immediately clear that he was interested in Duval—or . . . what's his name?"

"Salvatore Toone. But he really does prefer Wendell Duval."

"Oh, yes. Quite so. Toone. In any event, it was immediately clear that his real interest was in Toone." A strange look passed across Allan's face, which sent Maidie into whoops.

"There," she gasped, recovering herself with difficulty. "You see why Wendell should much prefer to be known as Duval. I truly despise people who are always quoting books, but like Squire Boobie he has a . . . a *ticklish* name!" and she went off into whoops again.

Allan, seized by a new thought, saw nothing so very amusing. "The man you're presuming was a spy never mentioned anyone named Toone. Odd. Did he know Duval was masquerading under an assumed name?"

Maidie wiped her eyes. "Oh, truly, Wendell's reasons for changing his name are too innocent for such a puffed up way of describing it."

"Nonetheless, I cannot think that the government would pursue young Toone—"

"Duval."

"Very well, Duval. Nonetheless, I cannot think that the government would pursue Duval for nothing more than opinions."

"He's written some radical poetry. And it's been printed, too—in some of those pamphlets he's always reading."

"Under his real name, or—shall we call Duval his *nom de guerre?*"

"Oh, I should think as Duval." Maidie was silent for a moment. "No, he uses Wendell Duval because of his poetic nature, not to hide his identity. Even though his *poetry* is terrible, he does have a very poetic *nature,* you know."

"I don't doubt it," Allan replied, doubting it very much. "Well, for the moment, we can at least agree that it is all very odd, can we not?"

"Oh, yes. Quite so."

Allan cast her an abrupt glance, but she turned up an innocent face to him, and a pair of suspiciously guileless eyes . . .

He hastily looked away. "Well, we must hurry on," he said, a little lamely. "I fear we are about to be rained on, and I'd like to find some shelter, however inadequate."

As the slope steepened, Allan stopped. "Look, that's a sheep trail just above us. How did we miss it?"

"A sheep trail?"

"Come. We'll follow it along the mountainside. The sheep will have picked out the best way." He took her hand and assisted her up the three or four feet of incline.

They soon learned that they had discovered a sheep trod across the scar of an ancient land slide. On one side rose a rocky cliff, on the other a precipitate slope fell away, covered with rocks and scree. The wind was rising, tugging at Maidie's skirts. Allan reached back to her. "Take my hand."

"I'm not afraid. I have no fear of heights."

"You unman me. How can I fulfill my prescribed role as protector of the tenderer sex if you reject my efforts?"

"Oh, in *that* case," she said cheerfully, "give me your hand. Shall I scream occasionally?"

"I'm man enough to do without that."

Once past the ancient slide, they found themselves in an outcrop of tall crags. "And just in time," Allan said. "The wind's already up. Let's hope we can find some shelter among these rocks."

Maidie's skirt swirled around her legs as the rising wind gusted through fissures and down rock chimneys and around boulders. She hugged her shawl tighter as he drew her against the outward-tilted face of a high crag where they were protected from the wind's force. "We'll wait here. It seems the best place."

They stood side by side, their backs to the rock. "I haven't been on this part of the Sagfel range often, but I came upon this outcrop from below once," Allan observed. "There's a shepherd's cottage not far from us. No one there that day, but inhabited . . ."

The rainstorm burst upon them. Protected though they were by the overhanging crag their hair and clothing were soon covered with a fine mist. Lightning flashes were followed immediately by thunder that echoed across the heights, the echoes drowned by succeeding crashes. As minutes passed, the lightning and thunder diminished, but the rain dashed against the crags in greater force, and soon water ran in rivulets at their feet and poured from the overhanging rock above.

"It's almost like being under a waterfall," Maidie said, in an awed tone. She shivered. "Oh, if I weren't so cold, this would be a most utterly *sublime* experience!"

Allan opened his jacket and pulled her into its warmth. His arms about her, he moved to shield her from the deluge. He offered no apology, and she seemed to expect none. She only said, "I was very cold, but I do want to see the storm, if you please." He shifted their positions, still keeping her within his arms, and resisting the impulse to either laugh, or kiss her, or both.

"Yes, indeed sublime, my most excellent companion to be lost with. However, as for me, I had enough of the sublime on the Peninsula when I was a soldier."

"Did you sleep on the ground under the stars? I've read that soldiers on the march bivouac in the open."

"Many times, but as often as not I was sheltered in some peasant's hut or rustic inn where the fleas were fierce."

"No, I suppose soldiering isn't the most pleasant way to live, especially since it's so easy to be killed or horribly wounded—when there's a war, of course."

The curve of her cheek and the corner of her lips were tempting as he looked down at her. "Yes, that does take some of the pleasure out of it. But one doesn't think about it much, you know."

"I should think one wouldn't." Maidie looked up at him. "I mean . . . it would be best one shouldn't . . ."

Another palpitating moment passed as Allan thought, I will not kiss her. With an effort he pulled his glance away from those wide, dark-lashed eyes. "We'll be drenched. I'm afraid you'll take a terrible cold. We must find that cottage as soon as this stops."

"Mmmmm," she replied. Wrapped in her shawl, his arms around her, and the heat of his body between her and the cold stone against which they sheltered, she felt warm and even languorous. She involuntarily snuggled more closely against him, and in response his arms tightened. They remained thus, each now more than ever aware of the other, not knowing how to break away from the heightened intimacy, not knowing if they wished to do so.

The rain passed as quickly as it had come. With a mixture of relief and regret, Maidie freed herself from his embrace, and stepped away from him. Loose strands of hair stuck wetly along her cheek, and her skirts clung around her legs. She pushed her hair back and shook out her skirts. "I must look a fright! I feel a fright."

"No," he said. "Just a wet duckling." With gentle touch, he brushed at one of those wet, curling strands. A dangerous business. He quickly withdrew his hand.

Allan removed his jacket. "Here, you're shivering."

"Oh, no. I couldn't. I have my shawl."

"Inadequate. You must take it, Miss Worthing."

She submitted. "Very well." She gazed up at him, wide-eyed and melting. "You are simply too masterful, Mr. Gilmichael." And then, unable to continue the charade, she laughed.

He draped the jacket around her shoulders and considered kissing her. "And you are simply too given to jest."

"I was jesting?" she asked innocently.

"Come along."

They walked on, Allan leading, and Maidie silent beside him.

In the odd way of the fells, by the time they had descended for a quarter of an hour they could see no sign of the storm except for the torrential rush of water in the beck they walked beside. Nonetheless, the sky remained low and forbidding. Allan estimated that they had no more than two hours of light. Although the storm had passed, the sun had already sunk behind the fells, and the eastern face of the range now lay in shadow, intensifying the chill. He had no concern for himself—he'd lived through much worse on the Peninsula—but he really had to get Maidie's clothes and shoes dried.

As the sheep trod crossed a clearly defined path, Allan stopped. "Here, my duckling, we take this path. I must get you to that cottage I remember. I'll break in if I have to. And then I'll leave you there and alert Emery."

"Prudence will have done so, I should think."

"Nonetheless, the storm is far from spent. And you're shivering."

An argument ensued that was only ended by a hail from a man who was approaching them rapidly across a heavily grazed hillside of short grasses.

Ten

"Halloo there," Allan called.

When the man reached them he stared for a moment before speaking. "You folks got caught in the storm, I see."

"Afraid so."

The man eyed Maidie. "She your sister?"

"No, just a stray I found wandering about the fells. She and her companion were separated. I offered to help her look for him, but afraid I mistook the way, too, and it was a considerable time before we could work our way back."

"Expect you was up around them batch o' ghylls and crags. "Lots o' folks get lost up there. Have to take so many turnings, folks lose their bearings. Well, come on up to the cottage. I expect my wife can dry you out. Make up some beds for you, too, if simple comfort will do you."

"Oh, dear, no!" Maidie cried. "We must really return home as soon as possible, if you could just be so very kind as to show us the way. My aunt and uncle will be frantic, and my companion—the one I was separated from—may be lying at the bottom of a ghyll with a broken head, or a smashed leg, or . . . or something terrible. Surely you can guide us down. I'm from Pennelbeck Farm."

"That so? Know it well. Know Mr. Clarke and Mrs. Fanny. You their young niece what's here to visit?"

"Yes, yes I am. Maidie Worthing, sir, and this is Mr. Allan Gilmichael. And you are?"

"Name's Stricket, miss, and it's a pleasure to meet you. Mrs. Fanny and him, her husband, they're right 'uns. But as to taking you down tonight . . . well, I'd like to, but it's too dangerous for laikers. Yan hardly knows what the weather will do here in the fells, you understand, but unless I miss my guess, there's more rain coming before night falls."

"Too dangerous for lakers? You mean too dangerous for even *you?*" Maidie turned to Allan. "Goodness, Mr. Gilmichael, where do you suppose we've wandered?"

"He means tourists, Miss Worthing. Laik is a local word that means play."

"Oh."

The shepherd smiled. "That's right. Too dangerous for laikers, them as didn't grow up on these fells. Come along with me now, and me wife will see to your comfort. Then I'll go down and let them all know you're safe, and that I'll bring you down come morning. And don't you worry about your friend. Sure to've been a party out looking for you when you didn't get home. If he was hurt, he'd have stayed in one place. It's wandering that gets folks lost."

Within less than a half-hour of easy walking they were in sight of a small well-kept cottage. Smoke rose from the chimney, and light from the fire within flickered behind the window.

"Here, Mother," the shepherd called as he opened the door. "I've broughten you some visitors."

Mrs. Stricket, who was stirring a pot hanging from a crane over the fire, straightened with a startled exclamation. "My, but you did surprise me, Father! And who might you have broughten on a night when we're eating nobbut oatcake and milk and a bit o' mutton stew? Not tet young rascal Mr. Wendell—" Mrs. Stricket stopped in mid-sentence. "Oh," she concluded as her husband stood back to let Maidie, and then Allan, enter the kitchen.

"Mother, these folks were caught in the rain up among the crags. This is Miss Worthing, tet niece of Mrs. Fanny's at Pennelbeck Farm. You mind you met Mrs. Fanny last year at the shepherds' fair?"

Mrs. Stricket made a rapid recovery. " 'Course I mind. I mind verra well. Mrs. Fanny's a woman as yan doesn't forget. But come in, child, come in! Forgive me scolding, but it amuses the young gentleman from below as visits us now and then. Caught in the rain, were you? And how did this gentleman here let that happen?"

"Now, Mother," Stricket admonished his loquacious wife, "why will you be blaming the gentleman afore you hear the story? Mr. Gilmichael, me wife is just showing her low opinion of the gentlemen in general, but she's a good woman at heart."

Allan stepped forward to shake hands. "I deserve your low opinion, ma'am, at least in this case. I found Miss Worthing lost on the fellside, and then I almost lost the way myself."

"It do be easy for yan not bred on the fells. But sit down, sit down. Come to the fire, now do." She put her arm around Maidie's shoulders to lead her to the fire. "Why, child, you're shivering like to shake apart. You'd have caught your death if Father hadn't found you."

"Oh, but Mr. Gilmichael was such a true knight that as you can see he gave me his jacket. Really, it's Mr. Gilmichael who I'm afraid will catch his death."

Mrs. Stricket turned to Allan with a broad smile. "Me apologies to you, sir. Now you come over here by the warmth, too. I'll just pour a little hot tea for you and then I'll find something to put around you while I dry your things."

"And I'll be going along to Pennelbeck Farm, Mother. Mr. Clarke and Mrs. Fanny must be worrit to death."

"Please don't forget to ask them if Chester is all right," Maidie begged. "That's Chester Califaxton. I was looking for him when I got lost."

"And my guess is that he was looking for Miss Worthing and no doubt got lost himself." Allan added.

"And don't forget, please, Mr. Stricket, to ask if Wendell—oh, you're acquainted with Wendell, aren't you, Mr. Stricket? Don't forget to ask about Wendell, because when we didn't meet him—Chester and I—as we were supposed to have done, he probably came looking for us. Or—" She abruptly closed her mouth. She could not voice another nagging worry—that Wendell might have come out the loser in his encounter with the spy.

"And perhaps *he's* lost," Allan finished. "Really, Miss Worthing, how could you manage to get so many people lost in one afternoon?"

"Now, now," Mrs. Stricket said, smiling at Allan over Maidie's head. "Don't you go scolding miss." She turned to her husband. "And you, Mr. Stricket, don't be standing there. Be on your way now. Mrs. Fanny must be near distracted."

"Yes, and she's—" Maidie caught herself. Would these people think her terribly ill-bred if she mentioned that Aunt Fanny was increasing? She didn't know enough yet about the local people and what they might think improper. But in whatever event, she really had no right to make her aunt's announcement for her. But she would *never* forgive herself if her escapade caused Aunt Fanny to lose her baby. She had heard that nervous strain could have such an effect, and even though Fanny had assured her that morning sickness was common in her condition, she couldn't help worrying when she saw how her dear aunt suffered. Maidie had determined not to think about it, or she might lose courage, but the worry she felt could no longer be suppressed. "Oh, I've really been very *wrong!* I didn't heed any of Aunt Fanny's or Uncle Emery's warnings." Before she could stop herself, two tears spilled down her cheeks.

"Here, here, miss," Mrs. Stricket said soothingly, putting her arm around her again. "Don't you cry. Your aunt will soon know you're safe." She looked up at Mr. Stricket. "That is, if this man here will get hisell agoing!"

"Yes, Mother, I'm agoing this minute. Just getting mesell an oatcake."

Allan, without thinking, had taken a step toward Maidie, but she wiped her tears away with her fingers, and smiled with watery sweetness at her hostess. "I'm all right. Truly. It's just that you're so very kind, Mrs. Stricket."

Allan turned to Stricket. "Now that Miss Worthing is safe, I'll accompany you. I've spent a good deal of time on the fells, and I shan't be in danger of misstepping."

"You're wet through, sir, and it's started up to rain again. Getting colder, too."

"I've spent colder and wetter nights—out in the open, rolled up in a blanket and with no fire."

"Soldier, were you?"

"Yes. And I've spent a night or two in the open right here on the fells. Thought once I'd never get used to a civilized bed again. So if your good wife can provide me with something . . . an old cloak or blanket . . ."

"Have you done for a fact? Cold nights out on the fells. Even tet Mr. Wudsworth never *sleeps* on the fells, though he do wander a fair bit at night."

"Good heavens! Will you go along now, Mr. Stricket?" his wife demanded. She bustled over to the kitchen table and took up several oatcakes to wrap in a clean cloth from the table drawer. "Now you can just munch on these as you go along," she said, handing the package to Allan. She took a heavy cloak from a chest along the wall. "Get along, both of you. Step careful, now, the way to Pennelbeck Farm can be dangerous in the dark and the wet."

Maidie went to Allan and offered him her hand. "I can't thank you enough, Mr. Gilmichael, for rescuing me. But I don't want you to risk a lung fever . . ."

"No danger, Miss Worthing, I assure you."

She smiled at him rather mistily. "Then I'll say goodbye, and thank you again."

His heart softened alarmingly as he took her hand and gazed down into the tear-brightened eyes with their heavy fringe of dark lashes. They weren't long lashes, and now he knew what he was reminded of. They brought to mind the kohl-painted eyes of houris in Turkish bordellos. He frowned. Not a proper thought.

Then suddenly the eyes gazing up at him were sparkling with mischief. "No, no, don't frown at me! I know how much I merit a rousing scold from my aunt and uncle. Nonetheless, when it comes to scolding, a little bit goes a very long way, I think, and I must thank you for not loosing the reproofs and reprimands I know very well you so longed to deliver. This time I freely admit I deserved them."

He'd just had his heart softened toward the chit, and now she was at it again! Reproofs you richly deserved, my girl, he thought crossly—and should have had bigger doses of when you were growing up. He chose, however, to reply with silence and a stiff bow. Had he turned back he would have been even more annoyed to observe the amusement in the dark lashed eyes.

They had reached the lower meadows when they heard distant halloos. Stricket answered, and within another twenty minutes they met Emery and Wendell, with one of the farmhands.

Once assured that Maidie was safe at the Stricket cottage, they could report that Chester was safe—that is, if he and his guide had not fallen into trouble. "He should be on his way down to Pennelbeck Farm, just as we were," Emery said, examining his watch by the light of the torch he carried. "We agreed to return at dark to the farm, rest until four in the morning and the first lightening of the sky. Meanwhile old Briggs and his son—they know every foot of these fells—would have been continuing the search through the night."

"You'll take the word to Mrs. Fanny, then," Stricket said to Wendell. "So I'll be back up the path to me cottage, where Miss Worthing will be happy to hear that Mrs. Fanny isn't worriting about her any longer."

"As fast as I may," Wendell declared. "Emery and Mr. Gilmichael can follow at a more leisurely pace. And thank you, Stricket."

"The missus looks for you to be stopping with us again soon," he replied.

"I can't thank you enough, Stricket," Emery said, as Wendell, after a hearty shake of the shepherd's hand, turned to descend. "Anything I can do to show my gratitude . . ."

"I'm glad enough to be doing Mrs. Fanny a good turn. She's a rare woman." He paused and, with a glint, continued, "Mappen that cow we was talking about could be sold for a good price . . ."

Emery laughed. "Why, you sharp fellow! Of course I sell for a good price. *My* good price. But I'll think about it."

"I'll be thinking on it too, and mappen we two'll come to an agreement after a spell."

The reunion of Maidie and her aunt was as joyous as it was tearful. Emery, who had been at pains to caution Fanny to remember that Maidie was a woman grown, and that her experience had probably taught its own lesson, nonetheless lectured gravely on what might have happened, with a rather overlong recounting of accidents and mishaps that had befallen local people and visitors in the course of the previous twenty years. Fanny refrained from chiding her niece, contenting herself with what she called auntish advice, and by the time the day was done had forgotten all of the strong admonishments she might have made.

However, when Maidie, following an uncomfortable and remorseful night, in an excess of repentance made unwise vows to be less impulsive and more circumspect in future, Fanny felt it necessary to deliver more, and sterner, auntish advice. She pointed out to Maidie that she hadn't a hope of fulfilling her promises. "My dear, the very impulsiveness and fervor with which you make these promises is contrary to the vows you are now making to consider consequences more carefully—to better regulate your mind. What I wish from you is a promise to hereafter think before you act; you are a clever, intelligent young woman, and your good mind can serve you in making decisions about the best courses of action and in meeting problems that inevitably arise. Now run along, do, for I begin to dislike myself excessively when I lecture."

"But you, Aunt Fanny—"

"No, no. I won't be held up as a pattern card. And I am more prudent than you think, or than Emery will believe. Now run along. But consider what I've said. And remember that I'll need your help this afternoon."

Maidie kissed her aunt and ran along to think over her advice. Control of passions, caprices, whims, and fancies, in pursuit of patience, prudence, and composure were the subjects of numerous uplifting books and sermons for young females, from which Maidie's progressive education had not entirely shielded her. All young ladies had at least heard of Miss Hannah More, a most learned adviser on education, who warned parents and teachers that the purpose of study for females was to rectify their principles, regulate and strengthen their minds, form habits of usefulness to others, and prepare them to be sensible companions to the men they married. Maidie now proposed to take such advice to heart.

For a day and the part of another she tried to determine if

regulating her mind meant that she should stop thinking about Mr. Allan Gilmichael—remembering the moments when she thought he would kiss her, how much she would have liked it, and wondering why he hadn't. And what fun it would be to go tramping across the fells with him! They could both carry knapsacks, with just the barest necessities—toothbrushes and changes of stockings—exclaiming at magnificent views, stopping at farmhouses for their meals. He would teach her to fish and to build a fire. And at night . . . well, there would be inns . . . and there would be soft beds . . .

She sternly told herself that such daydreaming was doing nothing to strengthen her mind—in fact was probably weakening it—and as she sat on the drystone wall overlooking the lake, she wondered how one actually went about strengthening one's mind. Did it mean reading philosophy? Or the economists? Or perhaps she should read Homer—except that she found him boring beyond endurance. Her erstwhile admirer, Lord Calvette, had told her that of course she would find Homer boring—nothing more natural—classical literature wasn't meant for girls. (What her Aunt Fanny, who was most particularly fond of the classics, had said to *that!*) She rather thought that Blake might strengthen her mind, because she had to think so hard to understand his poems. What could the man mean when he asked if he should sow a lapful of seed on sand . . .

> For on no other ground
> Can I sow my seed
> Without tearing up
> Some stinking weed.

But if one had to think so hard to understand, and still couldn't make sense of things, had one's mind been strengthened?

She was considering that philosophical problem and gazing blankly at the lake, when slowly an image she had been watching but not comprehending assumed the shape of Prudence Califaxton rowing a boat. Blake and philosophy were immediately forgotten, as she jumped up and ran to the boat landing.

"Oh, Prudence!" Maidie exclaimed, as she steadied the boat for her friend to alight. "I'm so glad to see you! I've had nothing to do for three days but reflect on my sins and help Aunt Fanny prepare for our guests—although what's to prepare for our very own family I'm sure I don't know, when we have guests all the time. You remember that my father and mother and aunt are coming?

They walked up the path arm in arm. Fanny, catching sight of them from a window, thought they looked a charming pair in their light summer dresses. So did Allan, standing on the farmhouse steps with Emery.

"Have you come to take tea with us, Prudence?" Maidie asked as they seated themselves on the wall.

"No, I just wanted to hear about your adventure on the fells! But Mama wouldn't let me come to you until today—and Papa doesn't know, for he's gone to Kendal on business."

"Are your parents being very unpleasant about our escapade, dear?"

"Oh, yes. Even John reproached me. And now Papa is come home, and *he* scolded me. Oh, Maidie, if you had heard what he said to Chester and me! It was truly dreadful. You can't imagine! But I wouldn't have cared at all, if we had just caught the spy!" Prudence tossed her head in a gesture of defiance. "I just wish I had been brave enough to help."

"Why, Prudence! I believe you would have liked to have been lost on the fells yourself!"

Prudence blushed, but chose not to respond to such a suggestion, which in point of fact was not too far from the truth. "Did you get a frightful scold, too?" she asked.

"No. Only a lecture about strengthening my mind. And I'm sure you're the very one to tell me how—or at least how to regulate it, which I believe must be the first step to strengthening it. I'm sure you must have a well-regulated mind!"

Prudence laughed shyly. "I don't know why you should think so, Maidie. My mother is always scolding me. I dream too much, she says, and don't pay attention."

Maidie forbore commenting that Mrs. Califaxton was a certified scold and not to be taken seriously. "No, no. I'm *sure* your mind is well-regulated—although perhaps not strong. I think mine might be stronger, although it still wants strengthening. But yours *must* be the better regulated! You were the only one among us who cautioned against chasing spies and warned that our plan was foolish."

Although Maidie spoke lightly, she was as mortified that it was Prudence who had recognized the faults in their plan as she was truly sincere in her praise of the girl.

Prudence refused to accept an honor for herself which simultaneously cast doubts on the wisdom of her lover. "Chester likes to say it's all Mr. Duval's fault, and that he won't listen to what he calls stuff about spies again. But it wasn't just stuff, was it, Maidie?"

Maidie shook her head emphatically. "Indeed not. The plan went awry because Chester and I took the wrong way. Although I do think that Wendell chose a place that was too hard to reach, and of course Chester and I should have made a practice climb with Wendell." She frowned. "Although how we could . . . for the spy would have followed us . . ." She gave up on what was now a useless line of thought. "Our plan was truly foolish, but the spy is not imaginary! And furthermore, I learned something I know you'll find interesting. It's also vastly amusing, although of course it was very good-natured of Mr. Gilmichael."

Maidie then related Allan's attempt to discover whether a person named Wendell Duval was under suspicion. "But of course to no avail, since as you know, Wendell's real name is Salvatore Toone."

"You told him Mr. Duval's real name?" Prudence asked, with a touch of censure in her voice. And then, with a touch of hurt, "He told you, too?"

Maidie had come dangerously close to revealing to Prudence that she already knew of Wendell's declaration of love. "Of course. His relatives all know. But I must learn to guard my tongue. I had no way of knowing that you also knew his correct name."

"Oh, yes, he did tell me," Prudence said, avoiding Maidie's eyes. "But I don't think it was right to confide in Mr. Gilmichael."

"Well, I do think that if Mr. Gilmichael exerted himself to discover the truth about the spy, he deserved to be told Wendell's real name, don't you?"

"I suppose," Prudence conceded reluctantly. "But what did Mr. Gilmichael say when you told him?"

"He said next time he goes fishing he'll go to Scotland."

"Oh." Prudence's hand flew to her mouth.

"No, no," Maidie laughed. "He wasn't serious, you know."

For two days Prudence had been consumed with curiosity about Maidie's sojourn on the mountain all alone with Mr. Gilmichael, but had felt it would be indelicate to ask. Nonetheless, curiosity will sometimes overcome delicacy, even in gently bred maidens. "Was it terribly embarrassing to be so long alone with him?" she asked timidly.

"Embarrassing? No, not at all. Mr. Gilmichael is a gentleman, and I assure you, he played his role as rescuer and protector so very properly you've no notion. But I do believe I fell in love with him."

"Maidie!! You haven't! You're funning!"

"You must be aware, Prudence, that any well brought up young woman *should* fall in love with the man who rescues her. Or don't you think so? But perhaps it was just propinquity. I'll have to think about it."

"You *are* funning."

"Sometimes I'm not sure whether I'm funning or serious, you know, so pay no attention to me."

"Are you . . . are you *compromised?*" Prudence asked cautiously, thinking perhaps Maidie might be putting the best face on it all.

"No, indeed. Surely, a gentleman would think twice before rescuing a lady if it would require he marry her. And when one contemplates the various specimens of manhood who might be our rescuers, I should think that we in our turn might often prefer not to be rescued at all!"

A light breeze wafted across the meadow and gently lifted their skirt hems where they sat on the wall.

"Let's go out in the rowboat!" Maidie exclaimed. "We can enjoy to the full this refreshing breeze. Do you think Mr. Wordsworth has anything to say about breezes? Aunt Fanny will invite him to call, with his wife and sister, to show Mama and Papa and Aunt Seraphina how conservative the Lake Poets are become. Mr. Wordsworth is campaigning for the Lowther's candidate in the election, you know."

"Mr. Duval says that Mr. Brougham, although not as democratic as he would like, is much preferable to the Lowther candidate."

"Undoubtedly," Maidie answered, distracted by the soft breeze in her hair and the beauty of the tranquilly shimmering lake.

They stepped into the boat, and Prudence took the oars. She guided the craft to the center of the lake, behind a small, irregularly shaped island called Krigsholme, out of sight of both the Califaxton residence and the Pennelbeck farmhouse.

"Nobody can see us here," Prudence remarked, removing her bonnet; but before pulling her skirts up to her knees, as Maidie had already done, she scanned the shores with guilty apprehension, as though her mother might somehow be able to see her straight through the verdure-cloaked island. "Mr. Duval says that holme means island in Norse, and that this lake and the island were probably the first settlement of a Viking named Krigs-something. Or so the rector told him."

"The rector must be a diligent scholar," Maidie replied, not attending closely. She moved her hand in slow circles through the cool water. "I suppose I could study the history of the Lakes to regulate my mind—mental discipline is supposed to be good for one, I believe."

Her curiosity satisfied, Prudence was willing to go on to subjects other than spies and compromised maidens. "Would you like to borrow Miss Hannah More's volumes on the—what is the title?—*A Modern System of Female Education,* I think it is. Something about strictures too. What does strictures mean, do you think?"

Maidie scooped up a handful of water and allowed it to dribble from her fingers. "I believe it means to limit something. Or I guess it also means to criticize."

"Well, whatever it means, my mother is always telling me that Hannah More says this or that about female education. It's funny because Miss More doesn't approve of Mr. Lancaster's system of education for the lower orders, and Mama does."

Maidie frowned at Prudence, only half teasing. "Aunt Fanny says we should not call the poorer and more humble people the lower orders. It degrades those who are often of better character than many lords. Hasn't Wendell given you his lecture on The Evils of a Hierarchal Society?"

Prudence blushed again. "Yes, he has. But it is difficult, you know, to learn new ways of talking."

Maidie sighed. She thought it might be even more difficult to learn new ways of acting. "Perhaps I will borrow Miss More's books on Female Education. I was just thinking about her. *My* mother always said that Miss More very rightly defended female intellect, but her ideas about what we may use our intellect *for* are too narrow. But if you are the result of her theories, then they must be worthwhile for slapdash creatures like me."

"I'm sure Mama will let you borrow the books, but you mustn't say you are a slapdash creature, or that I am perfect—for oh, I am not! I assure you I am not!"

Maidie, product of a progressive upbringing, was crafted of sterner stuff than the daughter of the scolding Mrs. Califaxton. "Oh, don't worry. We humans are so various, and there are so many theories about what we ought to be, that I'm sure nobody could be perfect—even you, dear Prudence."

Maidie languidly swished her hand back and forth, watching the ripples. The boat rocked gently. "Wouldn't it be wonderful to go swimming?"

"You can swim?"

"Oh, yes, since I was a child. Mama and I go to the seashore every summer. But this summer I was permitted to come to Aunt Fanny." Maidie leaned over the side of the boat, tipping it dangerously, to peer into the clear depths. "If we should capsize, then we would have no recourse but to swim." She grinned at Prudence as she straightened, until she saw stark apprehension in the girl's face.

"You don't swim, Pru?"

"No. Mama says—"

"But really, Pru, you shouldn't be allowed on the lake alone if you can't swim . . ." She paused a moment, considering. "I brought my bathing dress with me from London, and now that the weather's warmer, I'm going to get it out and go splashing. Perhaps we can persuade your mama to let me teach you. I taught another friend, and I'm sure you'd learn quickly. I'd looked forward to swimming with Aunt Fanny, but now she's—" Maidie clapped a hand over her mouth.

"Now she's what?" Prudence asked innocently.

"Oh, nothing . . . just that now she's so busy, she doesn't have time. She's writing a new series of articles for the *Examiner.*"

She did wish Aunt Fanny would openly announce her exciting news! It was so difficult not to let the cat out of the bag. But then, an unguarded tongue was one of those faults that she was certain Miss More would think young ladies should correct, so perhaps it was good practice to have a secret.

Prudence had been thinking. "You mean your aunt is expecting to have a baby?"

When Maidie wondered how she had ever come to know about her Aunt Fanny's interesting condition, Prudence rather thought it was Chester who told their mother, but she couldn't say for certain. But then, everybody knew. The postmaster's wife . . . Gossip in a small place like Sagpaw . . .

They explored, somewhat desultorily, the subjects of gossip and childbirth, until Maidie suddenly sat up. "Oh, dear. It must be time for tea! Do come, Prudence."

"I can't, Maidie." Prudence burst into tears.

"Why, Pru, whatever is it? Don't cry. Here, dear, take my handkerchief."

Prudence sobbed brokenly into the dainty piece of linen. "Oh, Maidie, I wasn't going to tell you . . . but Papa said I was not to see you or Mr. Duval ever again! He said Mr. Duval is a whippersn . . . whippersn . . ."

Maidie gently urged Prudence to make room beside her, and put an arm around her shoulders. "Whippersnapper?"

"Y-yes. And that if the G-government has put a spy on him there must be something b-b-b-bad about him, and oh, Maidie, you know that's not true, but Chester told Papa *everything*."

"Of course it's not true."

"But I *must* see him, because I'm *so* in love with him, Maidie!"

"Are you indeed! But how wonderful!" Although Maidie had been waiting for the confidence, she had expected the circumstances to be somewhat more joyful. "And of course Wendell is in love with you. How could he help but be in love with such a sweet ch—girl?"

Prudence was rapidly turning the handkerchief into a soggy ball. Her cheeks were still wet with tears, but she was no longer crying. "I know you were going to say child, Maidie. I know we'll have to wait until we're older. But I'm going to marry Mr. Duval, and I'll *elope* with him if I have to and even if Papa will never see me again!"

"Yes, dear, so you must, although I should think it uncomfortable to never see one's family ever again. But now let us think how we can soften your Papa's heart so that you may visit me, and I you. Then we'll think about Wendell."

"Oh well, Mama says she can fix that. She always knows how to manage Papa. She says she'll just remind him that you're an heiress, and that your papa is even richer than *he* is." Prudence turned an enquiring face to Maidie. "Are you richer than we are?" she asked naively.

"I'm sure I can't say," Maidie replied, repressing an urge to laugh. "I don't know how rich you are, you see. But yes, I believe my Papa is what is generally called rich, and since I am his only child, I am a considerable heiress. Unless he chooses to disown me for this scrape."

"Oh, would he do that? Is he an ogre like my papa?"

"No, you gudgeon. Of course he won't disown me. But what does my being an heiress say to anything?"

"Mama says that Papa would never forbid me to be friends with an heiress. And I thought, Maidie, that since Mr. Duval is your cousin . . ."

"Not really my cousin, Pru. He's Uncle Emery's cousin."

"Yes, I know. Oh, Maidie, did he get a terrible scold, too? From Mr. Clarke? Is he terribly unhappy? Papa denied him the house, you know, when he came to call." Prudence's voice broke.

"Yes, he had to tell everything. Uncle Emery demanded what he called a full and frank confession. Wendell had to confess that Mr. Gilmichael had suggested that the spy's investigation might have more to do with curiosity about his character than his political opinions, which had some weight with Uncle, for you do know that he and Mr. Gilmichael are great friends. But Wendell naturally found this interpretation insulting . . ."

"I should think so, indeed! Mr. Duval is upright beyond anything!"

"Yes," Maidie agreed. "Except for the nonsense about his name, which doesn't amount to a hill of beans." In fact, her uncle had had a good many things to say about the wisdom—or lack of it—in using a false name, but Maidie did not consider it important. "Wendell had a few pointed remarks to make about people who might be questioning his probity and character. But I rather think that the very idea that someone was actually spying on him, for whatever reason, aroused Uncle's ire sufficiently that he was not so severe in his strictures. There, you see! I've just used the word."

Prudence thought her dear Mr. Duval a much more interesting subject for discussion than definitions and usages. "Oh, I'm so glad he wasn't severely reprimanded. He's suffered so much!"

Maidie again forbore comment. Wendell was savoring the distinction of being the subject of spying and had borne with fortitude the rebukes delivered by her uncle.

"But," Prudence continued, "Mr. Duval is often at Mr. and Mrs. Clarke's. That is, because he's your uncle's cousin, and I can't avoid seeing him if you're my friend. And you *are* my friend! I've never had such a good friend before."

Maidie kissed Prudence's cheek. "What a nice thing to say, Pru. I don't think anyone has ever said anything so nice to me! But now I really must be going back. I'm already late for tea. Come to me as soon as your mama has convinced your papa that I'm worthy of your friendship."

"Of course you're worthy! Even if you weren't rich. It's just that Papa . . ."

"I know, dear. Papas can be dreadfully trying, can't they? But you know, I'm sure, that Aunt Fanny is planning a picnic for all the neighbors when Mama and Papa and Aunt Seraphina are here, and she spoke most specifically of inviting your family. If you can't come to me before that, we'll see each other then. And don't worry. We'll think of something."

"Maidie . . ." Prudence hesitated. "Maybe if you and Mr. Duval pretended, just a little, to be in love. Chester told Papa that Mr. Duval . . . that Mr. Duval *likes* me, you see. And . . ."

"He did? I declare, brothers must be quite as pesty as papas!" Having delivered herself of this startling discovery, Maidie frowned at Prudence. "But as for pretending I'm in love with Wendell, aren't we in trouble enough from our last scrape without engaging in another?" But as Prudence's lips began to quiver, and tears to gather in her eyes, Maidie impulsively took her hand and said soothingly, "No, no, dear. Don't cry again. Wendell and I will think of something."

"Please, Maidie, can you tell him for me that I will wait for him forever, and that I have always dreamed of a little cottage, with a cow and a pig . . ."

"Pru, you haven't the least idea what it's like to be poor."

"No, I suppose I am being foolish. But I don't need the luxury I have now. Mama has taught me to be a very good housewife. I am not unprepared. Will you tell him, Maidie? Please?"

"I can't tell him that you will elope with him. That would be wrong."

"I know. But you can tell him that I'll wait for him as long as I must. And that I am prepared to be a poor man's wife. . . . Well," she amended as she caught Maidie's skeptical frown, "to be the wife of a man of modest means. For I know that Mr. Duval is much too clever to ever be poor."

"No, it isn't at all clever of one to be poor." Prudence's puzzled expression gave Maidie a tremor of conscience. "But of course, my dear, I can tell him that you are prepared to wait for him to be rich enough to marry you."

"No, Maidie." Tears threatened again.

"I'm sorry, Pru. I'll tell him that you will wait until he can provide you with a home. But now I really must get back to shore."

Maidie waved to Prudence, sighed, and then turned to direct her steps to the house. Really, Prudence at times was hardly more than a winning child!

Eleven

The drawing room was filled with more than the usual number of callers when Maidie entered. Mr. Gilmichael, she immediately noted, was speaking to a lady in travel attire, who she supposed to be the owner of the smart vehicle drawn up just inside the short farm lane.

Although Allan's head was bent attentively to the bothersome woman, who was persistently describing her Lakeland tour for him, he had been surreptitiously watching the door for Miss Worthing. Since their parting in the shepherd's cottage, he had had only that one tantalizing glimpse of her, walking arm in arm with the Califaxton chit. He saw her as immediately as she saw him. He nodded to her, and she smiled in return.

Maidie went directly to the tea table to relieve Fanny. She hadn't seen Mr. Gilmichael since the afternoon on the mountain, and wanted an ordinary chore to occupy her when they met again. Really, she had been foolish to let her imagination run so loose, dwelling on his face and figure and on those moments on the fells when he could have kissed her—and even entertaining notions of setting off across the fells in his company and passing nights with him in rustic inns! Falling in love was making her shy. As well as raising turbulence in her veins!

Fanny readily relinquished the tea table to Maidie, and straightaway was off to mingle with the company. She abstained, however, from an exciting discussion of Shelley's *Revolt of Islam* and paused only briefly to listen to incensed denunciations of the government's efforts to control the press. Her target was Allan.

Although Emery described the man's politics as moderate and Whiggish, Fanny thought such a position of a more conservative persuasion than not. After all, Whigs differed from Tories only in exalting the power of the aristocracy over royal power—they were equally willing to suppress the People. And at the moment she had a very good use for a suitably conservative gentleman.

She skirted the room, refusing to be drawn into one of the perennial condemnations of tourists and villa builders, those late-coming invaders who threatened to destroy the unique charm of the Lakes. (Why was it, she wondered, that those who condemned so readily never felt themselves eligible for similar condemnation?) She needed Emery's assistance to detach the tiresome female from Allan, and for the moment had no time for discussions of any kind.

"Emery," Fanny whispered, tugging at his sleeve, "do come with me."

Emery excused himself and tucked Fanny's hand under his arm. "Well, my dear, I await your orders."

"I must extract Allan from the grasp of that overpowering female who has been monopolizing him for the last half hour."

"Do you wish to speak to the overpowering female, or to Gilmichael? Or are you attempting to deliver both to new conquests?"

"To Mr. Gilmichael. I'm afraid I must deliver the female into your hands. But I'm sure you'll be up to her weight, my love."

"Or her wiles. She looks as though she'd like to eat Gilmichael for supper."

Soon it was Emery who was bending his head to hear what the stylish lady was whispering about so intently. It seemed to have something to do with the bad roads and how overcome she was by the violence of the Lakeland scenery. It was not her idea of what the picturesque should be at all!

Fanny bore Allan away to an alcove, where they might hope for a few uninterrupted minutes. "Allan, dear, I must ask you a question, for which I hope you'll forgive me when I explain my predicament."

"Of course, Fanny. How may I serve you?"

"Are you by any chance a Tory?"

"A Tory? No. I believe I'm currently leaning to the opinion of my latest mentor, Mr. Godwin, who tells me that political parties are bound by their nature to exaggeration and distortion. So you mustn't think me Whiggish, either, but something on the lines of a cold, rational, analytical observer."

"I would never think it. In fact, I take you for a traditional sort of gentleman, whatever your politics, and eminently respectable. Which is just the kind of gentleman I'm needing to lend us respectability these next several days."

"Respectability! My dear Fanny, how could anyone think you not respectable? But what prompts this inquiry into my political views?"

"You know perfectly well that Emery and I are not considered respectable. If nothing else, we had too much admiration for Napoleon, and I think it exceedingly liberal-minded of you, Allan, to accept that we admired the man against whom you fought so resolutely for absolutely years and years."

It had in fact been difficult for Allan to accept that there were those in England who had favored Bonaparte's rule in France. But the past was past, and he had long since conceded that the self-proclaimed emperor of France had brought needed reform and modernization to an ancient regime. "As I've told you both, if anyone could have guaranteed that Bonaparte would confine himself to governing France and forget the lure of conquest, I would not have been averse to his return to power, since the French seemed to desire it."

"Yes, it must be admitted that he has that peculiarly unfortunate tendency to aggrandizement. But a discussion of Napoleon Bonaparte is not at all to the purpose now. I'm sure Emery has told you that we're expecting Maidie's parents and my sister Seraphina."

Allan acknowledged that Emery had indeed mentioned it.

"Sam—Maidie's father and my brother—seems to think that Maidie will fall under the spell of some demented democrat or prosy poet while under my roof, and I . . . I'm being sincerely honest with you . . . I'm trying to ensure that the company in which Sam finds her is all that's respectable. And Seraphina! You can't imagine how detestably starchy my sister is. I fear Sam will insist that Maidie return to London, but I do want to keep her through the summer. You do know that I'm increasing?"

Allan thought it diplomatic to deny previous knowledge of Fanny's promising condition, while admiring, as he always did, her refusal to follow the conventional rules of delicacy. He wondered if Maidie's direct approach to life came from association with her aunt. He responded to Fanny's announcement with a suitable expression of surprise and was launching himself on good wishes and felicitations, when she put her hand up. "Emery and I are happy, of course, but it's nothing so very great, you know. The commonest and most stupid female can conceive."

Allan could not help laughing. "Fanny, as our shepherd friend Stricket observed, you are a rare one."

"Did he indeed?" was all Fanny's comment. "In order to carry out my plan, I intend a *petite ruse de guerre*—which is to people my household with the most conservative of our neighbors. The Wordsworths and the Southeys may call—they are so depressingly Tory—but William is simply throwing himself into electing his patron's man, Mrs. Wordsworth tells us, and she is leaving directly to visit relatives, so I mustn't count on it. Will you stay? I'm having the Califaxtons for a picnic; Califaxton *père* is with the family again, you know, and will lend a touch of manufacturing-might to my party. And I'm having the rector. He can bore on at excruciating length about Lake history and geology. Everyone believes boring people to be conservative, you know, although of course it isn't true. And Wendell has promised me faithfully—*faithfully*—to control his political passions and inflammatory opinions while they are here. And if you were of the party, I know Sam would be convinced that Maidie is in no danger."

Allan thought Maidie might well be in danger. Hadn't Fanny noticed the flirtation she was carrying on with young Duval? The feeling that he suspected was developing in his own breast was not only of a different and higher order, but respectability itself—he was neither a prosy poet nor a demented democrat. "I fear I must leave the Lakes shortly, you know," he demurred. "I've neglected my affairs far too long."

"But I didn't know. Surely you are not leaving tomorrow! They come to us this week. I know that I'm asking the most immense favor, but I'm only asking you to grant me a week . . . Emery will scold me roundly for begging, but I do so want your presence."

Allan hesitated. A banker was all very well for a father-in-law, but if he should prove to be exceedingly vulgar, it might somehow rob Maidie of gloss. He did not want his growing feeling for the girl to be influenced either for good or ill.

Across the room Maidie was presiding at the tea table and chatting with the rector, who Allan knew from experience could indeed bore on about Lakeland history. She looked up, and smiled at him. He looked down at Fanny, who was regarding him earnestly. "How can I deny you, Fanny? You and Emery have made my time here more enjoyable than I ever expected."

Fanny, her purposes gained, after a brief expression of gratitude, was off to throw herself into a battle, any battle, leaving Allan to acknowledge to himself that it was a smile from across the room that had secured Fanny her ends. And if he knew anything at all about the language of flirtation, Miss Worthing had not merely acknowledged him as an acquaintance, but had acknowledged also an intimacy and understanding between them.

And if he was to challenge Duval for Maidie's affections, he should hie himself off to the tea table. Or was the better part of wisdom to walk out the door and never come back? He readily admitted that he felt a strong interest in the girl. A serious business, this parley between men and women, he mused. How many women had he met in the course of his life? And how many might he have chosen for a life partner? But for one reason or another nothing had come of those passing attractions—the woman's interest elsewhere, an unavoidable separation . . . After all, wasn't propinquity supposed to foster love? He believed Miss Worthing was willing to receive his attentions. But whether as just another flirtation to add more interest to her summer, or whether with a deeper motive, he couldn't know. Perhaps she didn't know either.

"I say, Allan, you look to be a thousand miles away. I've someone here I want you to meet."

Allan, feeling vaguely that he'd been caught mooning, responded with ready invention. "Just considering the delay in my departure that your wife has persuaded me into."

"A very persuasive woman, Fanny, although I wasn't aware you were thinking of leaving us. But let me introduce you to a future Laker, Sir Harold Mogglesby. He's planning to build a house on Derwent Water for which he claims superior piscatorial attributes. I'm recommending Ennerdale Water for the trout. Be that as it may, he accepted my offer of our spare room tonight, and will sup with us. Hope you can stay as well, although I must warn you as I've warned him that it will be plain fare." Allan permitted himself to be persuaded again.

He tried to make his way to Maidie, but was prevented by the intervention of the tiresome lady who had previously captured him, and who was soon making pointed remarks about his resemblance to the new Marquis of Enett, a resemblance she had immediately noticed once she stood across the room from him.

"Distant relative," he murmured. "Never met him, so couldn't say."

"Well, I can't say I've met him, either. However, I closely observed him at Lady Afton's musical evening several months ago, and determined that he doesn't resemble his brother Clarence in the least. I have little use for the aristocracy in general, but I knew Clarence well, and will bear witness that if we must have an hereditary peerage we could not have had a better representative of the class. England lost a fine man when that unfortunate accident snuffed out his life. Did you know him?"

Allan, although momentarily confused at being asked if he had known his own brother, attempted to halt this flow by breaking in to repeat that he had never had the privilege of knowing either the former or the present marquis. "Afraid I'm merely an obscure twig on the family tree, but I thank you in the name of the family . . ."

The lady was deflected rather than halted, and not a little provoked. "Just what branch of the family are you from, Mr. Gilmichael?" she asked, not disguising her curiosity or disbelief.

Allan reached into the back of his brain for some memory of distant relatives and their tenuous connections. "I'd need a genealogical chart to explain the relationship, which I fear would bore you exceedingly. The connection is, I believe, in the generation of our grandparents . . ." Better make it more distant yet, he thought—make it a more artistic deception. "No, on second thought, it is in the generation of our *great* grandparents. Great uncle. I believe a younger son from a second marriage."

"Rather a long time for a family resemblance to run true."

"Yes, quite."

He was saved from further elucidation by Fanny. She had more than once told her dear Emery that the discrepancy in their worldly fortunes was of no import in a marriage of true minds, and that it was adequately demonstrated at their afternoon entertainments. Emery's slight nod directed her attention to Allan and the persistent lady, and although she did not particularly note that he was uneasy, she certainly considered that he had suffered enough from the plaguy woman. She threw a last observation into the heated argument on the merits of the younger poets and went to Allan's relief, carrying the tiresome lady off to meet another guest.

Maidie was now occupied with a young woman, so Allan strolled over to a window where, should his reflections be again interrupted, he could claim to be observing Emery's fine herd of cows. It had been forcibly borne in on him that his masquerade was folly, and the sooner he put an end to it, the better. His resolution to mix with the local gentry only as common courtesy required had melted away before the tactful companionship of the Clarkes and their winsome niece. Which would eventually, as he should have known, expose him to someone who would recognize him, or who would not be put off by a claim of distant relationship. He might have told himself that he was too little known in the fashionable world, and that the literary and political enthusiasts who visited the Clarkes were in any event people not likely to move in that world; nonetheless, the curious lady had demonstrated the absurdity of his reasoning. There was no iron barrier between the aristocratic and literary world—or for that matter between the aristocracy and the radicals and reformers. Several aristocrats were outspoken Bonapartists, and Lady Stanley had spoken equally emphatically on the disgrace of excessively large fortunes. And wasn't there some gossip about Lord Cochran joining that South American revolutionary, Bolivar?

"Good afternoon, Mr. Gilmichael. Admiring Emery's cows? I understand you're staying to supper, too. I hope that later we may find some time for a discussion of Godwin's *Political Justice*."

Allan suppressed an exasperated sigh. He had begun to hope that this particular young man had decided to keep himself at home for once. "Hello, Duval. Afraid I haven't read enough yet to sustain a sensible discussion."

"Perhaps another time. But, indeed, sir, I hadn't meant to engage you in a political discussion. That I should even think of doing so was mere embarrassment. What I want to say—"

Allan knew what Wendell wanted to say, and hastened to forestall him. "If you were thinking of expressing gratitude for helping Miss Worthing—"

"Please pardon me, sir, but I cannot allow you to make my speeches for me. I do wish to express my gratitude, and acknowledge my folly and want of caution and consideration in putting Maidie—and for that matter, Chester Califaxton—in danger. I am well aware that she could have fallen, or been lost for an uncomfortable time . . ."

Perversely, Allan was determined not to accept gratitude for rescuing the troublesome chit. "If she had waited for Califaxton's return, there would have been no need for a rescue." Even more perversely, and quite gratuitously, he added, "She is a heedless child." He was aware of Wendell's surprise at such censure, and relieved to observe Emery approaching with Sir Harold Mogglesby and a purposeful expression.

"Everybody about cleared out," Emery said. "Let's go up to the Scriptorium and wait for Fanny and Maidie there. They can do the final honors."

Maidie was dismayed. She was ready to embark on a love affair, and now Wendell's presence was forcing a point of honor. If he had just kept himself conveniently at home, she would have had no need to discuss Prudence or even to think about her request that she pretend to be falling in love with him. Well, she just wouldn't do it! That was all. She'd tell Wendell everything that Pru had told her, and she'd offer to help, but she absolutely would not pretend to false feelings when her interest was beginning to be engaged by Mr. Gilmichael. How could she encourage him if she pretended to be falling in love with Wendell?

As the evening wore on she realized that she hadn't taken into account that Wendell had come to depend on her to listen to his odiously horrible love sonnets and to his besotted praises of his adored Prudence. Nor had she taken into account that his dependence would be all the greater for his rejection. Denied Prudence by her ogreish father, betrayed by fiendish Chester, Wendell was badly in need of comfort. He clung to her as unwelcomely as a barnacle. Where had he been earlier in the day, when they might have talked privately? Seldom had Maidie's good manners been so tried or her natural sympathy for the woes of others so severely tested. She would have rather had Uncle Emery's guest, Sir Harold, monopolizing her attention—Mr. Gilmichael could not imagine that she had any interest in *him*.

The party walked to the lakeshore to observe the changing appearance of its waters as twilight advanced into night. Wendell managed to walk by her side, whispering his troubles into her ear. They all then went to the barn for cups of fresh milk, with Wendell again at her side. And in the orchard, where they carried their picnic supper, he threw his rug down beside hers. It was out of all bounds aggravating.

She reasoned, somewhat desperately, that if she could just assure Wendell that she'd think of something, he would leave her alone. Immediately acting upon the idea, she suggested they walk to the lake again in order to speak privately. Although how would their departure look to the others? Or rather, to Mr. Gilmichael? What could she say to explain?

Wendell, who had no motive for subterfuge, simply jumped up, held out his hand to Maidie, and said, "Come on, Maidie." To the others he explained, "We're going down to the lake. Watch the moon rise." His explanation was freighted with unfortunate romantic implications, but Maidie could think of no remark that would reduce a moonrise over a lake to the humdrum.

"Wendell, for goodness sake," she scolded, as soon as they were out of earshot, "is it necessary to hang on my skirts so? I wish when we go back that you will let me speak to someone else! It is exceedingly selfish of you to keep me all to yourself just so you can talk about Prudence."

Wendell was fulsome with apologies, but rationally pointed out that it was Maidie herself who had suggested they stroll down to the lake. And furthermore, she had always been willing to listen before, and now that he was in such desperate straits, he would have thought she would be sympathetic and willing to help him. But if she wasn't, just say the word and he'd take himself off home to brood alone.

Maidie couldn't help laughing. "You are such a fool, Wendell! And if I were Pru's parent, I wouldn't let you marry her for another ten years. If you will just behave with more circumspection—"

"I will not give up my political ideals!"

"I'm not suggesting you do so. I'm just suggesting that you stop dramatizing yourself and try to regulate your mind a little. Oh, I didn't intend to lecture! I'll ask Aunt Fanny to give you the same lecture she gave me about regulating my mind."

"I can't help the way I am. Poets are sensitive, you know. More so than others. 'Vain was Caesar and Newton's pride; They had no poet and they died.' That's Pope. Or almost, anyway."

Maidie seated herself on the stone wall. "Pope? I thought only Chester quoted Pope."

"Oh, well, everybody quotes Pope." Wendell sat down beside her.

"But why are we discussing poets?"

"I don't know. You started it."

"I did not. You . . . Oh, of all the aggravating . . . I suggested we walk to the lake in order to most vigorously urge you to exert yourself to more composure. I've told you that Prudence is prepared to wait for you, and that she does not expect a life of riches. I've assured you that you'll see Prudence at Aunt Fanny's party. Mrs. Califaxton has accepted for the whole family. If you just comport yourself with some dignity . . . And now that Chester has told Mr. Califaxton that you like her—"

"Oh, God!" Wendell clutched his head in his hands.

"—you must try to show him you are worthy of her."

"How can I? If Chester told him the whole story he knows my political views. He will know that I'm spied upon, and he's just the kind of man who would think that just because I am spied on that I should be. Dash it, but I wish them both at old Nick! And if you and Chester had just had the sense to follow my directions—it's just because you got yourself lost on the fells that everybody knows—"

Maidie leaped up, and looking down at him angrily, stamped her foot. "Don't you *dare* blame me, Wendell Duval, or Salvatore Toone, or whatever your absurd name is!"

He caught her hand. "I'm sorry, Maidie. Don't know what I'm saying. I'm so infernally distraught. Anyway, the spy's gone."

She pulled her hand from his clasp, but sat down again beside him. "Gone! How do you know?"

"Well, I think he's gone. He didn't follow me, at any rate. So our trap would have failed, anyway. I haven't seen him since Blea How. Didn't even see him then, as a matter of fact. It was you and Chester."

"Maybe he did follow you, and he's still lost on the fells."

"No, he didn't. And I'll thank you to dispense with levity. It means he's gone to give a report to whomever he reports to. But," Wendell observed darkly, "he'll be back. There've been other times when I haven't seen him for several days."

For a few minutes Maidie had forgotten that she was anxious to return to the others, but there was really nothing more to say about either the spy or Prudence that hadn't been already said. She got promptly to her feet again and urged their immediate return.

"Here they are!" Fanny said to Allan, as Maidie and Wendell approached. "But I do urge you to stay and take a glass of wine with us before you go."

"No, I must be going. Letters to write." Allan was feeling peevish, and having some difficulty not showing it. He stood up.

Fanny held out her hand to Emery for assistance in rising. "Mr. Gilmichael has been waiting for you, Maidie, in order to take his leave. I've urged him to stay for a glass of wine, but he insists he must write letters."

"But my dear Fanny, you mustn't reproach me, when you are the cause of my departure."

"I?"

"I must notify my family that my return will be delayed, thanks to a very persuasive lady."

Fanny laughed. "Well, make your adieus to Maidie, then, and we will expect to see you again very soon."

Emery objected, "No, indeed, Gilmichael. We shan't let you go before we take our wine. Plenty of time to write your letters tomorrow. Come, Maidie, I need your persuasive powers, since Fanny has capitulated so readily."

"Fie on you, Emery," Fanny exclaimed. "What can one say when blame has been laid so clearly at one's door?"

Maidie, obediently, tried with all the means in her power to convey to Mr. Gilmichael a willingness—even desire—that he stay. Casting about for a sensible reason to ask him to delay his departure, other than that she very much wanted him to, she said the first thing that came into her head. "Yes, do stay. We haven't had an opportunity to discuss Miss Austen's novel, or—except too briefly—the poetry of Mr. Blake."

"No, Maidie . . ." Fanny interrupted. "I'm weary of thinking.

Let's turn to the most frivolous activity imaginable! Let's catch fireflies and put them in a bottle . . . I've been eager to catch one this last hour. We can drink our wine by firefly light. Maidie, run back to the house and bring an empty bottle. You'll find several in the scullery."

"Foolish Fanny," Emery chided. "You shouldn't be chasing fireflies. You might fall."

"I am perfectly all right. Run, Maidie."

Allan held a debate with himself. Should he offer to accompany Miss Worthing to the kitchen, or should he not? Should he encourage this activity, or support Emery? Which would give him more opportunity to flirt with the bothersome girl? He who hesitates is lost, and Maidie was gone.

She was soon back, with not one but three bottles, a decision made in the hope that she might manage to manipulate the party to her liking. Catching fireflies with Mr. Gilmichael might be frivolous, but it might also be romantic.

"Three bottles, Maidie?" her uncle asked.

"I thought it would be easier if we worked in parties," she said lightly. "We can put them all in one bottle later."

"Very wise," Fanny commended her niece. "But I'm afraid I have been commanded to stay just where I am, and although in the ordinary way of things—"

"In the ordinary way of things she takes commands from no one, least of all from me."

"I'm increasing, you see," Fanny announced to Sir Harold.

Unnerved, Sir Harold replied, "Oh, yes, I see. Or rather, I, yes, I understand. Yes, indeed. Best thing."

"Joining us, Wendell? Sir Harold?" Emery asked.

Wendell, mindful of Maidie's wish that he detach himself from her skirts, refused. "My thanks, but I'll keep Fanny company."

Sir Harold also thanked them, but refused the invitation.

"Much prefer to recline here on the grass and watch the moon ascend into the heavens. If you will permit me such indolence."

"So, it's just the three of us, unless you prefer to keep a moon watch also, Gilmichael," Emery said.

"Like Fanny, I haven't chased fireflies since I can't remember when. Not since my school days, certainly. No, give me one of the bottles. I'll contribute to the harvest."

"Give us each a bottle, Maidie. The three of us will soon have enough bugs to satisfy Fanny, I'm sure. Let's go down by the lake. Seem to be more of them down there. But watch for cow pats."

As the three hunters departed, Wendell turned his attention to Sir Harold Mogglesby. He would much rather have been catching fireflies, but he wouldn't have Maidie claiming he was hanging on her skirts. "I understand that you are a fishing enthusiast, Sir Harold," Wendell stated unctuously. "I have never practiced the sport myself."

"So I understand. I'm told that your interests lie more in the literary and political line."

Wendell turned a surprised eye on Sir Harold, who laughed and said, "Oh, I'm no radical in my politics that I should have read one of your literary efforts. A lady happened to mention your radical poetry this afternoon."

"A lady?"

"Yes. Singularly talkative woman. Drove a spanking outfit, however. Touring the Lakes with only a groom and a hired dragon, she told me. Both of whom she parked at the inn in the village before driving out here. A woman quite out of the common way. I believe you discussed with her a system of public education for the lower orders that would be independent of our established church?"

"Oh, yes. A Miss Levinge. She's an enthusiastic Lancastrian—as I am. She intends to open a school in Manchester, I believe. Of course, we both agreed that eventually the state should provide a basic education for all, similar to, but an improvement on, the practice in Scotland."

"But if it is God's will that some are born into poverty and others born to riches, should not the poor bear it with fortitude, and is it not ordained that the higher orders accept their ordained responsibility to govern?" As Wendell showed signs of outrage, Sir Harold put up his hand. "Oh, I am not opposed to working people receiving what is due them for their labor. Or against bettering the lives of the poor. I merely ask your opinion. One hears so many opinions, these days! So many minds simply seething with every species of innovation, you know, that a man hardly knows what to think."

Wendell replied with what he considered excellently cogent arguments on the possibilities for the regeneration of humanity through education, and the matchless benefits of a democratic system for ensuring the happiness of the regenerated. Sir Harold listened respectfully, interjecting only an occasional question, or a "very sensible" or "quite so, indeed."

Fanny, sitting quietly beside them, felt a twinge of unease. It did seem that their guest was encouraging Wendell to ever more extravagant and inflammatory utterances. "But I have heard," Sir Harold was saying, "that educating the lower orders would enable them to read seditious literature, and stimulate in them ideas of insurrection."

Fanny could remain still no longer. "The French who stormed the Bastille could read, Sir Harold?"

Sir Harold laughed. "Ah, another assault mounted. But I protest. I am only assuming the role of Devil's advocate. I have also heard it argued that society is best organized with a proper hierarchy of classes."

"Hierarchy be damned!" Wendell exclaimed, forgetting cogent reasoning. Nothing made him madder than someone calling honest workers and people who never had a chance in this life the lower orders.

"And are you a republican, then, as well as a democrat, Mr. Duval?"

"How can one not be?"

"Then you would overthrow the monarchy, and strip king, Church, and peerage of their governing powers?"

Fanny, now nervously anxious to divert Wendell, responded quickly. "Oh, I can't think anyone of sense would go so far as to reject a monarchy in England, where our monarchs govern on sufferance. The Regent rules by will of Parliament. Not to mention that we parted one king from his head and not so long ago sent another packing." It had most decidedly been time that she intervene.

Wendell would not be diverted. "I would dispense with monarchs altogether, not only in Europe where monarchy is more despotic, but here in England as well. I am not so foolish, however, as to suppose it immediately possible, now that we have helped a Bourbon return to the French throne. Royalty will go to the aid of royalty, while claiming to defend liberty. As our recent war proved!"

To Fanny's immense relief, she heard the firefly hunters returning. Ruthlessly interrupting Sir Harold, who appeared to wish Wendell to turn his attention to the problems of unmerited wealth and sinecures, she scrambled to her feet and called, "Have you caught many?"

"Enough," Emery called back.

"Now do get up, Wendell, Sir Harold. It's time for our wine, and for that we must return to the house. I hope, Sir Harold, that you are not so nice that you consider a kitchen unworthy of those who can read? Wendell, pick up that basket. And Emery, you take the rugs."

"But you banter with me, Mrs. Clarke. Has it not been said that truth emerges from minds scraping against each other?"

"I believe you refer to Mr. Godwin," Allan stated, repressing an impulse to wink at Fanny. Couldn't say he was behindhand in his education!

He might better have kept his mouth firmly closed, for instead of Maidie for companion on the short walk back to the house, Sir Harold attached himself to his side. "But it is why Mr. and Mrs. Clarke's teas, or suppers—or whatever their gatherings might be called—are so stimulating. Such a variety of company! Such cross-purposes and exciting ideas and theories! Simply electrifying!"

Allan considered a set-down, and then quickly reconsidered. He had chosen to meet the world as an equal, here in the Lakes, and was ashamed of his momentary impulse to exercise his privilege as a peer of the realm to indulge a longing to belittle preposterous fellows like Sir Harold. "Yes, very stimulating," he said mildly. "And when you consider that there is excellent fishing, and in such magnificent surroundings. Are you an admirer of the picturesque, Sir Harold?"

Sir Harold was, although he couldn't agree with all of Gilpin's principles. Of course, all theories were modified with time, as indeed the principles governing the picturesque had been . . .

Allan murmured appropriately, and considered Miss Worthing's graceful form as she preceded him. With Duval by her side again. The fellow was a pest. Now what was it he was murmuring in her seemingly willing ear?

Wendell was murmuring an apology. "Couldn't help sticking to your skirts . . . that fellow, Sir Harold . . ."

Maidie, wondering if messages could be sent from brain to brain, cut his apology off.

"Just don't talk."

Wendell was happy not to talk. His own brain was seething with the arguments he would deploy should he get Sir Harold in range again.

She could hear the low voices of the conversation behind her, and concentrated intently on her message. "I'd rather be walking with you, Mr. Gilmichael," she beamed silently backward. For good measure she turned, and sent a tangible smile straight at him.

Happily, one way or another, her messages were received. He stationed himself by her side as they drank their wine by the fitful and fading light of fireflies. But now she was exactly where she wanted to be, she found herself without anything to say. Her mind seemed to have gone blank.

Allan, laboring under a similar disability, took the easiest route. "I hope you have recovered from your ordeal on the mountain, Miss Worthing."

"Oh, yes. And how can you call it an ordeal? Although I am very sorry that I caused anyone concern for me, it was in truth a wonderful adventure! Someday I should like to climb to the very top of one of the peaks." But it was not practical to suppose that there was any chance of going climbing alone with Mr. Gilmichael. She cast about for some other activity . . .

With a disgraceful want of brilliance, he asked, "Have you learned to prefer the country to the city, then, Miss Worthing?"

"I always wished my father would buy a country property. But this is my only experience outside of London, you know, aside from summer visits to the seashore."

"And how would you entertain yourself in the country? You would miss, I suppose, the theaters and grand balls. And perhaps improving lectures?"

"Well, one does enjoy those activities immensely of course. Especially improving lectures. But in the country one can walk wherever one likes, read so many books, and dig in the garden. Aunt Fanny is teaching me the difference between a flower and a weed. And I would want a pond or a stream where I could fish . . ." *Aha!*

"I was not aware you had taken up fishing, Miss Worthing."

"Well, I haven't. But I would so like to learn . . ."

Allan knew as well as Maidie that they had managed to maneuver themselves exactly where they wanted to be.

Within minutes it was settled. He would call for her on the morrow, and with Fanny's permission they would begin Maidie's lessons. No reason for a chaperon, when they would be right in plain sight out there on Krigsmere, under the eye of any passerby, or Fanny herself.

"And have you any more novels to lend me, with which to divert myself when in need of relief from the political tomes that Duval plies me with?"

"I have just finished a diverting novel by Mr. Peacock . . ."

Fanny, engaged meanwhile in an effort to keep Wendell from voicing his radical notions so emphatically, was horrified to hear him invite Sir Harold to look over some of his political literature, and even more horrified to hear him add, "Some of the most powerful tracts I've loaned to some workmen from Kendal, but plenty left to give you a start in comprehending the need for radical reform . . ."

Emery, catching warning signals from Fanny, was not a little alarmed himself; distributing to laborers publications the government considered seditious was against the law. "Forgive me, cousin, but I was thinking of carrying Sir Harold off tomorrow to fish one of my favorite tarns. Fine angling any time of day— and a midday repast always willingly supplied by the farmer's wife whose house lies close by."

"I thank you all for your kindness, but I must be off tomorrow for London."

Emery frowned. "I thought you said you would be another week with us . . ."

"Perhaps I didn't make myself clear. I hope to return within a week. But tomorrow, indeed, I must be off to London."

Wendell bowed, and took an admirably terse leave. He'd put ideas in the fellow's head, anyway, he told himself with satisfaction.

Fanny, now it was no longer necessary to prevent Sir Harold from hearing more on dangerous topics, could turn her attention to Maidie and Allan. And was struck with the most entertaining notion! She bent a brightly interested gaze on Emery and Sir Harold, but her mind was wandering happily in thoughts of romance. When Allan stated that Miss Worthing had expressed an interest in learning something of the art of fishing, and that he had offered himself as teacher, she felt herself to have been perspicacious beyond the ordinary. The possibilities of romance ran such riot in her brain that it was not until later, as she was drifting off to sleep, that her uneasiness about Sir Harold returned.

The uneasiness drove away sleep. As she reviewed the conversation in the orchard she was even more certain that Sir Harold had been deliberately leading Wendell to express his political opinions, and in the most radical way possible. "Emery," she whispered, but his breathing remained deep and slow. Well, she needn't disturb him tonight, but tomorrow . . . Although she didn't believe it would be wise to mention yet what she suspected of love ablooming. On that thought she fell asleep.

Twelve

Maidie's eyes opened to bright sunshine slanting through her window. She sat up to enjoy a morning view of Krigsmere. The lake! Fishing lesson! She had overslept!

She dressed quickly, searched hastily and unsuccessfully for the novel she had promised Mr. Gilmichael, and then hurried to the library where she might have left it. There she came unexpectedly upon her aunt and uncle, still in dressing gown and night robe, drinking their morning chocolate.

"Oh! I'm sorry. I didn't know anyone would be here . . ."

"Yes, Maidie?" her uncle asked.

"I just wanted to retrieve *Headlong Hall* before going down to breakfast . . ."

"Peacock's latest? Saw it yesterday." Emery, after digging under a pile of newspapers, found the novel and handed it to her.

"Thank you, Uncle Emery." Blushing, she then reminded her aunt that Mr. Gilmichael had very obligingly offered her a fishing lesson. "But I wish to be certain that you have no need of me, Aunt Fanny, with Mama and Papa and Aunt Seraphina to arrive tomorrow."

"No, run along and enjoy yourself. But I'm afraid you'll first have to face Sir Harold at the breakfast table."

"If you had mentioned, Maidie, that you were interested in the contemplative man's recreation—"

Fanny hastily interrupted her spouse. "I've kept her too busy until now to even think about spending any time contemplating anything, let alone your favorite recreation—and with her young friends across the lake, it's a wonder she found a minute even today. Now run along, Maidie. You must have some breakfast before you go out." Really, Emery was so slow!

With interesting prospects for the morning ahead, it was with very little attention that Maidie faced Sir Harold across the breakfast table, and it was with a start that she realized he was waiting for a reply. "I'm sorry. Did you speak?"

"It was nothing of importance. I only said, a delightful evening last night."

"Yes, wasn't it?" Maidie applied herself to her porridge.

After a moment of silence, Sir Harold tried again. "You and Duval must be very good friends, Miss Worthing."

"Why should you think so, sir?"

"Two young people—I've always thought that young people preferred each other's company to that of their elders. But perhaps I err?"

"Perhaps. For indeed, I enjoy my aunt's company quite as much as that of many of my younger friends."

"Ah, but your aunt is so exceptional. Such a lively woman, and of such intellectual accomplishment! I have been quite awed, I freely acknowledge. Still, one supposes that she is often at her writing, for her prodigious production of work testifies to her diligence. But perhaps that is the case with Mr. Duval also?"

"Yes, he must devote time to his poetry."

Another short silence followed as Maidie refilled her porridge bowl.

"An interesting young man. We had a stimulating discussion last night. So well informed! I only regret that business calls me to London and that I could not spend further pleasant hours with him. Or some pleasant hours fishing with your uncle. *That* I regret to the extreme. I do dearly love pursuing the elusive trout . . ."

"I'm sure my uncle and Mr. Duval regret your departure. Although the trout may not."

"Oh. Ho, ho. So amusing, Miss Worthing."

Maidie closed her lips firmly. Quite unfairly she told herself that she did despise people who pretended that silly remarks were the best wit in the world.

Mrs. Eckston entered with a platter of eggs and ham in one hand and a pot of fresh coffee in the other. Sir Harold and Maidie served themselves, and eyed each other across the table.

The door opened on their silence. Allan stepped into the room. "Sorry to interrupt your breakfast, Miss Worthing, but Mrs. Eckston insisted that I join you and drink a cup of coffee. I apologize for arriving early. I believe my watch is becoming unreliable. Good morning, Sir Harold."

"Ah, good morning, Mr. Gilmichael." Sir Harold's glance, and the tone of voice in which he pronounced the simple honorific, Mister, held such a world of insinuation that Allan was immediately on guard—although the oily fellow's next statement was innocuous enough to satisfy a polite tea party. "And a beautiful morning it is!" he chirruped. "How I regret that I must make my departure from these enchanting hills and azure lakes so immediately. Such splendor lifts one's soul to such contemplative tranquility!"

Maidie was hard pressed not to laugh, and even more so as Allan replied with an excess of gravity that he too found that contemplating the lake and fell scenery was soothing. To avoid disgracing herself, she had recourse to the coffeepot. "May I serve you more coffee, Sir Harold?"

With a smile for Maidie, Sir Harold graciously assented to being served, but he directed his next statement to Allan. "Miss Worthing and I were discussing Duval's political interests. So exciting! So challenging! One goes through life simply assuming that the world is going along ever so nicely, you know, and then one meets a young man with a spark in his eye—"

"And a fever in his brain?" Allan interrupted.

"Oh, I would never say so. I would rather say with a brain in ferment; and so full of vigorous activity . . . so energetic in spreading his ideas. He has such a sufficiency."

Maidie looked up sharply. Had she detected a hint of mockery in his voice? But Sir Harold was flowing blandly on.

"And not only among those of us from the Better Classes, but among those who would never open a political work—and wouldn't comprehend it if they did. Not only is young Duval a scholar, but a teacher, an instructor of men, I would say. Meritorious, to put it simply."

No, Maidie concluded—no whimsy in this man, his description of Wendell overblown and distorted. "You asked if we are friends—Mr. Duval and I. I'm afraid I was distracted from answering by a lamentably vulgar desire for my breakfast. To answer your question now, Wendell spends much time lazing about the hills with me and with Miss Califaxton and her brother. The Califaxtons—our neighbors—you surely have noticed their house on the promontory across the lake? The elder Mr. Califaxton is a man of considerable manufacturing and property interests."

"Oh, yes. Considerable," Allan echoed cooperatively.

"We sketch, and read novels to each other. For all Mr. Duval's highflown talk he enjoys a good novel quite as much as we do, you may be assured!"

Rival or not, Allan had no stomach for spying, which Sir Harold's questions smacked of. "Duval has an interest in fell wrestling, and spends much of his time training with the locals. The Cumbrians, you know, are exceptional sportsmen. I understand he intends to participate in the village contests later this summer, preparing for the final event in the fall. Such a strapping, well set-up fellow—should be good at it."

"Indeed? I had no notion of it," was the all of Sir Harold's response to these testimonies to Wendell's frivolities. "I believe I'll just serve myself a bit more of that cheese, and this delicious ham. Made from mutton here in the Lakes, is it not?"

Allan set down his coffee cup. "I don't wish to hurry you, Miss Worthing, but it grows late . . ."

"Yes, so it does. I'll just run up and change my shoes."

While she was gone, Sir Harold reverted once again to Wendell's activities, seeming, Allan thought, to want to determine if he matched practice to theory. He answered noncommittally, until Sir Harold, tiring of that unproductive line of questioning, turned his insinuating remarks in Allan's own direction.

"And how are you enjoying your own holiday? Or should I perhaps say *respite* from the pedestrian responsibilities that *will* consume us if we permit. I assume you are, like myself, a property owner?"

"Yes. I am a property owner. And yes I enjoy a respite from time to time. I am particularly fond of angling. By the way, what length of line do you find best in our southern, more placid rivers? I assume of course that your property is in the south of England?"

The conversation quickly assumed the dimensions of a duel: while Allan attempted to determine just how much of Sir Harold's enthusiasm for fishing was genuine, Sir Harold attempted to trap him into a revelation that would suggest his true identity. By the time Maidie returned—and a devilish long time it seemed—Allan had concluded that Sir Harold was an indifferent angler, certainly no fly fisherman, and that his professed enthusiasm for a Lakeland residence in order to pursue the sport more seriously was pretense. But to what purpose? His interest was clearly in Duval, and the insinuations about his own identity merely symptoms of Sir Harold's annoyance at his failure to elicit information. But, again, to what purpose? First the ridiculous fellow in the wig, and now Sir Harold. Why such interest in Duval?

As they walked to the lake, Maidie stated emphatically, "That man is a spy."

"I should, by all that's reasonable, disagree. Although I can't credit a political motive, I admit that the man arouses suspicion."

"Have you written to your father's friend to ask if a Salvatore Toone is spied upon?" Maidie peeked up at him from under her bonnet. "Now that I have revealed to you Wendell's real name?"

"As a matter of fact, I have done so, but with Parliament approaching dissolution I doubt he will have time for further investigation . . ." Allan did not add that in this third letter, (written with some weariness) he had again mentioned that an inquiry of Bow Street might be productive.

"Couldn't you send another explaining how important it is? We mustn't let Wendell be arrested! He has no idea of leading any revolution . . . And even if he did, we should do our utmost to protect him from arrest and prosecution! Surely you can't think that it's wrong to speak freely as he does, and to urge the—"

"The regeneration of humanity?"

"Well, yes. Even though you may laugh . . ."

"I'm not laughing." He put on a serious face. "See, not the least suggestion of a smile. But now, Miss Worthing, let's forget Duval's problems and turn our mind to the important lesson on which we have embarked. How shall we begin?"

"Perhaps by getting in the boat?"

"That is a good first step. Have you learned to row yet, Miss Worthing?" he asked as he unshipped the oars.

"Aunt Fanny and I went out twice—but as you perhaps know, she hasn't been feeling quite the thing. And Prudence and I always meant to, but since I learned that she can't swim . . ."

"And you do swim?"

"Oh, yes. Mama and I have been going to the seashore since before I can remember. But I'm not at all certain I could rescue someone."

"I am relieved I shan't have to rescue you. Now, shall we begin your lesson?"

"That is why we are here, is it not?"

Allan ignored this patently false statement. "We're not likely to be so lucky as to take a trout. The best fishing is when there's a breeze—and earlier in the day. But perch are indifferent to time of day, and seem to feed anywhere. Not much challenge for the sportsman, but excellent for a beginner."

"Oh, dear, will this be too terribly tiresome for you, Mr. Gilmichael?"

"My pardons, Miss Worthing. I certainly didn't intend to seem so ungallant. There is much pleasure to be had in a leisurely day spent tranquilly contemplating—is that how Sir Harold phrased it?—this azure lake within its fearsome hills. And contemplating a lovely companion, I might add." Now here he was, dropping into idiotic gallantries again! He hastened to return to stilted commonplaces. "And even the most gullible fish can often provide a challenge . . ."

Maidie feared that his reference to a lovely companion was threatening to reduce her to simpering, something she absolutely never did, and hastily replied, "Aunt Fanny says that's the half of fishing—the enjoyment of the woods and streams—of nature . . ."

"Yes. And respite—again as Sir Harold puts it—from the burdens of responsibility. Your uncle and I find pleasure also in provisioning our own tables . . . Now, your first lesson: we'll use worms today. One also uses minnows and insects of various kinds, depending on where one is fishing and the type of fish."

Allan took a worm from the container at his feet. "Now observe how I do this. Then you may bait your own hook."

"*Worms!* I thought we would be using those artificial insects that you and Uncle Emery discuss so enthusiastically when you meet!"

"Fly fishing requires more practice than we can attempt today. But all anglers, whatever the hoped-for catch, and whether in stream or lake, use live bait."

"And if I have not the heart for it, then I am destined never to be an angler. Is that not so?"

But Maidie did bait her hook, and with sufficient skill to win praise from her teacher.

"Now, one casts one's line out. So."

Maidie's effort was less skillful than her baiting exercise, and she was required to cast again. She won no praise from her instructor, but was not asked to repeat her effort. They drifted easily, Allan making occasional corrections in their position by a casual application of the oars, reeling in line and casting again, at which Maidie slowly improved. By the turn of fortune commonly called beginner's luck, Maidie made the first strike—a matter for excitement as Allan gave her instructions for taking the fish. "Carefully, carefully—you don't want to lose it."

He was amused by her delight in her catch, and then her dismay as she realized that the fish would not passively give up its life. "Can't we knock it on the head, or something?" she appealed, looking up at him with those dark-lashed, houri eyes. She was really such a tantalizing morsel!

The boat had drifted close to the island, where overhanging boughs provided some shade, but as the sun rose higher even the perch seemed determined to leave off feeding and it was evident to both that fishing for the moment was over. Nonetheless, although there were only three fish in their basket, both could consider it a profitable fishing trip.

"Miss Worthing . . ." Allan began, as he again took the oars preparatory to returning to shore.

"Mr. Gilmichael?"

He ignored the widened eyes and suppressed smile. "There's little likelihood of catching anything more, and I fear you will find that the sun grows uncomfortably warm . . ."

"I am not such a delicate flower, sir, that I wilt in the sun. But yes, we must return, I suppose." She did not try to disguise her reluctance.

"Perhaps I could give you a lesson in rowing," he said, as he bent to the oars. "This evening, when it's cooler."

"Oh, yes, I should like that so much!"

Allan stepped from the boat to pull it close enough for Maidie to disembark. She gave him the fish basket and their gear, and then, accepting his offered hand, stepped ashore.

"Thank you, Mr. Gilmichael." But her hand remained in his as they stared at each other . . . he's going to kiss me! she thought. She caught her breath, and her lips parted.

Allan compulsively tightened his grip on her hand as he drew a deep breath to steady the pace of his heartbeat.

Maidie's eyes, still staring into his, registered her surprise as she tried to pull her hand free from his painful grip. He eased his hold, but did not release her hand.

"You . . ." she began, but the intensity in his face caused her to again catch her breath and the sentence to die on her lips.

"I can't kiss you here," Allan said, which was not what he had intended to say at all. The thought in his head had been that he should apologize.

"No," she breathed, and then she bowed her head against his breast. His free hand lightly caressed her hair. It was only an instant, so brief that any watchers might have wondered if their eyes had deceived them.

When her head came up again, he saw—not a maiden willing to fall into his arms, but an imp. He hastily released her hand.

"How *very* improper that would have been!" she exclaimed. "Really, Mr. Gilmichael, I can't think what you are about!"

"I apologize, Miss Worthing," he said stiffly.

"Whatever for?" She looked up at him, wide-eyed. "If you are apologizing for wanting to kiss me, my nose will be sadly out of joint!"

He restrained with difficulty the impulse to kiss her then and there, in full view of God and the Devil. "You tempt me, Miss Worthing! I would not wish such a sad fate for such an agreeable nose."

"Agreeable! What a strange choice of word! But I seem to be seeking a compliment on that feature, and I wouldn't for the world. But I shouldn't at all like it out of joint!"

Could she possibly tell him any more clearly? Those still intent eyes brought a faint heat to her cheeks. She looked away, to the hills beyond, bit her lip, and fell silent. There was not a doubt in the all of creation what his feelings were, or hers—at least as far as kissing went. She must put them on a steadier footing before they faced Mrs. Eckston, or Aunt Fanny, or one of the farmhands.

And they did have another concern. "I was thinking, before I was set upon so abruptly—" She caught herself up hastily. She must stop this teasing and provoking. "I was thinking that I must ask your permission to tell Aunt Fanny and Uncle Emery of your belief that Sir Harold is not a fisherman, and that you too suspect him of fell purpose."

"I had intended to speak to them about my already aroused suspicion of the man on our return." Why in bloody hell did the bulk of their conversations seem always to revolve around that clownish young man?

They delivered their catch to the kitchen, where Mrs. Eckston made a great fuss over Maidie's fish. "And Mrs. Fanny and Mr. Clarke are waiting for you in the Scriptorium. They said to tell you both to just go right up. My, my, Miss Maidie, it's as pretty a fish as any your uncle has brought me."

"It's only one fish, Mrs. Eckston."

"We mustn't praise her beyond her due, you know. One fish does not a fisherman make."

Mrs. Eckston laughed. "No. Now go on, both of you."

They passed through the library, and climbed the narrow spiral stair to the Scriptorium.

"What a comfortable room!" Allan exclaimed. "I must admire how you have converted this old Peel tower."

"We can't claim credit, I'm afraid." Emery laid his pencil down. "It was two owners before us—a prosperous farmer who owned the entire valley and an extensive sheep range. It was his successor who started the property on the decline. Mortgaged land to pay for some questionable improvements, and then an extravagant son . . ."

"Do desist, Emery! We didn't ask Mrs. Eckston to send them both up to us in order to talk about our farm, but about Wendell and that strange fellow, Sir Harold—a government spy if I ever saw one!"

"Did you ever see one, Fan?"

"Well, no. But if I saw one, I'm sure he'd resemble Sir Harold to an inch."

Maidie and Allan brought this discussion to termination with a description of their breakfast conversations with Sir Harold and their suspicions of his motives.

"You confirm what Fanny and I have feared. I walked over to Wendell's cottage after my breakfast to warn him that he may be under surveillance, but Old Peg says he left. To practice for a wrestling contest, I surmise."

"Mr. Gilmichael plans to send another query to his father's friend, don't you, sir?"

Fanny reserved speculation on this indication of influence. "Excellent. But without certain knowledge of Sir Harold's intent, Emery and I think that we absolutely must get Wendell away for a time. He could take passage for the South Seas on a merchant vessel under an assumed name."

"He already has an assumed name, Fan."

"Well, then, another one. Two as good as one, it's said. Of course, once one starts a deception, who knows where it will end? But to leave off irrelevant philosophical speculation, surely these preposterous prosecutions will come to an end! The government must see how dreadfully imperative reform is . . ."

"We must tell Papa, I think," Maidie hesitantly offered. "He won't approve Wendell's politics, but I'm sure he doesn't approve spying, and could help Wendell avoid arrest. Although Wendell is so foolish that he will insist on being arrested, depend upon it." Maidie turned to Allan. "And your father's friend perhaps could help."

"Perhaps."

"If we can find the ridiculous young simpleton . . . I do worry where he can have got to."

Further discussion proving unprofitable, and with nothing worthwhile to add to it, Allan excused himself. "I can see myself out," he assured them, but all insisted on accompanying him down the stairs, through the library, and into the kitchen. Fanny and Emery wanted to see Maidie's fish.

A steady rain set in shortly after. Maidie tried not to watch the sky too eagerly, but after an hour of intermittent squalls, between which a fine drizzle steadily fell, she despaired of another meeting with Mr. Gilmichael that day. During an intermission in the deluge, a note from the gentleman arrived. "Unlike the weather," he wrote, "I am steady in purpose, and when your parents' visit is at an end it is my hope that we may renew our lessons in Lakeland skills. Meanwhile, I should like to call this evening, if convenient."

This suggestion of a change in his plans—for hadn't he said he must leave them soon?—she would leave for pleasant speculation later and meanwhile indulge in anticipation of his evening call. But why did he come tonight? Only Wendell's affairs? Or to see her again? It was too early for a declaration.

Maidie was too unsure of her own heart to believe that Mr. Gilmichael could be certain of his. But that he wanted to see her—that must surely be the case, for he had not cried off the projected lesson, only postponed it. After a few minutes spent composing herself, she went to Fanny to inform her of Allan's proposed visit.

The rain at last stopped, but clouds descended the mountainside from the oppressive skies, to lie over the lake like a great white pillow. Maidie's spirits, however, were all sunshine.

Wendell, as it happened, had spent the morning bearding a lion. Craftily, he chose to approach the lion through the lioness. When the liveried footman answered the Califaxton door, he casually slipped a sovereign into the man's hand, and announced that he was calling on Mrs. Califaxton. The obliging footman, knowing full well who ruled this particular pride, showed Wendell into a sitting room, carried his card (on which Wendell had scribbled a most affecting plea) to his mistress, and then retired to contemplate how to dispose of his ill-gotten wealth.

It took very little time for Wendell to persuade Mrs. Califaxton of his sincere love for her daughter, and of the certain success of his lofty future. Mrs. Califaxton, who harbored a softness for the boy, and who prided herself on her democratic principles, promised to soon bring her husband around, and left him alone to contemplate his shoes.

"Won't do him any good," Mr. Califaxton warned her.

"If you have the sense you were born with, Mr. Califaxton, you will take my advice." She opened the door herself for Wendell, announced him, then left to listen at another door that connected the bookroom—where the interview would take place—with a smaller room beyond.

Wendell wasted no time in softening up his opposition, correctly assuming that Mr. Califaxton would prefer the direct and most economical approach. "Sir, I would like your permission to pay my addresses to your daughter."

"Well, I figured as much. I must refuse."

Since this was exactly what Wendell had expected, he was not cast down. "May I present my case, sir?"

"If it pleases you to waste your time."

"I know that my political opinions are offensive to some, and that I am liable to prosecution by the government . . ."

"You needn't waste your breath. My sons and Mrs. Califaxton have put in a word for you. I've no objection to your politics." Mr. Califaxton chose not to mention that his sons had suggested that Wendell's political opinions were still in the process of formation (John) and that it was all just bamboozle anyway (Chester). "In fact," he added, surprising Wendell, "I respect a man who's willing to face the consequences of his actions and of his convictions."

"Then I'm to understand that it is only my lack of fortune?"

"That's right."

"May I ask that before you refuse me on those grounds that Miss Califaxton be permitted to express her own desires in respect to an alliance with me? I do not anticipate, sir, that I will go through life penniless. I have an adequate education, and fully intend to pursue a career in law. Only after I am established in my profession will I consider standing for Parliament. As for my poetry, I realize that sacrifice I must. Miss Califaxton understands that I am not a rich man . . ."

"Love in a cottage, eh? Ain't what it's cracked up to be, I can tell you."

"No, sir. Neither Miss Califaxton nor I suffer from romantic delusions. If you would permit her to speak, sir, I'm certain she would assure you—"

Mr. Califaxton held up his hand. "No more need be said. Money should marry money. Pru's too young to know her own mind, whatever notions she may have put in your head. And I mean no insult, but an heiress is always a target for penniless young men."

"Excuse me, sir. I am not poverty stricken. I have an annuity that will provide for us in some comfort during my preparation for the bar, and will be an addition to our income thereafter. If I had not met Miss Califaxton, and had remained unmarried, I would have devoted the money to relieving the poor, but I well recognize that once a man takes a wife . . ."

"And what might the income be?"

"Five hundred a year, sir."

"Five-hundred-a-year?" Mr. Califaxton came perilously close to shouting. His face reddened alarmingly. "Have you rats in your head? Can you think I would give my only daughter away for five hundred a year!"

"But sir—"

"Don't speak!"

Mr. Califaxton rose to pace off his agitation. He drew a deep, calming breath before turning to Wendell. "What in the name of all that's sensible are you thinking of, man? I'll be frank with you. I expect my sons and my daughter to marry with the purpose of bringing capital into the family; I don't fancy my money watering some other field. I might forgo a fortune for a penniless duke or earl, but not for less. You have nothing at all to offer. Now leave me in peace." Mr. Califaxton drew another deep breath. He pointed to the door. "Get out."

Wendell tried desperately to keep his voice at a reasonable timbre. "I can only offer you my promise to care tenderly for Prudence, and that she will never be sacrificed to my efforts to bring about the greater happiness of humanity. And I should point out that when we marry, Pru and I, you will be relieved of one of your five heirs, not gaining a burden in my person. I have determined to refuse both a dowry and her inheritance, sir. I cannot accept—"

"That does it!" Mr. Califaxton slammed his fist on his ample and well-breeched knee. "I've dealt with plenty of jinglebrains in my time, but I have never before encountered such want of sense! I am astounded, Duval, that you have the temerity—no, I'll speak more plainly—that you have the *gall* to even propose such a course, or such a life for my little Pru."

"Sir, Prudence has a right to speak for herself."

Mr. Califaxton rose in purple wrath. "Get out of my house, you . . . you *nincompoop!*"

Wendell's frazzled nerves might have found some balm had he heard Mrs. Califaxton's caustic remarks, which were delivered immediately after he had left her husband's presence. The good lady burst from behind the door where she had been listening and sailed in to deliver a scold that even Mr. Califaxton, long accustomed to her tirades, found difficult to bear and impossible to ignore.

"How can you refuse such a sincere and honest man? He has been all that's forthcoming about his situation . . . He and Prudence would soon give over these follies of youth . . ."

Mr. Califaxton resolutely took up his newspaper and tried to let the tide of recrimination roll over him, until Mrs. Califaxton, irritated beyond endurance, snatched the paper from his very hands, and delivered herself of a lengthy scold on the subject of people who made their fortunes in trade and manufacturing opposing democratic inclinations.

"But that ain't the argument!" Mr. Califaxton shouted in exasperation. "The man has no money! I'm not going to see Pru married to a posturing, penniless, nincompoop politician."

"You are a fool, Mr. Califaxton, if you can't see that that young man is going to be important some day!"

"And you've been consulting the Gypsies. Or some other such nonsense."

"We'll just see about that!" she rejoined, and beat a dignified retreat to pen a note to Wendell not to despair.

* * *

While Wendell was working off anger and desperation by tramping through the rain at top speed to Patterdale, where he could expect a rousing match with one of his wrestling friends, Allan was devoting his afternoon to some profound and serious thought.

He was well on his way to being in love, and that meant paying formal addresses, which in turn meant speaking to guardians. And that in turn meant candor on the part of the suitor. Fanny's words had struck home. What was it she'd said? That once one starts a deception, who knows where it will end? It was time for him to stop this foolish business! The inquisitive lady, followed so closely by Sir Harold's suspicious questioning, demonstrated the flimsy structure of his masquerade.

Only Fanny and Emery were in the drawing room when the maid Stella announced him.

"Perhaps you should step upstairs, Fan, and see what's keeping Maidie," Emery suggested.

But before Fanny had stirred herself, Maidie came into the room, offering her apologies for not being present to also receive Mr. Gilmichael. Fanny immediately saw why her niece had been dawdling.

Although the extra care Maidie had taken at her toilet was obvious to Fanny, Allan's only thought was how charming and very pretty she looked. And, as Fanny also saw, that she seemed more demure and withdrawn than was her usual wont.

Emery, oblivious to such arcane matters, was prepared to address the subject of Wendell immediately. A second enquiry of Old Peggy had simply elicited the statement that there was no need to worry about Mr. Wendell; such a strapping big fellow could take care of himself. Emery wondered if he could have recognized danger, and gone into temporary hiding.

Fanny remarked that when Wendell had left them the previous

evening, he had not been suspicious of Sir Harold's motives. "Although I recognized his insinuating questions almost immediately. One must despise those who present themselves falsely. When imperative, in order to escape unjust persecution, but otherwise—no."

This was close to home indeed! Allan gathered his resolution. There was no postponing it longer. "Fanny, Emery, Miss Worthing, I have a confession to make about myself. I'm ashamed to tell you that . . . that I too am hiding my identity."

He had stunned his audience into silence, until Maidie exclaimed, in an attempt to relieve the shocked surprise they all were feeling, "Mr. Gilmichael, I will not be able to bear it if you're to tell us that you are a spy, too, or that your name is . . . is . . . Nero!"

He gave her a relieved smile. "No, not Nero. Nor Caesar, nor Augustus. And I am not a spy. Just pretending to be something I'm not. Or rather, pretending not to be something I am." How was he to make the announcement without sounding too impossibly lordly—er—no. Proud.

"Well, for pity's sake, what are you, then?" Fanny asked. "I'm simply fainting with unrelieved curiosity!"

Allan got up from his chair and paced across the room to stare out the window for a moment. He turned to face them. "I'm terribly sorry, but I am not a distant relative of the Marquis of Enett . . ."

Emery, with what Fanny thought a consummate want of intelligence, said in a puzzled voice, "But it's no matter to us whether you have noble relatives or not! I can't think why you should apologize."

"Emery, you are a worse simpleton than Wendell! But there, my dear, don't be distressed. I recall you were never at all good at riddles. If you will think only a moment, he says that he has been pretending *not to be* something that he *is!*"

Maidie's eyes widened as she caught the import of Fanny's words. "You are the marquis."

"Botheration!" Fanny exclaimed. "Must we now begin to address you as Enett?"

Maidie was overwhelmed by a vague, empty feeling in the pit of her stomach. A marquis! It was nearly as bad as a duke! How Papa would fuss! And, of course, perhaps Mr. Gilmichael—Lord Enett—or his relations would object to the daughter of a commoner . . . As Fanny and Emery declared their astonishment, she was silent, her hands clasped tightly in her lap. That he was casting surreptitious glances her way as he answered their questions only told her that he was thinking how he had deceived her of his intentions. But what intention? He'd only declared an intention to kiss her, which in her experience with gentlemen wasn't so very unusual.

"And you, Miss Worthing, you are silent. Have you suspected my perfidy?"

"No, my lord. Never."

"Please, Miss Worthing. Not my lord. Can't we remain as we have been?"

"But, my lord," Maidie answered, her nose considerably in the air (and out of joint, too, truth to tell), "how else can one address you? Mr. Gilmichael certainly won't do, and I couldn't presume to call you by your given name! Yet Enett is so unnatural to my tongue, so formal . . ."

"I think, Allan," Fanny put in, "that you should continue to be Mr. Gilmichael to the world at large. Here in the Lakes, that is. As I have said, who knows where deception will lead?" She caught her lip between her teeth. She was arguing against herself, as Emery would point out if she permitted it. "What I mean to say is that it would be ever so much better if Emery and I, after you have left us, should just let slip out—accidentally here and there, you know—your true identity. When you visit Krigsmere again, the world will be accustomed to it. But these last few days—for haven't you said that you must leave us soon?—we will just go on as we have been."

Emery's brow was clouded. With Maidie's father arriving on the morrow . . . "And Sam, you know . . ." he began.

Fanny rushed in before he made some horrid mistake and properly put his foot in it. "What has Sam to say to anything? I was thinking of the Califaxtons, who might be resentful, you do realize. And our poor dear rector. Not to forget how awkward socially . . . Think how harrowingly difficult it was for Allan to tell us—just three of us—in the most informal and friendly of surroundings . . ."

Emery was not so dense that he didn't catch Fanny's intent, although he might be missing her motive. Always awkward with Sam where the aristocracy was concerned! "Perhaps you're right, Fan. What do you say, Allan? You must be the one to decide."

"It will be uncomfortable and even embarrassing, I admit, and especially since Fanny means to put me on exhibit as a pillar of respectability."

The new and interesting turn of events drove Wendell's affairs from all their heads. Allan's explanation of his reasons for the deception was more immediately interesting than worrying about a romantic young radical.

Allan, on the other hand, was worrying because Maidie, unlike her aunt and uncle, seemed to suffer no curiosity. "Perhaps Miss Worthing will see me out?" he suggested. As they walked together to the door, he said, "You were very quiet tonight, Miss Worthing. Has my masquerade upset you? I assure you, I've regretted my foolishness over and over again—and condemn my duplicity severely."

"I'm sorry if I seemed upset. I was only surprised. But I must tell you that I'm not certain that you aren't different . . ."

"Different? No."

"Or I wonder if I would have behaved differently . . ."

"No. Miss Worthing . . ."

"Yes?"

"I believe now is the proper time to kiss you."

He dropped the lightest of kisses on her lips, whispered, "Good night, duckling," and departed, wondering how such a brief touch could so affect his heart. He believed that nonetheless he had passed off the tension between them.

As he walked homeward, he began to suspect himself of cowardice. If he kept up his pretense, denying his title, he would be deceiving Miss Worthing's father—the very one, if things went on as they had been, from whom he would be required to seek permission to pay his addresses. That would be maladroit, to say the least. But he didn't want to let Fanny down, and she seemed not to want him to reveal his true identity. Then he rebuked himself for blaming Fanny for his own weakness. Anyway, it was Maidie who was important. And for that matter, he had never heard of a banker yet who would refuse a noble alliance.

Emery said to Fanny, as they settled back on their pillows in their comfortable bedroom at the top of the Peel tower, "Really think it was wise, my dear, to argue Allan out of revealing his identity?"

"Of course it was wise. I promised Sam no aristocrats."

"Yes, but you couldn't know . . ."

"Anymore than I knew Wendell was a radical or fancied himself a poet when I promised Sam no poets or democrats? One look at Wendell's poetry and Sam will know that he won't be a poet long. But a marquis is a marquis. One can't give that up. All in all, I believe that Sam would prefer a deranged democrat."

"Yes, Sam has his prejudices. But only as it concerns Maidie. He might favor abolishing titles, in a theoretical sort of way, but he has no objection to business dealings with aristocrats, or to occasional social meetings."

"You know perfectly well, Emery, that he won't entertain a peer in his home."

"But again, that's because of Maidie. He doesn't want to provide any more occasions than necessary . . . Why are you looking at me that way?"

"Exactly."

"Exactly?"

"Precisely. If you will."

Emery sank back on his pillow. "You mean . . . ?"

"Yes, dear."

In the bedroom overlooking the lake, Maidie's thoughts were too tumultuous for description.

Thirteen

Wendell had not reappeared by the following day, but the arrival in early afternoon of Mr. and Mrs. Worthing, accompanied by Miss Seraphina Worthing, put an end to all efforts by those at Pennelbeck Farm to locate him—in fact rather pushed him out of their minds entirely.

The visitors arrived in a procession of three post-chaises: Seraphina and Mrs. Worthing occupied the first, Mr. Worthing the second, and two ladies' maids and a valet the third. A local cart drawn by one of the famous fell ponies followed, loaded with the visitors' traveling effects. The four matched bays, six outriders, well-sprung Worthing carriage (overly ample for fell roads), and a lesser vehicle for the servants and baggage were all comfortably housed at a Kendal coaching inn.

Maidie and Fanny, both on the watch for their guests, ran out to the lane gate to greet them.

"We'd have been here an hour ago," Mr. Worthing grumbled, as Mrs. Eckston and Stella, aided by one of the farm hands, began unloading valises, portmanteaux, and bundles, "except Phina and Tish would stop every five minutes to view the scenery in those damned colored mirrors!"

Fanny pecked her sister's cheek in greeting. "But haven't you heard, Phina? It is much more the thing with our tourists these days to examine views reflected in a silver belt buckle than in a Claude glass."

"Sounds even more foolish than I've found the Claude glasses," Phina sniffed, returning a stately peck. "And of course you would find fault, Fanny, before I've even set foot in your parlor."

"Yes, Fanny, you are very bad to tease us!" Mrs. Worthing exclaimed, as she hugged her sister-in-law. "And what is this exciting news that you tell us in your letters? Is it really true?"

"Yes, Tish, I'm increasing. But here is Emery to add his welcome to mine and Maidie's."

Later, as they all sat around the supper table, Emery said to Mr. Worthing, "Sam, you might be interested in seeing something of our industries. The pencil factory at Keswick? A visit to one of our sheep farms?"

"Excellent plan, although can't think the ladies would like it. They toted along a pack of guidebooks, so I suppose they've found some natural wonder they'd like to see."

"I was going to mention that there are many picturesque views to enjoy just by exploring the paths around Krigsmere and ascending some of our easier hills. And among our natural wonders . . . would you, Seraphina, and you, Tish, enjoy seeing one of our Druid Circles, not as massive or as impressive as Stonehenge, but of some interest. Or perhaps the great balancing rock at Borrowdale? Abbeys and castles? An excursion by boat the length of Windermere? There is also a grotto—man-made—but interesting nonetheless."

"And don't forget Colonel Braddyl's hermitage. He even employs a hermit to go with it!" Maidie exclaimed.

"Hmmmph—artificial hermits! I think not," Seraphina stated decidedly.

"And you *must* meet our neighbors," Fanny said. "That I insist upon. We will have an afternoon party, and if it's a clear day, we may set up a table in the orchard or on the terrace."

"Neighbors? Some of those peculiar poets and excitable democrats?" Mr. Worthing asked, raising a half-serious eyebrow at Fanny.

"Not at all! A gentleman of property, who is spending a holiday in the Lakes—an angling enthusiast like Emery. Then there are the Califaxtons who live in the house across the lake. You must have noted it—so prominent . . ." Fanny felt, rather than saw, Mr. Worthing's sharp glance at the mention of the Califaxton name. "And of course, our dear old rector, who knows absolutely everything there is to know about the history of the Lakes—Romans and Vikings and marauding Highlanders . . ."

"Phina enjoys picnics," Mr. Worthing said, implying that he did not.

"And Wendell, of course," Fanny continued, "if he returns in time." She was reasonably certain that Wendell would reappear in time, perfectly hale and hearty.

"My cousin," Emery clarified. "Young man named Wendell Duval. Actually a distant cousin. In fact, we aren't certain just how we're related, except, apparently, through some family named Toone in Sussex."

"Old family of woolen merchants," Mr. Worthing said promptly. "Died out now, just about. Except for a young fellow—"

"No," Seraphina contradicted him. "That's the wrong Toone . . . well, whatever are you giggling about, Maidie?"

"I'm sorry, Aunt Phina," Maidie said, attempting a contrite expression.

Seraphina nodded her acceptance of the apology. "You're thinking, Sam, of the Toones in Lincolnshire. However, they are related to the Sussex Toones, which is the noble family. I believe there's an eccentric old duke still living . . . somewhere in America I think. I've heard gossip that there was an enquiry in the Lords about the succession. Sissy Dunlopper knew them well— the Lincolnshire Toones, that is. Addicted to gambling, she says, and have quite brought the family to ruin. Except for one of the brothers . . ."

"Well, the Lincolnshire Toones then. I must say, Phina, I don't know how you keep all that nonsense straight. All I know is that young Everett Toone bought himself into Durkim, Findley and Biddle, then embezzled half their assets."

"A shocking incident. But as I was saying, one brother—that would be Everett's uncle—I understand led a quiet and respectable life as a provincial lawyer."

"Utterly shocking!" Fanny murmured. "But I must confess to you, Sam, that this particular connection of the Toones writes poetry, as I'm sure Maidie has mentioned. He has, however, committed no other crime against society, and none against property."

At Emery's sharp glance, Fanny laughed. "Emery knows how you feel about poets, Sam. But in truth, Wendell will not be a poet long. His poetry is, I assure you, a calamity—a disgrace to the English language and to all poets, even those of minor merit—past, present, or future. And I confess, Sam, that you will think him a democrat." Fanny gazed at her brother inno-cent-eyed and appealing. "But I couldn't know his politics when I was in London and had only known him a few days, now could I? But you must admit that Emery is a respectable connection, and I'm sure their mutual cousin in London even more so."

Mr. Worthing, already suspecting Fanny of some mischief, and not at all moved by innocent eyes, said, "I know any number of people with respectable connections, but with pudding-headed notions for all that."

"But Wendell is so undeniably young. His mind is not yet formed. His politics are like his poetry. Romantic and quixotic to an excess. But the years will add temperance to his character. He is in truth simply a delightful young man. I've come to love him."

"Yes," Maidie said. "And he is so determined to do some

good in the world, which is really most admirable, don't you think, Papa?"

"Oh, well," Mr. Worthing conceded. He figured that since the poet was a connection of Emery's there was nothing for it but to be charitable. "No harm in a young man sowing some wild oats. Although usually ain't in the field of poetry or politics." Then, remembering Maidie's presence, he lapsed into benevolent silence.

Fanny was satisfied that Sam could now be accustoming himself to the idea that he would meet a romantic, but certainly not dangerous radical. Although she might think her brother's notions of a proper marriage for his daughter foolish, she had great faith in his capacity to act decisively if Wendell should need his assistance. She must remind Wendell again to mute his opinions. But all in all, she foresaw no insuperable difficulties in persuading Sam to honor his promise to let her keep Maidie with her for the summer.

Mrs. Worthing had no opportunity to speak to her daughter alone until all in the household had retired for the night. Holding her wrapper close about her, she knocked softly on Maidie's door. "Is it too late for a little visit, my dear?"

"Never, Mama. I didn't come to you, for I feared you might be overly tired from the trip."

"No. As you remember from our excursions to the sea, your father so occupies himself with my comfort that I can never complain of fatigue, even when I might like to do so. It must have irked Fanny on your own journey here together, to be so cosseted."

Maidie laughed. "Yes, indeed. But Papa is Papa, and we can't change him. I do hope, though, Mama, that he hasn't come to take me home." Impulsively, she threw her arms around her mother. "You do know how much I love you and Papa, but I just

want to stay a little longer. Fanny can use my help. And . . .
and . . . I don't know how to say it. I like the country, Mama. I
feel so much more . . . more . . . free."

Mrs. Worthing kissed her daughter. "We miss you, of course,
but so will we miss you when you marry."

A conscious look that crossed Maidie's face and was instantly
gone suggested to her mother that perhaps there had been another reason than Fanny's convenience behind the plea, but she
did not question her. She had never forced a confidence from
Maidie, and in any event might have been mistaken. "But now
let us sit down and talk for a minute. Tell me what you have
been doing, and about the people you write to us about."

Fanny was at breakfast the following morning with only her
brother for company when Wendell walked in, looking as innocent as you please. Although, perhaps, also slightly wan.

"Wendell! Where have you been?" Fanny demanded.

"Where have I been? Were you looking for me?"

For a moment Fanny was at a loss to explain her emphatic
greeting—she couldn't speak openly with Sam sitting right there
with his ears sticking out a mile. "Yes, I wanted you here to
meet my family and Maidie's. Since you're part of Emery's family . . ." It sounded a weak explanation for such a demanding
greeting, even to her own ears.

Mr. Worthing rose and put out his hand. "So you're Emery's
cousin? Sam Worthing. Pleased to meet any connection of Emery's."

Wendell accepted the outstretched hand. He could not approve
of anyone as rich as Worthing was reported to be, but as Maidie's
father and Fanny's brother he unquestionably deserved polite
deference. "I'm equally pleased, sir. Fanny has been kindness
itself."

"Good morning, Papa, Aunt Fanny." Maidie bent to kiss her father's cheek. "Hello, Wendell. Where have you been?"

"This the young man you've been writing about, Maidie? The one who writes poetry?"

"Yes, Papa. Wendell often accompanies me and my friend, Miss Prudence Califaxton, on our walks."

"Just where *have* you been?" Fanny again demanded—curiosity, anxiety, and annoyance overcoming caution.

Wendell couldn't say that he'd been offering for a young lady, and subsequently working off his anger and disappointment with hard physical activity. "I just went over to meet a fellow in Patterdale. A wrestler. I told Old Peggy . . ." Wendell frowned. "Or did I? Was going to, but then . . ." He'd been so furious, so agitated after his interview with old Califaxton . . . "I'm sorry, Fanny. I fear I did forget to tell her where I was going. There was a. . . ." He paused, as he bethought himself. Couldn't mention reading radical pamphlets as excuse. "Er . . . I hope I didn't cause you any worry."

Mr. Worthing, listening to all this, studied Fanny suspiciously. Why so anxious to introduce this particular sprout? Sweet on Maidie? Maidie sweet on him? Fine, strong looking young man. Handsome as the devil.

Emery, who had just come in from a conference with his herdsman, looked in on the company. His greeting to Wendell was brusk. "You're back are you? I need to see you for a few minutes on a business matter."

Fanny was so anxious to participate in the coming discussion that she quickly found an excuse to leave. Maidie could think of no excuse for following them, since she'd only begun her breakfast. She was hard put to sit still as her Aunt Seraphina, who entered on Fanny's rapidly departing heels, undertook to relay the latest London gossip.

* * *

Mr. Worthing was luckier than Maidie in promptly securing the interview he desired. Emery soon returned to the breakfast room to announce that if Sam felt a farm tour was in order they could leave as soon as he completed some pending business with one of the farmhands.

"Anxious to see your improvements, Emery, but if Fanny is free for a few minutes, I can just talk over a little business matter with her while I'm waiting."

"She's in the Scriptorium. She'll be down again soon."

"No, no. I'll go up to her."

"Has Wendell gone, Uncle Emery?" Maidie asked.

"Yes. But he left you word that he'll return this afternoon."

Mr. Worthing, who heard this brief exchange as he was leaving the breakfast room, wondered once again if Maidie was sweet on the fellow, and it was foremost in his mind as he entered the Scriptorium, puffing lightly from the exertion of climbing the spiral stair.

"Say, Fanny, want to talk to you a minute. Without interruptions, if you please." He removed a handkerchief from his pocket, and wiped his forehead. "I admire your house, Fanny. Told you so before. But I'd do something about those stairs."

Fanny, who had been expecting that a *tête à tête* with her brother would have to be endured some time, smiled brightly, and gestured him to a comfortable chair. "I was just looking for a book of Wordsworth's poems for Seraphina. Well, Sam, what is it?"

"Now I want no dodges, my girl. I let Maidie come up here to meet some rich fellows named Califaxton. We hear in her letters a pack about this Wendell, who seems to run loose in your house. And his surname ain't Califaxton."

"No. You'll meet the whole Califaxton family at my afternoon party, and perhaps the young men or Mrs. Califaxton at tea one day."

Mr. Worthing gestured impatiently. "Straight to the point, Fan, if it's within your capabilities. How's it going? I'm not trying to get rid of the girl, you know that. Couldn't love a son more than I do our Maidie. But I won't say I wouldn't like to see her married to some worthy man. I took it into my head that maybe young Duval was sweet on her?"

Fanny had never liked to lie outright. She dodged. "It's so terribly hard to say with young people these days."

"Come off it, Fan. Don't play old lady with me."

Oh, well, if lie she must. "I assure you, Sam, I can't tell you. We see a good deal of the two Califaxton young men who are currently in residence, John and Chester, the former of whom I believe might possibly have a kindness for Maidie. We see more of Wendell, of course, because he is, as you learned yesterday, Emery's distant cousin. There may be something there . . . and although he isn't rich, Sam, it might please you to know that he dislikes his name. Wendell Duval is just a name he's using for a little time."

"Using a false name? Now what kind of lunacy is that? And why should it please me? I'd say it's suspicious."

"Not at all. He has a perfectly respectable name—Salvatore Toone. He just doesn't like it. Doesn't think it's sufficiently poetic. I told you that for all his remarkably sharp wit, he still demonstrates some lamentably youthful follies."

Mr. Worthing frowned. "Can't say I like it either. Salvatory. Sounds Italian. Don't hold with these foreign names." His eyes narrowed. "One of the Sussex Toones you say?" He was remembering that that was the line of noble Toones.

"So Emery's old relation in London wrote us, but so far removed that should you draw his blood you wouldn't find even a tiny tint of blue."

Mr. Worthing was half convinced that Duval (or Toone) was sweet on Maidie, and that Fanny was hiding it because he wasn't rich and had that distant taint of nobility. As though he didn't know the difference between a titled aristocrat and some eighty-second cousin! And the fellow didn't like his name. Now he thought about it, it was a circumstance in his favor, like Fanny said. "Well!" Hands on his knees, he boosted himself out of his chair. "Emery will be waiting for me. Taking me to see the improvements he's made here and then we're off to see the pencil factory in Keswick."

"Before you go, Sam. If I don't have another chance. You'll meet Mr. Gilmichael, perhaps this very afternoon—"

"Fellow that's here for the fishing?"

"Yes. You should know that he's a cousin of the present Marquis of Enett. I think it would be a great deal more tactful if you kept your opinions of the aristocracy to yourself."

"Don't want me to embarrass you?"

"No. Or embarrass him."

Mr. Worthing suddenly laughed. "Don't worry, Fan. I know very well how to hold my tongue. All I need to know is whether or not he's got any interest in Maidie. Has he been hanging around her?"

"Well, of *course* they are acquaintances! I couldn't shut her up, could I?"

"Doesn't look to me like you're much of a matchmaker, Fan."

"I guess not," Fanny conceded. "I'll go down with you. We're walking this morning."

Mrs. Worthing found it necessary to rest after the walk along the lake, since she particularly wished to be present if anyone interesting came for tea. Mr. Worthing might find penniless poets and demented democrats beneath his notice, but she expected to find them amusing. She did hope that one or two might call.

Fanny acknowledged that she too was uncharacteristically tired.

Seraphina nodded. "I recommended, if you recall, Fanny, that you remain at home. In your condition . . ."

"Yes, Seraphina," Fanny replied docilely. "I have learned my lesson." She did not bother to explain that she was only just coming to the end of terrible bouts of morning sickness, which had proved more draining than she had believed possible.

Seraphina, for her part, had no idea of resting (Seraphina never rested in the afternoon), but thought instead of sitting in the garden where she could read her guidebooks, renew her acquaintance with Wordsworth and Coleridge's *Lyrical Ballads,* and study the natural beauties of Krigsmere and the fells under the changing light of a passing hour. With that pronouncement, she went off to change into what she deemed appropriate attire.

Fanny suspected that what Phina really wanted to do was to inspect her linen closets. If she knew Phina—and she trusted that she did—she would soon be in the kitchen, interviewing her servants, and in any number of uncalled for ways snooping into her household arrangements. To be fair, Phina was not a difficult visitor or a dull companion; she was not only a vigorous walker, but she was also observant and interested in all that she saw or was shown. Fanny just wished that she wouldn't include her household as a subject of her interest.

These reflections were interrupted by Maidie, wishing to learn the outcome of the morning conference with Wendell.

"Unproductive to the highest degree," was Fanny's succinct reply. "The foolish boy fully intends to let government agents arrest him. If you can talk him out of such an extraordinarily nonsensical notion, Emery and I will be much obliged to you! We've offered to help him pay expenses for a time on the Continent. Wendell's never done a grand tour, and while it needn't be as extravagant as some youthful lord might undertake, he could benefit immensely from a more economical journey. After all, it doesn't cost a fortune to live in Italy. But Emery firmly refused to pay his passage to South America, where he declares he will join the Freedom Fighters."

If that doesn't sound just like him! Maidie thought, as she

retreated to her own chamber to wash her face and change her dress. She did hope Wendell would find time to call before any visitors came for afternoon tea and conversation. She devoutly hoped there would be no visitors of the sort that would give her father concern.

Wendell was as eager to talk over his difficulties with Maidie as she was to listen and exhort. He discovered her in the garden with Seraphina. Unable to think of any better strategy, he invited them both to a row around the lake. Seraphina benignly sent the youngsters off to enjoy themselves without her. She fully intended to take up sea bathing as soon as she found a house in Brighton, but until she learned to get about competently in the water she preferred to remain on dry land. And there was no harm in the two of them paddling around in full view.

As soon as they were well launched, Wendell said, "It didn't enter my mind for a minute that that fellow Sir Harold was a spy. Just because he wasn't sneaking around behind bushes and boulders . . ."

"Did Uncle Emery tell you that Mr. Gilmichael discovered that he knew very little about fishing, even though he claimed it was the reason he was visiting the Lakes?"

"But mind you, I wouldn't change a word I spoke that night! It is simply that as a politician I must learn to be more sensible of my auditors—"

"Listen to me! The man said he intended to be in the Lakes a week, but after he talked to you, he decided he had to go immediately to London. Did Uncle Emery tell you that?"

"Yes. Certainly. They told me everything they suspected."

Maidie was beginning to believe that Wendell's habit of self-dramatization might better be called self-delusion. "And you intend to do nothing?"

"What should I do? Emery and Fanny want me to flee, of

course. I prefer to face my accusers. How else will it be known that our government persecutes honest citizens who only wish for the greater happiness of all?"

"Oh, Wendell! No political statements, I beg you. I know your opinions as though they were my own. Better, I sometimes think."

"How can I tell you why I refuse to flee without making a political statement?"

Maidie controlled a strong impulse to shake him. After a moment spent staring at cloud shadows crossing the fells, she said persuasively, "But think of Aunt Fanny and Uncle Emery. Have you enough money to pay for your defense in court? Do you want to be sent to New South Wales? And what of your family?"

"Well, as to that, you should remember that Emery could very well disclaim any relationship to me, the connection is so distant. In truth I have no family now. No father, mother, brother, or sister."

"No one at all?" Maidie's annoyance was momentarily lost in her sympathy for this great overgrown orphan.

"Only other family I know about—or have anything to do with—is an old lady in London who told me I was related to Emery. Family calls her Miss Hattie. We all seem to be cousins, somehow, at about twenty removes. Although I dare say everybody in England is related if you go back far enough. She wanted to talk about Cholmeleys and Sussex Toones—or was it Essex?—who apparently add some lustre to my name." Wendell grimaced disdainfully. "But who cares a fig for dead ancestors, whether they're lords or thieves. No difference anyway."

Maidie demanded to know if he wanted to spend half the rest of his life in New South Wales, or to languish for an untold time in some odorous, pestilential prison, and that she wouldn't give him a shilling if he persisted in making an example of himself by not accepting her aunt and uncle's offer of assistance. Wendell countered that he could write pamphlets and poetry in prison, just as Cobbett did his *Political Register,* and that anyway, only thieves were sent to New South Wales, and he hadn't asked her for any money, and wouldn't take it if she forced it on him.

"I don't think you'll like jail all that much, and I think you're wrong about New South Wales, but if you're so foolish, I will say no more about it. But," Maidie brought out her last argument, "I'd think that you would consider Prudence. Do you think Mr. Califaxton would ever permit his daughter to marry a man who's been in prison? I think you are selfish, Wendell!"

Maidie had struck just where he had known she eventually would. "Don't you know I wish that for Pru I could be different?" he asked dramatically.

"So Pru must sacrifice, but you will not?"

"Sacrifice?" Wendell was prepared to tear his hair, but was unfortunately responsible for the oars. "I'll ask her if she loves me enough to love a jailbird, and if she says she cannot, I'll give her up, although I know I'll never love again so completely. So fully. So intensely! But she's young. She will love again. I can only hope that a small corner of her heart will be reserved for my memory . . ."

"Oh, stop being so idiotic! Upon my word, I sometimes wonder if you have the sense you were born with, or if it went straying when you learned to read!"

"You don't know what it is to love!"

"That may be so, at least how to love as you do."

They had at last arrived at the subject he had wished to discuss. He said soothingly, with just a touch of wheedling in his tone, "Don't be angry, Maidie. Please help me. I must see Pru. You can find a way. At Fanny's party. A few minutes in the library are all I'll need."

"You're impossible! Why should I help anyone so selfish?"

Wendell didn't answer immediately. Should he tell her that he had approached Mr. Califaxton and been dismissed? His longing to pour out his distress in Maidie's usually willing ear was powerful. So powerful that it all came pouring out.

She was not sympathetic. "Well, I must say! Anyone who hopes to be a politician ought to have more sense. Really, that was quite foolish, you know. What if Mr. Califaxton should prevent Pru from coming to Fanny's picnic?"

"Then that will be my opportunity to see her, and you will be relieved of helping me."

Wendell was prepared with several persuasive arguments, all of which he was required to use, but at last Maidie agreed.

I always do seem to succumb to his entreaties, she thought crankily. "I'll ask Mr. Gilmichael to help us, but I can't promise."

"Gilmichael?"

"I can hardly ask Chester or . . . or my mother, can I?"

"Your Aunt Seraphina looks like a good sort."

Maidie was beginning to wish she had never ever seen Wendell Duval. Or Prudence Califaxton either. "Row me back to shore, please."

Fanny, a basket of flowers on her arm, met Allan just crossing the terrace.

"How are you, Fanny? May I take your basket? I've come to offer my services—or simply to enquire after your health and that of your relations, if you have no need of me. But I am completely at your orders. Are your guests finding the Lakes entertaining?"

Fanny gave him a brief summary of the day's activities. "Sam and Emery haven't returned yet, but Maidie and her mother will soon be with us, I trust. My sister, Miss Seraphina Worthing, was just going into the drawing room to attend to two early visitors. A young gentleman from Windermere," Fanny elaborated with naughty intent, "who claims to admire my essays, but I believe admires Maidie more. And the rector—who as you know, is one of our regular guests. I'll present you to Seraphina as soon as she's free."

Seraphina, who had already freed herself from the two early visitors, was rearranging cups and plates for a more efficient service. She looked up as Fanny and Allan approached.

"Phina, may I present Mr. Allan Gilmichael?"

"Mr. Gilmichael?" Had she not been Seraphina Worthing she might almost have been accused of blurting the question. As it was, it was only too clear that she had been expecting a different name. In fact, she had been expecting Lord Enett to recognize her, if not remember her name. "But you—"

Fanny was quick to interrupt. "Yes, Phina. Mr. Gilmichael is a distant cousin of the present marquis. They are very like."

Openly, and skeptically, Seraphina studied his face. He met the inspection with a bland expression, but a very speaking eye. "Certainly you are remarkably like, you and your cousin," she said at last. "One would take you for twins."

Allan bowed. "So I've always been told." Although he had met her only once, he had recognized her immediately. He'd forgotten the name until this very minute, but he had not forgotten her. No one who met Seraphina Worthing forgot her. But why hadn't he recalled her when he met Maidie? . . . If he remembered the circumstances, he had been presented to Miss Seraphina Worthing at a boringly exclusive affair at the home of one of the kingdom's most self-exalted and rank-conscious peers. There had been no reason to connect her name with a well known banking house.

"And how does your cousin go on?" she was asking. "I met him once, I believe. One would not call him amiable."

Fanny, relieved, said, "I leave you two to get acquainted. I'll take my basket now, Allan. I must get the flowers in water." Seraphina was either taken in or had accepted the ruse.

Allan, speaking carefully, replied to Seraphina. "The marquis is much more . . . amiable these days. He finds he rather likes farming, although he has not come to enjoy the privileges his rank confers, or to accept the automatic deference rank elicits. Nor the restraint on his freedom. He is, however, at last resigned." Should he give her a hint that he was developing an interest in matrimony?

Seraphina could supply her own hints. "Many a man has found that a wife and a full nursery, with perhaps a mettlesome horse or two in his stables, will compensate for a restraint on his freedom."

Maidie walked in to interrupt this formal jousting, to offer her hand to Allan as prettily as her Aunt Seraphina could have desired, and she hoped with no show of confusion. His ambiguous kiss, at their last parting, had done nothing to relieve the tension between them. She was saved from any further reliance on her aunt's demanding social training by the entrance of Mr. Worthing and Emery, eager to relate their adventures and all the facts about poets and pencil manufactories that had come in their way that day.

Mr. Worthing distributed pencils to everyone. "Don't know how it is, but somehow you always end up with a collection of gewgaws and gimcracks when you make a tour—although I will say this: at least these pencils have some use."

Emery described their stop at Greta Hall, where they spoke briefly with Mrs. Southey, and Mrs. Southey's sister, the wife of the unfortunate Mr. Coleridge. Mr. Southey, poet, essayist, and historian, had then taken them to look at picturesque views and to hear his recommendations on Lakeland sights. They had gone on to Rydal Mount to look in on the Wordsworths. Mrs. Wordsworth was visiting with relatives, but they secured a promise from Mr. Wordsworth's sister that they would visit soon, especially since learning that Fanny was in an interesting way. They had also had a brief conversation with the noted poet himself, who was resting from his labors in favor of the Tory candidate.

Mr. Worthing was led to conclude that although prosy might describe either poet, neither was contributing to the population of deranged democrats or to the delinquency of the lower classes. "That Wordsworth fellow takes the prize," he told them. "Who'd ever think he wrote all that la-de-da stuff about birds and bees and idiot boys?"

Mrs. Worthing entered in time to hear the last remark, and coming up to her husband slipped her hand under his arm. "Are we discussing demented poets, dear?"

He patted her hand. "No, no. Just telling about our trip today. But I won't bore these folks with repetition. You must await your report until we're private."

"Sam, I must take Tish from you," Fanny said, "for I see John and Chester Califaxton coming across the terrace. I particularly want John to meet Tish. And I see someone has just drawn up in a curricle. Now who would that be? I can't possibly offer anyone a bed tonight . . ."

Allan was uncomfortably conscious facing the man who he would very likely be addressing on the serious subject of marrying his daughter, and was even more stricken with the knowledge that he would be presenting his petition under another identity. He felt both foolish and dishonest, and wondered why he had ever been so absurd as to deny his title, and so cowardly in submitting to Fanny's suggestion that he continue to do so. Mr. Worthing, on the other hand, was perfectly easy, chatting comfortably about Lakeland industries and the improvements in the farm since his last visit.

Allan's ordeal was not long, for Emery soon joined them. "Tomorrow I'm taking Sam to visit the Brownriggs up Pennelbeck Road, Allan. Nobody knows more about sheep farming in the Lakes than they do. Don't expect we'll be home before late afternoon. Care to come along?"

Fanny, escorting a tall, thin gentleman with a dyspeptic look, interrupted them. "Let me present Mr. Appleyard. He tells me that he is a great admirer of your histories, Emery."

"And so you should be, sir," Mr. Worthing said generously, "although if you ask me he goes too easy on bouncing kings out on their ears. But I've never been one to argue history. What's done's done. It's the here and now that interests me. Although probably would've been for bouncing old James myself—what was his number?"

"The second. Came after—"

"No, no, Emery. Don't need a history lesson, although there couldn't be a better man to give me one than you. Read some of your books. But Fanny, now. I've read her stuff too—makes me think that it's probably Cloud Cuckoo Land around here when I'm not visiting."

"Why Sam!" Fanny exclaimed. "Quoting Aristophanes! I didn't know you read the classics."

"Don't. But I did go to school. Lot you don't know, Fanny."

Chester paid his respects to Mrs. Worthing and Seraphina, and then to Mr. Worthing, and finally, finding Maidie for a moment unoccupied, asked her if she knew that Wendell had made an offer for Prudence. "Jinglebrain, *mon père* calls him. Can't say I could've found a better word. Of course, Duval doesn't know the governor the way I do, but if he'd asked my advice, he would've waited until he had something better to offer than five hundred a year."

Mrs. Worthing, standing by the tea table, told John Califaxton that she was looking forward to a longer discussion on the subject of Arianism when they next met at Fanny's afternoon picnic. Seraphina, who had taken over the coffee urn and teapot, privately cast her eyes skyward. Arianism! She handed Fanny a cup of coffee for the long, dyspeptic looking gentleman who had just intruded himself. Well, she knew Fanny kept her doors open most afternoons for whomever might be passing by, but . . .

Allan, holding Maidie's hand longer than was necessary, was saying, "I look forward to meeting you again on Thursday, Miss Worthing."

"Yes," she replied, making no attempt to withdraw it.

Mr. Worthing, who had moved hastily away from the historians, remarked to Fanny, "Should call this room your Babble-orium, Fan."

"But," the dyspeptic historian told Emery, "one must remember, when discussing Queen Elizabeth's foreign policy, that she was a woman."

Fourteen

The three days that followed were filled with tourist doings, as Mr. Worthing characterized them, even and despite one day of steady rain. Neighbors and friends came to call, including Allan, Wendell, and the Califaxtons, until Mrs. Worthing declared the Lakes the most friendly place in England. They were surprised by a visit from Dorothy Wordsworth and her brother, who walked ten miles in the rain to take tea with them, a feat that Fanny later assured her guests was in no way unusual. Seraphina surprised herself by accepting an invitation from Miss Wordsworth to climb Helvellyn with her on another visit.

"Phina's becoming a regular Amazon," Fanny remarked to Emery later. "I never thought to see the day when our dauntingly proper sister would enjoy climbing mountains! But then, I never thought I'd see the day when Phina would decide to take up swimming."

"Sam wonders if it might not be a certain age. He says he'll have to look out she doesn't run off with her coachman."

Fanny giggled. "Shame on you both!"

The uneasy fear that a brace of government agents would appear on their doorstep with a warrant for Wendell's arrest throbbed nervously at the back of their minds through all their activities and conversations. Every visitor, previously known to them personally or by reputation, was suspect. Fanny, in quiet moments, devised elaborate plans for sending government agents or Bow Street runners on unproductive chases around the countryside, or polished and rehearsed a proposal to her brother for aid in Wendell's escape. For his part, Emery planned a visit to a legal advisor in Kendell. And late at night in their tower bedroom they debated the wisdom of immediately Revealing All to Mr. Worthing.

Maidie was the recipient during these three days of distressed notes from, and unsought but urgent conferences with Prudence and Wendell, both harping on the same theme—that she help them meet privately when all were assembled at Fanny's picnic luncheon—and always couched in the most heartrending terms.

She replied to Prudence's notes and appeals with entreaties that she use her influence to urge Wendell to flee before government agents arrested him for sedition. "Only you, Prudence, can make him see where his own interests lie," she wrote. "Neither I, nor my aunt or uncle have been able to bring him to his senses." In reply, Prudence promised to do all within her slender powers to save her beloved from durance vile, if only she could meet him for the barest minute.

Mr. Worthing, responding to hints from Fanny, observed how often Maidie was to be found walking or sitting with Wendell and so began to see a confirmation of his original notion. He set himself to a close observation of the young man, and quickly concluded that for once Fanny wasn't lying, that the poetic posturings were those of a romantic youth. On asking to see some of his poetry he easily determined that it was as bad or worse than Fanny claimed, and that whatever his real name was, or whoever he married, Duval would have to find other employment if he was to make his way in the world. He himself might be only a banker, but as he had told Fanny, he knew good poetry when he saw it. It was unfortunate, of course, that Duval didn't command a fortune, but he came from a respectable (as opposed to the gambling and embezzling) limb of the Toone family. And

didn't like his name. Wouldn't be such a poor match for Maidie.
Not just what he'd like; didn't seem to have much interest yet
in down to earth matters. But as for his politics . . . Well, as he'd
said early on, nothing wrong with a young man sowing his wild
oats in radical politics. Better all around, in fact, than petticoats
or dice.

Mr. Worthing cautiously suggested to Mrs. Worthing the possibility of a kindness between the youngsters. "Mr. Duval's
rather young," was all the answer he received, but he set it down
to what he suspected was his wife's preference for a more lively
sort of fellow. That the young scrub was not—handsome as a
new penny—and a likable sort, too, but not an ounce of dash.
And he certainly couldn't blame Tish if she thought Duval too
young. He thought so himself. But if there was one thing sure
in this world, it was that everyone got older.

Mrs. Worthing observed later to Fanny and Seraphina that
Sam was good at divining a man's steadiness and his net worth,
but not always his romantic inclinations. Fanny and Seraphina
both nodded wisely.

And thus the day of the picnic dawned. Bright and sunny,
with a soft, refreshing breeze, it remained so as the hour approached for the guests to assemble. Fanny ordered the trestle
tables set up on the terrace under a marquee secured from rental
agents in Kendal, and put the hired servants to placing chairs
and rugs and cushions in the orchard and the garden. She then
sat down to wait comfortably until Mr. Worthing came in to
report that it looked like the first guests were arriving.

Maidie had spent nearly fifteen minutes with Mrs. Califaxton,
who was intent on scolding the weather, and with the rector,
who was pleased to tell them both about a ruin, which he suspected to be Roman, in the town of Ravenglass. They were joined
by the dyspeptic historian, returned from two days at Win-

dermere before traveling northward to view Hadrian's Wall, and more than eager to discuss Roman ruins with the rector. Mrs. Califaxton was willing to abandon the weather in favor of the Romans, who through folly and lechery had lost an empire. With the three guests so amicably engaged with each other, Maidie judged she could undertake her promised favor to the lovers.

It was not difficult to catch Mr. Gilmichael's eye, for each time she had glanced at him he had been looking at her. She excused herself and began an aimless stroll among the guests. He moved away from the group with whom he was conversing and ambled across the lawn toward her.

"You called me, Miss Worthing?"

"You are rewardingly observant, Mr. Gilmichael, and amiable in the extreme. I need your help."

"Perhaps you shouldn't judge my amiability until you have succeeded in securing my help."

"I know you won't refuse me. It's a case of love, you see."

Although Allan opened his mouth to speak, he discovered he was speechless. Was the bold chit actually telling him he was in love with her? But as the initial shockwave receded from his benumbed mind and reason returned . . . the imp was prattling on about lovers in distress who needed her assistance, and that she in turn needed his assistance if she were to help them.

"And who are these lovers?" What straits he must be in if any mention of love seemed to pertain to his own case!

"Prudence Califaxton and Wendell."

"Duval?"

"Hush! We mustn't appear to be conspirators, you know."

A surge of foolish relief had gone coursing after the shockwave. There had never been anything between her and the young fool after all! He had been a simpleton himself to even think it possible! She was too discerning to have fallen in love with a schoolboy. He offered Maidie his arm. "Would you care to stroll down to the lake, Miss Worthing?"

She placed her hand shyly in the crook of his elbow. He put his own hand possessively over hers. "Well, duckling?"

"I fear," Maidie began, her hand tingling, "that Wendell has rather rushed his fences by asking Mr. Califaxton's permission to pay his addresses to Prudence."

"Not a good campaigner, I should say." Allan drew Maidie's hand to rest more snugly in the crook of his elbow. "I take it he was refused permission and that he and Miss Califaxton are now under close surveillance by the elder Califaxton?"

Maidie sent a steadying message to her heart. "You are perceptive in the extreme. It seems that Mr. Califaxton has no objection to Wendell's politics (I suspect he thinks him only schoolboyish), but to his lack of fortune. He won't permit Prudence to throw herself away on five hundred a year."

"Capital or interest?"

"Oh, interest, of course," replied the banker's daughter.

"Not a princely sum, but certainly adequate for a comfortable living if there is no extravagance."

"Yes, except of course that Prudence is more accustomed to 'extravagance' than 'adequate.' But it's not for us to decide what they are to do. We can only give them the opportunity to decide for themselves."

Allan could not find himself out of sympathy with Mr. Califaxton. Not to mention the impropriety of secret meetings. "I can't like it, Miss Worthing. They are young, you must admit. And if her father—"

"And I can't like fathers deciding who a woman may marry! Mr. Califaxton told Wendell outright that his interest is not in Prudence's happiness, but that she bring money into the Califaxton enterprises. You must be shocked at the use of daughters as . . . as merchandise."

"I'm sure her father has warmer feelings for his daughter than that, and if Duval and Miss Califaxton have patience and constancy, he will soften."

"I believe that they wish to meet in order to pledge their constancy, Mr. Gilmichael," she said stiffly. She withdrew her hand from his arm, walking on at his side with her chin up and her lips tightly set.

He had angered her, but he nonetheless could not approve such a challenge to authority. He had been a soldier; he knew the importance of authority—as a commander, a landlord, and as the head of a family. He judged Miss Prudence Califaxton to be about the same age as his sister Julie—and she probably had just about the same amount of sense as Julie. His natural sympathies would of course be with her father.

Maidie was indeed angry. She forgot, in the passion of the moment, her own reluctance to arrange this meeting. It *wasn't* for Mr. Califaxton to choose Prudence's husband for her! And if this was what he had forced them to . . .

But she had another argument that was truly more urgent. She stopped to face him. "Since you are so nice, I think you should know that our conspiracy is more monstrous yet! I have told Prudence that Wendell refuses to flee from the government agents who are pursuing him, and that our best hope of saving him from prison is to convince him to do so. Perhaps she can succeed where the rest of us have failed. He says that he prefers to go to prison! But if they also speak of their love and their future, I will not object."

Allan was in love himself, and here was the object of his desire standing before him with a rosy flush of anger reddening her cheeks and eyes made brilliant by defiance. Her chin was up, and her bosom rose and fell with her quickened breathing. She was delightful!

He mustered one last objection. "I've agreed that I found Sir Harold's interest in Duval suspicious, but I can't believe that he has done anything to warrant arrest."

"Neither have others who now languish in our filthy and verminous prisons!"

"I would not incur your displeasure for the world, but—" At least he could impose a condition. "I cannot be a party to planning an elopement. Can you vouch for Duval?" He must find an opportunity to kiss her.

"Wendell is not so foolish that he would run away with Prudence. Or agree to do so should she desire it."

He capitulated. "Since Mr. Califaxton will not sit by and watch his daughter stroll off arm in arm with Duval I presume she must be on my arm?"

"Neither. I thought you and Wendell could wander away together, and then Prudence with me. When we are out of sight, you and I will discreetly withdraw . . ."

"But we will be compounding our perfidy, Miss Worthing. Not only will we be leaving a young couple unchaperoned who have been denied each other's company, but we will ourselves be unchaperoned."

"So we were for several hours on the fells, Mr. Gilmichael, and you were a perfect gentleman. I trust you to hold yourself to the same high standard of conduct today."

Was she roasting him? Her face was hidden from him by her hat. "Shall we set our campaign in motion, then?" he asked as he offered his arm again. As they strolled slowly back to the orchard, her hand once again securely within his arm, he outlined for her the movements required to win this particular campaign of deception. Once won over, he might as well enjoy the sporting aspects of it.

Six people had witnessed the scene at the lakeside, with mixed notions of its portent.

Seraphina exchanged a look with Fanny that confirmed a mutual, although unspoken belief that something interesting was taking place. Fanny's pleasure was more elevated, perhaps, for whether Allan was lord or commoner made not a particle of difference to her. Seraphina, although harboring some slight sympathy for her brother's aversion to an aristocratic marriage for Maidie, entertained pleasant thoughts of social triumph. Sam's marriage to a viscount's daughter was almost forgotten by society, but that his own daughter should marry a marquis! For one who loved society as she did, how agreeable to contemplate.

Mrs. Worthing, sitting with John Califaxton, had kept a motherly watch on her daughter all afternoon, and something in the attitude of Maidie and Mr. Gilmichael as they stood together by the lake made her again wonder . . . Her speculative gaze naturally drew John's eyes in the same direction, to confirm what he had earlier suspected. He'd seen it so early, in fact, that any thought he might have initially entertained about the Clarkes' charming niece had been quickly laid aside. John was a generous man, and as Mrs. Worthing turned her attention again to their conversation, he said, "An excellent man, Gilmichael. Was in the same regiment as my brother, who speaks highly of him."

Prudence and Wendell had been more consciously on the watch, but were so entangled in their own difficulties that they interpreted the conference by the lake solely according to their own concerns. They each watched anxiously as Maidie and Allan returned from their walk along the lakeshore, her arm in his and seeming in charity with each other. On receiving her smile, they both thought what an excellent friend she was.

Wendell hadn't dared approach Prudence that entire afternoon, or even Maidie, certain that Mr. Califaxton's baleful gaze would immediately immobilize him—and so he had found himself immobilized by Mr. Worthing instead. Seated comfortably on a bench shaded by an apple tree, the banker was engaged in a conversation with Chester Califaxton when Wendell strolled by, his thoughts on Prudence and their hoped for interview.

"Join us, Duval?" Mr. Worthing interrupted his thoughts.

Wendell had no desire to converse with a representative of the Rapacious Moneyed Class. But he was Maidie's father and seemed not entirely devoted to sitting on the necks of the poor. So courtesy triumphed, despite his burning need for immediate knowledge of the outcome of Maidie's conference with Gilmichael. He could see them through the trees. At least he could watch them and perhaps judge the outcome by their demeanor. He sat down on the grass in front of the bench on which Mr. Califaxton and Chester were enthroned.

Chester no more than Wendell felt at ease with Maidie's father—so much his senior and with little mutuality of interest. He had just been sitting comfortably by himself on the bench, resting from social rigors and debating whether or not to strike up a conversation with the rector's granddaughter—a pretty looking filly—when Mr. Worthing had sat down and asked whether he wrote poetry, too. He had been vehemently denying any such foolishness when Duval happened by. And looking like he had something on his mind, although he'd often wondered just how much of a mind the fellow had.

Mr. Worthing felt no reciprocal discomfort in the presence of callow youth. The only thought that crossed his mind was that it was a good opportunity to feel these two striplings out. Looked more like Duval had Maidie's interest than Califaxton, but he was far from sure of it.

He fixed his eye on Wendell. "Well, sir. How is it you find time to take your leisure here in the Lakes? Been to university, have you?"

Wendell rallied his thoughts. "Yes, sir, Oxford. That's where I came under the influence of the poetic mind. Not Pope and Milton, you understand, or any thanks to the old dons, but some of my set who admired Wordsworth and Byron. And I knew Shelley there."

Chester, affronted, said, "Nothing wrong with Pope. Or Milton either. Poetry wasn't invented by Wordsworth, you know."

Mr. Worthing turned his gaze on Chester with something akin to astonishment. "Now here's a sensible fellow! Have a fondness for Pope myself. So, Califaxton, what keeps you in the Lakes? Most sprouts your age with well-greased papas are on the strut in London."

Chester, who had decided that Maidie's father was not a man to be passed off with sham, answered frankly. *"Mon* . . . uh . . . M'father's got me rusticating, sir. I was on the town for a while, but got myself in a bit of trouble. Gambled a bit, overspent my allowance, went to the Jews—and as you know, sir, regular Shylocks—want their pound of flesh. Couldn't raise the wind—went to my father. Governor's not a bad sort. Paid up, but cut off my allowance. So here I am."

Mr. Worthing nodded. "Well, sir, I admire your honesty. But I have to tell you I don't hold with such talk about the Jews. If it hadn't been for the Rothschilds, d'you think we could have kept our allies supplied with gold, and kept their spirit up for fighting the French tyrant? I've many a time met the Duke of Wellington at Nathan Rothschild's table, and lots of other folk that're supposed to be among the best people—lords and ministers and their ladies. Now, it's nothing to me, you understand, that Arthur Wellesley's a duke. It's his military accomplishments that rate the respect."

No one who knew Mr. Worthing would have questioned this sentiment, or that he accorded respect only to those who proved deserving of it. Although neither Chester nor Wendell had had the honor of a previous acquaintance with the banker, they were not inclined to question it either, confining their comments to agreeable mumbles.

"As a politician, now." Mr. Worthing leaned back, very much at his ease. "Little too much the Tory, Wellington is, even for me. Of course, I don't hold with extending the suffrage and such nonsense as that—it's property that weds a man to the interests of his country." Secretly amused by this sally onto Wendell's turf, he glanced at him enquiringly.

Wendell, however, had caught Maidie's signal, and would have been hard put at that moment to martial any arguments at all on the subject of property and privilege. What a good fellow Maidie was. His brain was turbulent with his anxiety to speak to Prudence, his thoughts incoherent.

"But, as I was saying," Mr. Worthing continued, "it's not that I've met the so-called best people at Rothschild's table, because my idea of best ain't the fashionables, although there's those at Rothschild's table too. But there's men there that know what the world's about, and who're willing to serve their country and pay their debts, and women that know the back end of a horse when they see one, if you'll pardon that expression in regard to the ladies. No, I think I'm in the best company when I sit down to dine with Rothschild, or with Mr. Goldschmidt, Nelson's banker—God rest the good admiral. What a blow to the nation his loss was. Well, be that as it may. Goldschmidt, by the way, gives more generously than I ever did to the charities. It's what we do in this world that counts. What do you say?"

Chester suddenly came to the unnerving realization that he was being directly addressed. He nodded. "Exactly as you say, sir."

Mr. Worthing, with some effort, hid a smile. "But you were talking about the Jews screwing out the last percent. Now—begging your pardon, sir—that shows how innocent you are in the ways of the world. A banker thinks about the other partners, if he has any, and the security of the people's savings. He can't take your chancy loans, now, and risk depositors' money that way."

Wendell shifted his position on the grass and wondered how to make his escape.

"Say you're a pawnbroker, which some Jews are. And so are some Christians.

"Now, one of your bloods comes to you and wants to borrow five hundred pound to buy his doxy a new phaeton, or to pay off a gambling debt, or because he fancies a blooded stallion but can't afford it. He tells you as soon as next quarter's allowance, or next quarter's dividend comes in, he can pay up. Or maybe even that the old gentleman, his great uncle, is about to turn up his toes, and he's sure to inherit. That's a risky loan, see—otherwise he'd go to a banker, not to one of your money lenders. What's he got for security? A signet ring he inherited from his old grandfather, or some other trumpery thing. So the fellow charges him interest—plenty of ways to get around the legal interest rate that ain't illegal—and takes the family jewels in pawn, 'cause he's got a very good chance of never getting the money back. Not much different from what that fellow we were talking about at breakfast the other day did. That Everett Toone. And his grandpa before him, I'll wager. Put their land up for security to raise the wind to pay their gambling debts. But that's respectable. It's called a mortgage."

Mr. Worthing got up from the bench and stretched. He could see that Duval was ready to shoot off like a released spring, given the chance. Probably wanting to walk off with Maidie. "Well. I can see that you boys have had enough. Picnic's no place for learning the p's and q's."

"It's been instructive, sir," Chester said valiantly.

"Well, that's to be debated. But I want to recommend that you young fellows read the economists along with your radical political papers."

Chester recoiled. "I don't read radical political papers, sir. That's Duval's line."

Mr. Worthing eyed him. "Wouldn't hurt you. Reading don't hurt anybody." He smiled to himself as he strolled away, leaving the young men to escape to the company of their peers. He'd bet Maidie knew more about banking and how the world was put together than those two sprouts did.

Released from his ordeal, Wendell wandered aimlessly away, trusting to Maidie's arrangements, whatever they were, to rescue him. His trust was not misplaced. He was soon engaged by Gilmichael in a discussion of Godwin's radical thesis that women's favors should not be monopolized by one single man, a subject Allan had chosen as his own private revenge for being dragged into Wendell's distasteful affairs.

Wendell stammered inarticulately something about Godwin having modified his opinion in a writing subsequent to *Political Justice*—he couldn't remember which at the moment—to the effect that society had not yet attained a sufficient state of perfectibility . . .

"Let's stroll up the lane and discuss this more thoroughly, shall we?" Allan suggested, smiling to himself with as much wicked pleasure as Mr. Worthing had done. He directed their steps away from the rest of the party toward the back of the farmhouse. As soon as he was certain they were out of earshot of straying guests, he said, "We can leave marriage and the relationship between the sexes for another time. There's a bench in the yard behind the house where you and Miss Califaxton may discuss whatever it is you have to discuss. I must tell you, however, that I agreed to help arrange this private meeting with reluctance, and only because Miss Worthing assured me that you have no intention of suggesting that Miss Califaxton accompany you to Gretna Green."

Wendell did not like being lectured to but felt himself powerless to object. Beat him why Gilmichael was even willing to help, he was cutting up so stiff about it! He replied with injured dignity that he harbored no such despicable idea as an elopement.

"Now. You will be in view of the servants in the kitchens at all times. You should also know that Miss Worthing and I will be in the library, where, I just mention, there is a window overlooking the yard."

Maidie and Prudence were waiting for them, seated on the bench. Prudence rose, holding out both hands to Wendell, and he, forgetting Allan and Maidie, strode forward to meet her, catching her hands in his own and carrying them to his lips.

"Oh, Wendell, my dearest." Prudence whispered. Her eyes shone with tears. "My very, very dearest."

Allan cleared his throat, and spoke more gently than he had intended. "I warn you that you should be brief. Too long an absence . . ."

"Yes," Wendell said, not taking his eyes from Prudence, her hands still tightly clasped against his heart.

Allan offered Maidie his arm and they retreated, both feeling like intruders, their own emotions in sudden turmoil. Her hand trembled on his arm.

"My dear . . ."

She looked up at him then, her eyes wide, as bright with tears as Prudence's had been.

"My dear . . ." He was unable to think of any other phrase.

She quickly lowered her gaze. "We must remember . . . remember we are . . . chaperons."

"Yes."

They sat together in the library, tensely, trying to make conversation on any subject but the one that filled their thoughts, and counting the dragging minutes until they were released from this exquisite torture.

Mr. Worthing and Mr. Califaxton had found that they shared a number of interests, as Fanny had hoped they would. They did not, however, find those interests solely in the domain of Mammon as she had thought they would.

"That boy of yours," Mr. Worthing remarked, on encountering Mr. Califaxton again. "Lots of sense. Owned up fair and square he'd been rusticated." He added, with a self-mocking grin, "More in the intellectuals department than a lot of these bucks. Sat still and listened to an old banker like me talking about loans and interest. Wouldn't mind having a fellow like him at the bank."

Mr. Califaxton didn't bother to hide his disbelief. "Ain't what I usually hear about my youngest. Now, my oldest boy has a real head for the business, and steady as the day is long; I've another in the army—served his king well in the recent war. And John, although I can't like this nonsense about missionary work, has a head on his shoulders. A real scholar and a man to be reckoned with if you cross him. But Chester's always been a puzzle."

"Don't seem a bad boy to me. But then, I've only the one girl chick . . ."

The two gentlemen found much of interest in the subject of girl chicks, and the difficulties getting them settled in proper marriages—always a danger from heiress hunters. As they were finding themselves in such harmony, Mr. Califaxton was moved to unburden himself.

"Maybe you know, Worthing, that that fellow Duval's been after my daughter."

"You don't say! After your daughter, eh? I'd got it in my head he was after mine!"

"Well, whatever game they've been playing to make you think so, the impudent pup had the . . . the gall to ask permission to pay his addresses to my Pru!"

Mr. Worthing swallowed his disappointment. He hadn't been set on the idea, although he'd seen possibilities in Duval. Had counted a lot that he didn't like his name. "I wouldn't have had any objections to him marrying my little Maidie. He seems a likely enough young scrub. Doesn't have the smell of an heiress hunter. Emery vouches for him. They're cousins you know. And Fanny says . . ." Mr. Worthing caught himself. Better leave Fanny out of this; nobody in their senses would trust Fanny—as hadn't he just found out! And not for the first time, either. "Well, no matter what Fanny says. As I said, looks sensible enough underneath all that poetry folderol."

But Mr. Califaxton was reliving the monstrous moments he had spent with Wendell and was purpling up again. "Sensible! Ha! Now I've no objection to his poetry or his politics. It's his want of money—and common sense, too, if it comes to that. Had the audacity to say he didn't want any of my money—that he could support Pru on five hundred a year! Now where's the common sense in that? Or I should have said mendacity, for three to one he'd soon change his tune. Pru's worth more than some starveling politician with only five hundred a year. I expect the girl to bring money *in* to the family, not drain it out. I assure you, Worthing, I showed him the door in a hurry!"

Now here's a pretty piece of work, Mr. Worthing thought. Worthy young fellow like Duval. Or Toone. Whichever. "Well," he said tolerantly, "I wouldn't want my Maidie in a marriage she didn't like just because some fine fellow she did like came along, and my only objection was a lack of fortune."

"Pru's seventeen. Too young to know her own mind."

"She kicking up, is she?"

"Haven't told her yet. Thought I might make her stay home today, but Mrs. Califaxton wouldn't hear of it. Said she just might sneak off and meet Duval while I was over here filling my belly. My wife has a way of putting things pretty square on the mark."

"Yes, best listen to the women when Cupid's involved. But I'll tell you, it's a good idea to think back now and then. Mrs. Worthing's father wasn't any too happy when I made my proposals, you can bet. Viscount, you know. But he came around.

We even got to liking each other. But if he'd stood out against it, I'd have carried her off to Gretna Green and be damned to him—and to all the gossips besides."

Mr. Califaxton, who had met objections to his own marriage from Mrs. Califaxton's genteel family (who had led him to believe that generations of patrician and propertied forbears were spinning in their graves) thought it wiser to seek a change of subject.

But Mr. Worthing had not quite finished. It got his dander up, when he thought about it, that a perfectly respectable man and a relative of his sister's husband—practically one of his own family—wasn't considered worthy of that Milk and Water Miss old Califaxton had sired. Why, in comparison to his Maidie . . .

Allan happening by at that moment gave him to think he saw an opportunity. Might as well get another opinion. "Gilmichael, we're just having a discussion here, Califaxton and I. What do you have to say, sir, about girls who want to wed against their fathers' wishes? Given, of course, that it's an honorable and respectable man she's chosen? We've both got girls—Califaxton and me—that we have to get settled in the world, and we were just discussing the subject—in a theoretical way, of course. I suppose you have a sister, or some young relative you're responsible for?"

It seemed to Mr. Worthing that the question was more interesting than he had thought, for Gilmichael was looking very conscious. So he did have some young female under his wing, and giving him some trouble, too, he'd wager.

"I have a younger sister, yes," Allan said, rallying his forces. "I hope that she would choose someone I could immediately approve, but if not, I would certainly ask them both to wait for a period of time—prove their attachment . . ."

"And if there's some circumstance that you can't stomach?" Mr. Califaxton asked. "Something you're set against?"

"You defeat me, sir. The entire question is too theoretical. I'm afraid I must only say that I hope my sister never presents me with such a dilemma."

Mr. Califaxton, memories of his own hot youth stirred, and with Mr. Worthing's mention of Gretna Green on his mind, said, "Always a danger of a runaway marriage, you know. Not to be discounted."

"That's right," Mr. Worthing declared. "Can't discount it. Was just telling Califaxton here that I'd have run off with my Tish and society bedamned if her father had kicked up rough. Well, it's all theoretical, as you say, and I say there's not too much to be gained from theoretical talk. As I told Emery the other day, it's the here and now that interests me."

So the subject was dropped, to Allan's relief—his brush with headstrong youth and his disquieting minutes with the banker's daughter only minutes in the past. The three men stood talking amiably together until Fanny came looking for Allan.

As he walked away with her, Mr. Califaxton remarked to Mr. Worthing, "Gilmichael's a friend of my son—the one with the army. Says he's a distant cousin of some marquis."

"That's no recommendation to me. But he seems a sensible enough fellow."

"You one of those democrats?"

"No, but I'd say the aristocracy has too many privileges they don't deserve."

"Can't say I disagree with you, but a little bit of the blue never hurt a businessman's family."

Before Mr. Worthing could reply, they were set upon again by Fanny, who desired both gentlemen to come to their dinner, which was laid out on trestle tables on the terrace.

Fanny's party, as Fanny's parties often did, had tapered into a mellowing evening. As Mrs. Califaxton at last gathered up her family, Chester was discovered missing. A quickly instituted search found him in the library, absorbed in a book.

His mother was seriously shocked. "Chester! Put that book down this instant. Am I to be plagued with a second son whose nose is always in a book? Surely one is enough for any family! Put that book down, I say. Really, Mrs. Clarke, you can't imagine—bookish as you are—and without any children . . ." Mrs. Califaxton paused. "Without any children yet, that is to say, but you will learn soon enough how aggravating . . ."

Chester mumbled a denial of bookishness. He'd only been a little tired and had wandered into the library to rest a bit.

In fact, Mr. Worthing's discourse had lain on his mind all afternoon, rather jiggled around up there, and as the sun disappeared behind Sagfel, he wandered off to the tower library to search the shelves. He'd had an idea once to read the economists, but they'd proved to be incomprehensible as well as soporific. Of course, he'd been just twenty then, and hadn't known as much of the world. He pulled from the shelf a copy of Adam Smith's *Inquiry into the Nature and Causes of the Wealth of Nations* and, opening the book at random, read: "The great commerce of every civilized society, is that carried on between the inhabitants of the town and those of the country." That statement, at least, seemed both sensible and comprehensible. He checked the index for banks.

Chester had rendezvoused with Destiny.

Fifteen

A gentle rain fell on Krigsmere and Pennelbeck Vale as the long day ended. Some of the participants in the festivities were now soundly asleep, at peace with themselves and the world, their cares insufficient to prevent surrender to Morpheus. But others lay awake in the dark listening to the rain and the gentle soughing of wind in the trees . . .

Maidie now believed Allan Gilmichael, Lord Enett, to be necessary to her future life and happiness.

She was certain of his inclinations, was hopeful of his intentions, but uncertain of his circumstances. He had naturally been reticent when he was hiding his identity, and they had not, since her parents and Aunt Seraphina arrived, had opportunities for the intimacy that would permit revelations. Perhaps he had been promised to another before they met. A marriage of convenience for the purpose of heirs. Or the responsibilities that had fallen to his lot after the death of his brother would not permit him to marry for years yet. Or that with his elevation in rank he must seek a wife among the aristocracy, and a mere banker's daughter should not aspire.

She would like to stay at Pennelbeck Farm to aid Aunt Fanny during her pregnancy, of course, but she couldn't deny that between Mrs. Eckston, Mrs. Califaxton, a skilled midwife in Sagpaw, and a lying-in doctor in Kendal—and Emery so devoted—that Fanny could do without her very well. There were always young girls ready to hire out, who could perform the chores that she now did, and probably more efficiently.

But surely if her father intended to take her away from the Lakes, he would have told her before now, when there was only one day of his visit left. Or had he been waiting until the last minute in order not to spoil her pleasure? She must speak to him tomorrow morning . . .

She refused to think about it more, and dwelt instead on the many minutes passed in Allan's company during the afternoon . . . Maidie, ever the optimist, fell asleep.

Fanny was wondering why Sam had not suggested that Maidie leave her. Perhaps that hadn't been the purpose of his visit at all. Or perhaps she had passed muster. Allan had not yet spoken, she was certain, but if ever she saw a man in love! Fanny was not one to discount the advantages of propinquity or the dangers of separations in affairs of the heart. He hadn't given up the Huddleston house—trust Mrs. Califaxton to know. Interesting . . . Fanny too drifted off on the River Lethe.

Mr. Worthing, although Fanny didn't know it (and he had no intention of telling her) had a good reason for permitting Maidie to remain longer in the Lakes.

He had only the week before sustained an interview with Lord Calvette, Maidie's ardent admirer and frequent London escort, who had begged permission to address her when she returned. The permission had been summarily denied, although Mr. Worthing had condescended to give an explanation that a young lord, bearing responsibilities for perpetuation of a family name and title, could understand. Mr. Worthing had been at great pains to make it clear that although the Worthing name wasn't associated with either land or lineage, it was associated with solid financial worth and personal endeavor, and that Maidie must marry a man who would take her name.

Lord Calvette, to give him credit, was not snobbish, and read-

ily accepted the strange notion that even a commoner with no
claim to gentility except by marriage might be proud of his
name. He had expressed great pain that his suit was denied, and
was almost equally expressive in his understanding of the reason. Nonetheless, Mr. Worthing did not trust the fellow to keep
his distance once Maidie returned. Came down to the fact that
Calvette thought himself too much in love to be trusted. Furthermore, he suspected a want of firmness in his character. It
wouldn't do to throw Maidie in his way again so soon. Let her
stay until September, when Tish would be coming home from
Wales.

As for the Califaxtons, that looked like a dead end. A Califaxton alliance would have been agreeable from a financial point
of view, and after meeting the family he had to say he wouldn't
have been sorry if Maidie had chosen one of the boys.

He hadn't noticed any particular interest between Maidie and
either of them—the only two of Fanny's promised four in residence—and just like her to miscount. The older one was too
interested in religion. Going to be a tub-thumper in Scotland,
young Chester said. He'd be hanged if he could see how anybody
could spend all day discussing theology! John Califaxton had
sat the whole afternoon with Tish, and every time he'd gone near
them they were on some new and obscure point of doctrine. Of
course, he admitted, his own dissenting views were acquired
along with his wife, and were based more on his distaste for
unearned privilege as represented by the Church of England than
on any doctrinal convictions. More politics than theology.

Young Chester didn't seem to have an eye on Maidie either.
In fact, Maidie treated him more like a brother than a possible
suitor. Did seem a youth of sense (a conclusion that had surprised Mr. Califaxton, but then often a father didn't know his
own son), and he wouldn't have minded if he and Maidie had
hit it off.

Maybe he had missed something, with Fanny insinuating and

hinting that it was Duval who had Maidie's interest. Just what game had she been playing anyway? Throwing sand in his eyes? Maybe it was John Califaxton after all. He'd just bet Fanny thought he'd object to a tub-thumper. But would a suitor sit around all day with a girl's mother? Didn't seem likely. But why should Fan object to the younger Califaxton? Of course, John was more eligible . . . older and more settled. Young Chester was a trifle green, although just wanted some direction to get his feet set on the right path. Mr. Worthing concluded complacently that he could have him straightened out within a month if he had the chance.

Couldn't say he wasn't a little relieved that Duval had had his eye on the Califaxton chit rather than Maidie. He'd been willing to make allowances where Maidie's happiness was concerned, but he hadn't seen any spark of the banker in the boy.

"Tish? You awake?" he asked softly. Receiving no answer, he sighed, and settled himself for sleep.

Wendell, also wakeful, sat among his inflammatory pamphlets, an empty teacup in his hand, staring into the glowing coals—all that remained of the small fire over which he had brewed his tea. His thoughts were with Prudence.

He had laid his heart at her feet that afternoon. She had in turn given him her love, and her promise of fidelity through trials and sorrows. She would wait for him forever. Then she had confessed—looking so pretty and guilty—that Maidie had agreed to help them meet only if she promised to urge him to flee, and that it was awful of her to have lied to Maidie, but of course he must stand by his convictions and refuse to run away. She would be proud to marry a man who had been imprisoned for a principle—but it was just that she couldn't bear it for him. Wendell pondered for a time on his love's tender heart.

She had assured him that even though she was certain her father would be more willing to let her marry him after a time, and "after he comes to know you, dear"—if dear Wendell hadn't been in jail—although perhaps he would refuse to let her marry a former prisoner—but that it wouldn't matter, for she would wait for him forever. He realized, on thinking it over, that Prudence seemed to think forever might mean until she was thirty . . . when he'd be . . . he'd be thirty-seven! The calculation was discouraging and he chose not to consider it.

She would be more comfortable, she'd told him, if she did not have to break with her family, but she would if it was the only way. And then she'd been unable to hold back the tears. Ah, his lovely Prudence. Although she had quickly recovered her poise and taken his hand and begged forgiveness for her weakness, he had felt like the most unfeeling monster in the world. He had not been able to ask it of her. So brave and willing to sacrifice for him. Before he knew it, he was assuring Prudence that he would take flight.

But now that he had at last agreed, he didn't have any idea how to go about it. He supposed he should make his way to Liverpool and try to get passage to America, like Cobbett did. But to South America—for he fully intended to join the Freedom Fighters in Venezuela. Well, Emery and Fanny—and Maidie too—had been urging him forever to run from his persecutors, so let them figure out how it was to be done.

Wendell returned to pleasanter thoughts.

In the Califaxton household, Prudence recalled (with some satisfaction) her precious minutes with Wendell and dreamed of their future, while John considered his plans to remove to Scotland within the next few weeks. But it was only in Chester's bedchamber that a candle burned. Propped up on his pillows with John's copy of the *Wealth of Nations,* he had finished Banks, Bankers, Bank Notes, and Bankruptcy; read all the references under Interest; and was proceeding with Money.

And Allan Gilmichael, Lord Enett? He was reprehensibly asleep, not even dreaming of his true love.

* * *

Seraphina and Mrs. Worthing on the last day of their visit chose to rest, gathering strength for their journey into Wales. Mr. Worthing had a more active, and more interesting day altogether.

First, while he was drinking his morning tea, the maid Stella delivered a note from Chester Califaxton. "Hmmm," he murmured as he read it. Had the boy been awake, after all, while he talked of loans and interest? He called for paper and pencil, scribbled a reply, and gave it to the maid, Stella, for one of the farmhands to deliver. Then Duval had looked into the breakfast parlor, wanting Emery, and had been sent off to the library. After several minutes, the maid had appeared again, to tell him that Mr. Clarke would like him to join them.

"Have a problem for you, Sam," Emery said, the minute he stepped into the room. "My young cousin here has decided that flight is more prudent than martyrdom and probably more comfortable than jail . . ."

Mr. Worthing listened without comment to a fanciful tale of spies and political persecutions, and when it was concluded said, "Well, Duval. Really believe your opinions are odious enough to get the government after you?"

"Yes, sir, I do. I am a republican and a democrat; I believe the Church of England should be stripped of its role in government; like Mrs. Worthing I believe in civil rights for Dissenters and Catholics; public funded education for workers, and—"

"Yes, yes. I can see that you're a pretty radical fellow, all right. Not surprised if maybe the government put a spy on you. Now that don't say that I approve of spying on English citizens, for I don't." Mr. Worthing rubbed his chin, pursed his lips, and frowned, nodding to himself. "Looks like the best thing for you to do," he said at last, "is to lay low for a while, and let me make some inquiries. Know a few people who might be able to throw light on this."

"Allan Gilmichael made inquiries of a friend of his father in the House of Lords," Emery said, "but with the Parliament recessing, and the election . . ."

"Gilmichael. Hmmmm. Didn't you say, Emery—or somebody did at any rate—that he's related to the Enetts? They've got shipping interests. Might talk to him and see if he has any influence with the family. I've some connections myself in Liverpool. Ship you off to America for a while, Duval."

"South America, sir. If you'll excuse me. I shall join Bolivar and the Freedom Fighters."

"Now that don't sound sensible. Why not just run off to France? No reason political birds can't fly there as well as debtors."

Wendell maintained that it was South America or not at all, until Emery and Mr. Worthing, with an exchanged glance, decided to let the matter rest for the moment. A note was dispatched to Allan, begging his presence.

Allan, when he joined them, also saw fit to argue against South America, adding that one was as dead fighting in a noble cause as in any other. Wendell was adamant, and at last it was settled among them that he would accompany Mr. Worthing to London where he would quietly take rooms in an obscure section of the city and await word on his means of escape.

As Allan rose to go, Mr. Worthing said, "Walk a way with you, Gilmichael, if you don't mind company."

Allan accepted with expressions of pleasure, wondering if the banker had divined his interest in Maidie and sought a private interview. He was not yet ready to discuss his intentions, but he steadied his nerve and left the topics for discussion to Mr. Worthing.

"What do you think of that young scrub?" Mr. Worthing asked Allan as they strolled along the road toward Sagpaw. "Could see right away that you're a man of sense. Not that my brother-in-law isn't, you understand. But Emery and Fanny—well, they're always giving money to some poor scoundrel who's got himself in hot water—usually due to his own foolishness, I might add. They tend to take a . . . now I don't want to say over-excited view exactly . . . but sometimes aren't as logical as one might like. Think there's anything to this spy business?"

"I have to say, sir, that someone does seem to be investigating Duval. But whether it is initiated by the government . . . I just can't believe Duval is influential enough to be thought dangerous."

"Wouldn't hurt for him to lay low for a few weeks, however?"

"Probably a wise course until we can uncover who is behind these inquiries."

"Emery says you have connections in the government. Friend of your father, I understand? And of course your cousin—the connection with the Enetts. Think you can use it? I refer to their shipping interests."

"Yes, I can try." Allan hesitated. Why not make a clean breast of his identity this minute? Ask for permission to address Maidie . . .

"Well, that's settled," Mr. Worthing said briskly. "We'll both pursue our inquiries into this mystery and see about getting Duval out of the country for a time if we decide it's necessary. Nonsense, this South American business. You agree?"

"He may not be persuadable."

"I've a long drive with him tomorrow, and at least two nights on the road. I'll appeal to his attachment to that Milk and Water Miss of the Califaxtons. You know about that?"

"Yes. Miss Worthing mentioned it."

"And I'll take the responsibility for keeping him out of the public eye. Well, if that's agreeable, then I'll be saying good morning to you. But before I turn back . . ." Mr. Worthing produced a business card, on the back of which he jotted the address of his house on Bedford Square. "Contact me at the bank or my residence . . . Now just tell me where I can get in touch with you. Had a note from young Chester Califaxton that he wants to discuss something with me, and Maidie will be wanting to know how much longer I'll permit her to stay . . . arrange for a post chaise . . . busy day ahead." Mr. Worthing pocketed the scrap of paper from his notebook on which Allan had scrawled his Lakeland address, and stuck out his hand. "Between the two of us, we'll get to the bottom of this."

"I'll do all I can," Allan said. The opportunity for honesty and revelation had passed. Or so he told himself.

Chester entered his father's presence with a touch of trepidation. "I say, sir, may I speak with you a moment?"

"What about?" Mr. Califaxton asked suspiciously. When Chester requested an interview it usually involved money.

"I've been thinking, sir, about my future."

"Well, bowl me over!"

Chester disdained to recognize the sarcasm. His father had reason, he supposed, to think him a fribble.

"So, what have we to discuss about your future?"

"I spoke to Mr. Worthing this morning," Chester said, feeling valiant, "and asked him if he might be willing to take me on as an apprentice. The thing is, sir, banking sounds more interesting to me than manufacturing, and anyway, you've got Arthur. A fellow doesn't like to think about his progenitor popping off, but I thought if I invested some money . . . became a name in the bank, you know. And, well, I know that I'll be coming into money one day, and if I could borrow now against my inheritance . . ." Chester's argument trailed off. Dashed difficult talking about one's own father going West. Sounded downright mercenary, which for all his troubles with money back in his salad days, wasn't a right description of his character.

Mr. Califaxton was having a hard time coming to terms with this unexpected manifestation of ambition in his youngest and most difficult son. Gave him a lump in his throat. "Talked to Worthing about it, did you?" he asked gruffly.

"Yes, sir. Suggested I speak with you, and if you're agreeable, he'll take me in for forty thousand." As Mr. Califaxton began to color up, Chester held up his hand. "Now don't get into a taking, sir. He means after I serve a satisfactory apprenticeship. He said we—the three of us—must discuss the matter and come to some arrangement. He's got this notion that he won't have Worthing's Bank known by any other name than Worthing's, no matter how many partners he takes in, but I don't care about that. As long as it's all fair and legal." Chester waited for a reply, but none was forthcoming. Mr. Califaxton seemed lost in thought, gazing out the window, and drumming his fingers on his desk. "Maybe he'd agree to twenty thousand," Chester suggested tentatively.

Mr. Califaxton looked up. He hoped Chester wouldn't notice the tear in his eye. "Well, when does Worthing leave? Send a note along to him now. Ask him to share our mutton. Should have John's opinion, even if he ain't interested in business, he's a good head. And your mother isn't behind the door when it comes to brains. Shrewd as she can stand. After all, taking capital out of the business . . . Family affair."

"I don't think Mr. Worthing can spend much time today, sir. Leaving tomorrow and all. Said he'd call on us this afternoon, and if you're agreeable I can start my apprenticeship right away."

"Well, however." Mr. Califaxton got up to give Chester a fatherly clap on the back. "Won't use your name, even if you buy in? Looks to me like you should have been buttering up the daughter. Sprightly enough gal. Had plenty of chances, I should think . . ."

"You're right, sir. Should have been. But opportunity's past."

"Now what do you mean by that?"

"Wouldn't want to start any rumors, but I think her interest's already engaged."

"Hmmmph," said Mr. Califaxton.

That particular tranquility that follows days filled with people and activity settled over Pennelbeck Farm. Seraphina and Mrs. Worthing had proceeded in the Worthing carriage to their appointed visit in Wales. Mr. Worthing and Wendell departed by post-chaise to London. Chester, choosing to go on horseback, would follow in a few days to begin his unpaid apprenticeship.

A note went by express from Allan to the captain of a ship plying the waters between England and the Americas. A return express bore the news that the next Enett ship sailing had been delayed, but that Mr. Duval would be welcome if he didn't mind close quarters and the Spartan arrangements of a small crowded trading ship. The *Jolly Mistress* was no grand East India Company vessel, her captain added. Another express was sent off to Mr. Worthing.

A letter arrived from Emery's ancient relative, Miss Hattie, which he bothered only to glance through to assure himself of the old lady's health. It seemed to be exclusively devoted to more genealogy—she'd made a mistake, somehow . . . "obscure connection . . . not recognized socially by the family . . . etc.," to the effect that Wendell wasn't related to the Cholmeleys after all. He had more important things to do than bother with Wendell's ancestry.

The days passed, and although Allan had intended to leave the Lakes as soon as his conservative presence was no longer needed by Fanny, yet he lingered. He couldn't leave without coming to an understanding with Maidie. She seemed to be giving him every encouragement, but still he hesitated. He told himself he had to be certain. If he made his wishes known and she should reject him, he would be cast back again into that oppressive sadness, haunted by his brother's death and hating his responsibilities. It was easier to drift on, seeing her every day, but settling nothing.

Maidie was gratified that he remained, his attentions were certainly not wanting—but she was puzzled that he made no declaration. Why hadn't he spoken to her father? What was the matter with the man?

Allan found Fanny and Emery in the breakfast parlor drinking tea and sorting their mail.

"What a cold wind for July!" he said, as he joined them at the table. "And where is Miss Worthing? I've come to give her another fishing and rowing lesson as I promised her yesterday."

"She's gone to her room to finish a letter to her mother for me to post in Sagpaw," Emery replied. "She asks you please to accept her apologies, and she'll be down soon. You might as well take a cup of tea with us."

Fanny shivered. "It has become a terribly cold, depressing day, hasn't it? And it dawned so wonderfully pleasant! I'd hardly wish to be on the lake today, with this wind, and gloom, and rain in the air. Perhaps you'd enjoy yourselves more playing backgammon in the library." She shivered again, and hugged herself. "Dear Emery, would you mind getting my shawl from the Scriptorium? I asked Mrs. Eckston to build up the fire there, for I must begin that article the *Edinburgh Review* requested. But first this accumulated mail! Such a tiresome task! But how I ramble on . . . Emery . . ."

"I'll bring your shawl, Fanny," Allan offered. "I've already had three cups of coffee this morning—and no need to add a cup of tea."

As Allan mounted the spiral stair that led from the library to Fanny and Emery's Scriptorium, a quick footstep above alerted him that the Clarkes' housekeeper was hurriedly descending, her own errand completed. He moved against the outer wall to allow her to pass.

But it was Maidie who rushed upon him. He nearly reeled with the surprise. She too recoiled for a mere breath of time, and then fell headlong into his eager embrace.

Her lips opened to receive his impassioned kiss as naturally as though she had been born to it.

"Maidie, my darling," he whispered. She was warm, sweet, and pliant in his arms.

On a long breath her head fell back and he kissed her soft neck.

She caressed his hair and drew his head to her breast. "Oh, dearest, dearest," she said softly. He was ardent, strong, and infinitely tender in her arms.

He kissed her again, but when he would have stopped, she kissed him.

He held her from him. Time enough for her to learn how men were made when loving was afoot.

She strained against his hands, wanting to return to his embrace, but he took her face between his two hands, still holding her firmly from him, kissing her forehead, her closed eyelids, and again, gently, her parted lips.

"We shouldn't be doing this, my duckling." His breath was short.

"No." She drew a deep convulsive sigh. Then she smiled, straight into his eyes from where she still stood on the step above him. Her hand fluttered to her breast. "I am quite overcome!"

He caressed her cheek. "My dearest, I've business that must be attended at Thresseley, but I'll be in London at the earliest possible moment to speak to your father."

"Whatever about?" she asked, batting her lashes energetically.

He gave her a gentle shake. "Don't play the innocent with me, little imp. Teasing a besotted gentleman simply isn't done."

"I am compromised, then?"

He pulled her roughly back into his arms—heedless. "Yes . . . and yes . . . and yes . . . and yes . . ."

This time, they withdrew spontaneously from their embrace, dazed, staring into each other's eyes.

They were unaware that the intensity of their encounter lingered like ambient scent when Mrs. Eckston appeared below them around the curve of the stair.

She greeted them with aplomb. She was not particularly surprised at what she suspected had just occurred; she had some time since determined on nice Mr. Gilmichael as her favorite among those young males most commonly present on the premises. Mr. Wendell, although one couldn't help loving him, was too florid in his manners; and that Mr. Chester too young by far. She had a great fondness for Mr. John Califaxton, who she favored equally with Mr. Gilmichael, but in recent weeks it had seemed to her that Mr. Gilmichael was the more likely of the two.

"I was delayed in the kitchen and am just now on my way to build up the fire in the Scriptorium," she said. "I hope Mrs. Fanny hasn't seen fit to send you to do it, Miss Maidie! Such a botch as she makes, Mr. Gilmichael—or perhaps Mrs. Fanny remembered and was sending you to help? But I'll just go up and do it right now . . . unless you've already . . . ?"

"No," Maidie said, having gathered her wits to think and her forces to reply, "I remembered that I left my pen in the Scriptorium, but I must not have . . ."

Allan, succumbing to an unaccustomed schoolboy sense of having been caught out, said, "Mrs. Clarke was wanting her shawl, and I was just . . . I met Miss Worthing coming down . . . I'll just get it now. Miss Worthing . . ." He wanted to tell Maidie that they must speak together before facing Fanny and Emery.

Mrs. Eckston, alive on all counts, as Chester would have described her, said, "I'll get the shawl. You just wait here. And then you tell Mrs. Fanny that in two shakes I'll have the Scriptorium warm as toast."

"I'll come with you, Mrs. Eckston," Maidie said. "You needn't come back down these stairs just for that."

"Very well, dear child. Come along."

Allan and Maidie flattened themselves against the wall for Mrs. Eckston to pass, and Allan, his hand on Maidie's arm, mouthed softly, "I'll wait."

"Yes," she whispered.

She soon reappeared around the curve of the stair. The repetition of her earlier descent demanded a stealthy repetition of embraces, but warmer and more comfortable this time, as though all had been settled between them, permitting passion to await its time.

They entered the breakfast parlor hand in hand. Fanny—after one surprised second—rose and held out her arms to Maidie. "Well, my dears!" she exclaimed.

Emery looked up, astonished. "What? Fanny, what are you . . . ?" Then, as he remembered, "Ah, yes," he remarked, and rose, too.

Exclamations, congratulations and wishes for future felicity followed, until at last Fanny sent the newly-declared lovers away. "Go get in the boat and row yourselves into some rosy land. Or go into the library if it's too cold and choppy on Krigsmere. You will have much to talk about."

Neither Maidie nor Allan wanted any serious discussion of their future that rosy afternoon, but the day following—the day before Allan's finally determined departure—they turned their minds to more practical matters. Fanny had reminded Maidie of Mr. Worthing's prejudices, and so it was a somewhat sobered young woman who greeted her lover.

But she had no real fear of her father's disapproval; he had always been indulgent, and had let her make decisions for herself. Of course it was sometimes necessary to endure a storm if he didn't approve. But in this, the man she wished to marry, he would not deny her, for of course he would never ruin her happiness, no matter how exasperated it might make him for a time!

She told Allan, hesitantly, that her father had not welcomed aristocratic suitors. Allan was more interested in her former suitors and why she had rejected them. He had judged Maidie's father to be a sensible and well-bred man, and could not imagine any difficulty. If he were a mere second son with a trifling fortune, as he had been only two years ago—then a banker with an heiress for a daughter might well have cut up rough! But not now that he was a peer and could offer Maidie so much!

They were soon back in their rose-tinted world, with just each other, until Allan left—for a brief stay at Thresseley, and then to London.

The second event to interrupt the tranquility at Pennelbeck Farm was Sir Harold's return two weeks after Allan's departure, and openly asking for Wendell. Old Peg was the first to see him—and a mighty suspicious character she took him to be.

She arrived at the farm soon after in much disorder of person and bearing. Sir Harold, she breathlessly announced to Fanny, had come to the cottage, where she had been cleaning and scrubbing to make it all nice should Mr. Wendell return. He was asking for Mr. Wendell, and although she didn't know why Mr. Wendell should have left so sudden, when the rent was all paid and he intended to enter the wrestling . . .

Fanny interrupted to ask where Sir Harold had gone.

"Sent him to Sagpaw. And said Mr. Wendell was going on to do some walking about on the fells. So I could come this way to you." Old Peggy chortled, delighted with her ruse.

"You did just right, Peggy. Mr. Wendell is safe, I assure you. It is no business of anyone but himself where he has gone, or when he will return, and if Sir Harold comes again to the cottage, as he may likely do, just send him on to me. Mr. Clarke will make short work of him!"

Old Peg, grinning, departed with an air of relish for the coming encounter, but to her great disgust she was cheated of the pleasure. Sir Harold, discovering in the village that no one had seen Wendell for several days, muttered an oath, thought a few disparaging thoughts about overly-loyal servants, and set his steps in the direction of Pennelbeck Farm. Old Peg, on the watch, saw his approach with anticipation, and his passing with disappointment.

Sir Harold's first encounter at Pennelbeck Farm was with Maidie, working in the garden and thinking about her absent lover.

"Why, Sir Harold!" she exclaimed. "This is a surprise!"

"I am puzzled why you should find it surprising. I stated that I would return when my business in London was accomplished."

"So you did," she said unhelpfully.

Sir Harold was not feeling cordial, suspecting that the old hag of a housekeeper he had first spoken to had practiced a deceit, and that he had wasted time on a wild-goose chase. He made an effort at greater affability. "However, I will not engage in subterfuge. I have business with Mr. Toone, who has been calling himself Duval, and should I not find him here, then with Mr. Clarke. A business matter, you understand."

"Wendell isn't here," Maidie said.

Sir Harold turned an icy eye on her. "Then perhaps you can tell me where he is."

Her chin went up. "No, I can't. You should speak with my uncle."

Sir Harold's success was no better with Fanny and Emery.

"How may I serve you?" Emery asked, stiffly formal.

"I am hoping to speak with Mr. Duval. Perhaps you are more knowledgeable about his movements than your niece claims to be?"

"No, I must echo Miss Worthing. He isn't here. But if you will state your business with my cousin, I could in turn be more forthcoming, although in truth I can't tell you his whereabouts."

"I cannot divulge my business without divulging the identity of my client, who wishes to remain anonymous. I can go so far as to tell you that it is in Mr. Duval's interest—or—let us be as open about this matter as it seems possible to be—in Mr. Salvatore Toone's interest—that I contact him."

"Very well, I'll speak plainly with you, Sir Harold. If your client's notions of my cousin's best interests involve setting spies on him, I, for one, find it difficult to accept your protestations of benign intent. Until you can justify spying and underhanded dealing, we have nothing further to discuss."

Sir Harold was affronted. "Spying? I know nothing of spying. I admit readily that I came here to verify the quality of Mr. Toone's character, but I resent any such description of my activities as spying."

Emery shifted in his chair as an indication that he considered the interview closed. "I cannot believe, Sir Harold, that gentlemen would either engage in or sanction such actions."

Sir Harold, caught between his employer's requirement of anonymity and his own self-esteem, lost his temper. The accusation of underhanded dealing had struck to the quick. "I can only say that I hope you do not regret your refusal to reveal Mr. Toone's whereabouts. And I might add that I have never fallen into such an undisciplined set in my life—and I speak not only of the untested and over-imaginative theories that are bruited about on these premises every day, but that you have formed a community of lotus eaters—"

"Lotus eaters!" Fanny exclaimed, amused. "Obviously, Sir Harold, you have not eaten of our lotuses, for I detect no desire on your part to remain."

Sir Harold turned on her, infuriated. "I believe my reference is apt. Lying about on the grass in the middle of the night! Chasing fireflies! Phantom spies! As though no one among you had passed his thirteenth year! Encouraging young men to nurse notions against their best interests!" He halted abruptly, and took a deep breath. "I spoke in haste, and perhaps may be misinterpreted. I speak in this case of encouraging Mr. Toone to believe himself persecuted. Encouraging him to depart the Lakes, or to sequester himself nearby, and without informing his relatives or acquaintances of his destination or whereabouts. Or, perhaps, instructing them not to reveal it."

Emery, who was rapidly losing his certainty that there was any underhanded dealing of any sort, said, "We have spoken the truth—that we cannot tell you where Mr. Duval—Mr. Toone— is. However, I will give you the direction of my brother-in-law, Mr. Samuel Worthing, of Worthing's Bank. He may be able to give you the information you seek, if you in your turn can demonstrate to him that it is in my cousin's best interests. I can't do more."

Sir Harold left them, unappeased, still angry, but carrying Mr. Worthing's address in his portfolio. His departure left Fanny and Emery, and later Maidie, in consternation. They took counsel with one another, and their reluctance to accept Wendell's belief in persecution now began to seem to have been wise, and Allan's resistance positively brilliant.

"But there was a man watching Wendell," Maidie insisted when Emery questioned her. "Both Chester and I saw him."

"I don't doubt you, Maidie, but could it have been just someone curious about what you were doing, with your easels and portfolios?"

"Oh, Emery. Don't be ridiculous," Fanny said.

They concluded at last that Sir Harold's denial of any knowledge of spying was pro forma, for when they reviewed what he had said, it suggested that he *personally* had not engaged in surreptitious spying. They turned to speculating about how Sir

Harold was acting in Wendell's interest and who his mysterious client might be.

"Well, whatever it means, we must send an express to Sam, warning him about Sir Harold and asking him to inform Wendell," Emery said. "And what was the name of the ship?"

"The *Jolly Mistress*," Fanny said.

"And hope it reaches Papa before she sails."

"We should send an express to Allan also," Fanny said. "His ship, after all."

Sixteen

Despite Allan's haste to conclude an interview with Mr. Worthing, estate business could not be neglected. He had been making too many decisions for too long from too great a distance, and—as he wrote to Maidie—could not see his way clear to leave until mid-August at the earliest. "This is not what an impatient lover should be writing to the woman he hopes to marry; you will think me an indifferent lover, as well as a plodding, farmerish sort of fellow. But I am a farmerish sort of fellow, dear duckling, although I hope not plodding . . ." He ended the letter with such expressions of his regard that Maidie thought him a most satisfactorily impatient lover.

Allan's sister Julie plagued his busy days with begging and pleading to be permitted to accompany him to London. He at last agreed (if she couldn't wait until he was married, when his own wife would present her), but only if she succeeded in persuading their mother and sister-in-law to accompany them and to attend to the opening of Enett House.

"Do be quiet, Julia," Lady Enett said irritably. "August and September should be properly spent in the country, never in town."

Eunice looked up from her sewing. "My dear Clarence always said it wasn't worth being in town until the spring." The dog lying by her chair stirred at the sound of her voice. She leaned down to pet him, murmuring, "Clown wouldn't like London at all, would he?"

Julie, knowing these two very well, returned to plaguing Allan.

He received an express from Emery Clarke, describing Sir Harold's visit and noting that whoever had been spying on Wendell, it seemed not to be the government. "Ha!" he remarked to the assembled females of his household.

"Ha? What information is that monosyllable supposed to convey?" his mother enquired, with a fastidious curl of her lip.

"It conveys the perspicacity of your son," Allan said.

He left the table to compose a hurried express to the master of the *Jolly Mistress,* and a letter to the much put-upon Lord Blout thanking him for his efforts for Duval-Toone, but that the mystery seemed to be on the way to solution.

Allan heard no more of Duval's affairs, except an occasional word passed on from Mr. Worthing by Maidie, that Wendell was living quietly, and seemed to be spending his time with study and writing. A letter from Lord Blout conveyed apologies for his lack of diligence in the matter, and that he had been excessively occupied.

The damp, oppressive heat ended in mid-August, hay harvest was well finished, and the wheat harvest begun. Julie and Eunice brought in the first of the apples, and announced that there was autumn in the air. Julie intensified her pleading, until Allan, in exasperation, ordered his mother to accompany him to London—and in a stronger voice than she considered proper, as she sharply informed him. Nonetheless, she acquiesced, and he decided with some satisfaction that military training might be more useful than he had earlier thought for carrying out the duties of a patriarch.

At the end of the month, Allan felt that estate business was well enough in hand to make the remove to London.

"Now, Maman," he said, as they sat together in the drawing

room after dinner, "please inform me how your preparations for London progress."

Lady Enett embarked on what promised to be a lengthy list of excuses. Allan cut her short with a ruthlessness that surprised even himself. "We leave within two days, three at the most—and with whatever trunks you and Eunice have packed. And don't argue, Maman. My mind is made up."

"It's that banker's daughter! Might as well be a tradesman's daughter. No better!"

"Yes, Maman. It's that banker's daughter. And I'd marry her if she were a drapery clerk's daughter, so you must resign yourself. Don't forget that I was not long ago a simple soldier."

"A captain is not a simple soldier, and furthermore, noble blood flowed in your veins!"

"And perhaps noble blood flows in hers. Our aristocrats have never been averse to consorting with the lower classes in bed—now don't bridle, Eunice. Surely you are aware that the illegitimate sons and daughters of the nobility are legion? Perhaps one of Miss Worthing's ancestresses some generations back was set upon in the spinney by a lord."

Julie snickered; Eunice dropped her eyes modestly to her embroidery.

Lady Enett sniffed. "Diluted blood . . ."

"And her mother is a viscount's daughter—"

"Yes!" Lady Enett was suddenly galvanized. "And I've discovered who *they* are. Rank Dissenters of the worst sort! Who ever heard of anyone with any claim at all to gentility, let alone nobility, rejecting the Church of England?"

Allan threw up his hands. "I give up. We leave in two days' time. I warn you, Maman."

They arrived in London a week later. As soon as his mother, sister-in-law, and sister were settled and beginning to think about refurbishing their town house, he was free to call on Mr. Worthing. He sent a note to Bedford Square, and received in return a cordial invitation to dine. "Just the two of us," Mr. Worthing wrote. "Carrying on here by myself, but I think I can promise you a reasonable dinner, even though the ladies aren't here to order things."

Allan was shown directly into a comfortable library, well furnished with books and periodicals. An ormolu clock decorated with chubby cupids and nubile maidens ticked comfortably on the mantel; and an open window permitted a faint breeze from a rear garden to freshen the room.

"Well, Gilmichael! Welcome to London." Mr. Worthing shook his hand warmly. "Seen the morning papers? Who'd ever have expected such a thing?"

"Has something of importance transpired, sir? I've not had time for the papers this past week and more."

"Not heard from Emery?"

"Only some time ago that Duval seems not to be pursued by government agents. And a word or two since that he was discreetly sequestered."

"I was still trying to talk the young fool into flying to France when I received Emery's express to keep him in London. In any event, Enett got word to the master of the *Jolly Mistress* just before she weighed anchor for America—as you know, of course. Young Duval owes your cousin, and you, his thanks. No telling what would have happened if he had sailed."

"Sir, I should tell you—"

Mr. Worthing held up his hand. "No. No. Later. I beg your pardon for interrupting, but you haven't heard the ending of our spy story yet, which truth to tell, I can't wait to acquaint you with. You must have just missed my express to you in the Lakes. Sent two days ago—same time I sent one to Emery. But let's take a glass of wine. You will appreciate the fortification." Mr. Worthing poured two glasses. Handing one to Allan, he settled back in his chair. "Two, three weeks after I heard from Emery, this fellow Sir Harold Mogglesby calls at the bank, full of the good tidings he was bearing for Duval. Seems the old Duke of Toone. . . . I thought the fellow dead long ago, but I don't keep up on the aristocracy, and he didn't bank with me. What I mean is, I suppose the Jerseys knew he wasn't dead, since he banked with Child's."

"The Duke of Toone?" Allan didn't keep up on the aristocracy either.

"Looking for an heir! Of course he couldn't keep Duval—whose name, incidentally, isn't Toone any more than it is Duval . . . Damn confusing. Be that as it may, he wouldn't have been able to keep the young fellow from inheriting the title, even had he wanted to, once it was clear that his grandmother was legally married to the . . . let's see . . . duke's cousin. They only had one daughter, that would be Duval's mother, you see. But the Toone patent of nobility—or whatever establishes the dukedom—permits titles to pass through the female line. Never came up before, since there's always been a son to carry on. Seems the old duke lost his only son in some fighting in New Spain—with those freedom fighters Duval talks about, or some kind of revolutionists, at any rate."

"But if Duval was the legitimate heir . . ."

"Ah. There's our spy story. One for the scribblers. The old duke's been roving the world and making a fortune—trading in India, gold mines in Mexico, furs in Canada. Even a hint of piracy." Mr. Worthing shook his head. "You have to admire a man like that, who didn't let his title and name imprison him. Didn't let his name become a Bastille, as Hazlitt says. Odd thing. A downright crazy peer who should be locked up in Bedlam is still an aristocrat of the first order, but old Toone was a family black sheep—regular renegade, it seems. Family tried to get him declared incompetent to hold the title—big case in the Lords maybe twenty, thirty years ago. Well, I'm wandering. The point is, his fortune could go where he chose, independent of the title. Another glass?"

"But Duval? How has he taken the sudden wealth and rank he so disdained? He has my sympathy. You see—"

"Young Duval? Stunned, I guess is the proper word. I just heard it yesterday. All over the papers today! I can't imagine you missed it."

"So Duval inherits the fortune, too?"

"That's the way of it. Heir to a title, and what's more to the point, to a fortune!" Mr. Worthing shook his head again. "Came to see me yesterday. The old duke will stay with Child's, I suppose, but young Duval will be setting up with Worthing's."

Allan suddenly felt his mother's chilling stare on the back of his neck. He shook off the feeling. That the Enett shipping interests had declined under Clarence's stewardship was directly due to his reluctance to seek new business, a task to which he must soon turn his own attention. No different from Mr. Worthing's interest in a large new account. Maidie's father was a sensible, intelligent man; the room they were sitting in was well-appointed and in excellent taste; and he had married a viscount's daughter—a dissenting viscount, but a viscount nonetheless.

"I can see," Mr. Worthing said, "that you're as bowled over as I was. Seems the old duke favored rebellions and wants his heir to carry on like his own son would have done had he survived. Oh, not off fighting in rebellions, but using the money for good works. Wanted to make sure his politics were right. Doesn't that beat all? And if his politics hadn't been right, Duval would be a duke someday, but he'd have nothing to show for it but a run-down estate in Sussex, and not much of an estate at that."

Allan couldn't find a thing to say.

"And to think," Mr. Worthing mused, "that for a while there

I thought the fellow was sweet on Maidie. What a near miss that was!"

Allan again felt his mother's chilling stare on the back of his neck. Mr. Worthing was acting like the tradesman she had likened him to—sorry that Maidie had lost a fortune and a duke!

Mr. Worthing chuckled. "How I'd have liked to see Califaxton's face when he read the news! He won't have any objections now to that Milk and Water Miss of his marrying where she wishes, I promise you." He chuckled again, relishing the thought of the wealthy manufacturer's consternation on discovering that he'd denied his daughter a duke. "But as for our spy story—odd. I rallied Sir Harold about spying, and he damn near threatened me with a duel."

Allan's tongue seemed to be glued to his teeth, and even when he managed to get it unstuck he couldn't bring himself to broach the subject that had been uppermost in his mind when he walked in the door. His good breeding carried him through the evening, and he could say when he walked out the door that Mr. Worthing had shown no other vulgarities, and that their conversation—when he could keep his mind from roving—had been sensible and even elevated.

One of the Worthing lackeys secured him a hack, and he directed the driver to Enett House, but when it stopped at his door he changed his mind, and asked to be taken to the Service Club instead. He had not been long in that establishment, where he encountered several old cronies from his army days, before he was as properly foxed as he wished to be.

The following morning, despite a throbbing headache, Allan again steeled himself for an interview with Mr. Worthing. That he had even hesitated for a moment in gaining Maidie for his own was in the light of the new day inexplicable. And he had to promptly set straight his identity, which—equally inexplicable—he had been unable to do. The papers had already reported his arrival in London with his female entourage, and Mr. Worthing would soon put two and two together.

When he had finished his breakfast, fortified himself with coffee, and garbed himself in an appropriately sober manner, he set off to call on Mr. Worthing at his place of business. He had an idea that their encounter would proceed more expeditiously in a utilitarian atmosphere. He choked off the thought that perhaps he should begin by suggesting he might transfer his banking accounts to Worthing's.

Allan was shown immediately into Mr. Worthing's private office. The banker rose and held out his hand. "Well, Gilmichael, what can I do for you?"

"Sir, I have a confession to make, which I was too craven to do last night. Have you a moment?"

"Always have a moment for a sensible man. But a confession? Too much of the theater in that word. Sit down, sit down, and let's hear it."

"I must tell you first that I am Enett."

Mr. Worthing's expression metamorphosed from blank, to comprehension, to puzzlement. "You're telling me that the marquis isn't your cousin?"

"No. I am the marquis. You see, I never expected . . . I never wanted . . ."

"Ah, yes." Mr. Worthing was searching his mind for an old piece of news. "An odd accident. Couple of years ago?"

"Yes."

"You're the brother. Soldier?"

"Yes."

"Well." Mr. Worthing shrugged and spread his hands. "What can I say except what I've said already about Duval. Seems a foolish business. But I'd expect it of a young fellow like him. For a man of your parts . . ."

"I was as foolish as Duval, when it comes to that. I just

thought if I could have a little more time as an ordinary person . . . I sometimes nearly hated my brother for what he did to me."

Mr. Worthing frowned.

"Oh, I knew that Clarence didn't fall on those steps on purpose. My brother and I—we were always close. When I decided to visit the Lakes again, where we'd both enjoyed holidays together when we were young, and neither of us burdened with responsibilities . . . or a title . . ." Allan's explanation trailed off with a dismissive gesture.

It was nearly a minute, or seemed so to Allan, before Mr. Worthing replied. "Can't say that what you did was a wise thing. But no harm done. I can understand it. Glad you came to me before I figured it out. I saw in the *Times* that Enett—well . . . you—had arrived." A rueful smile touched his lips. "Guess I kept you from saying anything last night. Yes, I can see I did. You'll have to forgive me. Always talk too much when Mrs. Worthing and Maidie aren't with me. Well, resigned now, are you?"

"Thank you, sir, for trying to understand." Allan smiled. "And yes, I've found a reason to look forward to life again."

Mr. Worthing raised an enquiring eyebrow.

"You see, I've fallen in love with your daughter. With your permission, I would like to pay my addresses—"

"You *what?*"

Mr. Worthing had half risen from his chair. He sank back again, and from beneath a lowering brow, he asked in a voice from which all cordiality had disappeared, "Maidie has given you reason to believe that she would welcome your addresses?"

Allan, startled and confused, said, "Yes, sir. I believe so." He paused. "No. I am certain that she returns my regard."

Mr. Worthing precipitately abandoned his chair, which overturned with a crash. Allan rose to help right it, but was peremptorily prevented as Mr. Worthing righted it himself, setting it down with an even louder crash. He did not, however, sit. He paced. He pounded the desk. He raged. "Fanny. I knew! When I get my hands on her! The most untrustworthy, lying—yes—lying! My own sister . . . I should have known!"

He sat down, and with gimlet eye faced Allan. "Did Fanny know you were an aristocrat?"

Allan had been remembering suddenly what he had forgotten in those euphoric last days with Maidie—that her father objected to her aristocratic suitors. But somehow he'd thought that Worthing had objected to suitors who just happened to be aristocrats. That hadn't been what Maidie had said, or implied. But he'd thought . . . What he'd thought was that every cit wanted his daughter to marry an aristocrat.

"Well?"

He suppressed the shameful memory. Later he would examine it, and what it said of his own prejudices and character. But not now. "When I first met Mrs. Clarke, no one knew. Only a fellow officer, Lance Califaxton. Shortly before your arrival, as I recognized my growing affection for Miss Worthing, and out of respect for Mr. and Mrs. Clarke, I felt it necessary to confess that I was the marquis and not his cousin . . . to confess that I was I. So to speak."

"They all knew?"

"Only Fanny, and Emery, and Miss . . . Miss Worthing."

"And why weren't you introduced to me by your proper title?"

"Fanny thought it best—"

"Aha! Just as I expected. *Fanny!* Perfidious! Traitorous! And neither my wife nor sister—my other sister—Miss Seraphina Worthing—were informed?"

Allan was beginning to feel like a lowly lieutenant facing an interrogation by his superior for some dastardly breach of military discipline. "Miss Seraphina Worthing recognized me, I believe. I don't know if Mrs. Worthing was informed. But, indeed, sir, I must not allow you to think that Fanny—Mrs. Clarke—is to blame. I was too weak to overcome her objections."

Mr. Worthing paid no heed to Allan's defense of Fanny. "Phina too?" He shook his head, staring down at his desk. The first blaze of his anger had been replaced by a colder, more lasting fury. "So I've harbored more than one viper within my bosom."

Allan realized that it was time he take control of the interview. But even as he opened his mouth to speak, Mr. Worthing had forestalled him.

"No. You cannot pay your addresses to my daughter. I will not have an aristocrat for a son."

Allan went white. "You deny me?"

"I am denying your suit, yes."

"Will you also deny your daughter's happiness?"

"She's had other admirers."

"No doubt. Did she wish to marry any of them?"

Mr. Worthing's eyes narrowed. "Never had a chance. Shooed them off before anything could come of it."

"Commoners as well as aristocrats?"

"Maidie can marry where she wants. But no aristocrats." Mr. Worthing's tone was pugnaciously defensive.

Allan shifted his attack. "Why do you object to aristocrats?"

"All right. Answer me this. Going to let your son, supposing you have one, change his name to Worthing and join the bank?"

So that was it. A man without a son. "Be sensible, sir . . . Pardon me. I'll retract that. Of course I can't permit our first son to be anything other than what he will be—heir to the title and the future head of the Gilmichaels. But a second son, if he should be inclined."

Mr. Worthing was prepared to be sensible, even to overlook that *our.* Despite his anger, he was ashamed of his passionate denunciations of his sisters in front of this near stranger. He launched into the same speech with which he had rejected Calvette's pretensions, and was pleased he could end it on a more complimentary note than he had been able to do with that dimwitted young lord. "I can't say I wouldn't have been pleased to have had you for a son, Enett. Liked you right off. But my answer remains no. I'm sure that, on reflection, you'll understand." After all, Calvette had understood.

Allan's expression had been hardening into ice as he attempted to control his temper. He would not shout at Maidie's father. He rose.

"I have offered you our second son." Allan stumbled to a halt, feeling there was something vaguely reminiscent of sacrificial lambs in his phrasing. "I have offered to permit a second son to change his name," he restated. "I will not retract that pledge. But I also pledge to you, sir, that I will have Maidie, whether or not it pleases you."

"By God, sir, an elopement . . ."

Allan, when the mantle of command rested on his shoulders, was a formidable presence. He looked down a very haughty nose at Mr. Worthing, still seated behind his desk, and with such a withering stare that the banker, a formidable enough gentleman in his own right, was momentarily taken aback.

He too rose, putting himself on an equal footing. "I take that high and mighty stare to be a pledge of no elopement. But I warn you—"

"And I have warned you, sir. Good day."

Allan turned, and walked out of the office, his expression hard, and so grimly angry that he failed to see Chester Califaxton, who had raised his hand in greeting and, when unacknowledged, had gone hurrying after him.

"Califaxton! Here!" Worthing's head clerk recalled Chester to his lowly place.

* * *

Allan in after years remembered that day as one of blank spaces and blurred sequences, while those events that he remembered clearly he wished he could not remember. He spent the remainder of the morning in a state of cold and implacable anger to equal Mr. Worthing's, during which he made some attempt to comprehend the reports he had requested of his man of affairs in London on the Enett shipping interests. In midafternoon, he abandoned the fruitless effort, and wandered off again to the Service Club, where he partook of food, but also a quantity of liquor. By late afternoon he could not remember with whom he had shared food and drink, but he did remember a discussion having to do with honor and an impoverished earl who had made off to Gretna Green with a wealthy cit's daughter.

It began to seem a good idea to assure Mr. Worthing that he—Allan Gilmichael, Lord Enett—was an upright and honorable aristocrat, not like the despicable earl, and would win his bride by fair means. He ascertained by careful study of his watch that it was by now past bank closing time. He found a hack to drive him to Bedford Square, where he was informed that Mr. Worthing was not yet at home. "I'll wait," he said, and sat down on the steps. The footman, well aware that the guest of the previous evening was carrying a considerable load, remained in the open doorway, indecisive about the proper procedure. Allan informed him of his condition, assured him that the steps were comfortable enough, and told him to go away.

After the hazy passage of an undetermined time, a carriage drew up from which the worthy banker descended. After a moment of shocked surprise that his servants would leave a gentleman sitting on his front steps, he approached Allan and with a formidable frown asked just what he thought he was doing.

"Well, sir, I'm drunk as a lord. Ha, ha."

"So I see." Mr. Worthing motioned for his interested coach-man to wait.

Allan rose, teetering. "Wanted to reassure you, sir." He laid a hand over his heart. "Honor of my noble house. No intention of Gretna Green."

"I did not earlier doubt your word."

After further unproductive colloquy, in which Mr. Worthing kept his patience admirably, considering how deep Allan was in his cups, he attempted to persuade him to enter his own carriage to be taken home. Allan had no intention of being taken home, and craftily asserted that he preferred hackneys. Mr. Worthing, equally crafty, put his carriage completely at Lord Enett's disposal. Further polite offers and denials ended with his acceptance. Allan was driven in great comfort to the scene of his previous revels, but only after a dire threat to jump out of the carriage if his directions were not obeyed.

Chester in spare moments had been putting many twos and twos together, something he was getting increasingly good at doing, now he'd fired up his brains. It hadn't been difficult to see that, as the saying went, Maidie and Gilmichael were April and May. So when he saw Allan enter Mr. Worthing's office he'd had a pretty good idea about what would be transpiring behind the closed door, and was astonished when Gilmichael came out looking like a thundercloud. Or more like a fellow facing New-gate who'd been refused a last-chance loan on his expectations.

Chester's first idea, as soon as he was released from his bank duties, was to find Allan to offer any assistance in his power. What that assistance might be he didn't know, but Gilmichael was a good enough sort, friend of his brother, and Maidie liked him. He'd grown quite fond of Maidie. He didn't know where Gilmichael was lodging, but he'd seen in the paper that that distant cousin of his—Lord Enett—had come to town accompanied by a gaggle of females. So, logically, his first step would be to take himself off to Enett House to make enquiries.

He was told by the footman who answered the door that his lordship was out.

"Well, the thing is, I was just enquiring after his cousin. Know his cousin. Don't know Enett."

"Cousin?" The footman pulled his ear in lieu of scratching his head. "Don't know of any cousin."

The butler appearing at that moment, the question was referred to a more knowledgeable source.

"Lord Enett's cousins live in Yorkshire. He has no relatives in London."

"Believe he's a distant cousin, the one I'm looking for."

The butler stated that he knew of no distant cousins, and certainly not in London.

"I just saw him this morning, walking out of Worthing's Bank. Met him in the Lakes. He must have come to town without your knowledge. Perhaps you know what Lord Enett's club is. He ought to know where his own cousin is, distant or not."

The butler, who with Allan's man of affairs and estate steward had been charged with forwarding mail to the Lakes in packets addressed to plain Mr. Gilmichael, rightly felt that it was not his place to reveal, any more than to explain, his master's eccentricities. "I believe you might find his lordship at the United Service Club. Lower Regency Street."

When Chester finally located the establishment, he encountered difficulties, first in gaining entrance, and after he did so in making his errand known. No, he had not been a lieutenant in the Forty-second. He was just looking for Lord Enett. Or a Mr. Gilmichael—had been a captain in the army.

A passing officer in full regimentals stopped. "You mean Gilly? You looking for Gilly? He's over there. I was just going to hunt up a hack and take him home."

Chester, horrified, discovered that the gentleman slumped insen-

sibly in his chair was Gilmichael. An empty bottle and an overturned glass suggested a lengthy session with John Barleycorn.
He was staring blankly at the wall, but as Chester approached,
he lifted a finger and waggled it, mumbling incoherently. The
resplendent officer shook his head. "Drunk as Davy's sow.
Never saw him like this even in the worst of times on the Peninsula—or the best of times, for that matter, when we had cause
to celebrate. Could sit out any man in the regiment."

"I'll see him home," Chester offered. "No trouble."

"Good of you. I've an appointment at the theater. Wouldn't
have let him keep on like this, but hate to miss the play. Lives
in Portland Place. Enett House. Can't like to see old Gilly like
this."

Another four was ringing up in Chester's head. "Lives at Enett
House?"

"His house, you know."

Allan stirred. "Who's that?" Blurry eyes focused on Chester.
"Cal . . . f . . . f . . . f . . . faxton. H'lo. Drunk as a lord." Then,
scandalizing both Chester and the helpful officer, he giggled.
"Am a lord."

"I say, Gilly . . ."

"Not himself," Chester said.

"Cery nor," Allan confirmed.

"What did he say?"

"Said, 'certainly not,' " Chester replied, with the wisdom of
his reckless years at Cambridge.

The jolting of the hackney occasionally roused Allan, during
which periods of lucidity he revealed with tiresome repetition
that he was drunk as a lord, that Chester was apprenticed to a
monster of irrationality who wouldn't let Maidie marry him just
because he was a lord, that Chester was a good fellow to see
him home, and that he would never elope. "A promise," he mumbled. With an owlish squint in Chester's general direction, he
patted his chest in the vicinity of his heart and lapsed back into

lethargy. "Drunk as a lord," he repeated, rousing again. "Told him so." He mumbled on in disjointed sentences, until a complete notion of the morning encounter with Mr. Worthing was forming in Chester's mind.

He delivered Allan into the hands of the family retainers he had encountered earlier and those of a shocked elderly lady who appeared out of the gloom and who he took to be Gilmichael's— or Enett's—mother, and who seemed to think he was responsible for her son's condition.

"Haven't touched a drop," Chester swore, fishing in his pockets for a card. "Just bringing him home. Call tomorrow evening. Hope you'll tell him. Know he won't remember. Chester Califaxton, please to tell him."

Seventeen

On the street again, Chester dismissed the hack and set off on foot toward his lodgings. As he walked, he cogitated, and after a few blocks decided to look up Duval. Toone. Whichever. Downright corkbrained, all these people going around using false names and identities! Had been meaning to look him up ever since Mr. Worthing told him the fortunate fellow he'd read about in the papers was none other than Duval. Congratulate him on his good luck. Could marry Pru now.

The *Morning Chronicle* had reported that he was putting up at the Pulteney with the old duke while the Toone town house, which had been let out to rent for years, was being renovated. *The Times,* on the other hand, had reported they were residing at the Clarendon while searching for a suitable rental property. Of the two, Chester decided to try the hotel closest to where he stood, and as he walked along he continued his cogitations but in a new direction—he'd wager it was the old duke who put the spies on Duval. Just why, though, he wasn't able to figure.

He was soon entering the Pulteney, where on enquiry he discovered that the *Morning Chronicle* had had the right information. He was admitted by Wendell to what Chester judged were the finest rooms in the establishment. He stared around, admiring the luxury. "Slap-up quarters you have here, Duval!"

Wendell cautioned silence; the duke was asleep. After a whispered warning that the old gentleman slept very lightly, he was happy to accept an invitation to retire to a nearby coffee house. He put down his book and stepped into his bedchamber for a fresh neckcloth. Chester picked up the book. Godwin. Duval was still at it, he noted. Probably no cure for it.

Once on the street, Wendell accepted congratulations on his good fortune, but stressed the opportunities that it offered him to influence the course of England's future and the lives of the poor. As well as to wed the woman he loved.

Chester only with difficulty could recognize his sister in the panegyrics that followed on Prudence's beauty, modesty, and many virtues. Indeed, he thought it a service to Pru to protest that his sister was a good enough girl, but no angel. "Puff up any woman too much, Duval, and you're bound to be disappointed."

Wendell objected that some women were born with superior qualities and that if Prudence's own brother could not recognize those qualities he was to be pitied. But Chester only said succinctly, "See you ain't got any sisters. A word to the wise, that's all."

Wendell fell into a sulky silence, which Chester interrupted by asking, "What am I to call you, anyway? Toone? Duval? Got a title?"

"Viscount. But don't call me that. I refuse to use it. And I've learned as well that my name isn't Toone, you know, anymore than it is Duval."

"Ah yes. Paper—the *Times,* I think—said it was . . . no, no, I'll get it in a moment. Clackenham! That was it. And you will one day be Salvatore Clackenham, eighth Duke of Toone. By God, Duval, I'm impressed to know you."

Wendell ignored the compliment, not certain it was sincere— or even a compliment, for that matter. "The duke insists that I must retain the name Salvatore; he says that since my inheritance came through my mother I should honor the name she chose for me, which honored her own mother's profession."

"That was?" Chester had never heard of anyone's mother who enjoyed a profession. Or a respectable one, anyway.

"Opera singer."

"That so?"

"But he'd like me to change my surname from Clackenham to Toone, so I'd be Salvatore Toone, like I've always been, or thought I was. And eventually," Wendell added gloomily, "the eighth Duke of Toone." After a pause he said with a resigned sigh, "Why don't you just call me Duval, since you're used to it. I'm not ashamed to confess that I am still finding it all very difficult to adjust myself to."

They settled into a box at the coffee house, where Chester ordered a beefsteak and ale. Wendell, who earlier had dined sumptuously at the hotel, contented himself with a wedge of cheddar cheese with his ale.

Although Chester's purpose was to discuss the affairs of Maidie and Gilmichael—or Enett, rather—he was curious: how could a revolution-spouting leveler turn out to be the heir to a dukedom and a fortune?

"I hardly comprehend it yet myself. The duke's cousin—my grandfather—married an opera singer, and even worse, he was a Dissenter. Family—a number of sisters and cousins—cast him off for both offenses. A testimony, you will admit, to the nature of England's class system, and which demonstrates the connection between the nobility and the Church of England in controlling the people by means of religion."

Chester offered a demurral; he had no quarrel with the Church. But neither had he a quarrel with his steak, in which he was more interested than in politics. He did not press the point. "Cast him off, you say? But that don't change legitimate descent."

"There was a question whether my grandparents were legally

married. They were married in 1751 by a dissenting minister, and it was recorded in the Dissenter Registry. My mother was born a year later. But after 1753, all marriages except among Quakers and Jews had to be recorded in parish records and performed by an Anglican priest. Sir Harold Mogglesby—the duke's lawyer—convinced the Lords that if Dissenter marriages were legal in 1751, so was the Registry, and that my claim to the title was legitimate. Although I want you to know that *I* made no claim, and never would have! Well, not to make an epic of this, my mother was married in the Church of England; to a soldier, like my grandfather was."

Chester wiped his chin with his handkerchief. "Hadn't eaten since this morning. Could have consumed the whole animal." He beckoned a serving woman and ordered another ale and a wedge of Stilton.

"In any event, the inheritance of the title, after the duke's son was killed—fighting in a noble cause, you must know, the very cause to which I have been longing to make my small contribution—"

"Appreciate it if you could stick with just the facts. Got a few things to say myself. Can't sleep till noon, you know." Chester applied his knife to the Stilton. "Working man now."

"Nothing much more. Just that the line of descent for the title would have been thrown back to the descendants of the second son of the second duke—over two hundred years. Actually, fellow I thought was my cousin, it would have been. Nobody ever told me I'd been adopted. Bit of a blow. A distant relative—"

"Not that Everett Toone fellow! The embezzler? The one rotting in Newgate? Going to be shipped off to New South Wales?"

"Afraid it is."

"Well, good luck for you, bad luck for him. Although must be a queer fish. Congratulate your various progenitors on seeing to the legalities. But now I've got something to tell you."

Wendell would have liked to have talked more about the momentous changes in his life, but he had no desire to force his private affairs on anybody. And particularly, he thought loftily, on Califaxton.

But Chester had had another thought. "Suppose the duke put the spy on you?"

"Which one?"

"There was more than one?" Chester asked, amazed.

"Two." Wendell replied with a portentous nod. "You wouldn't know about Sir Harold, then."

"Sir Harold? All I know about is that hedgebird Maidie and I saw on Blea How. And who you got us traipsing helter-skelter all over the fells looking for."

"The duke says he didn't set any spies on me except his lawyer, Sir Harold Mogglesby, and even then it was right out in the open. But he agrees that it was certainly a queer business and is making enquiries."

They speculated on the queer business for a time, until Wendell had almost convinced Chester that the hedgebird had been in truth a government spy. "Of course, now that I am heir to a dukedom I am immune from prosecution. It is one of the reforms that I shall work for: an end to privilege, and that every citizen be equal before the law."

Chester was not a student of history, but he did know that various members of the nobility had in times past ended their days with their heads rolling off a block. But he had better things to do than argue with such a bag of wind. Chester thought unhappily about the long years ahead with Wendell as a brother-in-law.

It did not take him long to recount Allan's visit to Worthing's Bank, as pieced together from his sotted mumblings. "Never thought to see Gilmichael drunk." Chester paused. "Enett, that is. Suppose you didn't know that he's not his distant cousin after all."

"What are you talking about?"

"What I mean to say is that Gilmichael is Enett himself. Don't know why he wasn't owning to his title, but a fact nonetheless."

"Strange," Wendell mused. "Ashamed of it, perhaps. He was drunk you say?"

"Drunk is what I said. Not just a little bosky, mind you, but dead drunk. An awful sight. Not one I'd wish to see again."

Wendell suggested that it might have been a more pitiable sight than awful, but generally agreed that the very fact of such a man as Gilmichael drinking himself into insensibility undoubtedly indicated that his passions and sentiments were seriously engaged. And who would have thought that he was Enett himself and not a distant cousin, as he had been putting about?

"Probably my mother put it about. Friend of m'brother Lance's you know. But the question is, what's to do? Worthing won't have an aristocrat, and that's what Maidie's in love with."

"How do you know she's formed an attachment? Just because Gilmichael—Enett—asked to address her . . ."

Chester regarded Wendell witheringly. "Anybody could tell by looking at them! If you didn't see it you must have been blind. Thinking about yourself too much, that's what it was."

"If you're going to get insulting, Califaxton . . ."

"No insult. Had spies on your mind. Pru. Politics. Not room for much else I'd say." In truth, Chester didn't consider Wendell's head of adequate capacity to hold even that much.

"Well, first off," Wendell decided, "We had better write to Maidie."

"I figure that Worthing has already fired off something to Mrs. Clarke—sister, you know. And Maidie, too, most likely. Half expected to see him go tearing off for the Lakes before Enett was out the door. I don't say we shouldn't let Maidie know we're doing our best to help. Can offer our services to Enett, too—drag him out of gutters whenever he's under the hatches. But I was thinking . . ."

"Thinking what?"

"Well, Worthing's got no son. So he expects Maidie to bring one home for him who he can give his name to and who'll go into the business. Like my father. Expected Pru to bring money into the family. Well, you may have turned rich, but Enett ain't going to turn into a commoner. So we've got to think of some way around it."

They called for more ale and bent their minds to the problem, but except for the decision to send off an express to Maidie reassuring her that they were working on the problem, they formed no plan of action, and glimpsed no solution.

Allan woke once again with a throbbing head, and with a pain behind his eyes, a queasy stomach, his mouth foul, and a notion that he must have been and currently was a loathsome example of humanity. His resourceful valet, on being called to his aid, shortly returned with a preparation designed to mitigate the physical effects of his debauchery. However, a certain tightness around the good man's lips indicated that even had he also had a cure for remorse and shame, he would not have administered it. A fall from virtue, as virtue itself, was providing its own reward.

As soon as Hockings spoke, Allan winced. "Whisper, I beg you."

Hockings nodded, and drew open the heavy draperies, which squeaked loudly on the rods and set off a flurry of dust. Allan, wincing again, said in the dry croak that seemed all he was capable of, "A little compassion might not be amiss. I have been balked in love."

"Yes, sir. Very sad, sir." Hockings whispered, contriving to achieve a long face.

Despite himself, Allan laughed. "A gentle voice and a touch of sympathy will do." He put himself to the task of getting out of bed and donning the dressing gown that Hockings held for him.

"I have hot water ready for your shave, my lord, and have ordered water for the bathing tub brought up to your dressing room. A warm bath will do much to diminish the effects of your evening. While you are shaving and bathing I will lay out your apparel. May I ask what your intentions are for the day?"

An hour later Allan thought himself capable of cautiously taking some sustenance—a cup of hot black coffee and a small piece of toast—with perhaps a very thin spreading of butter on the toast.

He was surprised to find his mother in the breakfast parlor, drinking tea and looking over the morning paper. "Good morning, Maman." He poured himself coffee, steaming hot from a freshly brewed urn. They kept country hours at Thresseley, which meant the family was usually up and finished breakfasting by nine, and here it was closer to twelve. How quickly his mother was adapting herself to city schedules. He put two pieces of toast on a plate, but after reflecting briefly on the state of the inner man rejected any idea of butter, however thinly spread. He should have insisted on coming to town a year ago. If he hadn't been so selfish . . . He bent to kiss her cheek.

She accepted the kiss as her due, but her expression was not affectionate. She returned to her newspaper. After a few pregnant moments she remarked, not raising her eyes from the page, "A fine state you were in last night."

"I'm sorry that you had to witness it."

"If this is what coming to town will mean—carousing with those military friends of yours and swilling liquor half the night . . ."

"You need not fear a repetition. If you would care to discuss it, I shall be happy to do so, but perhaps you'd like to put the paper away first."

Lady Enett looked up, her face cold. She ostentatiously, and very deliberately, folded the paper and set it aside, before turn-ing, stern-lipped, to face him.

What was there to discuss, he wondered. He had taken so much liquor he had lost his senses and his control, something that had never happened to him before, and wouldn't again. What had he said to Chester Califaxton, that callow youth, who had somehow found him (why?), and brought him home? What had he said to his mother? To the butler and the footman as they bore him up the stairs? To Hockings, as he put him to bed?

"This is not an excuse, but there was a reason. Miss Worthing's father denied my suit."

"He *what?*"

Allan leaned his still aching head on his hand. "A man falls in love; the woman returns his affection; and *what?* is all their relatives can say? Mr. Worthing refused to permit my addresses to his daughter."

"A tradesman and a Dissenter dares to refuse an Enett?" Lady Enett was again galvanized—in truth, her blood hadn't coursed so vigorously through her veins for many a day. "I must say, England is coming to a pretty pass indeed when the riff and the raff of the nation can thumb its nose at the nobility! In my day there was respect for their betters. Why are you gaping at me like that? You look like a frog."

Allan struck his fist delicately on the table. "You are abso-lutely right, Maman. We can't let this kind of thing get out of hand. Such prideful behavior is unacceptable in the extreme."

"Well, what are you going to do about it?"

"I don't know what I'll do about it. Not yet. A campaign is required, which implies study of the terrain and of the enemy's forces, the development of strategy and a consideration of tac-tics, an assessment of one's own strengths—"

"Run away with the girl. Serve him right. And save you time and trouble."

Allan gazed speechless at his mother.

"Lily-livered lot, the modern generation. In my day . . ."

Recovering, he conceded. "Yes, Maman. But I've promised that there will be no elopement."

"And you call yourself a strategist? Now you have no threat with which to distract and worry the enemy, as you characterize that tradesman."

"He's a banker, a financier, if you will. Not a tradesman."

"Whatever . . . Now run along about your business. I'm taking Julia and Eunice shopping, and I have much to do to make this house livable again. Servants to hire—I can't run a household on this small staff we brought with us from the country. And I don't suppose you have noticed, but every carpet in the house needs beating."

Allan rose. "I leave you then to your tasks. I have a letter to write and business that must be attended, as well as a campaign against an upstart banker."

His mother detained him with a hand on his arm. "You were right that it was time we come to town. But it is very hard, losing one's child, even when that child is a man. You will forgive me, but I was prepared for your death—one must be, when there is war, you know. I would have grieved for you as intensely and as long as I have for Clarence, but it would not have upset my life."

Allan lifted Lady Enett's hand to his lips. "How can I not understand, Maman, when I too have found it so hard?"

She watched him go, and then returned to the paper. More about the old Duke of Toone—she had thought him dead long since, or possibly languishing in that ramshackle Tudor pile in Sussex. Must be eighty, if he was a day—and lost an only son in America. Poor man. The boy was a mere youth, it seemed. Just thirty. Had the duke taken a young wife at fifty? And how many bastards running around India and the Americas?

Julie bounced into the room with her usual impetuosity, Eunice and the dog Clown following more sedately behind her, to cheerfully interrupt her mother's musings. "What are you doing still in the breakfast parlor, Maman?"

"Waylaying Enett." It was the first time Lady Enett had referred to Allan by his title.

"He was drunk as an owl last night, wasn't he?" asked Julie, so savoring her starchy brother's fall from grace that she was unaware he had just been accorded his title and promoted to head of the family.

"Yes, unfortunately, he was. And don't use slang, Julia. And don't simper, Eunice. It is no great event for a man to come home drunk. And I won't have that dog in the breakfast parlor!"

Julie grinned. "But what a fuss they make! Eunice heard the servants taking him up to his bedchamber, just as I did. He was muttering and protesting, and that new footman was swearing . . ."

"He has had a disappointment in love. I trust that it won't happen again."

"Well, I should hope not. It must be terrible to be twice disappointed!"

Lady Enett frowned at her. "He will not drink to excess again."

"I know, Maman. I suppose it was that Miss Worthing he met in the Lakes that he has been so determined to marry? Has his fair one cried off?"

"No. The fair one's father. Some tradesman or other. He refused your brother's suit."

"I believe Allan referred to him as a banker," Eunice said.

"Refused *Allan?*" Julie exclaimed. "But every person like that wants to marry his daughter into the aristocracy."

"Never fear, we will find a way to put the upstart in his place," Lady Enett said darkly. "Well, why are you lingering? Where are your bonnets? Run and get them. And kindly send that dog out to the mews."

Now that she had encouraged Allan to fight for the girl, she'd like to see what she looked like. She knew personally none of her Dissenter connections, but she did know Seraphina Worthing slightly, and that her brother, evidently the girl's father, headed a reputable and well known banking house. An unexceptionable woman, received everywhere. Was there a chance she'd be in town? She would of course be unwilling to engage in outright defiance of her brother, but would undoubtedly be more sensible. Between the two of them . . .

Lady Enett considered her own about face, first in coming to town, which even in her youth she had never enjoyed, and second in accepting Allan's strange choice in marriage. Truth was, she was weary.

She could not approve that Eunice had so willingly reconciled herself to perpetual widowhood, and perhaps worse, assumed a die-away air to accompany it. Clarence would not have wished she behave so, of that his mother was certain. She was tired of Julia's restlessness; the girl was already nearly twenty, and needed settling. She was even tired of her own moping. And to top off the list in her catalog of weariness, she was to the highest degree tired of Allan's bad humor.

If he had been entertaining himself at Thresseley among the local wenches, she certainly had heard nothing of it. He might have been in better humor if he had. She had been most properly shocked by his wretched condition of the night before. And she was perhaps overly sentimental, but his maudlin mutterings had spoken to her of a man in love. But in love or not, he was a man and he needed a wife. And had she even the right to decide who might make a proper wife for a son of nearly thirty years?

They all needed stirring up (or settling down), when one came right to the nub of it.

Hang it all, she'd forgotten to tell Allan that that young man who brought him home would come around in the evening. Where had she put his card? She called a footman, and was told that Lord Enett was in the library. Hastily scribbling a note, she handed it to the footman to take to Allan.

Julie, tying her bonnet strings, looked into the breakfast parlor. "We're ready, Maman."

"Come along then."

I must discover, she thought, whether Seraphina Worthing is in town.

Lady Enett had no way of knowing it, but Miss Seraphina Worthing, although not then in town, soon would be. At that very moment Mr. Worthing's couriers were racing to the west and to the north—to the coast of Wales and the shores of Krigsmere—bearing summary commands to his wife, his sister, and his daughter to return posthaste to London.

Eighteen

The *Morning Chronicle* had named the correct hotel, but it was the *Times* that had accurately reported the reason for the duke and Wendell's residence there. At the very moment that Allan was leaving his mother, Sir Harold Mogglesby was signing a lease for an elegant furnished house just off Berkeley Square. Wendell suggested that it was perhaps overly elegant for two single men, but the old duke approved it, which decided the matter. They made the transfer of themselves and their meager effects immediately, after which the duke sent Wendell off to an employment agent to order a number of prospective servants sent around.

The duke, tall, and thin as a board fence (the *Times*), was even at eighty a man of decision. His health was frail, the effect of his years in the uncivilized world (the *Morning Chronicle*), but he himself chose to describe his frailty as simply a matter of accumulating years. "Wouldn't have lived so long as I have if I'd spent my life in this stink-hole," he had told both the *Chronicle* and the *Times,* a statement neither had seen fit to print, and which had afforded the duke a good laugh. He had a great fondness for disconcerting the press.

There were as well the requirements of personal elegance to be attended, and the duke soon had himself and Wendell engaged in selecting new wardrobes. Although more republican in char-

acter than was quite fashionable, the duke insisted that there
would be no stinting on quality, while Wendell thanked Provi-
dence that the severe styles introduced by Beau Brummel permitted him to dress more in accordance with his political
principles than might have been possible in the vanished era of
lace and satin. He was already the recipient of a fourth of the
duke's fortune (which he had placed immediately under the care
of Mr. Worthing's banking house), and thought it only fitting he
concede to all reasonable wishes of his benefactor—although
never, of course, conceding his principles.

, The duke also had affairs to arrange, and was anxious to re-
acquaint himself with London, which he hadn't visited for forty
seasons. He wished to discover if any friends from his rakehell
days, such as they were, had survived the years. He didn't have
much time left, he claimed, for enjoying the London world, and
before he and his heir journeyed down to Sussex to see what
was to be done about the neglected Toone holdings and getting
Wendell sent up to Parliament, he intended to ready a town establishment in preparation for a brilliant little season, as well as
more immediately for an entertainment in connection with the
arrival in London of his heir's future bride.

Wendell's first coherent thoughts after Mr. Worthing had delivered Sir Harold's note informing him of this momentous
change of fortune had been to reject it all out of hand on the
principle that wealth and rank corrupt individually, and together
promote degeneracy, dissolution, and depravity. His second
thought had been to accept a modest portion, and then immediately rush back to Krigsmere and Prudence. The duke would not
hear of it. Like it or not, Wendell couldn't avoid the title, now
his mother had been proven legitimate, and he might as well
have the money to go with it.

As to marriage, he argued that Wendell was too young; then
in the face of his new heir's violent arguments to the contrary,
he retreated to the position that the girl was not worthy. He

retreated even more rapidly from that position to disparagement of her father's grasping character and illiberal tendencies, objections which he recognized immediately were weak, contrary to his own convictions, and irrelevant to the case. "But not a penny will we invest in his manufactories," the duke decreed. "Any man who refuses his daughter to a worthy man because of a lack of fortune deserves censure, not reward."

Wendell could not object to that sentiment, and had gone off to write a long letter to Mrs. Califaxton; a briefer and more sober communication for Mr. Califaxton; and a tender note to Prudence to be delivered by her mother, and in which he again emptied his heart and asked her to set the date when she would at last be his.

In their spare time the duke and Wendell entertained each other with radical conversations. In the course of one such discussion, Wendell submitted Maidie's romantical problems for radical solution.

The duke listened to the story, and then said, "Tell you what. Let's go see Godwin."

There was nothing Wendell would have liked better than an introduction to the famous philosopher, but the duke, after considering the idea, suggested it might not be a wise course. "Better not. Hasn't his daughter, that one by the Wollstonecraft woman, run off with one of your poets? Might not be too sympathetic with headstrong girls."

"Oh, they're married now."

"Nonetheless, his feelings may remain raw."

Some time later, having given the subject further radical thought, he said, "Tom Jefferson—correspond with him regularly—argues for each generation choosing its course for itself, even to revolution and revolt. He was speaking politically, of course, but I think it might apply. What do you think of that, hey?"

"I am not familiar with Mr. Jefferson's writings—except of

course the Declaration he devised for the rebellion in North America. Will you call on Mr. Worthing with me? Perhaps you could make the argument more effectively. I am not certain just where Mr. Worthing stands on revolution, but I suppose he can't view it favorably. And I fear he thinks I am somewhat young and unformed; you know, sir, how some people believe that the young will be radical, but that we only need time to come to what they consider a more sensible view."

The duke nodded. "When we have ourselves nicely settled. A few days will not cool the ardor of true lovers, hey?"

Wendell and his newfound relative were finding themselves in tune on almost every issue, although Wendell tried to refrain from phrasing it in exactly those words. "Amazing, sir, that we agree so well," he said.

"Not amazing at all. I made sure my money was going where I approved. Couldn't stomach that Everett Toone fellow, who'd have got the title if I hadn't been sharp. But he'd have never got my money." The duke paused for a self-satisfied chuckle. "Now whose bank did he embezzle from?"

"Durkim, Findley, and Biddle."

"Suppose we should buy him out of jail—don't on an ordinary day approve that sort of thing, you understand. We'll pay Burkim, Dingley, and Fiddle back and spring the jackanapes."

"I believe, Duke, it's Durkim, Findley, and—"

"Yes, yes. We'll give him an allowance, find him a wife— some strong-minded wench—and set him to farming. Something to keep his mind occupied. I'll get Harold on it right off."

Wendell agreed that such a redemptive effort should be made. "It would indeed speak poorly for our efforts on behalf of the oppressed if we failed in our understanding of one of our family who has fallen into error."

The duke, thinking that his own redemptive effort might be to tone down his heir's highflown talk, said, "Speaking of our family, it's time we pay a call on Miss Hattie. Mother was a

Toone in the cadet branch. Traced down family gossip that led
me to you, my boy, and then connected it to the old scandal
about my cousin, your grandfather, and the opera singer. Beautiful woman, by the way. Well, it's been a long time. But if I'd
been in England, those prissy and prune sisters of mine would
have received her. I'd have seen to that. For a woman of her
years . . . I'm speaking now of Miss Hattie, and how she discovered you. She deserves our admiration. It was a close thing,
though. Saved us a lengthy hearing in the Lords, and perhaps a
fight in court."

And so Wendell and the duke set off to visit the ancient relative whose love of genealogies had helped discover a rightful
heir.

An elderly servant opened the door to them, and an even more
elderly maid took them to Miss Hattie's sanctuary. The room
was lined with shelves on which neatly labeled boxes shared
space with books in miscellaneous bindings. On a massive table
in the center of the room lay a great number of leather-bound
books the size of portfolios, a stack of writing paper, a water
glass filled with pencils, and a vase filled with rulers. Beside
the latter, a shallow dish held several large, gummy erasers and
a packet of pins.

The maid indicated two comfortable chairs beside a table on
which the implements for an elaborate tea were assembled. Opposite was a straight chair, which they presumed was reserved
for Miss Hattie.

She came into the room leaning lightly on a slender cane, an
old lady with white hair, wearing a tastefully modish lavender
dress. The duke rose and took her hand, which she offered to be
kissed, and led her to her chair.

"Edward, my dear boy, it is so good to see you again. And
you, Salvatore. How brown and fit you look! I couldn't have
done better than send you to your cousin Emery!"

"No, ma'am, you couldn't have, for I have met there the

woman I am to marry, and Emery has been as good as a brother to me."

"How proper. But I can hardly call you and Emery even cousins, now I've discovered that the only ancestor you share was born in 1570! The second duke that would have been. And of course, those who preceded him, probably going back to some cheating Saxon savage."

Wendell replied that he rather liked the idea of such an ancestor.

"The nomenclature for describing your relationship with Emery I fear would almost defy my considerable abilities," Miss Hattie said, ignoring the interpolation. "But how is he, and that charming scatterwit he married?"

Miss Hattie brewed the tea, chatting lightly of this and that. As they consumed the substantial offering of delicate sandwiches and small, delicious cakes, they sipped fragrant tea and conversed of books and political theories, until at last Miss Hattie rang for a servant to take away the dishes and cups and platters and urns. Then, turning to the duke, she asked, "You wish me to explain to Salvatore?"

Miss Hattie abandoned her chair and her cane to flutter about among her papers and books until she uncovered several pages filled with lines of descent and their ramifications. "You will see," she said, "that Everett's claim to the title was not insignificant." She sat down, and handed the sheaf of papers to Wendell. "You see, the second duke's second son, Reuben, had a great great great grandson, in direct descent. This was Henry, who was my own mother's brother, my uncle, and the first born of several boys—do you find him there? The second or third page, I believe."

Wendell thumbed through the papers until his eye lighted on a likely Henry.

"It was this Henry who married a Cholmeley, the great granddaughter of the eldest sister of the fourth duke. Do you see?"

"Oh, yes. Quite." Wendell nodded. What was clear was that it was too complicated to bother puzzling out.

"So my Uncle Henry's descendants had a claim to the dukedom through both the Toones and the Cholmeleys, for as you know, the dukedom could pass through the eldest female. Most unusual. I have seldom encountered such a condition. However, this made Everett the most likely heir. Imagine! An embezzler for a duke!"

"There have been numerous dukes who have committed worse crimes," Wendell remarked.

"Agreed," said the present duke. "But one would prefer even the worst of them to have some redeeming strengths of character—none of which could be discovered in Everett."

"Perhaps," Miss Hattie said, "Everett didn't know you had lost your son when he took the money . . . Oh, I don't mean it was right. Only that if he had had expectations, he might have been more circumspect. And then if he had inherited the title, although his character would be anything but sterling, he nonetheless would not have been an embezzler." Miss Hattie frowned. "On the other hand, perhaps he *did* know—"

The old duke gazed at her, astonished.

Miss Hattie made a small dismissive gesture. "Well then. Everett was the son of my uncle's first son, also a Henry; and Salvatore, as far as I knew, was the descendant of his second son, John, whose name was William . . ."

Although Miss Hattie had arrived at the man Wendell had always known as his father, his attention was flagging at precipitous rate. He opened his mouth, but closed it again when he realized that the duke was observing him with a most particularly warning stare.

"Then Edward—" Miss Hattie smiled at the duke—"then Edward wrote to me from America with a story about his cousin who married an opera singer, and I thought, my, but Salvatore is an odd name for William's boy. In any event, I discovered—you will not be capable of imagining the diffi-culty—that you had been, so to speak, willed to my cousin William—actually a second cousin once removed. You see, William was *devoted* to the opera, as you know, and was, I imagine, simply struck dumb when he learned that there was a singer bearing the name Toone. Oh, not her stage name, of course, but these men who hang about people like that are not always interested only in liaisons." She beamed at Wendell. "Your adopted father genuinely enjoyed artistic company, and came to know Lily Toone—your grandmother, Salvatore. Very famous in her day. And your mother, who also bore the name Lily. When poor young Lily was dying, she begged William to raise you as his own son."

Miss Hattie clasped her hands. "Oh! It was all so exciting! My heart simply raced when I discovered the truth. Such inter-esting people I was required to speak with—and then to learn almost at the same moment that your grandparents were Dis-senters! My heart nearly failed me."

The duke leaned forward to take the old lady's hand. "Ah that I had met you, Miss Hattie, when we both were young, and I could have carried you off to America with me. What a partner you would have been!"

Miss Hattie patted the duke's hand. "How gallant. I should have loved it."

The duke kissed her hand and rose. "We are tiring you, I fear, and Salvatore knows the rest of the story. But it was not in my power to explain what you have just told us."

Nor, thought Wendell, in anyone's power to remember it.

In another part of London, Chester Califaxton had just given his name to the footman he remembered from the previous day's adventure, and was told that he was expected. He was shown into the library with assurances that his lordship would be with him directly.

Allan was as good as his footman's word. He held out his hand to Chester with a welcoming smile. "I must give you my thanks, Califaxton. I understand it was you who saw me home last night."

"Yes, my lord."

"Come, we are old friends, and must not stand on ceremony with each other. Allan will do very nicely. And I may call you Chester? But let's sit down. Grateful as I am to you, I'm sorry your help was required."

"Can't say how surprised I was—never expected to see you with all three sheets in the wind. Well," he hurried on, "and can't say how surprised I was to discover you were Enett himself. Never occurred to me you might be your cousin. That's to say . . ."

"Even I was confused now and then, when I had to remember that I was my own distant cousin. But let me serve you a glass of wine."

They settled into their chairs. Chester set his glass on the table by his chair, then removed it again fearing he would stain the highly polished surface. (Lady Enett's servants had been at their work.) He crossed his legs, then uncrossed them to plant his feet firmly on the floor. He'd always found Enett intimidating, and adding rank to the equation didn't help—although plain as a pikestaff he was trying to put him at ease. He took a hold on his courage. "If you think I'm interfering, just say so. Promise you, won't say another word. But couldn't help learning about your trouble with m'employer. That's to say, you talked a lot."

It was difficult for Allan to discuss his private affairs, and even more difficult with a man he had always thought of as so much his junior, but he was indebted to him for a service, which imposed an obligation of civility. He could also remember trying to tell Chester his troubles, which in its turn imposed an obligation of candor.

"You know then that I asked Mr. Worthing for Maidie's hand and was refused?"

"Couldn't help it. Know why, too. Reason I called tonight. Fact is that I've got to know a little about the banks in town and who owns them and so on. To make a long story short, do you know Ransom and Morland's? It's a bank."

"No, can't say that I do."

"Doesn't matter. Point is, no one name of Ransom among the partners there. The Kinnairds have an interest through old Ransom's daughter—she married the seventh Lord Kinnaird. He was an active partner, and now it's the eighth lord. And Child's you know . . ."

Allan gazed bemused at Chester as he catalogued the banks in London, plus a few in the counties, in which the style of the name no longer reflected ownership.

"Thing is," Chester concluded, "don't see what the to-do is all about—except Worthing never had a son, and long ago he got this bee in his bonnet and can't get it out. He told me, when I requested an apprenticeship with the idea of becoming a partner, that he'd never have another style for the bank but Worthing's. I told him I wasn't interested in banking just so I could have my name on a sign over some door."

"Very sensible. And are you finding your work interesting?"

"An apprentice is a bit of a drudge, can't say otherwise. But I expected that. And I've got to know some other apprentices and clerks from Worthing's and some fellows from other banks. We all meet at a coffee house and, well, talk about banking and . . . things."

Although Allan showed no sign of wishing him gone, Chester nonetheless felt he had overstayed, and rose to go.

"No, no. Of course you must not go," Allan said. "You will take supper with us. My mother is expecting you. She wants to thank you. I suspect she believes that had you not brought me home last night, I would have been found robbed and beaten in some dark alley. I've been laggard in not taking you to her before now."

"Least I could do. But your friends wouldn't have let you wander off to get yourself robbed."

Chester basked in praises and kind attentions from the ladies for another hour. When at last he took leave of them and was standing with Allan at the door, he said, "If there's anything I can do . . . take messages to Maidie . . . whatever."

"I thank you, and I will call on you if there is need. In the meantime, I promise you I won't be idle in furthering my cause."

"Merciful Heaven!" whispered Mrs. Worthing. With trembling hands she opened her husband's courier-borne letter. And "Merciful Heaven!" she exclaimed again after quickly glancing through it. "Mr. Gilmichael has offered for Maidie and Sam has refused him!"

She sank into a chair, white and shaken. Her hostess, with a soothing murmur, hurried to secure a decanter from a nearby table to pour a restorative, while Seraphina, who had snatched the letter from Mrs. Worthing's trembling fingers, embarked on a thorough-going denunciation of her brother for a fool and a blackguard.

"He commands us—do you hear that, Tish? He *commands* us to return at once! And he has the presumption to denounce me—me—for not having warned him. If he weren't so puffed up with himself he might have seen, just as I did—I admit it— what was afoot between those two. But to . . . Tish? *Tish!* Are you laughing?"

"I just thought," said Mrs. Worthing, sobering, "how ridiculously pompous Sam can be. Ordering us all about like a . . . a potentate in an eastern seraglio."

Their hostess handed Seraphina a restorative identical to that which had brought the color back into Mrs. Worthing's cheeks, and poured herself a generous portion of the same. "I believe you mean that he's a regular Turk." She raised her glass. "To love, my dears. And defiance to all potentates!"

The three ladies drank to defiance, feeling ever so slightly wicked.

"And now what do you plan to do?"

Neither had any ready solution in mind, but find one they would! And return to London they must. Seraphina insisted that Mrs. Worthing remain behind to await the carriage, which Mr. Worthing's note had informed them was following on the heels of the courier. She herself intended to travel by post-chaise, and as far and as fast as possible each day—late on the road at night, and early off every morning. "I must get to London before Sam does something foolish," she concluded.

"And what could he do more foolish?" asked their hostess. "I can only think of a challenge, but gentlemen aren't ordinarily called out for offering for other gentlemen's daughters."

Neither Seraphina nor Mrs. Worthing had any idea what Mr. Worthing might do that was more foolish, but were certain he might do it.

And therefore, Mrs. Worthing insisted, she would make the dash for London with Seraphina. "I am perfectly well; it is just that I tire so quickly. If I find myself too fatigued, I shall rest at an inn until I am strong enough to go on. Likely we will meet our carriage on the road. But whether or no, I must make the effort. My poor Maidie will need me."

"But you will take my carriage, my dears!" said their hostess. "I simply insist. I will not let you leave my house otherwise. Now, do tell me, what is the objection to this Mr. Gilmichael?"

"He isn't a simple Mr. Gilmichael at all, but the Marquis of Enett," Seraphina told her. "Sam has never wanted Maidie to marry an aristocrat. He wants the bank to remain in his own name, you see, and an aristocrat . . ."

"But how foolish! My dears, Mr. Child, whose bank is as much of the first category as Worthing's, left his fortune to his granddaughter Sally. And Sally married George Villiers, who as you must know is the Earl of Jersey. So the Jerseys now direct the bank—Sally is head partner. We've known each other since we were children. But the bank is still called Child's, even though there's no partner of that name now."

"Surely Sam must know that." Mrs. Worthing sighed. "If we had had a son—"

"Nonsense!" Seraphina said. "Any boy with spirit would have hated banking."

"Nonetheless, I, and you too, Phina, have always understood Sam's objection. But I don't believe either of us thought that it would ever outweigh Maidie's happiness."

"It is abominably selfish of Sam," Seraphina pronounced, "and I, for one, will not countenance it."

And so the ladies set out for London early the following morning, waved off by their hostess with many wishes for their success in conquering the potentate and for the triumph of true love. "Remember. No one at Child's with that name," were her final words.

Mr. Worthing's second courier arrived at Pennelbeck Farm just as Fanny and Maidie were sitting down with Emery to enjoy a comfortable discussion of Wendell's prospective marriage. This latest news had been delivered that afternoon by Mrs. Califaxton, who had persisted in referring to Wendell as the future duke. She had treated them to a lengthy review of the circumstances, elaborated on her own discernment in having favored

Wendell from the very first, appended a lengthy scold for her husband (it would have served him right if Wendell had thrown Prudence over for a more exalted bride), and rounded the discourse off with her immediate plans to take Prudence to London as desired by her impatient lover.

Emery had stretched himself comfortably on a sofa with his hands behind his head; Maidie was curled in a chair; and Fanny had put her feet up on an ottoman and folded her hands over her belly. Now in her fourth month, she had felt the babe's first throbbing movement, and was anticipating another. A soft breeze, just touched with autumn, wafted in the open windows along with several moths that were now fluttering around the newly lit lamp.

Mrs. Eckston, looking nervous but trying not to, entered. "Excuse me, Mr. Clarke, Mrs. Fanny, but there's a courier here with a letter from Mr. Worthing."

"Indeed?" Fanny removed her feet from the ottoman. "Bring it to me please, and see that the man has something to eat and drink. Also you may direct him to the inn in Sagpaw. Tell him there may be a reply."

No one spoke as they waited for Mrs. Eckston to return with the letter, but Emery sat up on the sofa, and Maidie bit her lip.

"Thank you, Mrs. Eckston," Fanny said in a calm voice. Emery and Maidie watched silently as she opened it.

"Dear God. Allan has spoken." She looked up at Maidie. "My darling child, your father has refused him."

Maidie burst into tears.

"Oh, my dear," Fanny said, her voice faltering, "how is it possible? I never, in my heart, thought that he would put his own peculiar notions before your happiness."

She held out her arms to Maidie. Emery put his arms around them both, muttering comfortingly.

The tears did not last long, for Maidie had no more intention of accepting her father's refusal than going up into the fells and jumping off a precipice in despair. She waxed indignant. Fanny, once solace was no longer required, let her own anger bubble over. Emery asked to see the letter.

He permitted the two women a few minutes to relieve themselves of their exacerbated feelings, and then said, "Perhaps you would like to know the entire contents of Sam's missive? He summons you, Maidie, to London at once, and commands me, somewhat high handedly, I cannot help but feel, to escort you. And as for you, Fanny—it will take some time to digest his denunciations of your perfidy. I myself do not entirely escape censure, for he suggests that in future I look more closely to my wife's behavior. Well, Fanny, what do you have to say for yourself? And you, Maidie, what do you choose to do?"

"I of course will return immediately to London. I was to return within a fortnight in any event. But I cannot let Allan be intimidated by Papa. We must find a way—I must persuade Papa . . ."

"Never fear, Maidie," Emery said. "You have chosen a man accustomed to command, and not susceptible to intimidation."

Fanny again embraced Maidie. "Emery is exactly right—you need never doubt Allan's determination. And of course you must return immediately to London. I shall accompany you. I will not allow Sam to act the Turk."

"Fanny, I absolutely forbid it. I will accompany Maidie."

"Now who's acting the Turk?"

"But I can go with Mrs. Califaxton and Prudence," Maidie said.

It took much persuasion, but at last Fanny agreed that it was a sensible solution. However, she retired to the Scriptorium to write a red hot reply to Mr. Worthing, to be carried to him by his own courier, denouncing him and his Turkish notions in terms that rivaled the best of Mrs. Califaxton.

Maidie also attempted a letter to her father for the courier to carry back to London. The wastebasket was soon filled with her failures, until at last she contented herself with a simple reply, describing the proposed means of her return and the probable date of her arrival.

The following day brought word from Allan, who had not thought to employ a private courier.

My darling Maidie, I am certain that you will be receiving a letter from your father, perhaps on the same day that you receive this, telling you that I have seen him and that he has refused us his permission. As much as I have learned to respect Mr. Worthing in the brief time of our acquaintance, I cannot bow to his will in this matter. My dear, I am a man in love; had you been so unfortunate to have met me after I left him you would have said that I was distraught with love.

I will not *hope* that you refuse to accept your father's rejection of my suit; I will *believe* that you do. I will believe that you love me enough to withstand whatever time and separation is demanded of us before your father, in the face of our determination, capitulates to the happiness of his daughter. I wish to believe, you see, that I am as essential to your happiness, as you, my sweetest Maidie, are essential to mine.

We are not without allies. Your Aunt Fanny, of course; and, I trust, Emery; also, I believe, your Aunt Seraphina. My mother has already entered the lists on our side. Our newly wealthy and some-day duke, Salvatore Clackenham (surely you have heard that amazing news by now), must be our ally, as we were his. I admit that I was a reluctant ally, but that was when I thought that I only needed your acceptance to secure my own happiness. (And I admit as well that the shoe pinches infinitely more when it is on one's own foot than on another's.) Perhaps we may even count on Chester Califaxton, who I am ashamed to confess I have thought to be only one more muddleheaded youth, but who took the trouble to assist me in my despair.

I could write many more pages, my sweet, but whatever I might say would only repeat over and over what I have already said. I love you, Maidie, with all my heart, and will have you for my wife.

With cavalier disregard for daughterly submission, Maidie sent a letter on its way to him assuring him of her love, her determination to become his wife, and of her fortitude and patience while they demonstrated to her father their unswerving devotion. "I return by my father's command," she concluded. "Mrs. Califaxton is bringing Prudence to London at Wendell's urging, to begin plans for their wedding, and she has graciously permitted me to accompany them."

Emery sat down to write his own cogent and well-reasoned argument for the marriage, to also find its way by the regular post. He emphasized the happiness of the two principals, particularly the daughter who had always been as dutiful as she was cherished. He then resorted to historical examples of happy alliances between the bourgeoisie and various noble houses; and suggested that it was to the benefit of the nation to draw the landed interest closer to the industrial, commercial and financial sectors. He spoke strongly of Allan's upright character, the staunch service he had rendered England, and the competence with which he had shouldered the burdens of unexpected responsibility.

And that, he thought with some satisfaction, should adequately counter Fanny's letter, which he was certain had been full of scathing denunciations and emotional arguments that would properly set Sam's back up and do no good at all.

Nineteen

The first of the summoned to arrive in London were Mrs. Worthing and Seraphina.

The Worthing carriage, which as expected was met on the road, was a luxuriantly appointed vehicle, built to Mr. Worthing's own design, with the sole intent of making any journeys his wife undertook as comfortable and easy as possible. Mrs. Worthing therefore arrived in Bedford Square much less fatigued than would otherwise have been the case. She assured Seraphina that after a long nap and a bath, she would be perfectly prepared to do battle with the potentate.

After bidding her sister-in-law goodbye, Seraphina directed the coachman to carry her directly to Worthing's Bank. She would not let one minute more pass before confronting the potentate herself.

Mr. Worthing and his head clerk were standing at his desk studying the charts illustrating a reorganization in bank routine when Seraphina walked unannounced into the room. He looked up in surprise.

"Phina! You back? But what are you doing here? Who let you in?"

"I let myself in, despite that chattering minion outside your door who tried to stop me." She directed her stern gaze at the significantly more important minion who stood beside the banker's desk. The minion did not wait to be dismissed. With a muttered excuse he gathered up the papers and hastily slid past Seraphina. As the door closed behind him, she turned to her brother and fixed him with a severe and disapproving eye.

"All right, Phina. Out with it. Don't want you to burst."

Seraphina, incensed, said, "I am here because I have something to say to you that I prefer your wife not hear. Sam Worthing, you are a selfish, inconsiderate fool. How can you insult Tish so?"

"Insult Tish? What are you talking about? I would never insult Tish."

Seraphina drew off her gloves and placed them with her reticule on the desk behind which her brother stood barricaded. She folded her hands decisively. "Oh, yes you would. And have. You have wounded her deeply."

"By God, Phina, you're worse than Fanny. I know that you were on to Enett's game."

"Enett's game! What nonsense is that? Do you think that a marquis, with a rent roll of goodness knows what length, would be up to some game with a mere banker's daughter?" With a hmmmph and a shrug of her shoulder Seraphina dismissed that line of reasoning. "Enett could buy and sell you twice over."

"That's to be debated. And hmmmph all you like. Enett's fortune says nothing to the point. He himself told me that you recognized him. You knew my sentiments about aristocrats, just as well as Fanny, and I take it very unkindly of you—"

"It says one thing to the point. The man is in love with Maidie. But it does not speak to my point, which is that you insult Tish— making her so unhappily aware that she failed to produce a son for you to bully into the banking business."

"Now Phina, see here—"

"Don't see-here me. You are an unfeeling monster to treat Tish so."

"Damn it, Phina, you know I wouldn't hurt Tish for the world.

She knows I've never blamed her that we've not had other chick
or child than Maidie."

"Does she, Sam? And are you certain you've never, in your
heart, laid it at her door? I won't say any more on that head, but
I leave it to you to search your heart and then your conscience."

"My conscience is none of your concern, and—"

"Furthermore, there's no need to change the name of
Worthing's Bank just because you have no partner of that name,
as you know perfectly well. Child's—"

"Yes, yes. I know who owns Child's. Do you think I don't
know my own business?"

"I merely suggest that you reexamine your position in light
of what you do know. Now, when Enett spoke to you, did you
tell him your reason for refusing him?"

"Certainly I did, and—"

"What was his reply?"

Mr. Worthing shifted uncomfortably from one foot to the
other. "Don't remember."

"You're lying. I was always able to tell when you were un-
truthful. Not to mention that it strains the imagination to believe
you don't remember. You can remember what you had for breakfast on any specific day five years ago. But we will pass that
point by for now. Do you have any objection to Enett other than
his title?"

He clamped his jaws together and stared fixedly at his sister.
Then, for want of a better defense, exploded in anger, "Damn
it, Phina! You aren't the girl's father! She's my daughter, and you
have nothing to say in the matter!"

Seraphina was not overwhelmed by this show of aggression.
She sniffed. "Oh, don't think shouting will do you any good. I
am well aware that I am only Maidie's aunt. However, she does
have a mother. Does her mother have no say? Or only you, the
tyrant?"

"Phina, I warn you—"

"Don't issue empty warnings to me, Sam. You should know better. I again suggest you examine your conscience." Seraphina gathered up her reticule and gloves. She looked at her brother, at her most imperious. "Uneasy rests the head of the tyrant." Her departure, unruffled and majestic, stated clearly that right walked by her side.

Her mind considerably relieved, she directed Mr. Worthing's coachman to take her home. She allowed herself a faint smile, and muttered to herself that that should leave Sam with something to think about. Maidie had made a great coup, fixing the interest of such an exalted personage as the Marquis of Enett, a fact that she was not likely to overlook. But she was also truly fond of her niece, and wished to see her happy. Seraphina was quite certain in her own mind that she would have approved any reasonable suitor that Maidie might have favored. Except that silly ninny, Calvette, of course. At least she and Sam could agree on that.

She ordered her dinner for six o'clock, called for her mail, and asked that a cup of tea with milk and a plate of well-buttered toast be sent up to her bedchamber. After brushing out her hair and changing into a peignoir, she sat down to open such mail as had not been forwarded to her in Wales: invitations to sundry events from the few of her set who chose to spend summers in town, announcements of lectures, advertising circulars for all manner of useless things. And a note from the Dowager Marchioness of Enett.

Seraphina read the note, consumed her tea and toast, read the note again, and thought deeply. Then she rose, went to her desk, and taking pen and paper wrote a short reply.

Mrs. Worthing greeted her husband affectionately, and with her arms about his neck, told him how happy she was to be with him again. He kissed her, but she felt his reserve, and thought that he avoided her eyes.

Mr. Worthing was not a man to put off the unpleasant, and especially with Seraphina's death to tyrants speech still ringing in his ears. "Well, here's a pretty piece of work, Tish. Our girl's got herself mixed up with an aristocrat."

"Yes." Mrs. Worthing was not one to avoid the unpleasant either—only to approach it more cautiously. But if Sam chose to discuss it the minute he walked in the door, she would accommodate him. "Let's go into the library where we can be private."

She permitted him to describe his encounter with Lord Enett, to denounce Seraphina for a meddling old biddy, and to bluster about for a time before saying, "I'm surprised at you, Sam. I've heard nothing about Maidie, or what she might desire."

"It doesn't matter what her desires are. Maidie knew my sentiments, and has gone against my wishes. How can you call her a dutiful daughter?"

"I haven't called her a dutiful daughter. But one doesn't fall in love to specification, Sam. We long ago decided that since ours was a love match, that Maidie would marry where she chose." Mrs. Worthing was not averse to using wile to accomplish her aims. She smiled up at him archly. "Have you forgotten how it was with us?"

That he did not respond told her how difficult a battle this would be.

"Marry where she chose, yes. But not an aristocrat. I have said from the beginning; I will not approve an aristocratic marriage."

Mrs. Worthing argued for their daughter's happiness, reminded Mr. Worthing again of their decision that Maidie should marry for love. He countered that a summer acquaintance was insufficient for entering into a lifelong partnership. She reminded him of her own parents' objections to her marriage to him. He said that the circumstances in Maidie's case were different. She mentioned Child's Bank, and was told the example did not apply. She refrained, however, from mentioning her failure to bear a son for him—it was her own great sorrow and regret. She was too proud to use it as a weapon.

Mrs. Worthing could not know how accurately Seraphina's accusations had gone home. She sensed no change in his position—perhaps even a hardening of his resolve against the marriage—and decided that for the moment silence might be the better course.

She smiled at him sweetly and took his arm to go in to their dinner, saying, "It was good for me, Sam, that we permitted Maidie to go to Fanny and that she was unable to accompany me to the seashore. Otherwise I would never have known Wales and its beautiful coast. I had been getting quite set in my ways— which is the first sign of old age."

Mr. Worthing held her chair for her, and took his own place. Mrs. Worthing picked up her napkin and signalled the footman to serve the soup. "It's not that I dread old age, but only a certain symptom in myself that one often sees among the elderly—a tendency to be set in their ways, not open to new ideas. Wanting everything ordered just to suit themselves, without any thought of what other people might desire."

She gazed across the table at him with innocent eyes. "Do you like the soup? I thought you might. It's from a new recipe that Seraphina gave me."

Mr. Worthing said he liked the soup, and wondered why he had suddenly thought of Fanny.

Seraphina called on Mrs. Worthing the following afternoon before her engagement with Lady Enett.

"And how did it go with Sam?" she asked.

"Not well. I never thought I would ever say of Sam that he

was unreasonable, but I must say it in this case. And what a scolding you must have given him! He was quite beside himself."

Seraphina acknowledged what she took as a compliment with a grim smile. "Is there any word from Maidie?"

"She seems in strong spirit. She arrives within the week, Thursday at the latest, escorted by Mrs. Califaxton, who is bringing her daughter to town. Have you heard the news about that young Mr. Duval we met at Fanny's? It would be diverting, were we not in such difficulty."

"Yes—I amused myself last night with all the back papers. I'd heard somewhere about an enquiry in the Lords but didn't know the son had been killed, or that the old duke had been left without an heir. A great good fortune for Mr. Duval, or whatever his name is now. But I hadn't thought it diverting."

"But Sam was so impressed by Mr. Duval's dislike of his name that he was willing to believe that he might be an acceptable match for Maidie! When it was perfectly clear to me, at least, that the young man was eminently unsuitable. So prolix! And all the time Mr. Duval was heir to a dukedom!"

Seraphina and Mrs. Worthing enjoyed a pleasant laugh at Mr. Worthing's expense, and then got down to serious plotting.

"I have had a note from the Dowager Marchioness of Enett."

"Have you indeed? But that is interesting. I didn't know you were acquainted."

"We have met; although it would be more accurate perhaps, to say that we know of each other. She has never liked London. She has come to town for the first time in two years, with Enett and her daughter—Julia, I believe her name is—and her daughter-in-law, Clarence's wife, who had her come out perhaps five years ago. From an old family of large property in Kent—the Bushacers."

"But the note from Lady Enett?"

"Asking me to call later this afternoon. Contrary to what I

would have expected, she implies she has no objection to the
match. The former marquis made a much more suitable marriage
with the Bushacer girl, but of course one can't think it was a
love match."

Seraphina was graciously received by Lady Enett. They each
tried not to be too obviously taking the other's measure, but after
a delicate round of commonplaces and seemingly meaningless
observations, each concluded that the other was worthy of further acquaintance. They then arrived with admirable dispatch at
the subject which interested them both.

"Well, Miss Worthing . . . or may I call you Seraphina, since
I believe that we will soon be connections? And I would be
pleased if you would call me Margaret. Now, tell me, what are
we to do with your brother?"

Seraphina admitted that her brother had a tendency to be stubborn when crossed.

"I'd like to meet the girl. If I've ever seen her, I am unaware
of it. I am not in the habit of accepting invitations to grand
balls—to any of the sorts of events young girls are addicted to.
Don't like town affairs. Don't like crushes, and can't abide Al-
mack's. Or the patronesses either."

Seraphina chose not to comment on this observation, since
these were just the entertainments and people she found most
amusing. "I'd like to bring Maidie to meet you, but for the time
being it might be best not to directly defy my brother. And with
so many people still out of town, and so few entertainments . . ."

"Perhaps we can find some neutral ground."

Seraphina turned her gloves over in her lap, considering. "I
see from my mail that there are several lectures that might be
of interest."

"A lecture. Just the thing. Enett will escort me. Both the
young people accompanied by chaperones of the most respect-

able. Or do you believe it to be improper to conspire in aiding lovers to meet?"

"It is hardly a matter of serious consequence for your conscience or mine, for once the little season begins, Maidie will not be able to avoid meeting Enett."

"Agreed. Now, what lecture?"

"Mr. Hazlitt is lecturing at the Surrey Institution on the English poets. Repeating, I believe, his lectures of last March. Maidie returns no later than Thursday. So, the Friday lecture?"

"Excellent. I have always had a profound interest in the English poets."

Sometime later, when Allan was informed that he was required to accompany Lady Enett to a lecture, he was surprised, but when told the subject was poets, he was disbelieving. "When did you acquire an interest in poetry, Maman?"

"I have always had such an interest," Lady Enett replied. "I'm surprised you can ask. Now, what have you been doing to win over this banker whose daughter you're set on?"

It was not enough to please his mother, but Allan had not been idle. He had written two notes to Mr. Worthing, and although he did not suppose that the first, or even the second, would be opened—anymore than that he would be received at Mr. Worthing's home or his bank—he believed that one day curiosity would overcome his resistance.

"And I am just going to write him another," Allan said, dropping a filial kiss on his mother's cheek. "So if you'll excuse me, Maman."

"As I said before—a lily-livered . . ." But he was gone.

Allan drummed his fingers on his desk for a few minutes before setting to work on the third of his letters to Mr. Worthing. He again suggested that they meet and get to know each other, and emphasized that he did not wish to take Maidie from her family. In fact, he looked forward to the closest of ties and would never accept estrangement. "Maidie and I will pester you to death, as my old nurse would say." He signed himself, "Respectfully, Enett."

He was just sealing the letter when a footman knocked on the door to tell him that a Lord Blout was calling. Allan frowned in surprise. "Lord Blout?" He had thought him still in the country attending his political fences. "But bring him to me here immediately. No, wait, I'll go to him myself."

He hurried to the small front parlor, where he found his father's friend waiting. "Sir, I didn't know you were back in town. How happy I am to see you. And my mother will be delighted! But first, come into the library and take a glass of wine with me."

Lord Blout shook Allan's hand vigorously. "And I'll be equally delighted to see Margaret, and that little chit of a Julie, too. Wouldn't even mind saying hello to that lachrymose woman your brother married—what's her name? Never could remember. However, I have information for you that you requested of me, which we should discuss first. I'll take that wine now, though."

"You have discovered then that it was the Duke of Toone who set a spy on Salvatore Toone, alias Wendell Duval?"

"No, not at all."

Allan paused in the act of pouring the wine. "No?"

Lord Blout waited to reply until Allan handed him his glass and he had judged its quality. "Excellent. Excellent." Lord Blout was a shrewd and hard-working parliamentarian, a little stout and balding, who appreciated pretty women and sleek horses. But above all, he appreciated fine wine.

"Wanted to come as soon as I could—let you know why I was remiss in answering your letters." Lord Blout put his wine glass down and went to stand with his back to the cold fireplace. "We were privately looking into an enquiry in the Lords about a legal question regarding the succession to the Toone title, which I dared not inform you of at the time. But I was curious about who was spying on a young man who might very likely be our eighth Duke of Toone. No Government interest I could discover, so went to Bow Street, and set a Runner on the trail. Nothing definite, but reason to believe that Everett Toone—a distant relative—was paying the spy. You've heard that Toone's in Newgate for embezzling from Durkim, Findley, and Whatshisname? Well, I suppose it doesn't matter now, but as I said, wanted you to know I wasn't as behindhand as you might be thinking."

"But the reason?" Allan asked, with a puzzled frown.

"Obvious. Clear as a belljar what was happening—Everett Toone had got wind of the death of the old duke's son; knew he had a claim to the title—descendant in the cadet branch. But more important, in my judgment, knew it was in the duke's power to will his fortune where he would." Lord Blout sighed. "Amazing how difficult it is to keep secrets. Suppose some one of our clerks knew Toone, and saw his own fortune in the making. Well, to make a long story short, Toone's idea, it seems, was to discredit his distant cousin, Salvatore. Didn't have the money to pay a spy, slipped his hand in the money box at Durkim's, and there you are. Repenting in Newgate, and soon to be off for Botany Bay."

"Does the duke know this?"

"No. Does it matter?"

Allan considered. "I don't know. I called on the duke and his heir today, and I understand they're trying to get Everett Toone out of Newgate. Human reclamation I believe they call it. Both the old duke and his heir are highminded. May I reserve judgment?"

"The information is yours to use as you will. I know you'll use it wisely. Always were a good boy."

Maidie arrived in London fatigued to death. Prudence had valiantly tried to stem the flow of her mother's verbosity, although it was generally conceded in the Califaxton family to be a useless task. She was occasionally successful, with Maidie's help, in drawing her mother's interest to the scenery and its merits for sketching at some future date. Prudence had also made certain to have a supply of novels, for Mrs. Califaxton did read worthwhile novels, and had a most fortunate tendency to fall asleep over them.

For all such distractions, it had taken only one day of the familiarity of fellow traveling to bring Mrs. Califaxton to include Maidie among those eligible for her scolds. Nor was it long, given the intimacy and many hours together, before Maidie had revealed all to Mrs. Califaxton, for talk as much as the lady might, she was a willing listener when there was something she considered worth listening to. When she had heard the story, her response was to speak fulsomely on the republican spirit.

Mrs. Califaxton's version of republicanism was broad and inclusive, conferring worth on all citizens from the lowest and most impoverished to the most exalted in the land. Equality was at the heart of her life philosophy, and the implication certainly was that commoners should have no more reservations about marrying aristocrats than the reverse. The same was true in the matter of worldly comforts: money should be spread about by intermarriage between the wealthy and not so wealthy, as had been the case with Prudence and Wendell before his amazing elevation to heir to one of the greatest fortunes in the kingdom. However, she carefully pointed out, the Duke of Toone's wealth—at least as she understood it—was as much a product of his own efforts as the Califaxton wealth, and could therefore await another generation for redistribution. A good shaking up was the best remedy for any number of social ills, and she had never held with Mr. Califaxton's notion that it was a child's duty to marry for the purpose of furthering family interest.

As for Mr. Worthing's notions, they were too odd to be of any consequence.

When Maidie was at last let down on her own doorstep, Mrs. Califaxton said, "No, we won't come in, so don't bother to ask. I know your mother will understand. I'll call later."

Mrs. Worthing embraced her daughter affectionately. Then she held her away and studied her face. "You are all right, my dear?"

"Yes, of course, Mama. I'm sorry that Papa doesn't approve of Allan, but we are determined to marry. He can't force me to marry where I do not wish, nor can he prevent me from marrying where I will."

"Strong words, Maidie," her mother cautioned. "But let me call someone to carry your valises up. I suppose that the trunk is coming by wagon? We will talk after you've rested."

Later that day Maidie entered the small light-filled chamber they used as their sewing room, where Mrs. Worthing was busy stitching a shirt for Mr. Worthing. She looked up with a smile, and reached a hand out to her daughter. "Are you rested now, my dear?"

"Yes, Mama. Mrs. Califaxton is not an easy companion for a long journey."

"And the state of your mind?"

"It will relieve you, I know, that I don't intend to defy Papa outright—at least not before I have exhausted persuasions more in keeping with the respect and affection that a daughter owes her father, and, indeed, that I have for Papa despite the demands of duty and . . ." unexpectedly, Maidie's voice trailed off into a suppressed giggle. "Oh my, what an elevated speech! I must give up reading Hannah More."

"Hannah More! You have been reading *Hannah More?*"

"I thought it might help regulate my mind. But I promise, I'll read a chapter of Rousseau tonight in penance. Perhaps even a page or two of Plato."

"I recommend at least ten pages of Homer as well. Now, do

let us be serious. I would be very sorry if this caused a rift between you and your father."

"And you, Mama?"

"I am trying my very best to influence your father in your favor. My own family will of course have no objections, but I haven't yet spoken to them of it. I've hoped we could settle this without bringing them into the dispute, for you know how they and your Papa grate on each other, even when they try to be civil."

"Yes, I know. Aunt Seraphina?"

"Oh, Seraphina approves. How can you doubt it? And she has called on Enett's mother, who has not opposed the match. And that reminds me—Seraphina asks that you accompany her to a lecture tomorrow—something on English poets. She says she has developed a renewed interest in poetry since meeting Mr. Wordsworth and his sister."

Maidie had almost believed that with the cajoling, teasing, and rational argument that had always been so successful with Papa before, his resistance to Allan would crumble. She was surprised to find him immovable, hardened to any persuasion.

His first response was to storm and rage, but when Maidie seemed unaffected, and Mrs. Worthing remonstrated that the servants were certainly enjoying the drama, he assumed instead an air of righteous censure.

He was displeased rather than angry, he told Maidie. She had known that he would not permit her to marry an aristocrat, had known it since she was a child, and as soon as she had seen Enett's interest aroused should have discouraged him. She had deliberately ignored his wishes, could have saved herself from heartache, but had not, and must now suffer the unhappiness that defiance of her father brought upon her.

"I will marry him, Papa. Where my own heart is concerned, I cannot share your prejudices."

"And I will never give you my permission. That is my last word. We will not speak of it again."

Maidie turned at the door. "I hardly know you, Papa." Her eyes filled with tears. He had often been angry with her, and occasionally had flatly refused her permission for something she wanted to do, but always the reason had been because of his concern for her—not for himself.

And so, in vehement terms, she told Mrs. Worthing, who could only counsel patience, and that they would win Papa over yet.

Twenty

Mr. Hazlitt was a witty and popular lecturer, and the hall was so crowded that at first Seraphina, delayed in the traffic outside, did not see Allan and his mother. When she at last discovered them in seats near the aisle and to the front, the lecture had begun, and there was nothing for it but to listen. She whispered to Maidie that she believed Lady Enett and Lord Enett were seated several rows ahead, and wondered if the young lady sitting beside Lady Enett might not be his sister, Lady Julia.

Seraphina claimed later that she had profited greatly from the lecture, but Maidie could not have passed an examination on the subject for her life. Her entire attention was centered on the back of her suitor's head, with an occasional curious study of the back of his mother's head.

When the lecture at last ended, the applause finally died away, and people were making their way up the aisles to the exits, Seraphina put a hand on Maidie's arm. "Don't get up. Not yet." She began to peer at the floor near her chair. "Maidie, can you see my eyeglass case?" she asked.

Two gentlemen halted their progress, greeted her by name, and offered with great gallantry to crawl around under the chairs to find the lost case. Seraphina, annoyed, said, "You are too good, but before you risk your gloves and the knees of your pantaloons, I should again search my reticule." The two gentlemen waited, sneaking glances at Maidie and hoping for an introduction. After scrambling about in her reticule (to the detriment of all order) Seraphina took out the case and exclaimed, "How stupid of me! Here it is. Thank you. You have been kind."

The gentlemen did not wish to move on. Seraphina regarded them with a chilling stare. "Good night. Thank you again." Then, spying Lady Enett and Allan approaching, she exclaimed, "Why, Margaret! How delightful to see you. I had no idea you were interested in the poets."

"Neither did I," said Allan, looking at Maidie.

"Nor I you," Lady Enett said, addressing Seraphina. "But well met. Can you stop for a moment in the antechamber so I may present my daughter? I believe you know my son."

The anteroom proved to be too crowded for a woman who couldn't abide crushes, and there were too many people speaking in voices that were too loud and unmodulated to please Seraphina. It was impossible to discuss anything in such a turmoil; could Lady Enett offer them a cup of tea or a glass of wine in her own drawing room? Seraphina thought it would not be inconvenient.

Julie, who unlike Lady Enett did like poetry, had with her usual persistence wrangled permission to attend the lecture also. She hadn't expected to have the good luck to meet Allan's light of love too, and it was much against her wishes that she was ordered immediately to bed. She managed a covert wink at Allan and a raised eyebrow at her mother before dropping her proper curtsies to the guests. Lady Enett frowned severely, and reminded herself to speak to the baggage first thing in the morning to disabuse her of any idea that her mother was engaging in romantic plots.

Maidie did not need an explanation for how the chance meeting had come about. She was to be inspected by Lady Enett, and although Allan's letter had assured her that his mother favored their marriage, she felt herself to be in a quake. But Lady

Enett looked at her so kindly that her attack of nerves was quickly over, and she could say to her mother later that she believed she had acquitted herself well. Lady Enett, for her part, was pleased with what she saw. It was easy to see that Maidie was a well brought-up child, and she concluded that there was no fear that she would be unable to fill the position of marchioness capably. That her son was in love was not in doubt. He was perfectly correct as host, but his eyes betrayed him whenever he looked at the girl. Once satisfied on these points, she sent the lovers to the library with instructions not to linger for more than a few minutes.

The minute the door closed behind them Maidie was in Allan's arms.

They held each other tightly for only a moment, exchanging hurried kisses, and then separated, mindful of their elders. Maidie put her hand on his chest. "Oh, Allan, I've missed you." She meant that she had wanted him.

He covered her hand with his own. "And I you. I can't tell you how much. But come, my duckling, and sit down. We've not been given much time. I would never have believed that my mother and your aunt would indulge in such scheming and subterfuge."

"Your mother . . ."

"Approves of you." He drew her to the sofa, where she could rest her head on his shoulder as they talked, and where he could lightly kiss her hair from time to time. "My mother has given her consent. I believe she may be harboring an ambition to conquer your father. But now she has met you . . ." Obviously, anyone who met his dear one would love her.

Maidie was sorry to tell him that her father was constant in his refusal to listen to reason. "But I am determined, no matter what he says. We will elope. Papa is always saying how he would have run away to Gretna Green with Mama, if Grandpapa hadn't given them permission to marry."

"No, my dear. Perhaps that is only his way of telling the world how much he loves your mama. For we can't know that he ever would have, can we? And in any event, I've given my word that I will never carry you off to Gretna Green."

"You *what?* How could you?" She wrenched herself from the circle of his arm to stand angrily in front of him. "How *could* you?" she repeated, stamping her foot. "Whether Papa would have or not, he *says* it."

"Everybody is always saying *what?* to me," Allan complained. He caught her hand to draw her back down beside him. "No need for concern. We will win our way by other means."

She pulled away. "Now Papa will feel secure—we will have no threat . . ."

"Do you know, that is exactly what my mother said! It's just as I thought. The two of you will deal together famously. Come. I must have you back in my arms again or I can't think properly."

Maidie laughed, and complied, willing also to be kissed a few times.

"Now, my heart, think. He knows that I am a man of my word. But if he thought we might elope, he'd have to lock you up. But as it is, here we are together. And when people are back in town for the fall season, we can see each other even without the connivance of those two old conspirators giggling together in the drawing room." He bent his head to kiss her again. "Anyway, your father's position is untenable. We have his position invested."

"Invested?"

"He is surrounded—under siege by hostile troops. He has neither reserves nor allies to come to his assistance, so eventually he must surrender."

Maidie, amused, said, "And among the hostile troops we may count our families, Mrs. Califaxton—oh, very much so—and Wendell and Chester. Wendell has made me a very pretty and rather lengthy speech to help me keep my spirits up!"

"And more usefully, Chester's been at pains to undertake an investigation for us, and to tell me about the Kinnairds, and Sally Villiers—to hear him one would think that half the aristocracy is in banking. But I'm ever so trifling worried—you say that Mrs. Califaxton is among our allies?"

"Oh, yes. Very much so."

"Perhaps we should not foster that alliance. I refuse to be alienated from my future father-in-law. He likes me, by the way."

"Does he? One wouldn't think it to have heard him storm and rage."

"My poor darling. Does he make it so hard for you?"

"I believe I am making it much harder for him than he can for me."

A discreet knock warned them that they had overstayed their time. Allan halted Maidie at the door for another kiss. Then with his hand on the door pull he said, "One more thing. I have promised your father our second son, should that young man choose to become a banker. And he may change his name to Worthing with my blessing. Do you approve? I know I should have consulted you first . . ."

This was treading close to the careful cliff along which they had been walking. Allan, knowing it full well, kissed Maidie again quickly, and opened the door to escort her back to their chaperones—who were certainly pleased with themselves, but *not* giggling.

Mrs. Califaxton had waited only long enough to settle herself and Prudence comfortably at their hotel before setting out to deliver a good piece of her mind to Maidie's father. Like Seraphina, she chose to wait upon him in his counting house, where she intended to subject him to one of her ripest and richest scolds. She sailed past her horrified son, recognizing him with no more than a distant nod, to present her card to the assistant who guarded access to the banker's office.

Mr. Worthing, having had a taste of Mrs. Califaxton at Fanny's, although he took pains to show her every courtesy, did not welcome her into his private rooms with anticipation of any pleasure in the visit. He was not mistaken. She began immediately to berate him, ignoring even the most elementary courteous preliminaries.

"Mr. Worthing, I am ashamed of you! You men are all alike—using your daughters to further your own selfish ends. No better than degenerate Frenchmen!"

"Frenchmen?" Mr. Worthing had expected to be denounced again as a despot and a tyrant. "I confess myself at a loss, Mrs. Califaxton, to understand your meaning."

"Would you men have us in England marry off our daughters for your greedy, avaricious, worldly satisfactions—and then look the other way when they indulge their passions by taking lovers? I am telling you no more than I told Mr. Califaxton when he chose to deny a future duke permission to address our Prudence."

"Don't think he was a future duke then," Mr. Worthing interrupted slyly.

"That is beside all points. As I told Mr. Califaxton, the young man had promise, and I consider myself vindicated. But I am not here to discuss my own affairs, but your shameful want of republican spirit in rejecting an honorable and upright man just because he happens to be burdened with a title!"

Mrs. Califaxton, several paragraphs later, at last brought her scold to an end, and without a blink asked in a motherly tone whether Chester was behaving himself. She had a few words to say on Chester's failings, which Mr. Worthing would have to watch carefully, stated that he was on the whole, however, a very good boy, and departed with a nod and a final admonition to take to heart what she had just told him.

With a feeling of desperation, Mr. Worthing turned to his mail, hoping that he could bring his mind to bear again on his avaricious worldly affairs, only to discover that Enett had written him another letter. Damn his eyes! Main force couldn't persuade him to open it. He pushed it aside. But when all the other letters were disposed of, it lay on his cleared desk like a lump of bad food in his belly. It actually made him feel liverish.

The upshot was that he opened the letter, scanning it quickly, with the notion that if he merely skimmed over the words to capture the sense he would not be guilty of actually reading it. Despite himself, a chuckle escaped him. "Pester me to death, would they?"

He was beginning to feel he was being beaten about the head and shoulders by casual acquaintances as well as by his own family. Before he knew it, his employees would be after him, too.

And, of course, he was right.

It was his custom to invite new apprentices to dine with his family, and now that Maidie and Mrs. Worthing were home again he had issued an invitation to Chester. So it came about that that young man and Mr. Worthing found themselves sitting together in the banker's dining room digesting a very fine dinner and drinking an excellent burgundy.

And so it came about also that although Chester had provided Allan with an argument with which to confront Mr. Worthing, it was too good an argument to leave to him.

Mr. Worthing poured his guest a second glass of wine, and leaned back in his chair. "Enjoying your work, are you?"

"Yes, sir. Always did like figures."

"Getting acquainted with some of the other apprentices?" Mr. Worthing cocked an eyebrow at his youthful companion. "But I suppose you have some acquaintances in town already, from the days when you were spending your papa's money too freely."

Chester ignored this sally. "I've met a lot of good chaps from

Worthing's and some of the other banks. Fellow from Ransom and Morland . . . By the way, Ransom's have the same idea you have. Wanted to keep the style even when there's no longer a partner bearing one of the old names."

"That's true." Mr. Worthing's eyes narrowed menacingly. "Although I believe one of the present partners petitioned a while back to change his name to Morland."

"Just meant no Ransom." Chester had insufficient courage to pursue that line further. He cleared his throat and restrained an urge to finger his cravat nervously. "As I was going to say, didn't expect that all the work would be exciting. Mean to say, lot of drudgery in whatever one does, but if in general one likes one's work . . . That is . . ."

"Very true. That's a sensible way of looking at it."

Encouraged, Chester said, "Thank you, sir. Have to say for m'father, may have wrung his hands over me, but impressed on me that I couldn't expect to enjoy every minute of my life. Said I had to find something worthwhile to do. Said although he'd like me in the business with him, a man should choose his own path. Just took me longer to find it, you see, than it did m'brothers."

He realized that Mr. Worthing was staring at him skeptically.

"Know he kicked up rough with Pru. Mean to say, the governor likes money. As you know, sir, that's why he had me rusticated in the Lakes. Tolerant man when it came to schoolboy tricks—but not about squanderin' money. But about Pru, I said to him, looks like for a woman, marriage is her work. Mean to say, Pru can't study law or medicine. Only thing she can do is choose her own husband. Let him draw his own conclusions." Chester felt the ice beginning to crack beneath his feet, but he skated on. "Forgive me for saying it, sir, but that's the way I look at it. And with Pru weeping and wailing around the house— m'sister ain't ordinarily missish, you know. He would've given ground in the end. Know m'father."

Chester subsided. Couldn't even tell whether Worthing knew what he was talking about, but he wasn't looking friendly.

"Well," Mr. Worthing said, "found yourself a decent lodging? Not too far from the bank?"

As Chester walked home he reviewed the evening and decided he had not shown himself too badly with his employer once they got on mutually agreeable topics. Only thing was, didn't think he'd done much to help Maidie and Enett, and dashed if he could think of anything else.

Mr. Worthing had just fixed his attention on a sheet of figures when a clerk knocked on his door to ask if he would see the Duke of Toone and the Honorable Salvatore Clackenham.

He groaned. His business premises were beginning to be more like a coffee house than a bank.

He stood to greet them, shaking hands first with the duke, and then with Wendell. "Salvatore Clackenham! By God, Duval, if you don't settle on one name soon! Sit down. Sit down."

"Why not continue to use Duval, sir. A private name among those of us who met in the Lakes."

The duke said, "Have to thank you, Worthing, for assisting this young scamp. But we have just stopped for a minute to beg your presence at a small gathering in honor of Miss Califaxton and Salvatore. They're to wed soon—youth is all impatience, hey? Not like us old-timers who've learned to take it slowly, whether we want to or not."

Mr. Worthing didn't think he'd slowed down all that much, but refrained from saying so.

"We're on our way to leave an invitation in Bedford Square," Wendell added. "But the duke wanted to stop and give you your invitation personally."

"Believe I knew your grandfather, Worthing. Apprentice to one of the goldsmiths in Lombard Street. Jinkle? Jankle?"

"Jankling. But could hardly have been my grandfather."

The two older men fell into a rambling conversation in which the personnel of various London goldsmiths and bankers of the mid-eighteenth century onward were recalled and placed in their proper decade and geographic location, including their various moves from one house to another, their fortunes and failures. It was finally too much for Wendell's patience, and he took to shifting uncomfortably in his seat. He hadn't been getting enough exercise of late.

"Go on out and talk to that young fellow we met in the antechamber," the duke said. "Unless you've some objection, Worthing. If you do, he can just sit here and listen, or go outside and whittle."

Wendell chose, with Mr. Worthing's consent, to talk to Chester. Relieved of his presence, the two men fell into a discussion of the duke's youth knocking around town with bank apprentices and clerks, hanging about the docks, the trading houses and the coffee houses, getting an education while determining to recover the Toone fortunes by hook or by crook.

"If you'll permit me, wish to tell you how much I admire your spirit," Mr. Worthing said. "Was just saying to someone the other day that you didn't let your name become a Bastille. Not my words, but Hazlitt's—Round Table piece, I believe."

"Yes, a name can be a prison. An impediment. Too much importance given to names here in England."

Mr. Worthing cleared his throat. "Well. As I was saying, must not have been easy for the son of a duke. The title goes back to the sixteenth century, I understand. Not many of your class will condescend to dirty their hands with trade. Banking, now, that's a little different."

The duke smiled reminiscently. "In the end I had to leave England to do it. My father, the sixth duke, said it would kill him if I went into trade; and my sisters—well, you'd think I'd turned highwayman. They might have liked that better, the silly noodlings. Thought it romantic. But like I told Salvatore, each generation must reorder the world to its own liking. I admit that I made sure he was worthy of it before I declared him heir to my fortune. By that I mean that I wanted to be sure he was a man of the most unshakable faith in the perfectibility of humanity. But I've also said to him, and more than once, that he's not to be bound by my notions. The world moves on, and what seemed like the right thing yesterday may tomorrow seem false. No, the young have the right to their own destiny, hey?"

Mr. Worthing cleared his throat again and shuffled together the papers on his desk. "So," he said heartily. "You're going around to the house? Believe I'll call it a day and accompany you."

The duke got slowly to his feet. "We'll have the pleasure of your company then, and your wife and daughter, at our small entertainment?"

"To be sure," Mr. Worthing answered. "To be sure."

Twenty-one

Mr. Worthing was forced to face the unwelcome fact that Allan would surely be present at the entertainment honoring Prudence and Wendell. The duke had several times spoken of it, and how much pleasure it gave him to be able to thank all those who in one way or another had aided Salvatore.

He thus felt it necessary, before setting out, to caution Maidie that he expected her to be circumspect. "Don't want to see you offering Enett more than the most common civility," he said sternly. He was treated in return to such a glare from Mrs. Worthing, so contrary to her usual gentle expression, that it well nigh shriveled him down into his new shoes, while his daughter answered his command with only a defiant tilt of her chin. It was not easy maintaining his plausibility as a tyrant.

Then he had to run the gauntlet of a receiving line, shaking hands with his critics (the duke and Mrs. Califaxton). He presumed that his potential critics (Duval, Miss Milk and Water, and her father) would find an opportunity to put their noses into his business as well.

He presumed correctly. First Miss Califaxton came beaming and simpering on Duval's arm to tell him how very very happy she was, and that she wished *every* girl she knew could be as happy. Then Duval driveled some similar sentiment, in one of the most highflown speeches Mr. Worthing had ever had the ill luck to be subjected to.

He escaped from them to be almost immediately attacked by Mr. Califaxton who, after a hearty greeting, remarked even more heartily and with great relish, "Well, Worthing. Hear you're in the same fix I was not so long back."

"How so?"

"Got a girl who wants to marry where you don't like it."

Mr. Worthing directed a belligerent stare at the wealthy manufacturer from under lowered eyebrows. "How so?"

"Seem to remember you telling me you wouldn't refuse your own girl just because you didn't like the fellow."

"Don't remember."

"And didn't you mention to Enett that you'd have run off with Mrs. Worthing to Gretna Green?"

"May have. But Enett ain't going to." The minute it was out of his mouth he recognized his error.

"You sure?" Even had Mr. Califaxton not been well instructed by his wife, he would have enjoyed watching Worthing wiggle.

"Gave me his word."

"Man of his word?"

Mr. Worthing had backed himself uncomfortably into a corner, from which he was looking around for any possible excuse to escape, when he was providentially saved by Enett's own mother.

"Well, which of you is Worthing?" Lady Enett asked. "I'd guess you, sir. Certain look of Seraphina about you. And you must be Califaxton, father of the future Duchess of Toone."

Mr. Worthing and Mr. Califaxton acknowledged that they had been properly identified, and that they were pleased to make the acquaintance of the dowager marchioness.

"You'll pardon me for introducing myself, but age and rank have some privileges still in this country. Oh, I can see that our days are numbered. The Grim Reaper calls for us all, while the young and the upstarts are taking over the kingdom. People like you, Califaxton, marrying your daughters to dukes, and noble families like the Jerseys and Kinnairds running banks. Someone soon I expect we'll see women demanding their rights and rioting in the streets. Of course, the bankers have always called the tune—isn't that right, Worthing?"

"Well, it's true that bankers have always been essential to any prosperous community, but so have shoemakers."

"I suppose you'll be telling me that a well-run community requires a few beggars as well."

"No, that I would not."

Lady Enett turned to Mr. Califaxton. "You'll excuse us I'm sure, sir. We can perhaps chat together later about Mr. Owen's experiments in humane treatment of factory workers, but now I feel I must become better acquainted with this gentleman, who doesn't feel my son worthy of his daughter. If you'll give me your arm, sir?"

"No, ma'am . . . or, yes ma'am, I will be happy to lend you my arm, but no, ma'am I do not consider Enett unworthy of my daughter."

"Perhaps it wouldn't strain your republican spirit unduly to occasionally call me Lady Enett?"

Mr. Worthing suddenly laughed. "Not republican spirit, Lady Enett, but simple bull-headedness, of which I've been accused more than once these past few days."

"Then I needn't add my accusations. Why don't you let me take you to my son? I have met your daughter, and find her irresistible. I'm not surprised that Allan has fallen in love with her."

"My objections, Lady Enett, do not pertain to your son's character, which I believe to be upright and steadfast."

"And any other objection is foolish. But come, mere civility requires you acknowledge the boy. And may I say that if you esteem his character then your objections have no basis, for he

will do his utmost to honor you and your desires." Lady Enett
looked up at him and remarked shrewdly, "Those of us less
influenced by youthful heat than those two children may think
more rationally. Would not the connection of the Enett shipping
interests with the Worthing financial interests be a felicitous
union?"

Mr. Worthing looked down at Lady Enett. "One of the few
sensible words I've heard on the subject."

"My son's forbears financed pirates, and were well rewarded.
Enetts have been in shipping for three centuries."

"Pirates, hmmm?" He would enjoy knowing this lady.

Although Allan watched Maidie closely, he did not approach
her, and whenever she attempted to approach him, he moved
away, but when he saw her standing alone at the refreshment
table in the small drawing room, and Mr. Worthing nowhere in
sight, he couldn't resist snatching a few minutes with her.

"Hello, duckling," he whispered in her ear.

She turned around, surprised, and required to hastily swallow
a morsel of some faintly fishy substance she had unluckily sam-
pled. "What are you doing? I might have choked to death. I've
been pursuing you this half hour, and you have been avoiding
me."

"How are you, Maidie? Still constant?" He smiled down at
her. "I love you dearly, and would have been with you the moment you came into the room . . . But I was waiting until the
artillery could be brought to bear."

Maidie laughed. "Your mama?"

"Ah, so you observed?"

"She has certainly distracted Papa. He's no longer watching
me every minute. He instructed me that I was to show you no
more than common civility, but I shan't attend to that."

"Your duty is to defy your father, of course, but my duty is to prove myself worthy of him."

"Worthy of *him!*"

"So I must be circumspect, you see. But I would love you, my sweet, even if not worthy of you, and am so reprehensible I'd marry you anyway."

"Oh, I do dearly love a villain!"

"No you don't. You love a respectable farmer. But now let me take you to Miss Califaxton, for the old duke is beckoning me."

"Come into the library for a few minutes, Enett. Something best said in private, hey?"

In the library, the duke eased himself into a chair, muttering that the foul climate in the New World had ruined his knees. "Pull that chair over closer. Ears not what they used to be. Received your note. Suppose I know what it's all about. Everett Toone. Hey?"

"Yes. I came into some information since I called on you last week that I thought you should know. I wish to say first that I admire your desire to reclaim the man—"

The duke held up his hand. "No need for speeches. You want to tell me that Everett put a spy on Salvatore?"

"You know?"

"I wasn't going to stand for the government spying on my heir. Made some enquiries—one thing led to another." He chuckled. "Not going to tell Salvatore. Good thing to be suspicious of government. Guard against tyranny. And I don't want him to harbor a prejudice against Everett."

Allan was not certain he agreed with the duke's decision or his reasons. He said nothing, but his opinion was sufficiently clear from his expression that the duke nodded. "May be wrong—have been, many times in a long life. Assure you, I'll make certain Salvatore knows before I surrender the reins." The duke grasped his cane in one hand and the arm of the chair in the other, preparing to rise.

"May I help you, sir?"

"No, no. Can do it myself." With a grunt he pushed himself up. "One thing. You know the facts. If I shuffle off this mortal coil unexpectedly, leave it to you to tell Salvatore. Truth is, haven't much hope for Everett, but it's a man's duty to try, hey?"

Chester strolled across the room to join Prudence and Maidie. "Pru, m'mother wants you. Wants you to get acquainted with Enett's sister, Lady Julia. Lively girl. Just had a chat with her myself."

Maidie and Prudence embraced, and Prudence whispered, "Oh, Maidie, I am so *deliriously* happy!"

"Yes, I can see that you and Wendell are the happiest people on this earth."

"I would wish everyone such happiness, and especially you, Maidie. I told your father so. Right out. Was that not brave of me?"

Maidie squeezed her arm affectionately. "Yes, Pru. Terribly brave."

"Run along, Pru," Chester said, "and less in alt, beg you. Give me a headache. How are you, Maidie?"

They had been chatting comfortably for several minutes when Maidie interrupted, quite discourteously in Chester's opinion, to ask, "Who is that?" indicating with a surreptitious nod a foppish young gentleman speaking to her Aunt Seraphina.

"The embezzler."

"Who?"

"Shhhh." Chester frowned and shook his head in a slight negative gesture. "That's the fellow nicked the money from Durkim, Findley, and Biddle. Everett Toone. Duke got him out of jail. Bad bargain, if you ask me, but Duval will give you a lofty story about it, if you ask him. Don't recommend you do ask him, however."

"So that's Everett Toone! Wendell and the duke when they called recently said that they were hoping to redeem him, and Papa said—well, you can imagine how Papa feels about people who steal from banks. Anyway, he said—"

Chester suddenly grasped her arm. "Don't look. Your father is speaking to Enett."

"Chester! Where are they? Oh, I shall swoon."

"God's sake, Maidie . . . well . . . now see here, I don't like jokes. Bet you never swooned in your life."

At what point Mr. Worthing gave up he wasn't sure, although he thought probably from the moment Tish, the minx, looked at him across the table and told him she did not like the feeling that she (meaning he) was getting set in her (meaning his) ways. (He would never concede that Phina had had a hand in his capitulation; he'd had too much of her bullying when he was a boy. And as for Fanny, threw her letters away without a blink.) But he'd known from the minute he'd stepped out his door to escort Tish and Maidie to the duke's affair that he was in retreat. By the time he had been worked over by Miss Milk and Water, Duval, Califaxton, and Lady Enett on top of it, he was ready to surrender.

When an opportunity offered, he approached Allan. "Will you see me in the library for a moment?" he asked in a low voice. "Don't want to call any attention to our departure. I'll follow you shortly." When the door closed behind him a few minutes later, he said, "Well, Enett, it appears you've won. I've been outgunned."

Allan had been pacing impatiently around the substantial library table in the center of the room. He put one hand on it now, as though to steady himself. "Are you saying, sir, that you no longer deny my suit?"

"That's what I'm saying."

Allan turned away. "Sir, I . . . I . . ." He was more affected than he had thought he could be. He made a despairing gesture, as he turned to face Mr. Worthing again. "I had a speech prepared for this moment, but I find I am too overcome. Something about how deep my regard is for Maidie, and assuring you that you will never have cause to regret your decision."

"Had a speech prepared did you? Damn sure of yourself!"

"No, sir. I was sure of you." Allan smiled crookedly.

Mr. Worthing also found himself more affected than he had expected. Was losing his girl chick, but he had to admit that it couldn't have been to a better man. "We'll shake hands, then, and be friends," he said gruffly. He offered his hand to be tightly clasped in Allan's.

"An honor, sir."

"Well. Well. I'm sure you've no wish to spend any time jawing with me right now. Plenty of time for that later. You wait here then, and I'll send Maidie to you."

"One more word, if I may. About that night . . ."

Mr. Worthing raised his eyebrows.

"That night I accosted you on your doorstep, so disgracefully . . . I'd like to apologize."

Mr. Worthing waved his hand in dismissal. "No great thing. We all have our moments of weakness. Now, I'll go find Maidie. May take me a little while to cut her out of the pack, so don't get impatient. And after you've had a few minutes alone with her, I'll send Tish in to wish you both happy."

But of course, Maidie would have seen him talking to Enett— or his sharp eyed apprentice had. They were both standing near the door of the main drawing room, and the minute he showed his face, Chester said something to Maidie and walked away. Mr. Worthing put his hand on Maidie's shoulder. "Go into the library, Maidie. You'll find Enett waiting for you. But mind you, only a few minutes and I'll be sending your mother in."

"Yes, Papa. Oh, Papa . . ."

"No. No displays. We don't want to take the shine off your friends' party. Enough time to make our announcements. Run along."

As he surveyed the room looking for Tish, he wondered how in the world he was ever going to explain this to that nincompoop aspirant for Maidie's hand, Lord Calvette.

When Maidie opened the door Allan was waiting to enfold her in his arms. They held each other closely, without speaking, until at last he tilted her chin up to receive his kiss.

"Miss Worthing . . ." he said, still holding her close in his arms.

"Mr. Gilmichael?"

"I love you, imp. Will you marry me?"

"Does this mean we may now elope?" she asked, looking up at him wide-eyed.

He groaned. *"No! . . . No! . . . And no!"*

"I guess not." Maidie closed her eyes, and relaxed in his embrace. "But soon," she whispered.

"Before you drive me mad," he said, kissing her hair.

Epilogue

The felicitous union of Worthing and Enett enterprises endured a great many years—indeed, into the twentieth century, when both Worthing's Bank and the Enett shipping interests were gathered to different conglomerate and corporate bosoms.

As for Maidie and Allan, they were married at Christmas time, but they delayed their wedding trip until the spring so they could spend a long and happy two months in the Lakes with Emery and Fanny and their new little cousin. They tramped the fells together, with knapsacks on their backs and stout shoes on their feet, spending the nights in cozy inn beds. A few years later they built a house on Krigsmere, not far from Fanny and Emery, where with their jolly brood of youngsters they spent as much time as they could spare from the other demands of their busy lives. And when they gathered for tea at Fanny's they might find Wendell and Prudence, or Chester and Lady Julia, or one or another of the many Califaxtons. (Chester, that deserving young man, of course married Julie, Allan's lively sister.)

Thresseley was their primary residence, and Allan's primary interest. (Maidie preferred the Lakes, and her study of local history under the guidance of her uncle and, until he retired, the dear old boring rector.) Mr. and Mrs. Worthing became more frequent visitors at Thresseley and the Lakes as Chester Califaxton, who became a partner in Worthing's Bank in 1824, assumed more of the responsibilities.

Worthing's Bank, when at last sold to Barclays in the early twentieth century, was owned and directed by a tangle of Gilmichaels, Califaxtons, and Worthings that would have required the talents of Miss Hattie (whose mother was a Toone from the cadet branch) to unravel and explain.

Allan took his seat in Parliament, and pursued his duties with diligence and good sense, frequently consulting his old acquaintance, Wendell Duval. ("If the old duke thinks I'll ever call him Salvatore," Maidie had said, "he is dead wrong.") Maidie took her place on the Board of Worthing's Bank, and when Mr. Worthing died in 1850, only a few months after Mrs. Worthing, he had the pleasure of knowing that one of Maidie and Allan's sons, bearing the name of Worthing, sat by her side.

Not long after our story closes, the old duke died, at which time Salvatore Toone, known to a few friends and acquaintances as Wendell Duval, became the eighth duke. He was an active and diligent parliamentarian, and an orator of singular talent, speaking passionately in favor of the many reform bills introduced in Parliament during the nineteenth century. He did not, as Chester mentioned every now and then, lose any wind out of his bag, but neither did he grow more conservative as his elders had expected. His last speech, in 1862 (he died a year later), was in opposition to England's support for the Confederate States of America.

Wendell and Prudence lived happily together for a great number of years. It was just as Chester warned—that puffing Prudence up too much would lead to disappointment—and although Wendell held her in affection until the day he died, he wisely chose not to remember his glorious youthful expectations. As Maidie remarked from time to time, Wendell had a great capacity for self-delusion. Some said that his duchess wrote his speeches, and certainly those who knew them intimately knew that the hand at the helm belonged to Prudence—and a firm hand it was, too.

Everett Toone, the embezzler, proved impossible to reclaim, until at last Wendell reluctantly washed his hands of him, and sent him off to America with the promise of a substantial remittance each quarter as long as he remained out of England. He drifted ever westward, to end his days keeping a saloon on the Omaha, Nebraska riverfront. Boatmen and thirsty passengers often accused him of short change, watering the liquor, and other such perfidies.

We have said that no one who ever met Seraphina Worthing forgot her. She continued majestically through life, learning to swim in Brighton, enjoying the London season, visiting Lady Enett at Thresseley (and incidentally Allan and Maidie), and walking the fells with Fanny. With Dorothy Wordsworth (until that lady sank into her final long twilight of the mind) she learned to listen to the sounds and sights of the natural world. She lived until her ninety-fifth year, vigorous and opinionated to the last.

Allan's sister-in-law Eunice was eventually established in her own house in a village near Thresseley with her dog, Clown, ten or so other mongrels reclaimed from beggary, plus a number of lowlife cats, a few rabbits, and a flock of chickens. She never remarried, but acquaintance with Wendell and his reforming spirit inspired her to lead her own reform effort—to end the many cruelties to animals.

John Califaxton, whom Maidie might have fallen in love with and changed this whole story, gave up his missionary work in Scotland after a few years. He was active with Mrs. Worthing and others in bringing about the reforms, beginning with the first in 1828, that by the end of the century granted full civil rights to Dissenters and Catholics. He married at last, in his thirties, a most worthy lady, who stood by his side in all his battles.

And that poor nincompoop aspirant for Maidie's hand, Lord Calvette? Well, it shouldn't surprise us that he soon found another to love, whose father was happy to grant such an unassuming young lord his daughter's hand.

ZEBRA'S REGENCY ROMANCES
DAZZLE AND DELIGHT

A BEGUILING INTRIGUE   (4441, $3.99)
by Olivia Sumner

Pretty as a picture Justine Riggs cared nothing for propriety. She dressed as a boy, sat on her horse like a jockey, and pondered the stars like a scientist. But when she tried to best the handsome Quenton Fletcher, Marquess of Devon, by proving that she was the better equestrian, he would try to prove Justine's antics were pure folly. The game he had in mind was seduction — never imagining that he might lose his heart in the process!

AN INCONVENIENT ENGAGEMENT   (4442, $3.99)
by Joy Reed

Rebecca Wentworth was furious when she saw her betrothed waltzing with another. So she decides to make him jealous by flirting with the handsomest man at the ball, John Collinwood, Earl of Stanford. The "wicked" nobleman knew exactly what the enticing miss was up to — and he was only too happy to play along. But as Rebecca gazed into his magnificent eyes, her errant fiancé was soon utterly forgotten!

SCANDAL'S LADY   (4472, $3.99)
by Mary Kingsley

Cassandra was shocked to learn that the new Earl of Lynton was her childhood friend, Nicholas St. John. After years at sea and mixed feelings Nicholas had come home to take the family title. And although Cassandra knew her place as a governess, she could not help the thrill that went through her each time he was near. Nicholas was pleased to find that his old friend Cassandra was his new next door neighbor, but after being near her, he wondered if mere friendship would be enough . . .

HIS LORDSHIP'S REWARD   (4473, $3.99)
by Carola Dunn

As the daughter of a seasoned soldier, Fanny Ingram was accustomed to the vagaries of military life and cared not a whit about matters of rank and social standing. So she certainly never foresaw her *tendre* for handsome Viscount Roworth of Kent with whom she was forced to share lodgings, while he carried out his clandestine activities on behalf of the British Army. And though good sense told Roworth to keep his distance, he couldn't stop from taking Fanny in his arms for a kiss that made all hearts equal!

Available wherever paperbacks are sold, or order direct from the Publisher. Send cover price plus 50¢ per copy for mailing and handling to Penguin USA, P.O. Box 999, c/o Dept. 17109, Bergenfield, NJ 07621. Residents of New York and Tennessee must include sales tax. DO NOT SEND CASH.

ELEGANT LOVE STILL FLOURISHES —
Wrap yourself in a Zebra Regency Romance.

Taylor—made Romance From Zebra Books

WHISPERED KISSES   (3830, $4.99/5.99)
Beautiful Texas heiress Laura Leigh Webster never imagined that her biggest worry on her African safari would be the handsome Jace Elliot, her tour guide. Laura's guardian, Lord Chadwick Hamilton, warns her of Jace's dangerous past; she simply cannot resist the lure of his strong arms and the passion of his *Whispered Kisses*.

KISS OF THE NIGHT WIND   (3831, $4.99/$5.99)
Carrie Sue Strover thought she was leaving trouble behind her when she deserted her brother's outlaw gang to live her life as schoolmarm Carolyn Starns. On her journey, her stagecoach was attacked and she was rescued by handsome T.J. Rogue. T.J. plots to have Carrie lead him to her brother's cohorts who murdered his family. T.J., however, soon succumbs to the beautiful runaway's charms and loving caresses.

FORTUNE'S FLAMES   (3825, $4.99/$5.99)
Impatient to begin her journey back home to New Orleans, beautiful Maren James was furious when Captain Hawk delayed the voyage by searching for stowaways. Impatience gave way to uncontrollable desire once the handsome captain searched *her* cabin. He was looking for illegal passengers; what he found was wild passion with a woman he knew was unlike all those he had known before!

PASSIONS WILD AND FREE   (3828, $4.99/$5.99)
After seeing her family and home destroyed by the cruel and hateful Epson gang, Randee Hollis swore revenge. She knew she found the perfect man to help her—gunslinger Marsh Logan. Not only strong and brave, Marsh had the ebony hair and light blue eyes to make Randee forget her hate and seek the love and passion that only he could give her.

Available wherever paperbacks are sold, or order direct from the Publisher. Send cover price plus 50¢ per copy for mailing and handling to Penguin USA, P.O. Box 999, c/o Dept. 17109, Bergenfield, NJ 07621. Residents of New York and Tennessee must include sales tax. DO NOT SEND CASH.